I0638787

Captivated By Clio

A Modern Muses Story

Tanisha D. Jones

Tanisha D. Jones
Visit my website at www.TanishaDJones.com

Printed in the United States of America

First Printing: Nov 2018
DeLill Publishing LLC

ISBN- 978-1-7338085-2-1

"So, you admit there's a thing?" He teased, and she returned his cocky grin.

"You know there's a thing. There has always been a thing, even in college though you wouldn't admit it. You wanted me. You've always wanted me. Admit it." She waggled her eyebrows at him before biting into her croissant.

"I admit it. I want you, Clio." His voice was low, steady and hopefully seductive. She stopped chewing and studied him, and he saw a flicker in her eyes. A brief look of smug satisfaction flashed across her face but was quickly replaced by cool detachment. She swallowed and leaned back, her hands on the counter in tight fists. "But you knew that. You've always known. You just wanted me to say it, didn't you?" She shrugged.

"May I make a suggestion that hopefully will put an end to this *tension*? One that I think will benefit each of us?" He nodded again sipping his coffee waiting for this little nugget of genius. He assumed that she would say they had to cool it, to not get too close. He assumed that she was going to suggest that they keep their relationship strictly professional.

He'd assumed wrong.

"I suggest that as long as we're both comfortable with it, and that it doesn't become emotional or interfere with our work we can indulge in our urges whenever we see fit. Sexually I mean, no strings attached. That way we won't always be thinking about sex and we won't cause tension with the crew." His coffee went down wrong and he immediately began choking.

Chapter 1

"The *Pride*," Dr. Noah Toussaint's voice boomed across the auditorium, echoing off the high ceiling and walls. He moved across the stage, all eyes following him with intensity.

"Jean Lafitte's ship from his last days of "*buccaneering*" as he referred to it, was said to have left Galveston in May of 1821, loaded with treasure he'd looted before burning the Maison Rouge fortress to the ground. Supposedly, he was accompanied by his mistress and their infant son. Now as with most things about Lafitte, this could just be another legend. We can't be sure. We don't have the child's name. Nor were there any records to prove such a birth. We do know that Maison Rouge was destroyed," he pointed to the screen behind him and a picture of the infamous pirate flashed brightly in the dimly lit room. He nodded towards his assistant, who sat staring at her phone before she clicked a button on the remote beside her and an image of a plaque appeared commemorating the historic site.

"We can't even prove that he actually left with any so-called treasure because no one has ever found the actual ship. It also can't be proven that Lafitte escaped with or even had a mistress because just a year before he reportedly married Madeline Regaud, who also bore him a son, Jean Pierre Lafitte, that same year. It is well documented that Lafitte died while trying to overtake the largest Spanish fort in Central America. The fort at Omoa was set up to store the silver mined by the Spaniards before shipping it to Spain. What he didn't realize was that the Spanish were heavily armed and took down his schooner the *General Santander*. We do know that Lafitte was presumed dead and buried at sea in the Gulf of Honduras in 1823. Or was he? A burial at sea is a very easy way to fake a death. It's not like today where everything is proven with video cameras, recorded and shared via the Internet. Or even before this digital age when things were recorded on paper, documented and witnessed by dozens of people. How easy would it have been for him to fake his death and live out his years in the Caribbean with all of that silver and gold?" He paused, letting that little bit of mystery fall over the audience, when the heavy door at the back of the small auditorium opened and swung shut with a thud.

Damn, he thought as the little woman with drenched curls and tattered messenger bag slapping her thigh, stumbled in out of the rain. He thought she'd given up and gone away, but of course she hadn't. Because, she was the cherry on top of what had become the crap cake of his life.

It started when leaked excerpts from a manuscript he'd spend years writing mysteriously hit the Internet. A manuscript he'd submitted to the Wainwright-Magnus Endowment Foundation and received funding for an excavation in search of the Pride, the missing treasure and possibly the fate of the man himself. All his theories, years of work, work that he'd started even before his short career in the NFL had ended, had been discovered and practically eviscerated. The source of the leak had never been proven but Noah had an idea of who had been the culprit. A former student, a privileged, self-serving, entitled brat who thought he was more talented than he actually was. He'd been pissed when he hadn't garnered any favor with Noah. His work had been mediocre, poorly researched and lazily assembled. Just because his family's name was on a library or two, he believed he deserved better.

Noah had not.

That student, one Jackson Everett Blake, had graduated a couple of years ago and made a name for himself as a blogger, mostly discrediting or critiquing the works of others. He built his career on being snarky and rude, while never contributing anything substantial or original of his own. Yet, he had millions of followers, millennials who believed his word to be gospel. He had torn holes in Noah's theories so viciously that he had been made a laughing stock.

Until then Noah had been considered an expert in the pirates of the Gulf and Caribbean region, yet the with most things in this day of social media and global information, whispers and opinions become facts. All it took was a hint that perhaps he could be wrong, and his funding suddenly disappeared.

And so had his job.

Though he had to admit, when the new dean of his department had taken over at the beginning of the year, he'd felt his days were numbered. Even though in less than a year, he would have been a tenured professor.

There had been no definitive reason given other than vague references to enrollment being down. He knew that was an excuse, since all his classes were always full. There were waiting lists for his courses from the freshman level to graduate students. The problem was that most of his students were female, non-history majors who were using his class as an elective or just auditing the course.

He also garnered a great deal of attention from the athletic boosters and alumni having been a starting running back when he attended LSU in the early 2000's and spent three years as a pro. In his rookie year he'd made it as far as the playoffs, his second year he'd made it to the Big Game. He even had the ring and bank account to prove it. He had been the number two running back in the country, when he'd suffered a career ending injury in the fourth game of his third season. Instead of following the typical route of becoming a sports broadcaster or coach, he'd gotten a Master's in History, then his doctorate degree.

His firing had nothing to do with budget cuts or him being a newly formed pariah in his field. It had everything to do with the fact that he refused to be paraded around like a prized pony for alumni fundraisers and preferred spending his time writing and teaching. It did help that he'd become an expert in his field and somewhat of an intellectual celebrity. But academics didn't bring in big alumni checks from boosters and supporters. Some of that money, he was told, would trickle down to his department. It would be good for the entire university, they'd said. So, he'd done the job, let himself be brought out for any big money grab the administration had wanted until they began offering him up to any and everyone with the right number of zeroes in their checking account. It was the ring; the ring was worth millions to them.

After five years, he'd had enough, and had stopped allowing himself to be used whenever and however they deemed necessary. Alumni didn't care about their stable of prized ponies when the stud refused to be shown and pranced around. That had been the beginning of the end.

To compound the loss of his job and the stories calling him a fraud, he'd returned home three days ago only to discover his so-called fiancée, an Economics professor, in bed with the dean who'd made a show of firing him. In a matter of months, he'd lost his job, his funding, his girlfriend and since he'd moved into her house three years prior, his home.

"I told you moving into her place was a bad idea." His sister, and very recent teaching assistant Raina, had admonished while helping him move into her apartment. Technically, it was his apartment since he paid for it, but she had been more than happy to have him stay with her. That was at least the bright spot in what was otherwise a dismal existence as of late.

But now his tiny afroed black cloud was back. As had been her pattern, she would pop up after every catastrophe. It was like she was an omen, everything bad had begun right around the time she'd shown up. It had started with emails, constant and pleading for his attention for weeks. He'd ignored her, so she'd begun the calls to his office. Daily, he would get seven or more calls, one more frantic than the next. She'd showed up a week ago looking the picture of an insane stalker.

Now, during what was to be his final lecture, yet again she showed up. He'd tried to back out of the lecture, as he'd been unceremoniously fired, humiliated and dumped, but he was obligated. Had he known he'd be fired before he'd signed up for the series of lectures presented by the university, he would never have agreed. But like everything else in his life, he'd been forced to comply. If anything, he could go out on a high note, but here she was, the cherry on his endless months of misery.

Perfect, he thought. Raina cleared her throat and motioned for him to continue. He hadn't spoken for a full minute, his mostly female audience sat waiting, hanging on his every breath.

"Well, we don't know when he died exactly, but we do know that his legacy remains prevalent in southern Louisiana. How many of you have ever been to Lafitte's Blacksmith Bar in the French Quarter? If you haven't you should go and look. Maybe you'll run into the ghost of Jean Lafitte or one of his pirate crew. You never know." He winked at them then glanced down at his watch and smiled. "As some of you may or may not know, this will be my last lecture here." There was a startled gasp as many of the female students looked up at him in shock.

"Yes, the rumors are true, this is my last semester here. Onto bigger and better for all of us. But I must say, it has been a pleasure spending these years trying to shape your warped little minds." He clapped his hands together and bowed his head. "Have a great, safe summer break. It has been an honor."

The students filed out, some passing his podium and wished him well, others said good bye. A few propositioned him playfully, and he managed to smile and give an appropriately vague response, but he kept his eyes on the tiny figure at the back of the room. She adjusted her glasses and pushed her damp curls out of her face and took a deep breath. He could see her steeling herself for her approach.

He began easing away from the crowd, trying to make his exit without being rude. She held back trying, he assumed, to out wait the stragglers. Raina eased closer, her smile growing wider.

"That's her, huh?" She asked with laughter in her tone. Noah looked at his baby sister and nodded. Little Miss Jean-Noel had become the five-foot bane of his existence. At first, he thought her to be nothing more than an overzealous student, now he believed she may just be a borderline nut case. Or worse, an infatuated stalker, it wasn't like it was that far-fetched. He was a quasi-celebrity.

"You didn't say she was so cute." Raina teased, looking at the young woman who sat nervously adjusting glasses that were too large for her small features.

"She's not cute. She's an annoying ball of hair with googly eyes and a backpack." Noah muttered as he stuffed his notes hurriedly into his own bag.

"Messenger bag." Raina corrected. "If you ever took the time to notice," Raina put a finger under his chin and forced him to look at the woman. "You would see that she's pretty. Like really pretty." She was brushing curls away from her face and securing them with a head band. Her glasses were rain splattered so she removed them as well to clean the lenses with her shirt tail.

Noah squinted before adjusting his own glasses to take a good look at her. She was attractive in a sort of pixie-ish kind of way. He hadn't noticed her face before, probably because it was always obscured by her hair and those ridiculous glasses that made her look bug-eyed. Not to mention that she was always dressed in over-sized clothing, today a shirt three sizes too big, and a pair of cargo pants that looked as if they were held up by sheer will, her ever present bag was down to her knees. She looked like a kid playing dress-up in mom or dad's clothing.

But he had to admit, she was definitely cute and …familiar. Her eyes were almond shaped and tilted upward, her nose pert and pretty, her lips soft and full. She wore no makeup on her milk chocolate skin, but it didn't matter, she didn't need it. She looked up at him, squinting and her nose scrunched in the most endearing way. Yes, she was quite pretty, maybe even beautiful, he decided. Her eyes, he noticed even from this distance, he could honestly say, were gorgeous.

He knew those eyes.

She replaced the glasses and stared at him, the bug-eyed effect unnerving him. He wasn't sure, but he thought he might have physically recoiled.

"She's cute, but annoying. Always buzzing around making noise and just when you think it's gone it sucks the life blood out of you, like a mosquito…or little sister."

"Harsh," Raina laughed then stopped and cleared her throat as the petite woman approached. "Don't look now, but I think she's gotten the nerve up to approach. In coming…"

"It's a good thing I have to go." He shoved the papers into his bag and winked at Raina before heading for the nearest exit.

He only made it ten feet.

∞∞∞∞

"Go to Baton Rouge, he'd said, get in touch with that kid you wrote that paper with freshman year. He's the expert, right? It never hurts to ask, all he can say is no, right?" Right. She was going to kill Z when she saw him again, him and his stupid ideas.

She hadn't seen him for nearly ten years and in all that time he hadn't changed a bit. That wasn't entirely true, he was much better looking than she remembered. And taller. Or perhaps she'd gotten shorter, which she truly doubted. She was barely over five feet now, any shorter and she would have to have a booster seat.

No, he was taller, but still a complete ego-maniacal jerk. She watched him strut across the stage, his chest puffed up like a preening peacock. She'd wanted to throw her shoe at him and hit him in his stupid gorgeous face. He wasn't supposed to look that good in person. He was supposed to have bad skin and crooked teeth, and maybe even a crooked nose. Definitely bad feet and a potbelly. But no, he was better looking than he had been on TV or magazines.

Occasionally, when he smiled or chuckled, she remembered the Noah she'd known, sweet funny and smarter than any football player she'd ever met. Not that she'd known many, but he had been different from the start. The first time she'd seen him, he'd come sauntering into her American History class with such quiet confidence that every eye in the room followed him. She'd found herself paying attention to him more and more over the next few weeks, noting how he seemed to be distracted but was always able to provide the correct answer whenever their professor would pose a question.

The one day she'd managed to oversleep and arrive late to class had been the day the class had chosen partners for a research project. By the time she'd arrive, everyone else had paired off and she was forced to team with the only other person without a partner who was also the only person who managed to arrive later than she had.

"Well," he'd said, smiling at her in the charming way he had, "looks like you're stuck with me." She nodded resigned to the fact that she would be doing all the work. Until he showed up at her dorm room books in hand ready to work. He'd come over every few days at first, then every day after practice. They would lay on her bed and watch bad horror and sci fi movies, his favorites had been the cheesy 80's slasher flicks. They listened to music, he introduced her to old school R & B, while she schooled him on everything from British rock to hip hop. They were an odd couple, she the impulsive extrovert, he the more reserved introvert. After a devastating year, Noah had been her light at the end of the tunnel, her safe place. She had been so crazy about him and for a time, she'd believed he'd felt the same.

Until, of course, it had all come crashing down in the meanest spirited and hurtful way possible. Yet, here she was, those feelings of hurt and humiliation coming back in overwhelming waves.

Why she'd listened to her uncle was beyond her. She had never taken Z's advice on things like this and he blissfully stayed out of her business. Until now for some inexplicable reason, and she had listened like a complete moron. Now she was stuck with no phone, no credit cards, no identification. She was lucky enough to have a cousin registered at the university, so she had a place to stay, that was something.

She moved quickly across the quad in the heat, her legs burning from effort when the rain began to fall in fat, heavy drops. Weeks, she'd been trying to get a meeting with this man for weeks and he was completely ignoring her. She should have known he would be an arrogant, self-obsessed jerk. He had been before, and men like him rarely changed. If anything, they just become more arrogant and egotistical. She tugged at the waistband of shorts that were four sizes too big, tightening the belt that almost went completely around her waist.

Never again would she let her uncle book her flights. Poor Uncle Z hadn't flown commercial for as long as she could remember. None of them had really. They had people who did that for them. So, why, oh why had she trusted that man? Instead of booking her on a nationally known carrier, he used his 'friend' Ray's charter company. "It's a private plane, Birdie. A flight from the island to Baton Rouge will be quick and easy. A couple of hours at best. Trust me, sweetie."

Famous last words.

She should have known listening to Z was wrong when she'd arrived at the airport, scratch that, it wasn't an airport as much as it was a strip of dirt in a field in the middle of nowhere. Her second clue should have been the look of the plane, which looked as if it was held together with duct tape and wishful thinking. But she'd been desperate and had gotten onto the plane.

Ray had effectively gotten her to a small private strip in Baton Rouge...and flown off with her luggage. That was nearly a week ago and she'd been stuck. She'd had about thirty dollars cash on her, because in her infinite wisdom, she'd left her wallet and passport in her locked carry on, along with her contact lenses, cell phone, clothing and toiletries. Because as Ray had said, *"won't need that. I land at a private strip. No customs."* That statement should have sent up a ten-foot-tall flaming red flag, but she trusted Ray because Z trusted Ray. That had been stupid on her part. For all she knew she'd been flying with a drug smuggler. She used the phone in the tiny dingy office of the isolated little airport to chew Z a new one. He'd assured her that she would get her things by the next morning. He also assured her, he'd call her cousin Derrick to let him know she needed a place to stay. Derrick of the limited funds and no vehicle had a friend come and pick her up. Since then, she'd been stuck in Derrick's dorm room which smelled of sweat socks and old pizza.

She'd then called her sister at the apartment they shared in New Orleans, only to realize that Calli was in New York on a press tour. She offered to rent a car for her, knowing full well that Clio didn't drive. Hadn't since she was a teen. And besides that, she didn't have any ID, so she figured she might as well do what she'd set out to do. Even if she was wearing Derrick's clothes, which swallowed her five-foot frame. In a day or two, Noah would be leaving the university. She'd asked the administration if they knew where he was going, but no one had any information. None that they would give her anyway. And she couldn't really blame them.

She looked like a lunatic, with her wild hair, too big clothes and her "spare" glasses that made her look like a baby owl. She'd left her regular pair either at Uncle Z's place, at her apartment in New Orleans or anywhere in between. Hell, she could have left them in Sierra Leone, for all she knew.

"Fan-fucking-tastic," She mumbled before breaking into a sprint, her travel worn messenger bag slapping against her thigh. She'd managed to make her way into the History building just as the heavens opened and rain poured in heavy dark sheets.

Now she sat in the back of the dimly lit auditorium fidgeting. She hated the nervous tick but what could she do to stop it? She cleaned the lenses in her glasses, frowning at the huge frames as she did. Damn it, she should have put her contacts in instead of leaving them in her suitcase. Instead, in her haste to get to the air strip before Ray took off without her, she'd shoved her contacts into her suitcase, after she'd found these monstrosities called eyeglasses in her bag. That had started what would become the most frustrating and embarrassing week of her life. So far anyway.

The week wasn't over just yet.

She'd spent most of that time trying to get close enough to him to speak with him, when she wasn't yelling at Z or her sister's assistant on the phone. And he'd always had an excuse to avoid her. She knew she looked insane, hell if she'd seen someone like her stalking, and let's face it she was stalking him; she'd have called the police. She hadn't been back home to her New Orleans apartment since she'd visited her uncle in the Caribbean nearly four months ago. She didn't have her license or money. Her hair was out of control, she had to wear these stupid glasses that made her look like a cricket and the pilot had flown off with her luggage. She understood Dr. Toussaint's apprehension.

To make matters worse, he was freaking gorgeous. Not just handsome, handsome she could handle. He'd been handsome as a twenty-year-old kid but now he was drop-dead-lord-have-mercy-take-me-now gorgeous. He had been bulky, with an acne ridden face that was still fleshy with baby fat the last time she'd seen him. But now, she wouldn't have recognized him in a million years if she'd seen him walking down the street. When had he become sexy?

If she were like a normal person, she would have stalked his social media before meeting him, but she was trying to be a mature adult.

Ha! She had never gotten the mature part right and she barely passed as an adult, even on a good day. But she pulled up her big girl pants and walked over to him in a business-like manner, her documents in hand, her speech rehearsed and prepared to introduce herself.

"Dr. Toussaint," She started, when he'd turned to look at her and every thought evaporated into the ether. She'd had to crane her neck to look up at him, and her mouth had gone dry. Up close he was even better. Had he always been so tall?

His face was chiseled, the color of mahogany with eyes as dark as midnight behind neat, black square framed eyeglasses. He had a brilliant smile, perfect white teeth and a neatly trimmed goatee that drew attention to full sensual lips. His hair, which was pulled away from his gorgeous face, was in neat, thick jet dreadlocks that hung past his shoulders. He was more male model than History professor and she was immediately lost in the deep onyx of his eyes. Eyes that still hinted at the sweet, sensitive and somewhat shy boy she'd known. She opened her mouth and frowned when she couldn't form any coherent words.

"Yes," he looked at her, one brow lifted in question. His voice was like rich honey, and she felt her knees buckle. Her stomach twisted in knots, heat rose in her cheeks and she couldn't find her voice.

"I...I ...wow...yeah...Dr. Toussaint...do you..." Was all she could manage before someone bumped her and she'd dropped her papers. The wind picked them up, tossing them across the quad and she had gone after them, cursing as she scrambled. That had been a one-time incident, but it marked a trend in their interactions thereafter. Now whenever he saw the strange little woman, he avoided her. He'd duck into meetings or faculty only office spaces. He made sure he could extract himself from situations quickly and quietly. That had been her mistake, trying to get at him when he was alone or in an open space where he could easily avoid her.

He couldn't do that here and they both knew it. She'd noticed him tense when he spotted her entering the lecture hall. He was probably bracing himself for another run in with her.

This time, she'd had the advantage of time. She'd had time to sit and listen to him speak, to see how his students were completely enthralled with him, hanging on his every word. They weren't just there to stare at him, they were listening to him. And she couldn't blame them. Noah had always been a commanding presence but to hear him, so sure, so intelligent and authentic in his delivery, kept the entire audience captivated. She'd seen hints of his intelligence and wit when they were younger, but now he was so powerful, he demanded attention.

She waited, calming herself because it was now or never. She needed to get through to him before she had to contact Uncle Z and tell him they were on their own. She was waiting for everyone to leave, waiting until she didn't have any witnesses to her utter inability to speak with this man. But she needed him, and he was...staring at her. At least, she thought he was, she couldn't really make him out with her glasses off. When she'd finished cleaning the lenses she looked up and, yes, he was staring at her. She knew she looked a mess, she'd been caught on a downpour and her hair, which was already out of control, had fallen into her face.

But he wasn't looking at her with mild fear as he had during their last few encounters. No, he was looking at her with a spark of recognition. Was he finally realizing who she was? Her stomach twisted in knots and the memory of what had happened all those years flashed before her eyes.

She watched as he averted his gaze and mumbled something to his TA. She needed to get it together, she needed to take a deep breath and know that her attraction was not the deciding factor in her need for his help. She sprang to her feet and raced down the aisle as he stuffed papers into his leather briefcase.

The TA looked at her and nodded toward him, mouthing "he's leaving..." to her. Wait, was she helping her? Again, the TA gestured, this time with more urgency and Clio sprang to her feet.

She was in his path before he could take more than two steps, her documents in hand.

"Dr. Toussaint, you may not remember me, but my name is Clio Jean-Noel and I think I may have the key to finding the Pride. I know you're planning an expedition to Barataria Bay, but the ship is further south. I also know for a fact that your theory of Jean Lafitte not being buried at sea is in fact true. I know that you were planning on excavating a site and your funding fell through but I have-" He put a hand up to stop her rambling. She stared at his hand and gasped at the nerve of him.

"I know that you may think you have proof, kid-" He smirked.

"Obviously, you don't remember me because if you did you would know that I'm not a kid-" She said becoming annoyed. Sure, she was small, but a kid? Really? Apparently, Noah Toussaint was just as arrogant as ever. Now she remembered why she'd never spoken to him again since that first semester. Once a jerk always a jerk. But why did he have to be a good-looking jerk.

"But I am the foremost authority on Jean Lafitte" He continued as if she hadn't even spoken. "there is nothing you can tell me that I don't already know. And as for your theory, there is no proof that Lafitte made it that far in the Pride. Now, if you'll excuse me," He pushed her aside and gave her head a pat as if he were consoling a child. Brushing it off, she pushed forward, digging into her bag she began retrieving charts and papers to show him.

"If you will just take the time to look at my documents, I think you'll be -"

"I don't have time right now and really if you wanted to get my attention this – act of yours isn't going to work. Now as I said," He was trying to dismiss her as a crazed fan or stalker. She stood her ground, blocking his grand exit, her frustration after weeks of being dismissed and ignored bubbled over into pure rage.

"You egotistical... It's one thing to not remember me, Professor but to talk down to me shows me that you are still a self-important ass. Unlike you, Dr. Toussaint, I have someone ready to fund my expedition to search for the Pride based on *my* research, can you say the same? I've read your work, and I know that the critics have torn you apart over your theories, but- I thought you would want to prove yourself to be right just so you can rub it in the faces of those same critics, you ginormous douche canoe." She reached into her pocket and tossed a heavy gold coin at him. "How many of these have you seen Mr. Foremost authority? I guess the adage is true, those who can't do teach." She turned to leave, but whipped back around on him so quickly, he took a startled step back. "I hope spending the next thirty years teaching remedial history at some fifth-rate community college brings you all the adoration and teen aged panties your heart desires. And by the way, it's *Doctor* Jean-Noel, you pretentious...twat! "

She turned around and stormed out of the auditorium, making as much noise as she had when she entered.

∞∞∞∞∞

"I guess she told you," Raina whistled and continued collecting her things.

Noah stood stunned, his eyes on the heavy gold piece in his hand. He flipped it in his palm testing the weight and staring at the raised lettering and date embossed on the coin, 1820. Raina moved beside him looking at the coin he held. "What did she mean about remembering her? Do you know her?"

"I don't think so. Maybe she was a student or attended a lecture I gave." He mumbled trying to avoid the subject. He focused on the gold in his hand, testing the weight, holding it up to the light.

"She seemed pretty adamant and she knew you more than a student would, Noah. You really pissed her off and from the sound of it, not for the first time. Dr. Jean-Noel? Why does that name sound so familiar?" Raina took out her phone and began to type.

"Here we go, Dr. Clio Jean-Noel." Raina whistled, and bells went off in his head. He did know her. "Master's degrees in Sociology and Ancient History, and a double doctorate in Anthropology and Archeology. You should definitely know her name. She is responsible for unearthing artifacts that are on display in museums in London, New York and the Smithsonian. And you attended LSU at the same time. Well, for a little while anyway. She finished undergrad at Columbia, got her doctorate from UC Berkley, then research at NYU. She did a fellowship at Oxford, then worked as a consultant for the British Museum. She's even a polyglot, six languages. She's like a rock star, a real-life Indiana Jones or Lara Croft." Noah looked at Raina's phone, watching her scroll through the stories and articles about the tiny woman who'd just stormed out of the room. He felt a knot tighten in his chest. He'd had the one person who could probably verify his work, redeem his good name, just fall out of the sky and he'd dismissed her.

"And you pissed her off. Not smart, Noah." Raina said and continued to pack up. "That coin, I guarantee is real. I'd bet my life on it. "

He ran his thumb over the coin and stared at the insignia. It was worn in some places, making the writing nearly impossible to read. Like the woman who'd just stormed out, the insignia looked familiar. He pulled out his journal, flipping to a picture. When he found it, he held the coin next to it. Raina looked over his shoulder and whistled. The coin was a match to a print of a coin that had been unearthed on the site of the destroyed fortress of Maison Rouge. "It looks like..."

"You need to catch her before she leaves this campus and apologize for being such a... what did she call you? A douche canoe?" Raina laughed as she walked past him.

"I was not-" He was ready to argue when Raina spoke up.

"Yes, you were. And she called you on it. It's about time someone did." She was out the door before he could respond. He stared at the coin in his hand flipping it over again and again.

If this was real, he thought, and then she could help him find the actual Pride. They could make history and he could get his reputation back. And he'd let her just storm off.

∞∞∞∞

She was crying like an idiot. She hated crying, but she didn't know what else to do.

But what had she expected? She looked like a homeless person with an obvious mental illness and she wanted him to jump at the chance to go in search of buried treasure with her. Of course, he wouldn't listen to her. She wouldn't listen to her. She was exhausted and frustrated and angry with herself for not thinking her plan out fully before contacting him. Her sister Calliope always said she acted before thinking, and here she was doing it again.

"Hey, are you okay?" Clio started at the soft concern she heard in the voice behind her. She turned to see the TA approaching, her pretty face full of genuine concern. The TA moved closer, putting a comforting hand on Clio's shoulder. She wanted to move, to hide her tears from the young woman, but she didn't. That would be rude, and this girl had done nothing to her.

"I'm sorry he's such a raging jackass." The TA said, giving Clio a sympathetic look.

"I didn't mean-" Clio started, shaking her head. Yet again, her mouth was getting in the way. She needed to learn to bite her tongue.

"No, you're right. He's my brother so I can say it without guilt or embarrassment. Noah is a raging ego maniacal jackass. It's from years of everyone telling him how wonderful he is at everything. Sometimes he needs to hear he's being a damn fool. I'm Raina, by the way."

"Clio Jean-Noel." Clio couldn't help her smile at the younger woman. Raina was pretty and now that she looked at her, she could see the resemblance. They had the same silky dark hair, Raina's in naturally springy curls around a softly angular face. They had the same dark, intense eyes and full lush mouths.

"I heard. I must commend you, not many people would dare speak to the great Dr. Noah Toussaint in such a way. I really like how you shut him down." Raina laughed. "Most of the time, he's not like that. He's a sweetheart really, once he gets his ass off his shoulders." Clio couldn't help the soft chuckle that escaped. She removed her glasses and wiped away her tears, sighing heavily.

"I'm usually more diplomatic but trying to talk to him has been hell. It doesn't help that I look like an insane homeless bug-eyed hobbit." She said. Raina burst into a fit of laughter.

"Bug eyed hobbit?" She repeated and laughed harder.

"I told her she looks like a cross between a cricket and a troll doll." A male voice startled them both and Clio shook her head at the young man as he approached. Derrick Hendrix came jogging up to them dressed in cargo shorts and a t- shirt. He was drenched in sweat or rain, his smile brilliant as he bound closer.

"Hey, what are you doing here?" Clio asked curiously, trying to wipe away the tell-tale signs of her breakdown. The last thing she needed was him trying to play protective hero. But she needn't worry, Derrick was more focused on Raina, who looked down at her feet shyly.

"Your luggage is finally here, and Calli had her assistant reserve a room for you. I'm going to take you to your hotel and then I'll drive you home tomorrow."

"Why didn't they call me?" She wiped her tear streaked face with the back of her hand.

"We have been, all of us, for like two hours. I think your phone died again. Birdie, I've been telling you all week you need a new one." He looked at Raina and smiled. "Hi."

"Hi," she said suddenly shy. Clio halted her search for her cell phone and looked from Raina to Derrick and back again. They stared at each other shyly but said nothing else.

"Oh, Raina Toussaint, this is my cousin Derrick Hendrix,"

"I know who she is, she's in my aerospace engineering program." Derrick said, just as Raina spoke.

"I know who he is, he's in my aerospace engineering program." They both managed to look surprised by this little revelation, but also very pleased. "Derrick is my competition for a summer internship at the Stennis Space Center." Raina said with a shy smile.

"I have to work extra hard to keep up." They continued to stare at each other in obvious infatuation and Clio couldn't help but smile at them. The pure innocence of their obvious attraction was heartwarming. She wondered if she'd ever looked at anyone the way Raina looked at Derrick. She doubted it. She was not one for goo-goo eyes and wistful sighs.

She shook her head just as she found her phone. Sighing in exasperation she realized that Derrick had been correct.

"Dead," she confirmed, and Derrick gave her a sympathetic smile.

"You look exhausted. I have an Uber to take you to your hotel. You ready?" She looked up at her younger cousin and nodded.

"You need a nice hot shower and a nice long nap. Come on." He placed a protective arm around her thin shoulders and hugged her to his side.

"Again Dr. Jean-Noel, I'm sorry about my brother. I'll try to talk to him-"

"It's fine and its Clio. Thanks Raina but I'm going to go to my hotel and lick my wounds. At least I can say I tried." She waved tiredly and let Derrick turn her in the direction of the parking lot.

∞∞∞∞

He found Raina standing just beneath the portico watching a young man cradling the petite Dr. Jean-Noel to him and walk her down the steps from Webster Hall toward a car, one of the few remaining in the parking lot. The rain had stopped but there were puddles along the path. He gingerly lifted Clio with one arm so she wouldn't step into the ankle-deep water and carried her to the car. She dangled like a rag doll, her feet swinging as he hoisted her like a child. She was so small next to him and he was so careful and protective of her. It was by far one of the sweetest things Noah had ever seen.

"That the boyfriend?" Noah asked his tone quiet and somewhat reproachful. Raina glanced at him from the corner of her eye. He knew that look and he braced himself for an onslaught of obscenities. But she surprised him.

"That's the cousin," she said, folding her arms across her chest and staring at him.

"Why is he carrying her?" He asked.

"Because you made her cry and she's exhausted and stressed out and you were a jerk to her. He's taking her to her hotel to rest. You should be ashamed of yourself. How could you be so rude? And arrogant? And just a big- dick? You were raised better than that." He gave her a knowing look and she sighed. Their father had been a proud an arrogant man, if anything Noah had acted exactly as the man who'd raised them. "Anyway, you should go to her hotel and apologize..." She looked at her phone, her fingers moving over the screen with practiced ease.

"I don't know which hotel..." He managed to look sheepish and smug at the same time. Raina knew this little trick of his. Look just apologetic enough to get by on his charm. But unlike most women in his orbit, she was not charmed by Noah. She knew him too well to be sucked into his little games. Besides, she'd been around when women wouldn't give him the time of day, when he was a scrawny, pimply history nerd in middle school. He would not get off that easily.

"She's staying at the Renaissance downtown." She looked at him with a satisfied smirk.

"How did you do that?" Raina shook her head and gave his arm a sympathetic pat.

"Because unlike you, dear sweet clueless brother, people actually *like* me." He lifted an eyebrow and she sighed. "Her cousin told me."

Chapter 2

"I'm sorry it went so badly, sweetie. When are you coming home?" Calliope sighed.

Clio stared at her reflection in the mirror as she detangled her wet hair. She looked down at her phone which sat charging on the bathroom counter, her older sister's pleasant voice filling the room. She'd taken a long bubble bath, letting hot water relax her tense, tired muscles. She'd taken off the bug-eyed glasses and found her regular glasses, the ones that made her look human. She'd also found her contact lenses, thank god.

"Tomorrow, Cal. I just need a burger, a mindless movie and a good night's sleep. I think I'll take a day or two to figure out my next steps before I get started. I may have a bit of time before that imbecile Garrett Matthews starts his expedition. I wish I'd never showed him my notes, that underhanded, shifty eyed little -" She bit back the litany of vulgar names she had for her former colleague and one-time boyfriend. Sort of. It was more of a friend with benefits situation, apparently it benefited him more than her.

How was she to know that he'd take some of her notes and pass them off as his own to get his own funding. She wouldn't have cared if this was any other research, any other excavation. She'd worked with him for years, so for him to take something so personal had shown him to be nothing more than an opportunistic snake. Too bad he didn't get everything, the glory hungry simpleton.

But if he hadn't been so greedy, she wouldn't be here trying to get Captain Fantastic to work with her. The big stupid bastard-hole.

"I never liked him." Calli was saying, "He had a ghoulish smile. Too much of his gums showed and he had tiny teeth. Sure sign of a psychopath." Clio sighed and shook her head.

"Anyway, looks like I'm going to have to navigate this one alone since Dr. Doom brushed me off. I guess I wouldn't be so pissed if he wasn't so damned sexy. I must say, he was nothing like the kid I remember. Why couldn't he be like a balding overweight middle-aged creep?"

"Dr. Doom sounds mysterious. And sexy you say? What's his Facebook?" Calli asked.

"He doesn't have one. I think he may have Twitter, but he doesn't have a lot of social media. Which is weird. Don't you think that's weird?" She slipped on her favorite fleece pajama bottoms, a tank top and a pair of fuzzy socks. Now she was combing through her hair, which hung to her shoulders in thick damp waves. Her curls would be back to their lustrous bounce by morning. She was finally starting to feel like herself again.

"Do you want me to drive up and pick you up? Maybe we can hit the Mall of Louisiana for some retail therapy? Maybe have a nice lunch? Or, you can put your big girl pants on and actually drive yourself. Like a grown up."

"Clio, you are well aware that I only pretend to be a grown up. And why do I get the feeling that you're avoiding work?" Clio laughed.

"Because I am. But I have an excuse, a real excuse... my publisher hated my first draft. So much for that. I have to start over and it's giving me a headache. Anyway, do you want me to pick you up or not?"

"Not. I'll rent a car and driver. It'll be fine. But you can get the crew together so that we can figure out what I'm going to need for this trip. I have to get started if I want to beat Garrett out of the gate. The jerk. Also, find out about all of the permits and any paperwork or contracts we would need. Titus should have a handle on that, so just check with him." There was a soft knock at the door and her stomach immediately rumbled. "I think my food is here." She picked up the phone and headed to the door of her suite.

"Will do and please, tell me you're eating actual food and not ice cream and pie for dinner."

"I ordered a cheeseburger, fries and a chocolate shake. See, covering all of the food groups like a grown up." Clio opened the door and all of her light-hearted mirth evaporated.

"Damn, Calli, I'll call you back. It seems that I have a giant dick at my door." She disconnected before Calli could press her for follow up on that statement. She stared at him, her arms folded across her chest, her anger suddenly rising.

"What the hell do you want?" She asked a rather flustered Noah Toussaint.

"I came to apologize for being such a jerk- wow you look completely different. Less deranged...I mean .... This is coming out wrong. I bought these as a peace offering," He said awkwardly handing her a bouquet of flowers. Nothing extravagant she noted, just a bouquet one could pick up from any decent grocery store. But they were bright and pretty, and it was full of sunflowers. She liked sunflowers.

"Thanks," She took the flowers and slammed the door in his face.

∞∞∞∞∞

16

He was too stunned to move. She'd closed the door in his face; well he thought it was her. The woman who'd answered the door looked nothing like the bug-eyed ragamuffin he'd spoken to earlier. He wasn't sure if he was more surprised by her appearance or by the knot that tightened his stomach. He'd known the moment she'd looked up at him with those striking eyes who she was, and he dreaded coming here tonight.

They'd had a class together years ago when she was a freshman and he a big-man on campus senior. They'd been partnered on a project and had gotten along well. Clio, of course, why hadn't he remembered her, he wondered. But she had looked different then as well but smart as a whip. She'd looked rather boyish then, but he'd liked her. He'd liked her a lot. He'd even taken her to a party...

He groaned and closed his eyes, banging his head on the door. Her anger towards him now was completely understood and justified. The dog party.

Every year there was a party just before Winter break, a party he'd never attended because he had a full course load and was never one for drinking or loud parties. But that year his teammates had insisted he come, and they had insisted he bring '*the cute little freshman*' he was spending so much time with. He had. And he had regretted it ever since. He'd also never seen her again after that night. No wonder she was so pissed.

Not only had he been a major jackass back then, he'd been one all this week.

He lifted his hand to knock again when the door was thrown open and she stood with her hands on her hips. She was tiny but athletically built, her hair was pulled back in drying waves that framed her face. She traded out the buggy eye glasses with a stylish pair that flattered her features. Her full lips were pursed in anger and her brow was furrowed in frustration. She was more than cute, he realized, Clio Jean-Noel was absolutely stunning.

"Okay, apologize and it better be a good one because you were a complete dick to me. Then and now." She was looking up at him, tapping one fuzzy sock covered foot on the carpet.

"Can I come in?" He asked, suddenly feeling conspicuous standing in the hallway. A couple walked past eyeing him curiously.

"Depends on the apology. I'm still waiting Professor." She said. He looked down at her and had to fight the urge to smile. "You have a minute. Come on; make it quick my dinner is on its way."

"I am truly sorry for what happened today and, in the past, as well. That was completely unconscionable and I have regretted it every day since. I really liked you and, in my defense, I had never been to that party before. I would have never taken you if I would have known what it was. I liked you too much for that, you were my friend. And I should have taken the time to listen to you and not been quick to be such a dismissive asshole. I sometimes forget that I am not always the smartest person in the room. Please forgive my arrogance and disrespect, I'm sorry I upset you so much. And I'm sorry that I didn't remember you." He said.

She tilted her head, watching him intently but remained silent. When the elevator pinged down the hall, she glanced in that direction briefly before sighing.

"Did Raina make you come here and apologize? Because I've never known you to apologize even when you knew that you were wrong."

"She suggested that I was acting like..."

"A damn fool? An arrogant douche? A jackass? Colossal dick? A full-on bastard?" She asked, and he chuckled.

"Jeez, I wasn't that bad. But I was rude and dismissive and even a little condescending and for that I truly apologize. And if you have the time, I would like to hear what you have to say." She nodded at the room service waiter who came closer and waved him in, but still hadn't agreed to let Noah enter. He was staring at her, he knew it, but he couldn't help it. This woman was a far cry from the meek young woman who'd stalked him around campus. Or the kid who had been infatuated with him all those years ago.

"On the apology scale, I guess that was a seven. Come on in. You hang in the hallway much longer, people are going to think you're a hooker or something." She said and allowed him into the suite. He followed her taking a seat on a sofa in the living area, his eyes roaming over the hotel suite with interest. The Renaissance Hotel was one of the more expensive in the area and a suite like this had to cost a nice bit of money. He took note of her laptop which was set up on the table and the hundred-dollar tip she handed the server before he exited the room.

"Okay, now that you're here let's set a few ground rules. You act like a jerk, you are out. If you decide you want in on this, you must go all in. If you decide that you don't want to, we go our separate ways and never see each other again, but you say nothing about what I'm showing you. And the most important rule of the night," She said taking a seat opposite him before removing the cover from her tray. "Don't touch my fries." She teased, before taking a huge bite of her double stack double cheeseburger. He shook his head when she moaned in ecstasy and closed her eyes. The burger looked huge in her small, delicate hands. She took two more gigantic bites before placing the sandwich back on the tray and taking a long swallow from her milkshake.

"How can you eat all of that?" He asked when she began to slather her fries with ketchup and mayo. She paused and looked at him before groaning

"Don't tell me you're one of those people?" She whined.

"One of what people?" He asked.

"Those health nuts who only eat kale and organic carob. The ones who instead of eating sausage and eggs for breakfast or a nice big medium rare steak for dinner will drink beet juice and have a Portobello mushroom and call it a steak? I hate to tell you; a mushroom is not a steak. And bacon makes everything taste better."

"I eat healthy." She looked at him over her glasses and nodded.

"Of course, you do. But you're missing out on the best parts of life. That's probably why you are the way you are." She snorted and began devouring her fries.

"How am I?" He asked and found that he was smiling.

"You know, clenched. You're all bound up, restricted. Tightly wound. I could probably get a diamond if I shoved a lump of coal up your bum." He chuckled and shook his head.

"You've changed since the last time I saw you...knew you." He corrected, hoping it didn't sour her playful mood. He'd just managed to get back into her good graces and he didn't want to ruin it now.

"You didn't know me back then either. Not really." She said, popping a fry into her mouth. She folded her legs under her and leaned back against the sofa, her hair drying in springy dark curls that framed her face. She'd lost the chubby cheeks she'd had then, her cheekbones more defined, giving her face a regal look. He'd never imagined that she would become this sultry, earthy beauty; a fiery and determined young woman. He'd liked her then. Now, he was completely enthralled with her.

"I knew that I wanted to know more. Whenever I was around you, I felt that I could really be myself. That I didn't have to pretend to be anyone other than myself. I wanted you to know the real me. And I wanted to know everything about you." She looked at him, her head tilted to one side, as she studied him. He couldn't get a true read on her emotions, her face was completely blank, devoid of any hint of emotion. Finally, she sighed and shrugged.

"You should have tried harder." She said popping more fries into her mouth.

"Well, maybe this time I will." He said. She smiled and continued eating, not mentioning the implied intimacy of his statement. He could have continued down that road, opening old wounds but that wasn't why he had come. He took a deep breath and looked at her meal. Just watching her was enough to give him indigestion.

"What I actually meant was how can someone so tiny eat so much?" He said changing the subject to something lighter.

"I have a fast metabolism." She mumbled around a mouth full. "You didn't come here to discuss my eating habits. You came for this." She wiped her hands on a wet nap, dried them on a linen napkin and reached for her tattered messenger bag from the table beside her chair. He pushed her food aside, making room on the coffee table for the papers and notebooks she pulled from the bag.

"I've gone through these papers hundreds of times, they've all been authenticated. But I know more about ancient civilizations and indigenous tribes, I needed someone who knows pirates. It took a lot for me to even consider approaching you, with everything that happened. But," She took out what looked like a family bible which had been marked at a certain point and placed it gingerly on the table. He moved closer to get a better look and caught a whiff of her hair. He'd never in his life been turned on by the smell of sunshine, strawberries and French fries in his life. Until now.

"I put on my big girl panties and here I am. I figured if anyone would appreciate this, it would be you, Professor. I'm putting a lot of faith and trust in you. Don't make me regret it."

He looked at the list of births and deaths listed in barely legible scrawl in fading ink when a name caught his attention.

"Claude Laffite born 15 February 1821, son of Angeline Noel and..." He looked up at Clio who continued to eat her burger. "Jean Laffite, died 1837." By the spelling of the name alone, he knew that he was reading something incredible. The double F's in Laffite was the correct spelling; it was how the privateer signed his own name. The spelling had changed when he'd come to America, as most names did. This was real, he realized.

"Keep reading," She waggled her eyebrows at him before taking another bite of burger.

"You say that this is real, but how do I know that? You could have just created all of this ..." He stopped talking when he saw her expression. She was looking at him thoughtfully as she chewed. After she took her time swallowing and sipping her milkshake she exhaled.

"True. I could have gone to some great forger and had them create this tattered journal and family bible. I could have gotten this letter aged and had the authentication documentation falsified. I absolutely could have planned this just in case someone wrote a book to debunk your theories and cost you your position at the university. I could have made sure that I came here, just when your life was in an obvious downward spiral, lost my luggage and stalked you for a week, not to mention the month of emails and phone calls, just to present you with false records. Yes, that is what this is. I did all of this, including wearing clothes five sizes too big that smelled like sweat socks, having no money, no wallet, no underwear and following you around like a deranged psychopath all so I could get embarrassed once again by the same person who embarrassed me years ago. Yup, sounds like something I would do. Because, you know, I've spent every waking moment thinking about you and how I would exact my revenge, for what ten, eleven years? That is exactly what I'm doing now." She took another bite of her burger, her expression unchanged and he felt like a complete ass. She hadn't raised her voice or changed her tone, but each word dripped with dry sarcasm. He felt his cheeks warm as embarrassment rushed over him. Once again, he was thinking far too highly of himself. And once again Clio Jean-Noel had put him in his place. "I have no reason to lie to you, Professor."

"Call me Noah." He desperately wanted to hear her say his name. She'd called him everything, but his name and he wanted to hear her say it. He could just imagine her purring his name, her hazel eyes sparkling.

"Anyway, you didn't have to come here. You don't have to listen to me. But this is real. If you don't believe me, I will go with you to whomever you trust to have it authenticated. If you aren't interested, I can find someone else, someone interested in the possibility of what I'm offering you. You are more than welcome to leave and never speak to me again. If you're worried about leaving your family-"

"It's just Raina and me. And she's about to leave for a summer internship." He blurted. Her brow raised but she pressed on.

"What I am offering, suggesting, is that you take a chance and see if that what you've believed for all of these years is real. I'm offering you possibilities." He watched her face light up, her eyes sparked with gold fire and her smile widen as she spoke. She was infectious, her enthusiasm catching, and his stomach fluttered with long dormant butterflies. Just like that, he felt the embers that he'd thought long dead by this pixie of a woman who he'd fell for when she was a sprite of a girl. This was who he knew she would grow to be, smart, self-assured and full of sass.

"I'm very interested in the possibilities. And please, call me Noah." He insisted.

"Okay, then pay attention and keep reading," She tapped the book with one finger, that twinkle was back in her eye, a smirk on her lips. "Professor." She coaxed in a tone that was teasing but made the hairs on his arms stand up. He looked at her, her smile radiant, her eyes dancing with curious excitement.

He moved down the list following the tabs which were green to follow one branch of the family tree. "Philippe Jean -Noel married Rosalie Blanchard 21 August 1901, Ambrose Jean-Noel son of Philippe and Rosalie...born 18 July 1904, Kingston Jean-Noel son of Philippe and Rosalie born March 22, 1910...died October 30, 1984 Juniper Jean-Noel daughter of Philippe and Rosalie born December 4, 1912..." Again, a switch in branches and colors, this time red following Kingston, then shifted again to his son Brennan Jean-Noel and then finally to his sons. Noah swallowed hard as he read, his throat suddenly dry. He glanced at Clio for a moment then continued to read.

"Son Zeus Jean-Noel born May 3, 1958.... Son Apollo Jean-Noel born August 24, 1962...died June 3, 2004. Daughter Athena Jean-Noel born September 9, 1964.... Apollo Jean-Noel married Lila-Rose Claiborne February 19, 1983..." He slowly turned the page, knowing what he would find on the next page and his stomach sank. "Lila-Rose Jean-Noel, died June 3, 2004. Daughter Calliope Jean-Noel born July 18, 1984, daughter... Clio Jean-Noel born March 9, 1987, ... son Archimedes Jean-Noel born October 22, 1993...died June 3, 2004." He sat back, his hand over his mouth to keep it from dropping open. He looked at her, then down at the page again.

"Do I have your attention now, Professor?" She asked. He looked at her, her green gold eyes dancing with sheer delight. How could he have forgotten a woman with eyes that vibrant and a smile so beguiling. He would never again in his life see something quiet as lovely as Clio Jean-Noel.

"Yes," he said, "you have my full attention."

∞∞∞∞

"Are you sure about this? I mean just yesterday you referred to her as a crazy person, and I quote "an annoying mosquito.' Now you're ready to drop everything and follow her out of the country?" Raina sat on the bed watching him pack. "Don't get me wrong, you need a little adventure, especially after three years with the ice queen. But this is very impulsive."

He shook his head, not even bothering to correct her. As far as Raina had been concerned, his ex was the epitome of academic elitism. Catherine was beautiful, intelligent and extremely condescending and judgmental. She had tolerated Raina, believing his sister to be crass and immature. He had spent most of their relationship playing referee between the two. As much as he hated to admit it, he was thankful that it would no longer be an issue.

"I was wrong. I can admit that." Raina opened her mouth and he put a hand up to stop her. "About a lot of things. But once I actually sat down and listened to her...this is something I have to do. In college, she was one of the most intelligent people in the class. She set the curve. Clio is like ...the LeBron James of Archeology. And yes, I'm willing to drop everything because there is nothing left to drop. I don't have a job, a home, a girlfriend or any prospects..."

"You have me." He paused long enough to look at his baby sister and smiled.

"I would never drop you. But in a few weeks, you'll be off on your own adventure. It's about time I start doing the same. Clio is giving me the chance to do it. If she's right, this would have a huge impact on history. And she's offering me a chance to be a part of it."

"And she's cute." Raina teased. Noah exhaled avoiding her intense scrutiny, not wanting to reveal anything. The last thing he wanted was Raina and her bizarrely accurate intuition to pick up on the fact that he was hiding something. Part of the reason he was ready to follow Clio was because he wanted her. He had never wanted a woman the way he wanted Clio. He'd spent the better part of the night, breathing her in. She was smart and sarcastic, sweet and funny. When he was with her, he was completely at ease. They had stayed up all night talking, not only about the journal but about any and everything. But the turning point had come at the end of their night together.

He and Clio had poured through the delicate tattered pages of the journal. Piecing together a rudimentary understanding of what was written, which was a major task. Many of the pages were damaged, in other areas the ink had faded, and in some cases the penmanship was simply atrocious. The sun was just coming up when they finally took a break, Clio yawning and stretching.

"Are you in, Professor? I have less than a week to get started and I need an answer." She'd rubbed her shoulders and rotated her head before looking at him. Her curls flopped down over her forehead, covering one eye and she blew it out of her face. He couldn't explain why, but that simple action had made his skin heat and tightened. He swallowed and cleared his throat before reaching for a water bottle and taking a huge swig.

"Why the rush? Can I have a day or two-" She shook her head, closing her eyes.

"The rush is because my former partner stole some of my research and some of my crew and a great chunk of funding that was earmarked for this to start his own expedition. Fortunately, he doesn't have some very crucial information, because I falsified some of it. Unfortunately, he's already started his expedition. I have to get started as soon as possible and I spent too much time on you. So, are you in?" She looked at him, her features soft, almost angelic, those large doe-like eyes searching his face. The full force of her gaze, full berry colored lips parted invitingly and he leaned in close, his heart thudding against his ribs as he covered her mouth with his. She tasted of chocolate ice cream, her lips softer than he'd imagined. She leaned into him, parting her lips to coax him in deeper. He slipped his tongue past her teeth to the delicious warmth of her. He sank his fingers into her soft curls, pulling her closer. She clutched his shirt, returning the kiss with a fervor he hadn't expected.

Finally, he released her, his body thrumming with a need he'd never experienced before. His body was hard, his skin hot and he wanted more of her. He gently cupped her cheek and searched her face. She was smiling at him, a cheeky knowing smirk that made him groan inwardly. Damn, she was cute.

"So, I take that as a yes?" She asked breathlessly.

It had taken all of his will to leave her then. At that point he would have done anything she asked, gone to the ends of the earth at the crook of her finger.

The last thing he needed was for Raina to know about that. He would never hear the end of it. He leaned over and kissed Raina on the top of the head.

"I've spent my life reading about places, adventures, expeditions and I've never been anywhere. I do the same thing day in and day out, I'm predictable and boring, Raina. I do everything I'm supposed to do never what I want to do. I've wasted my time looking for the perfect time, perfect place, planning and plotting and what has it gotten me? Nothing. Clio is offering me the chance of a lifetime. I have to take it."

"I get it. And it doesn't hurt that she's cute." He tossed a shirt at her.

"She's more than that, smartass. She has this way of talking about all of this with such passion..."

"Okay, what color are her eyes?" Raina asked. He stopped and looked at her. "Come on, if you're going on this trip purely to prove your theories, tell me about her eyes." He snorted and shook his head. "I'm serious. Tell me, her eyes are?" He shrugged, the image of her face coming to mind.

"Well," He started "they're brownish, with green, actually more of a bronzed green with flecks of gold and copper..."

"You mean hazel? She has hazel eyes?" Raina teased.

"What?" He asked fighting a smile at her glee.

"The color, it's hazel." She chuckled. "I'll be damned, you really have a crush on her." He shook his head. He did sound like a gushing schoolboy even without mentioning that he and Clio had stayed up all night talking. He had never been with a woman he could talk to so easily, so comfortably without feeling like he had to dumb himself down. That she didn't laugh, that she guffawed and snorted without remorse and continued to eat as if it were her last meal. In addition to the burger, fries and milkshake, she'd demolished a hot fudge sundae and two slices of apple pie. She'd explained her deranged appearance and her persistence at pursuing him to get him to listen to her. She wanted him to be a part of her expedition and she would do whatever it took to get him on board. Even if it meant embarrassing herself.

"I'm an adult, I don't have crushes. I just find her kind of amazing. My interest in her is purely professional." Raina nodded, looking him in the eye. He avoided her gaze, focusing on the task at hand.

"And what color were the eyes of the last person who offered to fund this little excursion?" He stared at her, trying to recall the face of the investor he'd spoken with about his grant. He couldn't remember anything other than it was a woman with dark hair.

"Okay, easier question. What color are Catherine's eyes?"

"Grey. I know that. They're grey." She snorted and shook her head.

"Her eyes are brown. Those grey eyes...are contacts. You were with her for three years and you never noticed that but one night with Dr. Jean-Noel and you know that her eyes are gold and copper. If that's not a crush, I don't know what is." She laughed harder as she exited the tiny guest room.

Chapter 3

She'd told him to meet her in the hotel lobby at eleven, yet here he stood waiting for her to make an appearance. He turned to face the elevators as they pinged to alert everyone within earshot of their arrival. The doors opened, and he waited as guests filed out, none of whom where Dr. Jean-Noel. He glanced at his watch then at his phone when her voice startled him.

"There you are, I've been waiting in the coffee shop for like twenty minutes." She handed him a paper coffee cup and adjusted the bag on her shoulder. She seemed to struggle under the weight of the cumbersome duffel, so he gingerly took it for her. She looked up, her brow furrowed them smiled.

"Thanks, Professor. I'd forgotten you were a gentleman." She said before drinking her coffee. She wore a short flowy sun dress in a vibrant shade of yellow that brushed the tops of her toned thighs and flat beige gladiator sandals. Her mass of curls had been pulled into a neat puff on top of her head and from her ears hung great gold hoops. She wasn't wearing her glasses and he got the full effect of her beauty. How could he have forgotten a face and smile like that? He smiled at her and again her brow creased curiously.

"What?" She asked, her eyes sparkling as the afternoon sunlight that filtered into the lobby. The light caught the gold and copper flecks in her eyes making them shimmer. She had high cheekbones and her ears stuck out a little. She was small, but muscular, compact and curvy. Damn, he thought, just damn.

"You're kinda cute and sexy when you don't look like a homeless crazy lady." She shook her head and slipped on a pair of gold framed aviator sunglasses.

"Professor, I'm always cute. The sexy just takes some people a little longer to notice." She headed for the exit. He watched her slim hips sway as she walked away, her tiny frame moving with seductive purpose. The way the hem of her skirt brushed against the back of well-defined thighs the color a smooth milk chocolate had a hypnotic effect on him. He unconsciously tilted his head to the side, as if he were trying to get a peek at what was beneath the flowing garment.

"I know you're enjoying the view, but we need to get moving." She called without breaking stride and he felt his cheeks heat with embarrassment before following her out the door. Yes, she was sexy, he thought. Definitely sexy.

∞∞∞∞

Clio leaned back in her seat, her legs crossed at the ankle, her bare feet on the dashboard of Noah's Mercedes. They'd been on the road for twenty minutes and already she'd fiddled with the radio, reclined her seat, asked for food and had to make a bathroom pit stop. Noah turned to look at her before pushing the ignition to restart the motor for the third time.

"Is there anything else you need? I mean the ride is just an hour long and already you've put us behind schedule." She lifted her sunglasses to stare at him.

"We don't have a schedule." She said.

"Didn't you tell your sister that we would be there by twelve?" She sat up, pushing the glasses up on her forehead.

"I told her that because my sister works on Calliope-time. In her mind that's somewhere around one thirty. Right now, she's either still in bed or out shopping. She has no real concept of time. She's chronically late for everything. Even when she's at home. I guarantee she's at the supermarket or something right now. It's like a disorder. When Calli tells me, she'll be somewhere at three, she actually means four thirty. Anyone who knows her, knows she'll always be late and adjust accordingly, like setting a clock ahead. It makes life so much easier."

"That makes absolutely no sense." Noah grumbled as he pulled the car out of the gas station parking lot.

"Maybe not but it works for us. Somewhat. You'll see when we're on the boat." She slipped the sunglasses down and relaxed into the peanut butter leather of the seat. Noah couldn't help but smile at her ridiculous logic. She was a doctor and she spoke of time as if it were an abstract construct.

"So, does your investor understand Calliope time?" Noah wondered out loud.

"He is well versed in all of our idiosyncrasies. But just so you know, I'm never late. For anything. Ever." That managed to raise an eyebrow.

"Not ever?" She looked over her lenses at him.

"Never. There are always consequences for tardiness. Time is something you can never replace, I never waste it. When I work, I'm on military time, precise to a fault. Titus is one of the few people who can reel me in when I go off all half-cocked, he knows what buttons to push and he knows which strings to pull. And he has a way of working on Calliope time to his advantage. It's a thing of beauty." She sighed. Noah looked at her out of the corner of his eye, his curiosity piqued.

"Have you known Titus long?" He wondered briefly if Clio's mysterious benefactor may have had a romantic connotation and he felt a strange twinge, an emotion he'd never really experienced before. Was he jealous? Shaking it off, he decided to change tracks, there was no reason to go down that rabbit hole.

"Pretty much my entire life. His parents and mine were really close. Our fathers were best friends." He nodded, looking at her briefly before turning his attention back to the stop and go flow of traffic.

"Okay. I have a question for you. Why did you run off at the coffee shop the other day? I mean if you would have just said who you were and what you wanted you wouldn't have spent all that time stalking me. That woman and you- just don't add up."

"I freaked a little because I wasn't expecting you." She turned her head so that she faced him, but with her mirrored sunglasses on he couldn't see her eyes. Her face was relaxed, her tone flat giving no hint of the emotion behind the statement.

"But you came looking specifically for me." He looked at her again, trying to get a read on her, but his own reflection stared back at him in those glasses.

"No, I wasn't expecting you to look like you just walked off the cover of a magazine. I was expecting Noah the kid from college. You know, still slightly awkward goofy grin, hopefully a crooked nose a cauliflower ear or something. It threw me off for a second that you'd grown into an actual man. Then I was so busy trying to fix it that each time I made it worse. It didn't help that I was exhausted, and the pilot had lost my luggage and I was wearing Derrick's shorts as pants. In case you hadn't noticed, I was a little frazzled. The fact that I'm on a time crunch has me a little tender as well, so seeing you again really shook me. Which is strange because nothing shakes me, and I was once propositioned by a Saudi sheik with a ruby the size of my fist to become his mistress. My reaction was purely visceral, animal...sexual."

"So, you were attracted to me?" He asked, holding his breath. What was wrong with him? Good lord, Raina was right. He had a schoolboy crush on Clio. She turned away from him, a smile playing at the corners of her mouth.

"Sadly, yes. Very. Until you acted like an arrogant self-important ass. Kind of put a damper on the flame." She leaned forward, rummaging through a bag of snacks for chips.

"What about after we kissed?" He coaxed wanting, no needing her to continue.

"Let's just say you managed to get the kindling to smolder. We'll just have to wait and see if you redeem yourself." She gave him a coy teasing smile that made his skin tighten. He could see his reflection in her glasses, unable to read her eyes. But that smile did wonders. If he could've he would've crossed his legs to hide his growing erection. Instead he decided to concentrate on something else. Something other than her bare legs and the rise of her skirt as she twisted in her seat. He would ignore the memory of her mouth, warm and sweet.

"So," he began instead changing the subject completely. "The coin? The documents why are you just coming across these right now? Why hasn't anyone looked for them before?"

"I guess we never believed it. I mean how many times do families claim to have some famous ancestor. I never believed it, none of us really did. It's not like we had any proof, it was just a story we'd been told all our lives. But with that bible I had my first hint that it might be true."

"How did you find the bible and journal?" He asked.

"I had just finished a dig in Brazil and on my way home, I went to see my Uncle Z. He had been renovating my great grandparents' home in San Juan. I was helping him clean out the attic and found the bible in a box full old books and journals. Once we found that, we knew all the stories had been true." She explained how she and her uncle had torn through the family home, through boxes and trunks finding more and more proof. She was so stunned to find out that one of the greatest historical discoveries had been right under her nose and they'd never known.

"We found the coins last, with this." She dug the journal from her bag and ran a gentle hand over the cover. She smiled, carefully opening it, running her fingers over the sharp scrawl some in English, the rest in Creole and French.

He kept sneaking peeks at her, watching the way she delicately turned the pages, her fingers skimming the words. She lovingly caressed the pages, before finally closing the book and hugging it to her chest.

"If you have all of this, why do you need me?" He finally asked.

"Even though I'm a descendant, I'm not an expert neither is anyone in my family. My uncle Z is a retired family practice doctor and my sister has a Master's in literature. My father might have known more, he was the academic. According to Z he would listen to my grandparents' stories for hours on end. But since I never met them, and my parents are gone, I was at a disadvantage. I don't know that much about pirates and even less about Lafitte. There are some passages that I don't understand. There are hints and clues throughout his journal that I need help deciphering and with you being an expert I figured you would know more about the man than I do. You were the only person I know who knows everything there is to know about pirates. You were always talking about them and when I heard that the investor had to pull out and I figured you owed me one. It is, after all, the very least you could do. And here we are." She sighed and yawned.

"Take a nap." He said, when he noticed traffic slowing to a crawl, then just stop. They had run into the mid-day gridlock that seemed routine on the road to New Orleans. It was either the grand exodus of students returning home after spring semester, commuters getting a jump on the weekend or the ever-present road work. No matter, they were parked for the foreseeable future.

"Looks like this may take a while." She nodded. He had more questions, but within a few minutes, he could hear the soft even breathing that signaled she had fallen asleep. He watched her, her sunglasses were askew, her lips slightly parted as she slept. Gingerly, he removed the glasses, putting them neatly on the dashboard and stared at her. Her lashes were long enough to brush against smooth cheeks, her lips were a natural shade of berry pink that seemed to beckon him. He'd lied to her. Well, not really, he'd just omitted the fact that he'd liked her all those years before. He'd liked her but thought that she was too good, too sweet for someone like him. Even as a freshman, she'd been brilliant and though his friends hadn't been able to see it, he'd always found her to be beautiful.

But she had been just a girl then, now she was a full-grown woman and he couldn't stop staring at her legs. They were lean, smooth, the color of milk chocolate glistening in the sunlight. She was small, but curvy. He watched her, his palms itching to touch her, run a hand up toned chocolate thighs, he wanted to hold her face and kiss her, taste the sweetness that was her mouth. She shifted slightly, the strap of her dress, slipping from her shoulder exposing the lace covered curve of her breast and he stared, willing the strap to fall further. She even smelled good, like strawberries and gardenias. Everything about her intrigued and enticed him and he wanted her so much. He grunted, shifting to keep the growing erection that strained against his shorts at bay. That hadn't happened in a long time. He hadn't been so attracted to anyone in such a visceral way since, well since he'd known her before. What was it about the pixie of a woman that sent him into hormonal overdrive whenever she was near. What was it that made him ache for her so much, even after all this time? He didn't know, but he did know that he wanted to kiss her, needed to kiss her. Just once, then maybe he could keep his urges under control.

He licked his lips, leaning close enough to smell the sugary coffee on her breath. He brushed his fingers along her cheek, feeling the velvety softness of her skin. He tilted his head, ready to brush his lips against hers when a horn honked behind them.

He leapt in his seat, jamming his head on the roof of the car with a bone jarring thud. Cursing under his breath, he put the car into gear and rolled with the suddenly moving traffic. He snuck a glance at Clio to see if the blaring interruption had woken her. She'd simply shifted in her seat, and turned her face toward the window, still soundly asleep.

∞∞∞∞

What the hell was that? Clio's mind screamed as she stared out of the window, watching the sky whiz by, her heart racing. He was about to kiss her. Again!

She hadn't been fully asleep when he removed her glasses. She'd known they were askew, but she left them in place to block the blazing afternoon sun that filtered in from the windshield. She was going to say something snarky about him, but he'd leaned closer stroking her cheek.

His touch was so gentle, but it sent a wave of electricity through her that was like nothing she'd ever experienced before. She'd dared open her eyes, just a bit, so that she could see his face and she was stunned by his expression. He wasn't wearing his glasses, not that he needed them. She knew vanity glasses when she saw them. Noah's eyes, in the light were a clear deep whiskey brown, and the way he was looking at her made her stomach twist in knots. His skin was like rich dark coffee and he smelled amazing, like honey; and his hair, those thick dark locs, which were always pulled away from his face smelled of coconut. Why hadn't she noticed that before, she wondered. He'd leaned in, licking his lips before lowering his mouth. She'd held her breath waiting for the feel of his mouth on hers when that damnable horn had shocked them both.

He'd bolted upright, cracking his head on the headliner of the car, mumbled something and quickly moved the car forward. If she hadn't been so startled, she would have laughed but she'd taken the time to turn in her seat, knowing she needed to hide her expression.

She tried to take a deep breath without letting him know that she was awake, but her mind was already running through what-if scenarios. What if he'd kissed her the way he'd kissed her the night before? Granted, that had come as a total surprise, but she'd leaned into it. It had started soft, gentle but demanding more of her. She'd parted her lips, allowing him further access until she felt like she'd melt into a puddle of mush in his arms. Damn, a kiss like that could only lead to something she didn't think she was prepared for. She still hadn't completely forgiven him, she didn't trust him. Not yet.

But damn could the man kiss. If he kissed that well, she could only imagine what he would be like in bed. Her cheeks burned as less than pure thoughts invaded her imagination. She closed her eyes and tried to put those thoughts out of her mind. He hadn't kissed her and that was that. It was possibly just a lapse in judgment on his part or wishful thinking on hers. Who knew? All she knew was that her supposed faded attraction wasn't as dull as she believed.

Sure, the shock of seeing him after all this time had given her a tingle. Butterflies, like anyone seeing an old crush. Was it a crush? She had been infatuated with him all those years ago, but now she was older and, hopefully wise enough to know that she was not Noah Toussaint's type of woman. She was a novelty, a curiosity, the grown-up version of the ugly duckling he'd taken to a 'dog' party. She'd heard rumors about the unnaturally mean-spirited game, but to be a part of it had left her shaking and in tears as she left to walk back to her dorm. She hadn't

30

even cared that it had been the middle of the night or that she had to walk nearly across campus to her room. Alone. Devastated.

Just the memory of that had just about extinguished the brief flame that had begun in her stomach. But he touched her, gently tugging the hem of her skirt down. It had shifted, rising when she'd turned in her seat. He'd tugged, pulling it down so that it covered her exposed thighs, protecting her modesty. The tips of his fingers gently brushed her bare, sun kissed skin sending a new wave of heat from the pit of her belly to her cheeks.

'*Damn*,' she thought, '*damn you, Noah Toussaint for making me want to kiss you. Again.*'

∞∞∞∞

"Your name is Clio," Noah said as he stretched his legs. "And your sister is Calliope, you have an uncle named Zeus and you live in Olympus Apartments on the corner of Athens Road?" Clio looked at him over the hood of his car and smiled.

"Don't forget my aunt is Athena and my father was Apollo. It's kind of poetic, don't you think? Come on." Noah lifted their bags out of the back seat of his car once they made their way across the parking garage. He had to admit, he was very impressed by the apartment building Clio called home sitting a block off St Charles Avenue, it was a newer more modern structure with the name in fanciful script across the awnings. The area was very upscale and trendy and didn't fit his image of Clio Jean-Noel. As he drove past the little bistros and upscale shops of the neighborhood, he felt a little out of place here. When he'd begun searching for a parking space on the street, Clio had presented him with an entry key card for the secure parking garage. He waved the card at the sensor and a voice seemed to come from the heavens.

"Sir, you are not authorized to use that card to access this building. It is assigned to a resident." An authoritative male voice boomed. "And you are NOT that resident."

"It's me, Neil." Clio leaned forward, facing some unseen camera and waved. Noah looked up trying to see what she saw and saw nothing but the cement support beam.

"Ah, Dr. Clio. Didn't see you there. Good to have you home, look forward to hearing about your trip." The heavy iron gate rolled back allowing them entry.

Now as they walked through the cool indoor parking garage, he looked around at the cars stored there. All of them were expensive foreign cars, besides the BMW's and Mercedes', he noticed two cars sitting side by side that stood out even in a den of excess. One was a navy-blue Bentley Continental GT 8 convertible the other a

31

black Spyker C8 Preliator Spyder neatly together in a corner, pristine in their perfection.

"Nice cars," He said as they stepped into the elevator. "Expensive like sell your first born to buy one, but nice." She followed his sight line and smiled just as the elevator's doors were closing.

"Thanks. I think their pretty but completely impractical. We never use them. You want to drive one? Push five." He turned to look at her, his eyes wide with surprise. When he didn't move or speak, she continued.

"Well, you'll have to ask Calli about the Bentley. Push the button." She motioned to the metal panel near him again. Numb and confused, he pushed number five then continued to stare at the tiny woman beside him who hummed to the elevator music and absently dug through her bag for her keys. "I think they're a real waste of money. Calli rarely drives because she'd rather ride her Vespa. And I don't have a license. I'm barely home anyway. But I was told that they are a good investment, so we keep them. They're pretty at least." She mumbled. When she looked up at him, she frowned.

"What?" She asked. He was staring at her flabbergasted.

"What do you mean you don't have a driver's license?" He asked. "Everyone has a driver's license."

"Everyone who drives." He gasped, and she stared at him. He looked at her as if she were an alien being. "I'm not the only person in the world who doesn't drive, Professor. There are entire countries full of people who don't."

"But you can drive? I mean you know how? Right?" He asked. She rolled her eyes.

"I was a teenager in the United States, so yes, I can drive. I am fully capable. I just don't. It's not a big deal." She mumbled.

"I just think it's weird. I mean you travel around the world and you don't drive."

"It's not a big deal. I mean it's not like I need to drive in the jungles of Indonesia. And there is like fifty ride share services. What can I say, it's my one fault?" He had more questions, but he let it drop. There was something else there, something deeper than her simple explanation. "Sorry for snapping." She said in a low voice, her eyes averted. "I just don't like talking about it."

"You are ...not what I thought you were." He finally spoke when the elevator car stopped, and the doors silently slid open.

"I rarely am what anyone thinks I am. Makes life very interesting. Come on," She stepped into the hallway of the obviously luxe apartment building. He stood just outside of the elevator doors, weighed down with bags, completely confused. She was definitely different from the girl he'd met in college. She was more...just more. More confident, self-assured and there was a depth to her he would have never imagined. Smart and funny were only the tip of the iceberg with her. He couldn't wait to uncover the rest.

"Are you going to stand there all day or are you coming in?" She asked, unlocking one of the doors.

∞∞∞∞

"Lucy, I'm home!" Clio tossed her keys and her bag on the kitchen counter and turned to look at Noah who looked around the living room. He set their bags down and eased around the room, staring at family portraits that hung on the wall behind their sofa, then moved to look at the bookshelves that lined one wall. He seemed surprised, removing his glasses to look at the titles on the spines of the neatly ordered rows of books.

"Not what you expected either?" She asked, and he shook his head. The room was open, decorated in shades of grey and white with a decidedly feminine feel. Artifacts from her travels were peppered throughout the place, not too many, as to overpower the room, but enough to make it feel welcoming and distinctly homey.

"It's not. It's too...normal." His expression was so serious that she couldn't help but smile.

"Why is that surprising?" Before he could answer, Calliope Jean-Noel floated into the room like spring. She was a beautiful, curvy, blaze of color and dancing emerald eyes. Her face was full, the color of cappuccino and fully made-up, her left arm from her shoulder to just above her elbow was tattooed with creeping thorny vines of blood red roses. She was stunning.

"Hummingbird, I missed you so much. Are you okay? You look great. What did you bring me?" She hugged her sister, lifting her off the ground before she spotted Noah. She gave Clio a sly glance before narrowing her eyes and placing her hands on her hips. Having a woman who looked like she looked scrutinize him made him visibly squirm. "Wow, Birdie, thanks. He looks delicious. Can I unwrap him now or should I wait until later?"

Clio and Calli chuckled at the goofy grin that spread across Noah's face. If she didn't know better, she would have sworn he was blushing. It was cute on him. It reminded her of the kid she'd known before, not the stuffy pretentious professor. He should be like that more often, the way he was when he'd kissed her in the early hours of the morning. She shook herself back to now, the last thing she needed was to go down that road.

"Noah Toussaint, this is my big sister Calliope Jean-Noel." Noah took Calli's out stretched hand and nodded. Calliope studied him, openly inspecting him, her eyes roaming over him from head to toe in silent judgment. She came to stand before him, her lips pursed, her eyes studying his face with quiet intensity. She folded her arms across her chest and nodded.

"Hmmm" She sighed, then looked back at Clio. "The creep?" Clio nodded but busied herself with her luggage. "Uh huh. I've waited a long time to meet you. What you did to Clio, after everything we'd been through the year before..." Clio cleared her throat and Calliope closed her eyes and took a deep breath before continuing. "It hurt her. I mean really hurt her for a long time. She's grown a lot since then. I hope you have as well."

"I have. And I assure you, I've apologized and if I could take it back, I would. It cost me a chance..." He stopped, his eyes falling on Clio. She felt her heart skip a beat, the way he looked at her, the intensity of his gaze was unnervingly direct. "At something wonderful."

Calli turned to look at her, her expression mirroring Clio's. She'd felt it too, she'd felt the attraction, the tension between them filling the room, making the air heavy. Clio inhaled, and averted her gaze, her face feeling flushed. She slunk into the kitchen in search of sweets. She found a tray of freshly baked cookies. She loved Calli's cookies.

"Ooookay. I'm only going to say this once, Professor Toussaint, so listen up. My baby sister thinks she needs you for this little treasure hunt of hers. Even after you did what you did, she's trusting you. If you do anything and I mean anything to hurt her, I promise you, I will cut your balls off and shove them down your throat. Do I make myself clear, sir?" He swallowed hard and nodded. As pretty as she was, Noah got the distinct impression that Calli was the type of woman who didn't deal in idol threats.

"Crystal." He nodded. She smiled, a bright welcoming smile that was like the summer sunshine. "Okay then," She smiled, "Clio don't touch those cookies they are for the meeting." She said without turning to look at her sister. Clio shoved an entire cookie into her mouth and managed to look completely innocent.

"She's giving me those big wide puppy eyes, right?" Calli asked Noah who nodded. "She's been pulling that since she was two years old. Don't let her innocent face fool you, that one is as devious as they come. And twice as smart." Calli smirked as Clio began to protest.

"Lies!" Clio yelled as she pulled Noah toward a short hallway. "Lies, don't let my sister corrupt you. She's a devil woman." Calli laughed, a loud boisterous full bodied laughed that made Clio chuckle.

"Come on, you will be sleeping in my bedroom." He looked back at Calli who narrowed her eyes, then pointed to her eyes with two fingers, then pointed at him before running a bright red thumb nail across her throat. He swallowed hard , grabbing their bags and allowing Clio to drag him along behind her.

∞∞∞∞

He looked back at Calliope before following Clio down the hall to the bedrooms. She was the complete opposite of Clio yet there was no mistaking their genetics. They both had almond shaped eyes that slanted upward giving their faces and exotic look. Both had gold and green in their eyes, though Calliope's were a deeper shade of emerald and Clio's were more bronzed hazel. They laughed alike and had the same full lips, only Calli was much more voluptuous where Clio was athletically built. Calli was soft curves and bright red lips, Clio was all natural and smelled of cocoa butter.

"Your sister…" Noah started as he followed Clio into her bedroom, pausing when she turned to complete his thought. She was standing with her hands on her hips, her expression not quite a grimace or a smile, but a confusing combination of both.

"Is sexy, I know. I hear it all the time. Clio, your sister is so sexy, so gorgeous…"

"That's not what I was going to say." He said, looking down at Clio. He put their bags on a chair near a window that faced St. Charles Avenue. From this vantage point he could see the busy street below, the olive-green streetcars and bustling traffic surrounded by old world mansions and elaborate gardens. While the living room looked like a hodgepodge of the sisters, this room was definitely Clio.

The walls were a soft shade of denim blue, the headboard a deeper shade of blue that was somewhere between navy and midnight and seemed to have an almost Hindu design painted in white. Her comforter was plain white cotton and the wall art were photographs in heavy dark frames. He looked at them and realized that these were taken during her trips. The room even smelled of her, rich and earthy with floral undertones.

"Really?" She said with a snort. He turned to see her seated on the edge of her bed, undoing the buckles on her sandals. "You would be the first." She kicked her shoes off and pulled the band from her hair and her curls sprang free. She ran her fingers through her hair, tousling thick chestnut curls before turning to her dresser to take out her earrings.

"She is, there is no denying that. But she's not really my type." He said, his tone lower than he'd intended. She smelled good, and her hair wasn't just chestnut but also had touches of blond and mahogany. The light that streamed in from the window gave her that same sun-kissed angelic glow he'd noticed in the car.

She turned to look at him, her mouth moving but all he saw were soft, berry pink lips and the hint of her tongue as she asked a question. She'd tasted of whipped cream and chocolate when he'd kissed her earlier. When he'd held her, she'd felt right in his arms.

"Hello," She was waving her hand at him in an attempt to get his attention. He was immediately aware of the fact that they had been in the middle of a conversation when his thoughts had taken a detour.

"I'm sorry, what?" He blinked and cleared his throat trying to ignore the stirring in his groin.

"I was asking what exactly is your type?" She asked. He cupped her cheek, closing the distance between them. She took a step back, but bumped the dresser, her eyes wide with surprise.

"I think you know." He lifted her, sitting her on the dresser so that he could kiss her. She melted against him, her hands sinking into the hair at the nape of his neck. She parted her lips, allowing him access the warm sweetness that was her mouth. She wrapped her legs around his hips, pressing herself against him. He groaned gripping her hips and ground into the soft heat at her apex. She rocked against him, making it impossible for him to think.

He released her mouth, his lips moving down the column of her throat, one hand cupping her breast, his thumb circling a hardened nipple through the delicate material of her dress. The thin strap slipped off of her shoulder, exposing the velvety skin beneath. He trailed hot kisses across her flesh and she arched into him, her hips rocking against him. She was so warm, so soft that he felt light headed.

"We're either going to have to stop," He whispered, lifting his head to look into her amazing eyes.

"Or?" She teased, running her fingers over his bottom lip. He swallowed and tried to smile, but it didn't work, he could only look into her eyes, completely lost. She raked her bottom lip with her teeth and smiled. She shifted her hips, slowly, deliberately and he inhaled sharply. Her fingers sank deeper into his hair, her expression decidedly devious.

She leaned close her mouth at his ear, her breath tickling his cheek. She gently tugged his earlobe with her teeth, sending tendrils of heat to every nerve in his body.

He took a step back, but not far enough to break contact. He couldn't move even if he wanted to, he was frozen, the feel of her touch searing him. She smiled, a hungry little smile that made him realize that she was loving this, she enjoyed teasing him like this. She liked the fact that he wanted her, she knew that she had all of the power. For some inexplicable reason, it made him want her even more.

"This is strictly a business arrangement, professor." She whispered, her breath, sweet and warm against his lips, and he instinctively leaned in, but she was gone, stealthily slipping off of the dresser and out of his embrace.

"You can take a shower if you like-bathroom's through there. If you need a nap feel free," She indicated the bed with the wave of her hand. "We won't be meeting the rest of the crew for a few hours." She grabbed clothes from her dresser and headed toward the door, not bothering to even look at him. He was glad she hadn't, the evidence of his arousal standing at full attention and throbbing. Noah was stunned, he stood with his body aching his mind spinning the feel of her still lingering on his skin, skin that felt as if it had been set afire.

"Your sister was right," He finally managed before she left the room. "You are devious."

"Just a little," she shrugged before closing the door to give him privacy. He stared at the closed door, everything in him screaming to follow her, take her in his arms and kiss her until she was weak and boneless. That would show her.

Show her what? He thought, that he was a fool. This was strictly a business arrangement and that was his own fault. Not only had he apparently screwed up in college, he'd screwed up again when she'd crashed back into his life ten years later. When would he stop being such an idiot and think before he spoke? Once again, he'd ruined something before it ever got started. Raina had always told him he was too arrogant and self-important for his own good.

"Not all women are going to drop their panties just because you smile in their direction. One day you're going to meet your match and she won't be swayed by your pretty face. You're going to have to work for it." She had told him that more times than he cared to remember. As usual, Raina was the smarter of the two. Once again, his little sister was right.

"You're here to work, Noah. Just work, nothing else." He told himself, then a mischievous smile began at the corners of his mouth. Yes, he had work to do, lots of lost time to make up. He'd let Clio Jean-Noel slip away once before, he wasn't going to let her slip away again. He couldn't but he definitely had his work cut out for him.

"*Better get to work then, Toussaint,*" he thought. Smiling he sauntered into the bathroom, humming to himself.

∞∞∞∞

Clio leaned against the closed bedroom door, her eyes closed as she tried to collect herself. Her heart was racing, her body humming with an electricity she had never experienced before. It had taken a Herculean effort to pull herself away from Noah. She should have known better, but she just couldn't resist. Something about being so close to him made her let her guard down. She was thankful that her legs hadn't buckled when she walked away.

Damn, she touched her kiss swollen lips. Why did he have to be such a damn good kisser? This was the second time in less than twenty-four hours that she nearly dropped her panties for the man. He made her skin tingle, her breath quickened and everything else in her liquefy into a pool of unabashed sexual heat.

37

"Damn," She whispered and leaned against the closed door. Knowing that he wanted her, after all these years, after what he'd done, had made her giddy and careless. And hell, she couldn't deny it, it made her hot. She fanned herself with the clothes she had clutched in her fist, realizing that she had grabbed a t shirt and panties, no bottoms. She would have to go back in there. She turned to face the door, her hand on the knob when she heard the shower.

He would be naked by now, wet and hard, the water glistening on cocoa colored skin. She couldn't go in there, not now. Not with her libido in overdrive, she couldn't trust herself. When he'd kissed her, she'd lost the little control she'd had with him.

Why had she leaned into him, inhaling that coconut and honey smell he had and why did he smell like that? Men were supposed to smell like spice or musk, something earthy not sweet. She hadn't meant to wrap herself around him like cling wrap, but there she had been, legs akimbo, her hips writhing against his obvious rock-hard crotch like some wanton hussy.

Her cheeks flamed anew at the memory of him so hard, pulsing against her. She could feel his shaft against her, layers of denim and cotton keeping him from slipping heavy and hard....

"Whatcha doin?" Calli's head appeared around a corner, like a specter. Clio yelped and nearly jumped out of her skin. She waved at Calli motioning for her to quiet down while clutching her chest to keep her heart from leaping from her mouth.

"Shh. Nothing. Why are you sneaking up on me like that?" She asked in a harsh whisper.

"Excuse me for being in my own hallway. Why are we whispering?" Calli mimicked her tone, confused.

"Because I don't want Professor know-it-all to hear us. He just...kissed me."

"Ooh, bad kisser?" Calliope shook her head in exaggerated despair.

"Absolutely not. Good kisser. Like, dangerously good. Like make the hair on your neck stand up and your knees go weak good." She closed her eyes and began to fan herself again. Her sister stared at her in confusion, trying to decipher how Clio wanted her to react.

"And that's a problem because?" She leaned against the wall, folding her arms across her chest and waited. She was humoring her. She'd become a pro at it, ever since they were kids, the ever-mature Calliope would strike the same pose and wait for Clio to spout her nonsensical logic. Rolling her eyes, she relented and tried to explain.

"I don't want him to think I'm into him. That I'm still that gawky kid from college lusting after him." Clio hissed.

"But you are. You always have been. You watched every game he played, bought every book he's written, read every paper-" Calli said. Clio rolled her eyes and grimaced.

"But I don't want him to know that." Clio snapped. "I need this to be strictly business. I don't need him getting the wrong idea about what this is. I have got to be the one to set the boundaries of this relationship."

"Will that be before or after you sleep with him?" Calli laughed.

"Before." Clio answered honestly. "Then I can rub his stupid gorgeous face in the fact that he has no effect on me whatsoever."

"But he does. Obviously." Calli chuckled.

"Anyway, he's here to work not get his groove back. I'm not going to be his sexual diversion or whatever. If he thinks that he better think again. I will not be sucked in by him again. This time I call the shots. Me."

"Well that's mature." Calli frowned.

"I never claimed to be mature, Cal. I'm using your shower and borrowing some clothes." Calliope glanced at the clothes Clio had balled in her fist, then back at her sister. "I didn't grab any bottoms."

"Wow, he's that good of a kisser?" Clio narrowed her eyes at Calli who couldn't stop the knowing smile that spread from ear to ear. Clio hated that smile. She had often referred to it as Calliope's know- it- all grin. Calliope had been giving her that stupid grin for as long as she could remember.

"Shut up." Clio mumbled turning to go into her sister's bedroom.

"I swear smart people are so stupid." Calli called after her just before she slammed the door.

∞∞∞∞

Clio stood in the doorway staring at the man, correction, half naked chocolate fantasy, laying across her bed asleep. In the living room, their crew, what was left of it anyway, had gathered earlier than expected, eager to meet the famous Dr. Noah Toussaint. She'd frozen in the doorway, staring at the long, leaned muscled beauty that was Noah. She closed the door gently as not to wake him, and pressed herself to the cool wood, silently studying him.

He lay on his back, one arm thrown across his eyes, his chest rising and falling with each breath. His hair was loosely hanging to his shoulders and his feet were still on the floor. It looked as if he'd sat on the edge of the bed, intent on closing his eyes for a moment and had drifted off. The late afternoon sunlight cast the room in a soft amber glow and suddenly everything felt dreamy. She was staring, she knew, but she couldn't help it.

She moved closer taking in the corded muscle of his arms and thickness of his thighs. His abs were clearly cut, and he had that delicious V that pointed to what she could only assume was as beautifully made as the rest of the well sculpted man. He had a scar on his right knee, long and precise, from a surgery she assumed. She had to admit, his career in football had done his body extremely well. Except for his feet. She stared at his mangled toes and frowned. She supposed that it was normal for football players to have bad feet and knees, the years of hard work and injuries. She supposed he was lucky because the rest of him was pretty fantastic. He shifted and the towel that was loosely tucked at his narrow hips shifted exposing him.

She inhaled sharply in surprise but couldn't turn away.

"Get a good look?" His voice was thick with sleep and startled her. She took a step back, tripping over his duffel which he'd carelessly left in the middle of the room. She could feel herself falling, when large hands grasped her around the waist. He was on his feet, holding her steady losing his towel altogether in the process. Her breasts were crushed against him, her face only reaching the middle of his chest, she had to crane her neck to look at his face. Breathless, her eyes wide with the sudden realization that the only thing between her and his growing erection were a pair of thin khaki shorts.

"You okay?" He asked. He was looking down at her, his locs brushing her shoulders. She nodded dumbly, her palms flat against his chest. "Are you sure?"

Again, she nodded, her eyes locked with his. Her body was hot, her cheeks flushed, and she could feel her throat tighten. His arms tightened around her waist, holding her closer still. She licked her lips and opened her mouth to speak but only a small sigh escaped. He was looking at her with an expression that she was sure mirrored what he saw in her.

"You can let me go now." She finally managed.

"I could. But what would be the fun in that?" He said, and she watched the hint of a smile tease the corners of his mouth. He was goading her, and he was hard, his erection pressing into her with a growing urgency that made her heart rate speed up. Her skin was hot, her breath quickening in nervous anticipation.

"You're playing with me, aren't you?" She asked, and he smiled. When his mouth covered hers, she clung to him, and let out an involuntary groan when he slipped his tongue between her teeth, he tasted of mint and sugar, just delicious.

Her arms snaked around his neck, sinking into the silky softness of the hair at the base of his neck. He moved his hands down and cupped her cutely rounded bottom, urging her to wrap her legs around his waist, which she did willingly. He released her mouth for a moment, catching his breath, but she wasn't quite finished with him.

"We've got to stop doing this." He breathed, closing his eyes when Clio cupped his face in her hands.

"I know, right?" She brushed her slightly parted mouth against his, the tip of her tongue teasing him before delving into the sweet warmth. Her hands moved down his chest, raking his nipples and it was his turn to let out an involuntary moan.

When she finally came up for air, he stared into her eyes, his breath coming in great strained pants. She searched his expression trying to get some read on what he was feeling, but his face was blank. She cleared her throat and eased out of his embrace, taking a careful step away from him. She looked at him. He stood before her in utter magnificence, his body hard muscle and sleek planes. She had the sudden urge to run her tongue over every inch of him. When her gaze drifted lower, to his unrelenting erection, she stared, the room suddenly too hot and small. He was physical perfection. She exhaled and ran a hand over her brow and turned away.

She looked back at him, his eyes locked on hers as he slowly reclaimed his towel, a self-satisfied smirk on his face. She shook her head, running her hand through her hair in an attempt to clear her head.

"I was coming to tell you that the crew is here. We're waiting for you to get started. Calli made dinner if you're hungry." He was staring at her, his face a mask of calm that made her a bit uncomfortable. She couldn't tell what was going on with him, it was as if some sort of switch had gone off.

"Is that the only reason you came in here?" He asked. She swallowed hard, her eyes on his chest. He took a step closer and she froze, unable to take a step back.

"Of course," she snorted, trying to make her tone light and casual.

"Then why can't you look me in the eye?" His tone was teasing. She looked up, pursing her lips and lifting one eyebrow.

"Happy?" She asked. He reached up, gently stroking her cheek with one finger.

"I would be happier if I could kiss you again." His voice lowered to nearly a whisper, his dark eyes intense and she knew that if she didn't step away, he would do just that. Problem was, she knew that if she allowed him to kiss her, it wouldn't end there. She'd want more, she'd need more. He stroked her cheek, his thumb teasing her kiss swollen lips.

"You taste just the way I thought you would, just like some exotic tropical fruit, sweet, a little wild, delicate, addictive. I want to know if you're that sweet everywhere." He had moved closer, leaning forward, his mouth dangerously close to hers. He was going to kiss her again and she would let him. She would let him do that and so much more. Her bones felt liquid and her body burned. Swallowing, she managed a coy smile.

"Okay, good to know. You can come out once you're dressed. And once you're a little less- excited." She said finally and turned to leave the room. She was nearly to the door when he spoke again, that teasing tone back. But his words set her blood on fire.

"Clio," She turned to look at him. His jaw was set, his posture stiff and he made no attempts to hide the evidence of his arousal. "You always kiss me back, you know." She didn't know what to say so she just left the room.

∞∞∞∞

Well, Noah thought as he hurried to dress, that had been a mistake. He'd thought that if he kissed Clio, that his re-emerging infatuation with her would be quelled for a while, but he'd been so wrong. He'd kissed her three times now and it just made him want her even more. She was so soft and warm; her skin was like satin and her mouth...he needed to stop thinking about this. His skin felt hot, and his stomach was twisted into knots because he had never wanted a woman the way he wanted Clio. He just couldn't understand it; she wasn't his type. She had never been his type, not really. He dated tall, willowy model types not annoyingly smart-assed pixies, yet he felt his body tense the moment she walked into a room. It was primal the way he wanted her.

He put all thoughts of the smell and feel and sweet lord, the taste of Clio Jean-Noel out of his mind. They had work to do and from the sounds of laughter coming from the other room, he had a crew to meet. Slipping on a pair of jeans and a t-shirt, he padded barefoot into the living room to meet the people he would be spending at least the next month with in what he assumed were close quarters.

Something was wrong, he knew that as soon as he stepped into the living room. Clio was pacing back and forth chewing her thumb nail. Three people he assumed were part of her crew were looking just as anxious as she was, but they remained silent. There were two women, one with short, spiky hair, her deep brown eyes wide with worry, the other pale with jet black hair and heavy bangs. The only other male in the room sat beside Calliope on the sofa. They seemed only slightly less agitated than the others.

"What do you mean? The whole crew?" A husky, heavily accented male voice echoed in the silence of the room. Clio paused her pacing long enough to look at a laptop that sat open on the bar that separated the kitchen and the living room.

"This is the crew, or what's left of it. Garrett took everyone else. Now I just have a tech, a historian, an archaeologist, a diver and ..." She looked at her sister and sighed in defeat. "Calliope."

"Hey!" Calliope shouted indignantly. "I'm useful. Sometimes."

"Anyway," Clio continued, noticing him for the first time. She nodded to Calli who patted the spot next to her on the sofa. He happily sat, feeling less like an interloper on this tense exchange

42

"Apparently, he made the rest of the crew believe this was a solo trip. He's even got some pseudo-history expert with him. He convinced the crew, my crew, that he was lead and that the contract they signed with me extended to him as well. He poached my fucking team, Titus."

"Then they are in breach of contract. I will get my people on that. The real question is, what are you going to do? Are you still doing this?" Clio stopped pacing and straightened her back. Her entire demeanor, her aura completely changed, and Noah found himself enthralled.

"Hell, yes I'm still doing it. I will not let that pimple on the ass of history take credit for my family history. There is no way he'll get away with this and he better hope your people get to him before I do. Find me a crew, a competent crew that can be ready to set sail in three days. Get the ship ready and make sure it has everything I need. It will be a cold day in hell before I let him get away with this. And he better pray to all that is holy that I don't find him, that forked tongued bastard. If I get my hands on him, two hundred years from now they will still be finding his body parts in the Caribbean."

Noah didn't hear what was said after that because he was too focused on Clio. She had a fire in her that re-ignited the fire in him. Her eyes blazed, nostrils flared as her anxiety gave way to anger and pure determination. Anger on anyone else of her size would be adorably comical, but on Clio it was damn intimidating. His body sprang to life, the familiar tug in his groin started again. He shifted in attempt to hide his growing arousal.

Clio ended the call and turned to look at them, her hands on her hips. She exhaled and looked over the small group, scratching her head before she spoke again.

"Okay. I guess you guys noticed our guest. Dr. Noah Toussaint, this is part of the team that will be accompanying us to the Caribbean. The best part. Mina," Clio pointed to the dark-haired young woman, "she's our marine archaeologist. That strapping young fellow is Javi, he handles all of our tech and audio-visuals, and this rather vivid beauty is Teri, she handles all matters mechanical. Everyone, Noah our Lafitte expert. He's going to help me pinpoint exactly where the ship went down." They waved politely and smiled at him.

"Are we going to talk about the crew?" Calliope asked, rising slowly. She gave Noah's knee a pat and motioned for the kitchen. "You must be hungry. I'll get you something." He had to admit, the aroma wafting from the kitchen had made his empty stomach growl. Not to mention that he hadn't eaten all day. Food sounded amazing.

"Titus will do what Titus does and we will have a crew. It's just a minor hiccup. Now, let's get started." Clio was saying as she moved across the room. She was wearing tiny khaki shorts and a pale blue t-shirt, her curls a glimmering halo around her face. Kneeling at the coffee table a few feet in front of him, she gave him enough room to eat from the heaping plate of food Calli handed him as she rejoined the group. Clio sat on her haunches, her perfect ass and straight back facing him, tempting him. She glanced back over her shoulder at him briefly then turned back to the group.

He looked down his mouth watering at the fried catfish, homemade mac and cheese, and peas. He dug in, listening to Clio as she began. As she spoke, he became aware of the group hanging on her every word, listening intently, only nodding occasionally as she explained her plan of action. He found himself smiling. She had always been the smartest person in the room.

Chapter 4

"Okay," Clio began unfolding the sheath of papers she'd shoved into the journal for safekeeping. "I've looked at all of the locations mentioned. He talks about Grand Isle, so I think we'll have to head down there in the morning maybe in the next day or so, while Titus gets the crew together. He also mentions Puerto Rico, Jamaica, Haiti and Hispaniola quite a bit."

"Do you think that whatever is supposed to be in Grand Isle is still there? Could it have been pushed into the open ocean by the current or even sunk further into a crevasse or something. You know, the landscape of the ocean floor changes just like it does on land. We're talking about nearly two hundred years of erosion." Mina said, sipping a glass of red wine.

"What do you mean?" Clio asked, rising to her knees to get a better look at the map they'd spread out on the low coffee table. Noah's eyes drifted down her back to her firm, round bottom but only for a moment. Calli was watching him, a knowing smirk on her lips. She didn't say anything, just smiled and sipped her wine. He cleared his throat and leaned forward, pointing to the map.

"I think what she's saying is that if Lafitte's ship really sunk in the Gulf then with the centuries of land development, soil erosion, not to mention the number of hurricanes and storm systems that have battered the coast, the entire thing could have shifted with the current. The current in the Gulf feeds into two other currents. If it was picked up by southernly return flow, it could be anywhere between Iceland and Chile. If it was caught in the North Atlantic system it could have gone as far east as Europe or, and this is very unlikely, the coast of Africa. But since the current tends to be a loop, more than likely, it would have moved more toward the Caribbean." He sat back and continued to eat, aware that they were all looking at him as if he'd grown a second head.

"Pretty and Smart. Birdie, I think we have a winner here?" Calli teased and he felt his cheeks warm.

"Didn't you say something about Lake Borne and Shell Beach? Maybe we should check there first. Or even Galveston?" Mina suggested, and the others nodded.

"A few years back after Hurricane Katrina, some treasure hunters combed that entire Galveston area. They scavenged for the better part of a year hoping the storm had churned something up, they didn't find so much as a doubloon." Noah said. "Lake Borne has never produced anything and Shell Beach, very unlikely anything would be there. There may be something in Grand Isle, but chances are very slim. Simply because of the erosion and the number of storms that have battered the area."

"So, we still need to check out Grand Isle, right?" Clio asked.

"Maybe. I mean it wouldn't hurt. And we have a couple of days, right?" He agreed.

"So, you'll come with me?" She turned to look at him then, her face open and excited. She placed a hand on his knee, waiting for him to respond verbally. The muscle in his thigh tensed involuntarily, a spark of electricity making a beeline for his crotch.

"I'll come with you." Though he intended it to sound nonchalant, it hadn't. He could feel the tension in the room as everyone seemed to focus on the two of them in quiet anticipation. Clio opened her mouth to speak but stopped. He could see that she was debating on what to do next. She turned back to the map and cleared her throat, her hands raking through her hair.

"Okay, now that that's settled...This is a list of supplies we will need to get before we head down to Puerto Rico. That's where Titus has the ship docked. Javi, are you still set to fly out in the morning? I know you have somethings to set up, but without the crew-"

"I'm still going out in the morning. So is Teri. We have a lot to do and a short time to do it." Javi's voice was soft, quiet and a little on the unhurried side. From what Noah had witnessed, Javi didn't seem to let anything ruffle him, even in the face of a major crisis, he remained completely mellow.

"Great. I think we're getting the big boat this time, he said it's wi-fi ready and that we have everything in order, but I want you to be sure. Just in case." Clio handed each of them a sheet of paper.

"I'm heading out with them as well," Mina said. "I want to get my sea legs again and help with the excavation equipment, get my maps and gear...you know the drill. And I want to go over the maps and plot a course with the captain. Is it Doug again? Or did he jump ship with the rest of the traitorous bastards."

"Doug is still with us." Clio smirked, but continued reviewing the supply list in front of her.

"I'm flying out as well. Going to help I mean." Calli said. Clio looked back at her in utter shock.

"You're coming? I thought you were trying to get started on your new book."

"You're a writer?" Noah asked around a mouth full of food. "What do you write? Would I have read any of your work?" Calli managed to blush slightly and quickly dodged the question.

"Maybe, it's mostly young adult mysteries but lately I'm stalled. Maybe a change of scenery will help get my mojo going again. And I'm a certified scuba instructor, so I am *actually* useful despite public opinion." She sighed, and Noah realized she hadn't really answered his question. He looked around at the faces of the group to see if any of them had noticed. If they had, they didn't let it show because they were all paying close attention to Clio's schematics and diagram of the boat and what was needed where.

He turned his attention back to his food while he listened to Clio, Mina, Teri and Javi talk logistics, equipment, and supplies. They spoke in terms that Noah didn't understand but from what he gathered they were all very skilled and knew exactly what was expected. At one point, they began completing each other's thoughts while pouring over the layout of the boat.

"We do have a slight problem, Birdie." Javi was saying, his eyes shifting slightly to Teri.

"The damage to the mini-sub during that rock slide on your last excavation was more extensive than we thought. The entire computer system, the navigation and rover are all shot. I contacted "the man" and he said a new one wouldn't be a problem once you called to verify which one you need." Teri blurted.

"How much are we talking?" Clio sighed, rubbing her eyes. Javi handed over a slip of paper and she let out a long, low whistle.

"Jesus on a tricycle, did you tell him it was this much? And what are all of these additions?"

"That is the added tech, the video monitors, the recording equipment, it has to be large enough to fit at least three people and communicate with the ship. It has robotic manipulators and a remote rover. Titus said he could do it and have it installed by the time we get there, but as he put it, *'I need the Hummingbird to tell me herself.'*" Javi calmly explained.

"If you say we need it, then I say we need it. Anything else? Someone want a gold-plated helicopter?" Clio mumbled.

"Now that you mention it," Calli teased and Clio shot her daggers. She immediately demurred and sat back, her hands in her lap, her lips pursed in attempt to stifle a smile.

"Any serious requests?" No one responded, so she continued going over the list, which seemed to be unending. She shifted, and Noah watched her roll her neck and rub her shoulders a few times, but she continued speaking. When she began kneading the muscles of her lower back, he was tempted to massage her aches away. He could just about feel the taut, silky skin beneath his fingers. The thought of running his mouth along the curve of her spine, made his mouth water. Damn, he was getting hard again, and in a room full of people he didn't even know. What was wrong with him? He shifted the plate in his lap, hoping to mask the growing erection, when he realized Clio was turning to talk to him.

"Is there anything you need before they get going, professor?" She was looking at him with those incredible hazel eyes. He was confused for a moment before he noticed the others gathering their things to leave.

"Um, no. It was nice meeting you guys. I look forward to working with you." He managed. Javi nodded at him with a knowing smirk. But gratefully said nothing.

"No need to get up. Birdie, we'll see you at the end of the week? Calli will you be on time tomorrow?" Javi leaned across him to give Calliope a kiss on the cheek. His eyes on Noah letting him know he'd seen everything. Noah felt his face flush and adjusted his glasses.

"Of course I will. I'll be ready to leave at eleven." She proclaimed proudly. The three shared a look then looked at Clio who shrugged. Mina placed a hand on Calliope's shoulder and smiled for the first time that night. The expression lightened her face, and for the first time revealed to Noah that she was younger than he'd first thought.

"That's great, Cal. But our flight is at eight," Calliope stared at her dumbfounded.

"A.M.? Since when?" Calli snorted.

"Since always." Teri laughed as they exited the room.

"I'm going to walk them out." She rose to walk their guests out. On her way she grabbed Noah's empty plate and he casually dropped his hands into his lap. "Apparently, there are details that need clarification."

Noah didn't move until he heard the front door close and the muffled voices fade away. Clio turned to look at him. She took a sip from her wine glass and sighed before she spoke.

"Now are you ready to do this Professor? It's time for us to get busy." Clio said. He stared at her for a moment not sure if he understood her correctly or if his mind had begun playing tricks on him. It was the first time they'd been alone since they'd kissed in the bedroom and that was all he could think about.

"Do you read Haitian Creole or French?" She asked.

"What?" He blinked, then noticed that she was opening the journal and he sighed, shaking his head at his own wishful thinking. He eased off of the sofa in order to sit beside her on the floor to get a better look at the journal. They were alone, the silence in the apartment making it seem more intimate. She looked at him, her face soft relaxed and he thought she looked like that girl he once knew.

"French? Creole?" She asked pointing to the faded curling script on delicately worn paper.

"Um, no. Strictly English." He said.

"Well, that's why I'm here." She gave him a smile, the first he'd seen since her exit from the bedroom earlier. "We have a lot to do in a little bit of time. Let's get that big brain of yours working."

∞∞∞∞

Clio could feel his eyes on her the entire time she was going over the technical aspects with her crew. She'd expected Noah to interact more, but he'd remained quiet, listening to them go over their business. He laughed at a couple of Javi and Teri's bawdy jokes and complimented Calliope on her cooking, but he never said anything to her at all. It had freaked her out a little, to be honest.

She could feel his eyes on her back, the heat from his gaze distracting her from her work. That last kiss had thrown her into a tailspin and she wasn't sure how to handle it, how was she going to work with him if he continued to look at her as if she were the last meal of a dying man.

"This is the section I'm having trouble with, I believe that there is a hint in here but I'm not sure. Lafitte sent letters to his brother Pierre often and in this passage, he mentions a map to paradise in case he was captured or killed, so I'm not sure exactly where to look. I figured the way to the Pride is in here somewhere. I just need to know exactly where to look so we don't spend months going in circles. Look at this–" She pointed to a small drawing along the margin, a symbol that she could never really make out. It looked almost like two inverted sabers forming a point. Noah adjusted his glasses and stared at the crude drawing.

"This looks vaguely familiar. It looks like the flag of the Cartagena Republic. Lafitte sailed under this not a pirate flag around the same time he dropped the second F in his name. He called himself a privateer and no one would really take notice when they saw this flag on the horizon. It made his pirating easier, I suppose." He was saying when she laughed.

"Why do you wear those?" She finally asked when he looked at her.

"What?" He leveled her with a gaze that made her pause for a moment. He really was a beautiful man. His face looked as if it had been carved from marble, his eyes that smoldered whiskey brown made her stomach flutter in the most ridiculously annoying way.

"The vanity glasses?" She said around the growing lump in her throat.

"What makes you think they're vanity glasses?" He inched closer, the scent of him filling her senses making her a bit light headed.

"You're talking to someone who's had to wear glasses for the majority of her life. I know vanity glasses when I see them. Not that you look bad in them, I'm just curious. Is it a fashion statement or something else?" He studied her face for a

49

while, his expression masked. She squirmed a little under his scrutiny and hated herself for it. She straightened, jutting out her chin and waited for him to respond.

"Long story." Was the only response he would give before turning his attention back to the journal. It was as if something in him had closed off and made him pull into himself. She supposed it wasn't her place to pry, but Noah was proving himself to be quite the conundrum. He was sexy and intelligent but withdrawn and introverted. He'd been a star football player with millions in his future only to give it up after an injury that was by no means career ending, to become a history professor. Of all of the things he could have done, he could have been, he went into academics. He was extremely good looking and aware of his effect on the opposite sex, yet he ignored the women who'd practically thrown themselves at him. And now he was hiding behind his glasses, glasses he didn't even need. Everything about him screamed superstar and he seemed to be doing his best to fight it.

"I've got time." She gently nudged him, but he didn't waver, didn't even register her teasing tone.

"What does this say?" He pointed to a passage just beneath the symbol. Clio leaned in closer to see, and she could have sworn he sniffed her hair.

"You really don't like talking about yourself, do you?" She asked.

"There isn't a whole lot to tell. My mother died when I was ten. My father died my rookie year in the NFL. It's just been Raina and I since then."

"You never really fit, anywhere do you?" She asked, and he sighed.

"Not quite. Now, the journal?" He looked past her, turning his attention to the journal letting her know that conversation wasn't going to happen. Not tonight anyway.

"Umm, let's see... *I have sent Renato to Pierre with instructions on safeguarding this plan. He has been instructed to place these papers and mark the location, brand it with his irons to lead the way if it is ever lost.* Does that mean something to you? Who is Renato? My field of study was more ancient civilizations than pirates."

"Renato Beluche was one of Simon Bolivar's admirals, he worked briefly with Jean and Pierre. There is a house on Dumaine street that he lived in that was said to be a smuggling front. There are conflicting stories about that, but the house is still there. Pirates and smugglers used to have hidden rooms and guide posts like the underground railroad, little symbols and sayings that would lead them to safety and let them know who they could trust. Usually, it was carved into a brick or wooden beam." Noah answered, his voice at her back making the hairs on the back of her neck rise. She shivered as the memory of his mouth, hot on hers, made her skin heat.

"Do you think he had this Beluche hide something in the house?" Clio asked, the excitement welling up in her stomach. She loved this part, the trail of tiny clues. She knew that it could be a dead end, but just the excitement of finding the first of what she hoped to be many breadcrumbs made her a little giddy.

"Maybe but that place is a museum now. Honestly, if anything was there, with restorations and remodels, it's highly unlikely it would still be there." She shook her head, smiling more to herself than at him.

"They restore, they don't remove. Anyway, if there is a brand on one of the bricks it could still be there. Back then most of the structures were brick with a kind of stucco overlay. They would want to restore as much of the original structure as possible. And what ever they remove, they store somewhere for historical significance or some nonsense. We at least have to go look." She was rubbing her lower back again. She'd been sitting on her knees too long and now she was stiff and achy. She absently massaged her own back, trying to relieve the tired muscles, her face buried in the journal as she searched for more clues.

"Here, let me help." Clio heard the rumbling of Noah's deep voice move closer. The touch of his warm, powerful hands on her skin made her let out an involuntary moan. He began kneading the stiff muscles of her lower back. The feel of his hands on her skin made her whimper. Her head fell forward, her eyes drifted closed. He was sitting behind her, his long legs trapping her between him and the coffee table as his hands continued their delicious assault. Not that she was going to move, she was reveling in the feel of his hands on her aching, and now hot flesh. His fingers were strong and hard, but he wasn't rough as she would expect from a former athlete. He had a gentle touch and worked on the tight muscles until she grunted her approval. She could feel him move closer until the heat of his body warmed her back.

"What else does it say?" His voice was low, husky and warm, tickling her ear as he read over her shoulder. He moved up to her shoulders and neck and she moaned as the tension released her body going liquid. She eased back, resting against his chest as he worked a particular knot in her shoulder.

"That feels great." She whispered just before his lips brushed her neck. Her pulse jumped, and her eyes opened wide, but she didn't move, she couldn't. His mouth was hot, soft on the sensitive skin just beneath her ear. Her eyes slowly drifted shut, and she found herself tilting her head to give him more access.

"It says that? Really?" He teased, and she couldn't help her smile. "What else does it say?"

"This," she heard herself saying, "is probably not a good idea." His teeth gently tugged at her earlobe making her sink into him, her eyes drifting closed again. One arm curved around her waist and pulled her back so that she was sitting in his lap. He was hard, the length of him pressing against her own moist heat. She rocked back, enjoying the feel of him, her body tingling.

"Probably not." He agreed, inhaling sharply when she began the slow sway of her hips. He held her tight, his mouth on her neck, his hips matching her movements. She reveled in the feel of him, every tiny moan of approval that escaped him. His hand moved from her waist to cup her breast through her shirt, his thumb tracing delicious circles over her raised nipple.

"We should get back to work.". She let her head fall back against his chest, her lips parted as a wave of pleasure washed over her. She felt the snap on her shorts release and wondered for a brief second why had he done that when his hand slipped past the lacy waist band of her panties. She inhaled sharply when he touched her, her body shaking as he toyed with her. Slowly, he stroked her until her body began to shudder.

"Uh huh," He breathed into her hair, pushing his hips up against her heat adding to the tantalizing friction. She swallowed hard, trying to clear her mind and think of actual words as her body hummed against him.

"This is not really conducive to what we're doing." She murmured in husky tones.

"I think it's very conducive to what I'm doing." He said turning her head so that he could cover her mouth with his and all of her resolve evaporated. He felt so good, his body hard, his touch gentle. She arched into him, wanting him to continue his exploration as she savored every teasing touch. And he willingly obliged, his hand moving beneath her shirt, past the silken material of her bra until he cupped her bare breast in his palm. The feel of his palm against her tightened nipple sent a shiver through her. She reached back, sinking her fingers into the hair at the nape of his neck. He gently nipped at the pulse point in her neck. She was breathing heavier, practically panting when his free hand moved past the waist band of her shorts. She held her breath knowing that if he touched her there, his hand moved any lower, she would be lost.

"Clio- Oh- I'm - uh- going to go pack and get some sleep. Yeah. Early morning. Keep...doing ...working...I... good night." Calliope rushed past them and into her room like a brilliant rainbow. Her bedroom door closed with a slam. They sat frozen for a moment too stunned and embarrassed to move until Clio burst into laughter. She could feel Noah chuckling quietly at her back.

"Okay," Noah sighed, reluctantly removing his hands, grunting as she slipped off of his lap. "I feel like I was just busted making out with the babysitter." He mumbled, dropping one last kiss on her shoulder.

"Calliope, queen of bad timing." Clio sighed, looking back at him. "Back to work, professor. This time, try to keep your hands to yourself." She took a deep calming breath, silently thanking her sister for her timing. If Calliope hadn't burst into the room, she would have straddled Noah and rode him to the heavens.

"I make no promises." He said but shifted so that he could sit beside her. She peeked at him through her lashes, her cheeks still flush. Damn Calliope for walking in when she did. And damn her for letting it get that far.

∞∞∞∞

"Are you sure this is the place?" Noah asked staring up at the French Colonial home. The plaque near the entrance gave a brief history of the museum that had been named *Madame John's Legacy* and declared it a national monument. He stared at the second-floor veranda and the pale green shudders, squinting against the morning sunlight. He was in a foul mood, not bad really, just frustrating. He's spent the night tossing and turning in Clio's bed, surrounded by her. It hadn't helped that whenever he closed his eyes, the image of her body, hot and wet writhing against him flooded his memory.

He'd finally given up on sleep and just lay staring at the ceiling. He couldn't understand why he wanted her the way he did. Everything about her, her voice, her smell, the way she took charge her presence filling the room. He'd been with Catherine for years and he'd never craved her the way that he craved Clio.

He'd laid awake until he heard Clio trying to get Calliope out of the apartment and into a car for the airport. He could hear them arguing before the sun rose, Clio going through a list of necessities and Calli checking off as she did. When the phone rang at five thirty, she was ready to go, only to return to the apartment twice for something she'd forgotten.

By six, he smelled fresh coffee and some sort of sweet baked goods drifting into the room from the kitchen. When he entered the kitchen in flannel pajama bottoms and a t-shirt, he instantly remembered what it was about her that attracted him. She was freakin adorable. Not to mention the fact that she was probably the smartest person he'd ever met. She was seated on a bar stool, glasses firmly in place, her hair a mess all over her head.

"Morning." He mumbled, before pouring himself a cup of coffee. She looked at him over her glasses and smirked.

"Sorry if we woke you. I love my sister, but she is the most scatterbrained person I've ever met." He nodded his agreement before taking a sip of the best coffee he'd had in a long time.

"How can she be a writer if she's that scattered?" He asked.

"Nature of the beast, I guess because she's also the smartest person I've ever met. Other than our early morning shenanigans, how did you sleep?"

"I didn't." He said honestly. She paused with a buttery croissant halfway to her mouth. That was the wonderful smell that had finally coaxed him from bed. Not just the aromatic French roast, the sweet buttery smell of baking bread had permeated the apartment.

"I'm sorry. Is my bed uncomfortable? The mattress is kind of stiff, its rarely used. I'm never home for more than a few weeks at a time-"

"It wasn't the mattress." He said, and she met his heated gaze. She didn't blink, didn't falter as the gaze lingered. But he could tell, by the look in those sun kissed eyes that she was thinking about it, all of it.

"This thing between us, you're going to have to control it a little better. I mean, last night my sister walked in ..."

"So, you admit there's a thing?" He teased, and she returned his cocky grin.

"You know there's a thing. There has always been a thing, even in college though you wouldn't admit it. You wanted me. You've always wanted me. Admit it." She waggled her eyebrows at him before biting into her croissant.

"I admit it. I want you, Clio." His voice was low, steady and hopefully seductive. She stopped chewing and studied him, and he saw a flicker in her eyes. A brief look of smug satisfaction flashed across her face but was quickly replaced by cool detachment. She swallowed and leaned back, her hands on the counter in tight fists. "But you knew that. You've always known. You just wanted me to say it, didn't you?" She shrugged.

"May I make a suggestion that hopefully will put an end to this *tension*? One that I think will benefit each of us?" He nodded again sipping his coffee waiting for this little nugget of genius. He assumed that she would say they had to cool it, to not get too close. He assumed that she was going to suggest that they keep their relationship strictly professional.

He'd assumed wrong.

"I suggest that as long as we're both comfortable with it, and that it doesn't become emotional or interfere with our work we can indulge in our urges whenever we see fit. Sexually I mean, no strings attached. That way we won't always be thinking about sex and we won't cause tension with the crew." His coffee went down wrong and he immediately began choking.

She raced to him, patting him on the back as he sputtered and tried to catch his breath. She was stronger than she looked and pounded on his back like a jack hammer until he caught her wrist.

"I'm good." He half chuckled. "I just...you surprised me is all."

"Oh. Well that wasn't my intention. But I mean if you want to think about it, that's fine. Take your time. I'm going to get dressed. We have some things to do." She walked away then, shoving the remnants of her croissant into her mouth before disappearing into her bedroom. He stared after her, unable to form words or thoughts beyond the offer of sex whenever the 'urge' moved them. Talk about an offer he couldn't refuse.

Now they stood in front of the historic site, preparing to go on a treasure hunt, and all he could think about was her proposition. He'd been staring at her ever since she'd returned from the bed room, dressed in another pair of barely their shorts, this time in blinding white and a hot pink halter top that tied at the base of her neck. She slipped a pair of pink sneakers on and tied her curls with a pink and white polka dot scarf. Following her lead, and that of the ninety-degree weather, he'd opted for cargo shorts, sneakers and a t -shirt, his locs pulled back. He hadn't expected the unbearable heat at eleven in the morning, but it was New Orleans in May, so he counted himself grateful that it wasn't mid-July.

"This is the place. You're the expert on all things pirate, haven't you been here before?" She was incredulous. It made him a bit nervous to have her stare at him as if he had spouted a second head. Out of habit, he adjusted his glasses and cleared his throat.

"I've never been to the French Quarter." He confessed. She stared at him, her mouth agape in pure shock.

"What do you mean you've never been to the French Quarter? Aren't you from New Orleans? And you played pro ball here, you've at least gone to Cafe du Monde, right?" Again, he adjusted the glasses.

"No, my family is from Donaldsonville and we only came down to visit family, but never in the city. My father was a very strict, religious man, in his eyes everything was sinful. Technically, I've traveled all over the country. But outside of a classroom or a football stadium, I've never really *been* anywhere." He had never confessed that to anyone before. Confessing it to someone like Clio, who'd been everywhere and done everything, he felt less than worthy. He waited for her to laugh or giggle, but she didn't. She lowered her sunglasses and looked at him, her expression morphed from surprise to sadness to elation.

"Oh sweetie, the things I will show you." She was smiling at him, a big brilliant smile that made his chest tighten. She was so excited and eager to get started that he couldn't help but smile at her enthusiasm. She took his arm and led the way into the museum and he couldn't help but share her excitement. "Come on Professor, it's time to start our adventure."

∞∞∞∞

"This place is immaculate, how are we going to find anything in here? And with all of these people milling around." He grumbled, and Clio couldn't help smiling. He was cute in his clueless way and she found him fascinating. Noah was a clean slate, he'd missed so much in his life. She was going to make sure that this was going to be the most exciting time of his life.

He stood in the middle of the room looking around at the other patrons milling through the building, their foot falls echoing on the hardwood floors.

"It's probably on one of the bricks or the flagstones out back." She said, squatting down to look into one of the many fireplaces. From her purse, she found a flashlight and used it to look up the chimney for anything. "Some of these bricks are new. Actually, quite a lot of them." She duck walked further into the opening, looking up her lips pursed in concentration.

"I think many of them had to be replaced after a fire. You look ridiculous." Noah took her arm and helped her to her feet.

"I look like exactly what I am, an archaeologist. You being a historian should be doing the same thing. Come on." She took his hand and pulled him to another room. They checked all of the fireplaces, then went outside to inspect the patio and kitchen. Noah protested, complaining that the out buildings were off limits. But she persisted, pulling him into the tiny out building that was once a kitchen but was now being used for storage.

"It says prohibited on the sign." Noah pointed at the sign on the door and she shook her head.

"If I paid attention to signs, I would never find anything. Besides, who's going to stop me?" She continued picking at the lock with some tool she pulled from her tote.

"We're going to get arrested. This is a national museum; we could go to federal prison." He whined. The door swung open, she blew a raspberry and waved a dismissive hand at him.

"Relax. If anything, we'll be asked to leave and then we'll leave. I have been asked to leave some of the best museums and historical sites in the world. It's no big deal. Just think of it as a scavenger hunt." Clio said as they began their search. The kitchen really wasn't meant for visitors, it was dimly lit and hadn't been cleaned in quite a while. She took another flashlight from her bag and handed it to him, pointing to the other side of the small space. It was musty and full of cobwebs, the floor a patchwork of broken cobblestones and earthen bricks. She looked down at the floor, the cobblestones had been worn smooth, glinting black in the light. In some spaces there were bricks that had cracked from years of wear and erosion. She moved to the farthest wall, methodically running her light over the bricks row by row. "The bricks back here are older. Look at how they aren't uniform like the others. These weren't factory made, these were man made."

"How do you know this?" He asked, awe in his voice.

"I read. The bricks in the fireplaces in the main building are perfect rectangles, uniform, same size, same color. They were factory pressed. Older bricks were handmade, sun dried, and they didn't start building homes with brick until the late 1780's I believe. It looks like they tried using that method, the sun-dried bricks, on the floor. Look at the corners, there's brick residue because they weren't the stronger paving bricks. They probably began to crack within a few months. Looks like they either pulled up most of the floor or covered it with cobblestone." She let the light beam move into the corners of the room. "This place burned down a couple of times, right?" She asked.

"The original building burned down around 1780. They rebuilt this structure in 1788. It actually survived another fire that took out most of the Quarter." She looked over her shoulder at him, a smile on her lips. He was getting into it. Sure, he was terrified, but he was also having fun. "And it's supposed to be haunted by Renato Beluche." He added.

"Well, I wish he would show up and tell us where to look. It would make this go a lot faster." Noah snorted his agreement just before he stubbed his toe on something and tripped. He caught himself, his palms flat on the back wall.

"You okay? Be careful." She cautioned. "I can't carry you out of here if you knock yourself out."

"I think I found something. Bring the light over here." He motioned for her to join him on the other side of the dimly lit room. She rushed over with her flashlight, focusing the beam where he was pointing. When he'd stumbled, he'd grasped the wall and found what looked like an imprint on a brick.

"Hold this." She gave him her flashlight and rummaged through her bag until she found a small brush and gently ran it over the mark clearing it of debris. Once she was satisfied, she took out her smart phone and snapped a couple of pictures. Two quick flashes illuminated the room and they had to squint until their eyes readjusted. Once her pictures were taken, she gently ran her fingers over the mark.

"It's the same marking as in the book. It's loose. I think this maybe a false front." She put the phone back into her bag and used her nails to dig into the softened mortar. She tugged and saw that it was indeed a false front, Noah flashed his light into the void so that they could peer inside.

"What is that?" He asked, the light landing on a pale cloth. "Shouldn't you use gloves or something?"

"It's fine. It's wrapped in some sort of cheese cloth." Clio reached inside, gingerly taking it into her hand then froze. She looked at him and he nodded that he could hear hurried footfalls crossing the flagstone courtyard from the main house to this building.

"Someone's coming." She shoved the cloth into her bag and Noah hurriedly put the brick back into place. Noah grasped her hand and headed for the door, both of them screeching to a halt at the sound of someone approaching.

"Now what?" He asked, the panic rising in his voice. The footsteps were getting closer. Clio turned to him, her fingers loosening the tie of her top at her neck. "What are you doing" He hissed when she undid the button on his shorts.

"Just follow my lead. Okay? Now, kiss me." She said a bit breathlessly.

"Now?" He stared at her incredulously. Frustrated, she grasped a fist full of his t-shirt and pulled him closer, her voice a harsh whisper.

"Just do it, Professor. And make it good." She put her hands on his shoulders, hopped into his arms and wrapped her legs around his waist. He didn't have time to react because she was kissing him, her tongue assaulting him. He grunted and went with it.

"Grab my ass." She mumbled against his mouth and he happily obliged.

The door was thrown open and a beam of blinding light was shone on them in the dark recesses of the room, followed by a disapproving grumble.

"What the hell– y'all have got to get out of here with that. Out." The guard was yelling at them at the top of her lungs. "Out!"

Chapter 5

Noah sat across from Clio unable to contain the smile that had been on his face since they'd been thrown out of the museum. She'd taken him through the Quarter showing him things that he had only read about and people he would have never imagined existed. She'd taken his hand, her fingers linked with his, her face alight with excitement.

"Come on, I'm going to take you to one of my favorite places. And we can see what this is." She'd patted the bag at her hip, that ratty old messenger bag that she wore like armor. He'd followed her to Bourbon street where she guided him through the summer tourists as they stopped to look into the opened doorways of strip clubs, jazz bars and restaurants. They turned on a side street and continued through the quiet neighborhood of homes hidden behind stone walls coming to what he first thought was a house but realized quickly, was a restaurant. From the second-floor balcony came laughter and the clink of glasses and dishes as the diners up there ate, laughed and looked over the street performers below.

She urged him into open French doors to a room that was lined with full booths and tables and a long bar of polished wood and brass fixtures. The aroma of something wonderful wafted in from the kitchen each time a server entered or exited.

"Well I'll be damned, look what the wind blew in. Hummingbird!" A robust man made his way around the bar and scooped Clio up into a bear hug. She was swung back and forth like a rag doll, laughing. Noah stood back and watched how every employee and a few of the patrons, came to greet her with hugs and kisses.

"Big Ant, this is my friend Dr. Noah Toussaint, Noah this is Big Anthony Walker, my *parrain*." Big Ant, as she called him, grabbed Noah's hand and pumped vigorously. He was a tall man, with a wide smile and wavy hair that he wore brushed into a high pompadour which added a comical look to his round jovial face. Noah got the impression that Big Ant always had a smile on his face.

"Well, Hummingbird got herself a doctor. Noah Toussaint you said, why does that name sound familiar?" He asked and before Noah could respond, Big Ant slapped his shoulder hard enough to leave a bruise. "Toussaint? Played wide receiver at LSU like ten years, ago right? I remember you set a few records in your years with the Tigers, saw you take that nasty hit in that game against the 49ers. So, you went to med school after the pros?" He had placed an arm over Clio's narrow shoulders and guided her to a booth at the back of the room, Noah followed unable to get a word in.

"He's not that type of doctor, Big Ant. He's my kind of doctor." She corrected.

"Oh, so he a super brain like you?" Ant laughed

"I don't think anyone's a brain like Clio." Noah finally said before easing into the booth across from Clio, who if he didn't know better, was blushing.

"Yeah, you right," Big Ant laughed. "You want the usual, Birdie or do you need a minute?"

"Yes, the usual and can we get onion rings too? Oh, and please, please tell me Glenda is in the kitchen." He started walking away, that ever-present smile on his nutmeg colored face.

"You know it. Be right back." He disappeared into the kitchen.

Noah turned to Clio, watching as she carefully removed the cloth from her bag gingerly placing it on the table.

"You said Big Ant was your ...what now?" He asked.

"Parrain." She mumbled, her attention on unwrapping whatever precious treasure they had just discovered.

"What?" He asked not sure what she was saying.

"Parrain. You know, godfather. He and my dad were good friends." She looked up at Noah, her brow furrowed in confusion. "You don't know what a parrain is? What were you raised Amish?"

"I was raised...my family was very strict. We didn't really get to do much of anything but go to school and church." He shifted uncomfortably in his seat.

"How strict?" She asked, and he could tell she was genuinely interested.

"No friends, no radio unless it was gospel or classical. We were only allowed three hours of television during the week and that was very restricted. Football was my way out. It was the only activity my father allowed because it made him look good. Anything that made him look good to his friends was allowed. Pretty wife, fancy car, adorable precocious daughter, football star son. On the outside, perfect family, on the inside a nightmare." She was staring at him, her eyes narrowed in thought. The waitress arrived with their beers and onion rings, but she never took her eyes off of him and it made him shift uncomfortably in his seat. He adjusted his glasses and her frown deepened.

"I don't get you, Professor. You're extremely good looking," He blushed, "but you hide behind those glasses. You're a great athlete but gave up millions to teach, you know everything about pirates and traveled across the country, but you've never been anywhere. You're arrogant but shy. What happened to the Noah I knew in college? You were so bold and brash then."

"But I wasn't, not really. Ever since I first ran with a ball, I've been labeled a star. In high school I was treated like a star and then again in college. I was always presented as the next big thing. No one really cared about anything other than how fast I could run and catch a ball. It was all image. My dad loved that. All he cared about was how popular he became when I joined the team. Something for him to brag about. He wasn't impressed with grades. Not my grades anyway. It wasn't manly to be smart, I had to prove my masculinity. Being smart was great for Raina but I needed to be a star. Talk about projecting your dreams onto your kids." He leaned forward and took an onion ring, sipped his beer, but he didn't look at Clio. He needed to purge, tell her everything before he lost his nerve. He took another sip, rolling the bottle between his palms, his eyes on the label watching the colors blend together.

"I worked non-stop, if I wasn't in class I was on the field or training or studying, no girlfriends, no friends, no parties. After my mom died, I started taking summer courses while everyone else was on break. By the time we met, I was a semester away from my BA, when I was in the pros I was still working on my Master's, then my doctorate during my down time and off season. I played long enough to earn a couple of big endorsements, invested smartly and made enough money to take care of my sister. When I got hurt, I retired. It wasn't a career ending injury, but I had made enough money, and I never really cared about football. My dad died my rookie year, so I didn't have him to disappoint. I was able to do something I really wanted to, so I started to teach. At first, I was a novelty, no one really took me seriously, I mean an ex-pro ball player as a history professor? I was kind of paraded around to alumni and they would crack jokes about my classes being "*jock*" courses. You know the classes they give athletes, kind of easy **A** courses. But I was serious, and I wanted to show that I was more than just a muscle head with a made-up position to keep me around to get more money from boosters. When I noticed that most of my classes were full of female students, well that just made matters worse for my legitimacy. I started wearing the glasses to be taken seriously as Dr. Noah Toussaint, not former pro Noah Toussaint and not as '*Professor Hotness*' or whatever. I've heard the nicknames. When I started seeing another professor, she helped me focus, got a few of my papers published. Then I got a few more, then a few articles and then my first book, so I became an academic celebrity of sorts. It was working pretty well, until it wasn't anymore."

He met her steady gaze, in this light her eyes were more gold, and her lips were tinted a deep raspberry. She touched his hand, her thumb stroking his sun warmed skin. That small touch sent a tendril of heat through him, working its way up into a true flame in seconds.

"I don't know why I told you that." He confessed. "I have never told anyone all of that. Not even Catherine."

"And who is Catherine? She sounds fancy." She tilted her head to one side, a devilish smile on her face, her eyes wide. She had a wicked look in her eye and he realized too late that he had just opened another can of worms.

∞∞∞∞∞

Clio just about bounced out of her seat when their food arrived, and all Noah could do was stare. He looked at her over the platter of fried seafood. Shrimp, soft shell crab, catfish and oysters were served with hot, tarter and cocktail sauces in little glass bowls. The waitress placed two small dinner plates and utensils before each of them and gave them fresh beers before hustling back to the bar.

"This is your usual?" Noah gawked at the platter then at her.

"Uh huh. Now, back to Catherine..." She said loading her plate with fish and shrimp. He watched her mix a bit of all of the sauces together in an empty bowl that had been placed beside her plate. She proceeded to dip her food into it before turning back to him. He was looking at her with those soft translucent brown eyes as if she were some sort of alien creature.

"Until recently, Catherine was my supposed fiancée. Why does everyone call you Hummingbird?" He began loading his own plate. She paused mid chew and stared at him.

"Don't change the subject." She waved her fork at him.

"I've talked enough, your turn. So why does everyone call you Hummingbird?"

"My mother used to call me that when I was little. She said I fluttered from place to place, never staying in one place too long, always active, always busy like a little hummingbird. The name kind of stuck. How long were you together?"

"A little over three years. Do you have a boyfriend?" He countered.

"Fine time to ask." She snorted. "No, I don't do boyfriends. How long were you engaged?"

"A year. What do you mean you don't do boyfriends?" His fork hovered over his own plate as he waited for an answer. She shrugged casually and speared a shrimp with her fork.

"Just what I said. I don't do boyfriends. I'm never in one place long enough to sustain a relationship. They either get jealous or we drift apart. So instead of dealing with that heartbreak, hurt feelings and jealousy, I just don't do boyfriends." She popped the shrimp into her mouth and chewed happily.

"Maybe if he were serious, he could go with you on these trips." He said.

"Haven't found a worthwhile guy yet who would give up his life to follow me around the world. I did date my former partner for a while, but he wanted more than I did, so he stole my crew and research..." She clinched her fists, closed her eyes and counted to ten. "Anyway, It's no big deal, professor. I date, just nothing serious. Next question, I know you have one."

"What's with the Greek names?" She watched him enjoy his food, his guard completely down with her. She thought that it was so strange that he was such a complete contradiction. By his outward appearance, he looked every bit the worldly, sophisticated professor, but he was so vulnerable, so innocent almost childlike.

"My grandmother had an affinity for Greek mythology. My parents wanted to carry on the tradition. How long ago did you and Catherine split and why?"

"A while ago, she was sleeping with my new boss. I came home early after I'd been told I was fired, which happened the day after I lost my funding. Walked into our house and found them in our bed. Needless to say, I moved in with Raina last week." She stopped chewing and looked at him. He continued eating as if nothing happened. When she didn't say anything, he looked up at her quizzically.

"Last week? Like last week last week?" She asked, and he nodded, and she sat back, thunderstruck. "So, when I showed up it was like the crazy clown topper for what had been the shit pie of a week?"

"I wouldn't have put it that way, but yes. But you were also the light at the end of the tunnel." She continued to stare at him, watching him eat with a vigor she hadn't witnessed before. Suddenly, he seemed lighter and he was smiling as he ate. There was something quite charming and alien about Noah. He was almost awkward when he was outside of the classroom, around people in social situations, he was so shy and withdrawn. She'd noticed it the night before, the way he sat back and listened only speaking to Calliope and Clio when needed. And now, he'd just told her he'd caught his girlfriend cheating and there was nothing. No sense of shame or embarrassment about the situation, at least not when it came to her. He seemed to like talking to her, she thought.

"Are you okay? I mean you just found out your girlfriend of three years, the woman you were going to spend your life with, was cheating, but-"

"Why did you disappear on me after that party? I looked for you for weeks. I needed to apologize, I didn't know that party was a real thing." The question came out of left field and she was thrown off guard. She didn't have time to think, so the truth came out before she could divert.

"Why would I stick around? You were the only real friend I had there. My parents and brother had died and Calli was in New York. We needed each other then. Besides, I heard you tell your friends that we weren't even in the same league. One of them even called me an ugly little mutt." She said, and he dropped his fork.

"I never -" He started.

"I have an eidetic memory, Noah. You said, *"She's not my girlfriend, we aren't even in the same league"* and that you wouldn't dare try to sleep with me." She watched his expression change from confusion to downright anger. He carefully placed his palms on the table and looked her in the eye.

"Are you going to deny it?" She asked, feeling the pain and embarrassment knot in her stomach. Her eyes burned but she refused to cry in front of him. She had cried over Noah exactly one time and there wouldn't be a repeat of that.

"No. But, I think you misinterpreted it." He said, and she was stunned. "I'd never been to any parties before, I was all work and it was the first time I actually had someone I was excited to go with. And what you heard may have been out of context and clouded by the punch you were drinking. I did say we weren't in the same league," He took her hand and she tried to pull away, but he held her fast. "What I meant was you were too good, too special to want someone like me. I wouldn't dare try to sleep with you because I wanted more than that. Even then, I knew that you were something special, someone I cared for. Why would a girl, a woman as smart, as funny and talented as you want anything to do with a scholarship jock who spent most of his time running full speed into another man? You were my unicorn."

She wasn't sure she believed him, but then why would he lie. She stared at their hands, his covering hers, making it look tiny in comparison. His touch was like velvet, his thumb stroking her knuckles and she felt the familiar stir low and warm begin it slow burn down her thighs. His voice was low, earnest, his eyes locked onto her, forcing her to meet his gaze.

"I went to apologize that night, but it was after curfew and your RA wouldn't let me in. The next day I went back but you were gone. I would have never taken you to that party if I had known what it was." She thought about that, the kindness in his eyes and realized that she believed him. She couldn't reconcile that boy with this man. They were two entirely different people, like her, he'd grown. This was a Noah she liked, open playful and incredibly sexy. She slipped her hand from his, the warmth from his touch still lingering on her skin.

"Water under the bridge. It was a long time ago and we were both stupid kids." She said and popped a fry into her mouth. She wasn't angry anymore. That had been years ago, and she had suffered more humiliations and heartbreak since then, at least he was man enough to admit he was wrong.

"I doubt you were ever stupid. Just so you know," His tone was light, almost teasing. "The guy who called you an ugly mutt- I broke his collarbone that night. Accidentally, of course. He was out for the rest of the season." He sat back, leaning against the dark leather of the booth, a beer bottle to his lips.

"What did we find in the wall?" He asked purposely changing the subject. He was watching her as intently as she was watching him and something in his gaze made her shiver. There was a hint of anger in him, something dark and dangerous that he kept just below the surface. She lifted on eyebrow and shook her head, so the professor had a bit of an edge. She had to admit, it made her like him a little more.

∞∞∞∞

They sat staring at the small stone key and an aged peace of parchment that sat on the table between them. The sun had moved across the sky, casting shadows on the already dimly lit corner of the room. Noah picked up the key, testing the weight and turning it in his hand while Clio gingerly held the paper up to the light.

"I don't get it." He said, "did we leave something behind?" He watched Clio as she flipped the paper over then waved at their waitress who hustled over almost immediately.

"Can I get a shot glass of lemon juice and a lit candle, please?" The waitress looked at her curiously, shrugged then went behind the bar to retrieve her order. Even though the waitress had looked at her like a crazy person, Noah knew immediately that Clio believed there was a message hidden on the page.

The waitress returned and Clio dipped her napkin into the juice and wiped it across the paper. When she finished, she looked up at Noah, crossed her fingers and slowly lowered the delicate paper over the candle, careful not to let the ancient parchment get too close to the open flame.

Words began to appear, delicate almost feminine script slowly emerged, and Clio's face lit up. When she smiled like that she looked like an elf or fairy, Noah decided. That smile had melted his heart years ago and now it made his body ache for her.

"What does it say?" Noah asked, leaning closer to get a better look at the page. "Is that French?"

"*Oui,*" Cllo giggled and read the message in French. Noah tossed the key into the air, caught it and watched her mouth move. Listening to her speak in the foreign tongue sent his libido into overdrive. Her normally raspy voice seemed deeper and sexier in French. She looked up at him and sighed before translating for him.

"It says, *metal meets stone under cross and bones, making the light brighter than bright, makes secret what is hidden to those who do not see beyond the fires. Here lies the map to paradise.*" Clio looked at him, puzzled.

"Any clue of what that means?" Clio asked while Noah flipped the stone key in his hand. He paused, contemplating the riddle and watched Clio read the message again, her lips moving as she read silently. She looked up at him, the flicking candlelight dancing across her face in the dimness of the booth. She licked her lips and her brow furrowed in mild confusion.

"Anything? What are you thinking?" She asked.

"I'm thinking about coming over there and kissing you. I always want to kiss you." He watched gooseflesh rise on her skin and her face relax. He leaned forward placing his elbows on the table and looked her in the eye. She sat back, her fingers tapping on the table a wickedly sexy smile teased one corner of her delicious mouth.

"If you can figure this out, you'll get more than a kiss, Professor." To punctuate her point, she placed one bare foot on his crotch. He looked down to see the pink polish of her toenails wiggling against him, making him hard instantly. He briefly wondered when she'd taken her shoe off, but that thought evaporated when she added a little more pressure. She used her tiny foot to slowly stroke him, pressing into his growing erection. His knee jerked upwards, shaking the table hard enough to draw Big Ant's attention from behind the bar.

"It's a reference to Pierre Lafitte's Blacksmith shop. It's still on Bourbon street, but it's a bar now." He moaned, grasping her foot in one hand. He didn't push her away, but he did stop her teasing. She slipped away, disappearing briefly beneath the table. He caught his breath, not sure what she was going to do next, when she reemerged, shoe in hand.

"So, our next clue should be there. Ready? Let's go" She asked while she put everything back into her bag. Noah narrowed his eyes and shook his head. His body was one raw nerve and if he stood right now, everyone in the room would know what he had thought she'd slipped under the table to do.

"Just, give me a minute." He groaned.

∞∞∞∞

The streets of the Quarter were filling with people as the sun moved lower in the sky casting a deep orange glow over the city. Noah watched the crowds, a beer in his hand as he waited for Clio to finish an intense call with Calli. She looked at him over her shoulder, leaning against a wall, his legs crossed at the ankles. He looked relaxed and dangerously sexy, watching her the way he was. She noticed a few women checking him out, openly ogling him as they passed, some even flirted, but other than a brief nod, he was completely focused on her.

It was strangely titillating.

"So, it looks like it may be another day or two on the crew. But the good news is, my spies tell me that Garrett's progress seems to be stalled. Something about his research ship being in dry dock for a couple of weeks. There was some sort of breach in the hull." Calliope chuckled.

"You don't say? And how long will it take to repair this breach?" Clio glanced back at Noah who sipped his beer, his eyes piercing. He swallowed and licked his lips. She looked away, trying not to get caught up in his smoldering gaze. And boy could he smolder.

"About two weeks." She giggled, and Clio couldn't help but join in. "So, how are you two doing on your little scavenger hunt?"

"We've found something. We're close, Calli. I can feel it. We abandoned the Grand Isle lead. Noah thinks the clues we need are in the city." Clio gushed.

"What else have you been feeling since I've been gone? Have you corrupted the professor yet? Touched his naughty bits?" Calli teased and Clio felt her cheeks warm.

"No. But if I did, I wouldn't tell you anyway. Keep me updated on the crew and I'll see you in a couple of days." She ended the call before her sister could press her any further. She didn't want to explain the deal she'd made with the professor. She also didn't want to think about the fact that they would be alone in the apartment tonight.

Just her and the sexy Dr. Toussaint alone, nothing stopping them from indulging in their urges. Why, oh why, had she suggested that? It was stupid and reckless and the thought of it made her tingle all over. She looked over her shoulder at Noah. He was beautiful

"Noah!" the excited voice of a little girl of about seven, echoed down the narrow street. She came racing toward him in bright yellow shorts, and sunflower hair bows. Her smile was blinding, and she ran with a slightly awkward gait. He turned to her, his own face breaking into a smile that she had never seen before. He squatted so that he could catch her, before swinging her into the air in a wide arch.

"Kylie McCloud, I don't believe it. And look at this hair. You look amazing. You've gotten so big." The girl, Kylie began to speak, rambling and Noah listened, laughing and nodding. A woman came running up behind her, laughing and slightly out of breath. She stopped, placing her hands on her hips as she caught her breath. Noah nodded towards her but continued listening to the little girl as she spoke animatedly about something.

"I, I'm Clio, Noah's friend." Clio extended her hand once the woman caught her breath "She's yours I take it?"

"Yes. I'm Randi. That is my Kylie. We were on our way back to the hotel for her medication and a nap." She laughed. "She spotted him when we left the restaurant and raced down to see him. He's always been her favorite." She said.

"Her favorite?" Clio asked. Her favorite what, she wondered. Favorite uncle? Impossible. Raina was his only sibling and she doubted this little girl was a history buff or football fan.

"Um, yeah. When we go on their annual trip to Disney in the Fall. Noah does all of the princess stuff with her and a couple of the other kids. She said he's best to watch the parade with because she gets to ride his shoulders and see everything."

Now she was completely confused. Disney? Princesses?

"I'm sorry, what?" Clio asked

"He didn't tell you? Of course, he wouldn't." She sighed, shaking her head. "We met Noah through Emma's Angels, his charity. He and his sister run it for kids with leukemia. Kylie was one of their first. He spends so much time with those kids, hours at a time."

"Charity?" Clio repeated, turning to watch Noah and Kylie interact.

"He started it the year before he retired from the NFL. They cover the bulk of medical expenses for her and a few other kids and takes a yearly trip to Disney world. My husband and I wouldn't have been able to get through this without him. She's been doing so much better since we met him. She's finally in remission. Noah is Kylie's hero. She's just about adopted him." She chuckled. Clio looked at Noah with new eyes, feeling a new warmth for him.

"Why is it Emma's Angels?" She asked absently.

"For his mother. She died of leukemia when he was really young." Randi said.

Clio felt her heart swell as she watched Noah. How had she not known about this side of Noah. It was completely unexpected and amazing. She watched his animated conversation with Kylie, the two laughing at private jokes, Noah hanging on every word. He was so engaged, so in-tune with the girl that she believed he would be an incredible father. He absently ran a hand over Kylie's hair before giving her another hug and walking over to them. He spoke to Randi, hugging her with a familial grin. They spoke briefly about her husband and being in town for work, but Clio didn't hear a word. She was watching Kylie who looked up at Noah as if he'd hung the moon.

One day, his own child would look at him with awe and wonder, she was sure of it. Noah would be an amazing father, especially to a little girl. She could see him with a little girl with chocolate skin, eyes like his and dark curly hair. She absently ran a hand over her own curls and paused, her heart dropping to the pit of her stomach. *'Don't you do it, Clio.'* She told herself, *'Don't you dare.'*

"Ready to go?" He asked, and she realized they were alone. She turned to see Kylie hopping happily away, holding her mother's hand.

"What?" She asked, looking up at him. Her heart was thudding in her chest and something hard had settled in the pit of her stomach.

"I asked if you're ready to go." He repeated, smiling at her.

"So, you're just going to ignore the fact that you have a charity that takes care of sick kids? All you need is a freaking kitten and like to cuddle and you'd be perfect. What else are you keeping from me?" She teased. He sighed deeply, placing a hand on her shoulder.

"I run a charity for sick kids, it's no big deal. Actually, I have a board who runs it. I just show up to play with the kids. That's all." He shrugged nonchalantly.

"That's all." She repeated.

"Okay, my mom was a classically trained pianist and taught me the classics, Liszt, Rachmaninoff, Chopin, Scriabin and my favorite, Haydn. Now there, you know everything. There, everything in a nutshell." She stared at him hoping her mouth hadn't dropped open from shock.

"You are quite something aren't you, Professor?" She asked, and he gave her a lazy shrug.

"I have my moments. So," He clapped his hands together, "What now?" He changed the subject before she could ask the litany of questions that ran rampant through her mind. Instead, she moved closer, standing on tiptoe so that she could gently brush her lips against his.

"You are not what I expected." She said, echoing his words. He smiled, resting his hands on her hips.

"I'm rarely what anyone expects." He chuckled.

∞∞∞∞

They rounded a corner and came face to face with Lafitte's Blacksmith Shop Bar, one of the oldest buildings in the French Quarter. The bar sat on the corner of Bourbon and St. Philip streets, a small French colonial building with four sets of French doors that stood open, three facing Bourbon street. Since it was a warm evening, tables and chairs had been set up on the sidewalk outside beneath old-fashioned lanterns. They stood across the street waiting for a tour group to pass, when Noah grasped her fingers. She looked up at him, and he just smiled, before leading the way into the dimness of the bar.

Music poured into the street mingling with the conflicting melodies from other venues in the area. Inside, there were no electric lights and the place was small, with a few people listening some local musician she had never heard of sang and played a piano loudly. The shudders were all open, the cool late afternoon breeze blowing into the hot dankness of the building.

"How can anyone see in this place?" Noah mumbled, indicating that the only real light in the place coming from behind the bar. They needed to get started soon because in a little over an hour this tiny room was going to be packed full of locals, tour groups and summer vacationers.

"Where do we even begin looking?" Clio asked her eyes adjusting to the dim lighting.

"Okay, Professor, where am I looking?" She looked up at him, waiting for his response but he seemed deep in thought. He was staring at the ceiling, the exposed and worn wooden beams which seemed only a few feet from the top of his head. She followed his gaze craning her neck until she felt as if she would fall backward.

"You okay?" She placed a hand on his arm when he didn't speak for a while. He looked down at her and smiled.

"I just can't believe that so much of this place is still here, that this is where Jean and Pierre worked and moved and smuggled. I just - I am in awe." He sighed and seemed to shake himself. "Okay, enough of that. What we're looking for is probably there." He pointed to the fireplace in the center of the room. "It looks like the oldest thing in the room, and its load bearing. It was probably where the original forge was, just by its positioning, it was the focal point of the space. It has to be there. So how are we going to handle this?"

"We're going to get a drink." She pulled him towards the bar, which was relatively new to the place. She ordered Sazerac with an extra shot of Bourbon for each of them and eased onto one of the vacant stools. He sat beside her, still holding her hand, his thumb slowly stroking her knuckles.

"What did Calliope say?" He was looking down at their linked hands, his voice low again. She leaned forward, intent on keeping their conversation private.

"She was telling me that everything will be ready to go when we arrive. Titus has a crew, they should arrive in a day or so. And that Garrett's crew has been detained for a while. There was a problem with their ship." Their drinks arrived, and she warned him that the drink was made with absinthe then downed most of hers with one hearty swig. Noah sipped his, his eyes on her face as she did.

"I take it, this was a Titus induced problem?" She shrugged. "So, this Garrett, he was your partner? What happened?" He turned in his seat, moving closer to hear her over the growing noise. She shrugged, looking into her own glass as she thought of how to answer that tactfully.

"Garrett and I met in grad school. He is very charismatic and charming and has more confidence than smarts. He is one of those people who has to latch on to someone else to get what he wants."

"So a con artist?" Noah said, and she pointed to her nose after taking another healthy swig from her glass. "Doesn't seem like the type of person you would associate with." She shrugged.

"I knew who and what he was. I thought as long as I knew, and he knew that I knew that he was harmless. And he was fun. Don't get me wrong, he wasn't an idiot, he was smart enough and he knows the work. But when he wanted to make our casual arrangement permanent, I cut it off. He was looking for something that would set us up for life. He wanted a home, a family with a stay at home wife, while he ran a gallery or curates a museum."

"And that's not what you want?" She looked into his eyes, the soft light made them look darker, almost jet black. His gaze never wavered, and she fought the urge to look away.

"I'm not built to stay in one place for too long, Noah. I am who I am, and I love my life. I can't force myself to be anyone else and I wouldn't ask that of anyone else." He sipped his drink but said nothing. She signaled the bartender to refill and sighed. "I guess he took it harder than I expected, and he stole my research and tried to pass it off as his own. Mostly to get back at me."

"What if you found someone who would be willing to travel with you?"

"I haven't found anyone like that yet. Oh, in the beginning, they're all for it, a life of adventure, traveling the world. But after a while, they all want to plant roots, have stability, a home base. I haven't gotten there yet. I may never get there."

"That's why you don't do boyfriends." He said, his breath against her ear. She looked at him, his face was so close, she could taste the bourbon on his breath.

"It makes life a lot easier." She whispered. She waited for him to reply, but he didn't. He just watched her mouth, his eyes scanning her face in a way that was unnervingly sexy.

"So, is that all Calliope had to say?"

"She did ask if I've had sex with you yet." She said, and his brows shot skyward.

"Yet?" He asked.

"I told her not to worry about it. I won't corrupt you." Her bravado was completely false, but she didn't think he noticed. There was no way she was going to let him know that she hadn't been able to keep her mind off of being alone with him. She was at moments excited by the prospect, then she would become completely self-conscious her insides twisting themselves into knots.

"What if I were the corrupter? I may have a trick or two." He brushed a stray curl away from her cheek and her skin pebbled into gooseflesh.

"I'll just bet you do. I'll bet you're full of all kinds of little surprises?" She teased, her own brows lifting in mock exaggeration. She looked up into the depths of deep brown eyes and stuck out her chin defiantly.

"I guess we'll see won't we." He sipped his drink. She finished her drink, ordered another and turned her attention back to the task at hand.

"I have an idea on how we can search that fireplace in plain view of everyone in this room and not get thrown out." She waggled her eyebrows at him and smiled.

∞∞∞∞

Three very potent drinks later, he noted, she was on his shoulders pretending to read the plaque bolted high on the chimney. He had shaken his head at first, knowing that a man carrying a woman on his shoulders in the middle of a, now crowded bar, would look out of place.

"Psssh," She waved him off, "this is New Orleans, baby. Nothing is out of place. I once saw a man dressed as a devil, complete with red face and horns riding a bike down St. Claude avenue at nine a.m. on a Thursday morning. Compared to that this will be nothing."

He'd lifted her easily, but her ascent to his shoulders had been awkward, and in some ways strangely erotic. She perched on his shoulder, his thick locs resting on her thighs so he could feel the heat from her core on the back of his neck and he wobbled slightly. That could also be from the drinks, the effects of absinthe were a little unnerving to say the least. It was making him horny, well hornier than he'd already been, if that was possible. Her thighs were tight on his neck and he swallowed hard, while trying to keep his mind and body focused on the task at hand. He'd imagined having her thighs around his neck, but this was not quite what he'd had in mind.

She sank her fingers into his hair when he began moving closer so that she could use her flashlight to read the words in the dark. He wanted to close his eyes and revel in the feel of her fingers in his hair but wouldn't dare. He didn't want to drop her. So, he stood waiting, smiling at a couple of patrons who looked at him curiously, shrugged and continued on their way. One young man asked what she was doing, and Noah explained that she was too short to read it and insisted on climbing on his shoulders.

"And Clio gets what Clio wants." He said. The young man, who looked like he was barely old enough to drink looked at Clio's thighs and pert buttocks and smiled.

"I would give her whatever she wants too." Then he rejoined his group, only glancing back occasionally at the couple near the fireplace. He couldn't really see what she was doing, only feel her moving slightly as she searched. He felt like an idiot but the feel of her all around him was worth it. He could easily turn his head and nibble her inner thigh, run his tongue along the silky flesh, among other more inappropriate things. His grasp on her thighs tightened until he thought he would leave marks. But she didn't seem to notice, or if she did, she didn't say anything.

"Got it. It's a map, kind of. Coordinates but it's ripped, a piece is missing." Clio whispered and handed him a folded piece of paper. He took it and shoved it and the flashlight back into her bag. He was going to squat down and let her dismount carefully, instead she swung one leg over his shoulder and managed to awkwardly slide down his body. He held her around the waist, loving the feel of her lithe body moving over him. Her feet touched the floor, but he wouldn't let her go, he wanted to keep her pressed against him. He felt her nipples harden under his steady gaze and fought the temptation to cup her breast in his palm. He tensed as his body came to life his obvious arousal pushing against her stomach.

He cupped the back of her head before leaning over to kiss her, his tongue sinking into her bourbon and absinthe flavored mouth. She stood on tip toe so that she could returned the kiss, her mouth hot and hungry for more. He stopped, taking a deep breath and looked into her upturned face. She really was quite beautiful, with delicate features and eyes that made his pulse race whenever she looked at him.

"I wish I'd taken the time to get to know you in college." He whispered. "I mean really know you." He ran his hands up her arms, caressing her sun warmed skin, then cupped her cheek. She was soft, her skin like velvet under his fingertips. Everywhere he touched sent a current of warmth through him, his mouth suddenly dry and his body aching for release.

"How on earth could I have ever forgotten your eyes?" He ran a finger down her cheek to her chin and tilted her face up. "But I promise, I will never be able to forget you again."

"I think," She said, her palms on his chest where he was sure she could feel the pounding of his heart. "It's time for you to take me home, professor." She looked up at him through her long dark lashes and he could feel himself nodding dumbly.

During the ride back to her apartment he'd been tense, feeling as if he'd burst out of his skin from the anticipation. They had taken a taxi, since he was sure he was more than a little drunk and Clio wouldn't drive. Not that she was in any condition to drive herself. He'd spent the twenty-minute drive through Friday night traffic trying to calm himself. She hadn't helped by sitting practically in his lap, her fingers gently caressing the hair at his nape. Nothing had ever felt so good, no one's touch had ever set him on edge the way she did.

She kissed him in the elevator with such passion and pure need, that he had to push her away to catch his breath. Holding her at arms-length, he practically whimpered when she'd bitten her bottom lip and looked at him with eyes that had darkened to a deep bronze.

She'd made a beeline for the shower as soon as they'd entered the apartment, claiming she needed to clean the grit and sweat from the French Quarter off of her. She'd kicked off her shoes at the door, dropped her bag on the sofa and pulled her shirt off right outside of her bedroom door. She looked back at him as she unzipped her shorts, then disappeared into the darkened room. He took a step closer, trying to get a glimpse of her when a shaft of light from the bathroom brighten the room enough for him to spot dark lacy panties on the floor. The shower started, and he heard singing, off-key and occasionally muted, but singing, nonetheless. Images of her naked body, slick with soap, the sweet smell of her and the taste of her lips. He waited for as long as he could, which felt like minutes but in reality, couldn't have been more than a few seconds before he followed her lead, leaving a trail of clothing along his path to the shower. She'd said no strings, strictly business.

And Noah Toussaint was all about business.

Chapter 6

The bathroom was full of steam, the sweet smell of her soap and Clio's humming. He could see her silhouette behind the steamy shower door, and just watched her for a moment. Enjoying the shadowy image of her naked body as she let the water run down her back. He opened the door and waited for a cloud of steam to dissipate before stepping in behind her. She looked back at him, a sexy smirk on her lips.

"What took you so long?" She asked handing him a soapy loofah. He took it and watched her pull her wet hair over her shoulder, giving him full access to her sleek backside. He took his time working the soap down the smooth bronzed skin of her back, stopping just at the curve of her luscious buttocks. When he moved further into the spray of hot water, she turned to face him. Her body was perfection, her breasts the perfect size to fit in the palms of his hands, her nipples tightened begging for his touch. Her stomach flat and smooth, a rivulet of water running between the valley of her breasts to the small neatly manicured thatch of hair at her apex. He moved one soap lathered hand between the valley of her breasts, down over the stomach, stopping just above the neatly trimmed cleft, then repeated the journey up to her neck.

She took the loofah, allowing him use of both hands on her supple skin. He ran his hands over her shoulders, up her neck then sunk his fingers into her hair and pulled her to him, kissing her with a need that consumed him. He couldn't think, every sense was filled with Clio.

She began to soap his chest and abs with slow, long smooth strokes of the loofah. The rough texture against his hot wet skin made every inch of him tingle. Once she'd gotten a good lather on him, she discarded the loofah and used her hands, her fingers leaving trails of heat in their wake. He watched her small hands move over his skin, exploring every inch of him. When she reached down, cupping his hardness in her hand, he groaned. Her palm was slick and warm with soap, moving over his hardened shaft until he could no longer stand it.

He lifted her, his mouth on the sultry flesh on her neck, one hand on her breast, his palm teasing one hardened nipple. She wrapped her legs around his hips and pressed her moist core too him, teasing him. He took her nipple between his lips, suckling, teasing her with his tongue until she moaned and arched into him. He pressed her back to the cool marble of the shower wall and the tip of his shaft pressed against her, hard and throbbing. She rolled her hips, her body like warm satin moved against him him causing a delicious friction that made him vibrate.

"Wait, Clio sweetie..." He lost all semblance of calm when she trailed her mouth along his neck and shoulders, had nails raking his chest setting his skin on fire. She reached between them, slowly guiding him into her.

"I want you so much." She purred. He buried his face in the curve of her neck, tasting her skin, his palms teasing her tightened nipples. She shifted again, and he slipped deeper into her, she was achingly hot and tight against his shaft. She made a noise, a soft grunt before she lifted her hips, then moved back down taking him in deeper and deeper with each downward thrust. He tried to still her, hold her so that he wouldn't drive into her, he wanted to savor every stroke. But she shifted, rotating her body to take him in to the hilt, her body like hot liquid around him and he could no longer stand it. He braced himself, placing a hand against the wall and drove into her, his hips pistoning against her. She moved with him, matching him stroke for frenzied stroke. He ground his hips, wanting more and she purred her encouragement, matching his rhythm. She met each stroke, her body vibrating around him, taking him deeper until he couldn't think, he was lost in the feel of her. She was on fire and she began moving faster, her hips rotating in the most dangerously delicious way. He couldn't think beyond the feel of her, the taste of her and he wanted more. He searched for her mouth, finding it tasting her sweetness. He grasped her waist, driving himself faster and deeper, harder until her body bucked against him.

The fire that burned in her spurned him on making him even harder, if it were possible, all semblance of restraint, of control gone. He made a noise, a guttural growl that came from his toes before he grazed one tightened nipple between his teeth. She cursed and fisted her fingers in his hair, her body slithering against him in agonizing bliss.

"Like that," she moaned against his ear. "Just like that. Just like that, just...like..." She gasped her legs tightened around him just before she moaned long and hard, her eyes closed and mouth open. She came hard, everything in her became molten liquid as a mass of tremors made his knees buckle before he was lost in his own bone rattling climax. Her thighs trembled, and she made a soft purring sound against his neck, her nails leaving crescent marks in his shoulders. He shook, every muscle stiff as he exploded inside of her.

He held her riding the aftershocks that shook her every so often. She buried her face in his neck, taking deep calming breaths. It took him a moment to compose himself so that he could speak. He'd never experienced a need so powerful, so all-consuming and it shook him to his core.

"I'm sorry. I just wasn't expecting ... to want you so much. Should we be worried?" He kissed her neck and she leaned into him for a tick, enjoying the feel of his mouth on her skin.

"I'm on birth control." She breathed, still clinging to him. She trembled, and he held her tighter. He reached behind her and turned off the water before carrying her out of the shower, gently setting her on her feet before wrapping her in a towel.

He dried her hair, kissing the tip of her nose before reaching for a towel for himself. She stood looking at him with a peculiar expression on her face.

"What?" He asked.

"There is one more rule to this arrangement," She said suddenly serious.

"What?" He asked, a tendril of anxiety creeping up his spine.

"Please don't fall in love with me." Her tone was filled with a sadness that made his heart ache.

∞∞∞∞∞

He was watching her. Even with her eyes closed, in the darkness she could feel his steady gaze on her face. Sighing, she turned to look at him, the moonlight casting a strange shadow across his face. His locs hung loosely around his bare shoulders, his eyes again black as pitch, his jaw set.

"What?" She asked, and he physically started. She stifled a chuckle and rolled toward him.

"You've been staring at me for a good five minutes, professor. What's going on with you?" He gently pushed the covers off of her, exposing her bare skin.

"I didn't mean to wake you," He kissed her shoulder.

"I wasn't asleep. Are you going to tell me why you're staring or just continue to be all weird and stalker-ish?"

"That's not a word." He chuckled.

"Maybe not but it kinda perfectly describes you right now. So, what's up?" His hand continued its delicious journey down her side, pausing at the curve of her breast before moving to her hip.

"Same thing that was up an hour ago. The same thing that always seems to be up whenever you're around. I can't sleep because of you." He took her hand, kissed her palm then slipped it beneath the covers so that she could touch him. She smiled, moved closer and gently ran her hand down the length of him until he moaned.

"Is that so?" She looked under the covers.

"It's becoming a problem. I mean, how can I be around you when I'm like this?" He nuzzled her neck, drawing her closer still. "You drive me crazy, Clio. Always have."

"Really? I was waiting for you to admit that." She tightened her grip slightly, adding more pressure to her stroke and was granted a sharp inhale. She kissed him, teasing his bottom lip with her teeth. "Tell me more." She whispered, her body hotter and wetter with each of his moans of approval.

"I have been dying for you to touch me since that first night I kissed you." He kissed her shoulder again, his teeth teasing her skin.

"I've never wanted anyone this way before. Every time I look at you, I just can't think of anything else. The way you smell, the feel of your skin, the gold in your eyes." She continued her slow languid strokes until his breath hitched in his chest. She eased closer to him, feeling the heat from his skin, her lips on his chest, her other hand pushing him back onto the pillows. She moved down his body, her mouth trailing feather light kisses down his chest, the nails of her free hand raked across his nipple. He flinched and sucked in air.

"Really?" Her voice was husky with her own growing arousal. Watching him, the way he smiled and practically purred at her slightest touch. She moved lower, her lips brushing just below his navel.

"Uh huh," He trembled when the hand that was deliciously stroking him, coaxing him to the edge of release, was replaced by the warmth of her mouth.

∞∞∞∞

His phone was ringing, even from the sex induced coma like slumber, he could hear the familiar trill of Raina's ring-tone. He groped in the dark for the night stand, his hand grazing velvety smooth skin. He opened his eyes and saw Clio asleep beside him, the covers in a tangle around her waist, her bare back glowing in the moonlight. She looked ethereal in slumber and he smiled, remembering the feel of her mouth on him. It sent a tremor through him and he fought the urge to stroke her naked body until she came hard and long.

But annoyingly, the phone was still ringing. He could see the light from his phone on the table beside Clio. Reaching across her, he snatched it and swiped to answer.

"Raina, it's the middle of the night." He tried to whisper. Clio turned to face him.

"Is something wrong?" She mumbled. He was already getting out of bed, searching for pajama bottoms.

"No, go to sleep. I'll take it in the living room." He was struggling to pull his pants on, hold the phone and leave the room at the same time. Instead, he tripped

77

on something in the dark, his legs got tangled in his pants and he stumbled out of the room. In the dark, he hit his foot on the corner of a table, sending a shock of pain up his leg.

"Damn it, Raina what's wrong?" He asked between sharp curses.

"Is it true that you took off with some woman to go look for buried treasure?" He looked at the ID on the phone before he spoke. He had been right, it was Raina's phone number, but it wasn't his sister on the phone.

"Catherine, what the hell are you calling me for? It's the middle of the nigh for Christ's sake. And why are you on Raina's phone?"

"She took it from me, the devious heifer." Raina speech was slurred and slightly muffled.

"I'm bringing your drunken sister home. She was out celebrating some internship and..."

"She got it? That's amaz—" He rubbed the sleep from his eyes and was staring at the clock on the wall above the sofa when she cut him off.

"And when I took her phone to call you, she informed me that you weren't in town. She told me that you had gone off in search of treasure with some random woman who'd stalked you for the better part of a week. I know that couldn't possibly be true. The Noah I know would never do something so ridiculous. Not my Noah."

"I'm not your Noah, Catherine. I'm not your anything, you kinda killed that when you fucked my boss!" His anger surprised him. He'd never confronted Catherine about her infidelity, he'd simply walked out. He'd taken his things and gone to Raina's without saying a word. But now, a little after three in the morning, he felt as if he could break something.

"You have the nerve to question me? I am a grown man, Catherine. I've been one for a very long time and I don't answer to you for anything I do. You have no fucking right to ask me one thing about what I'm doing or who I'm doing it with. Now put my sister on the phone, you pretentious, pseudo intellectual—" He searched for the correct term, the perfect topper to what he hoped would be a scathing burn.

"Douche canoe?" Clio sleep rusted voice filled in the silence of the living room. He spun and found her leaning against the door frame in one of his t-shirts. Her hair was a pillow matted mess, her eyes still heavy with sleep.

"Douche canoe!" he barked, nodding at her.

"Is that her? Who is this woman, Noah? What has she done to you because this isn't you—" She was still talking, and he could hear Raina in the background mumbling something muffled and incoherent. He no longer heard her because Clio was coming toward him. She gave his chest a gentle pat before moving past him and into the kitchen. She opened the refrigerator and bent over to look inside. He watched, his eyes taking the journey from her bare feet up her legs to that perfect derriere.

"Noah!" He frowned and looked at the phone in his hand. From what he could gather, Catherine was asking him a question. Clio opened a soda and took a long sip as she crossed back to him.

"Did you even check her credentials? She could be a con artist or a serial killer for all you know. She could be using you to get you to pay for this foolishness then take off never to be seen again. I only have your best interest in mind. I mean after all these years, I do still care about you. You can't go off on this wild goose chase just because she says she may have ..." Clio smiled sleepily, kissed his cheek and handed him the soda.

"Come back to bed." She whispered, before kissing him once more.

"Bed?! Are you sleeping with her?!" It was more of an accusation than a question. Noah took a deep breath before he responded. "Is this because of what I did? Noah, I apologized. It was a mistake."

"Yes, Catherine, I'm sleeping with her but surprisingly it's not about you at all. You give yourself way too much credit. And if she's a serial killer, that just means I die a very happy man. Thanks for driving Raina home." He disconnected the call before she could respond turning his phone off for good measure.

He snuggled close to Clio in the dark. He sighed, wrapping his arms around her and closed his eyes.

"So, that was Catherine?" She asked.

"Uh huh,"

"She's really pissed, huh?" She yawned.

"Yep," He could feel her smiling even though she had her back to him.

"Because we had sex?" She continued.

"Among other things." He was smiling now.

"Good," She took his hand, moving it from her waist to cup her breast. "Wanna piss her off some more?"

ထထထထ

The smell of fresh brewed coffee coaxed Noah out of what had to be the best sleep he'd had in years. He stretched his sore muscles and couldn't help the smile that seemed to etch itself on his face. He lay naked, the sheets twisted around his hips, early morning sunlight warming his back. He couldn't remember ever feeling this happy and relaxed. Every muscle in his body screamed when he moved, but he really couldn't care less, for the first time in years he was genuinely happy and excited to start the day. He could hear Clio in the living room excitedly yammering with someone on speaker phone. There were several voices and they all seemed

79

really excited about something, often speaking in unison and on some occasions finishing each other's sentences. He made his way into the bathroom to wash up before going to investigate.

He padded into the living room a few minutes later after he'd taken a quick shower and brushed his teeth. He dug a pair of sweats from his bag and made his way into the kitchen where Clio sat with her laptop open, video chatting with Calliope and the crew. She was wearing a yellow tank top and Harry Potter pajama bottoms her hair a mess of wild uncombed curls. She looked radiant and he fought the urge to scoop her up into his arms and take her back to bed. He just couldn't seem to get enough of her.

"Well good morning, Noah." Calli called when he moved close enough to be picked up by the camera.

"Good morning Calliope," He waved and absently kissed Clio on her bare shoulder. She in turn handed him a mug of coffee. He took a sip and winced, then stared at the dark, lukewarm liquid she'd given him. It was black, strong and left a strange taste in his mouth. How she could drink this dark roast without cream and sugar was beyond him. He turned his attention back to the video chat when Calli spoke. Calli was on the deck of a boat from what he could see, her green eyes shaded from the morning sun on the water by red heart shaped sunglasses. Behind her he could see people moving around, Javi and Teri lugging some very expensive and high-tech gadgetry in the background.

"What was that?" Calliope asked.

"So," Clio quickly changed the subject. "Calliope was updating me on their progress. She says that Titus is finishing up the last of the paperwork needed for the new crew and that all of the equipment is being loaded now." She squealed, kicking her feet and he laughed. She was so damned cute, and he wanted to kiss her.

"That's great," He poured cream and sugar into his fresh cup of coffee. "Did you tell her about the map and the key?" She had just taken a bite of her toast and nodded.

"I was just getting to that, bae. Calli has some intel on the Garrett and his crew." She waved him over so that Calli could see both of them.

"Wait a minute, hold up, flag on the play. Clio Jean-Noel did you just refer to the professor as bae? What happened?" Calliope asked lifting her glasses, so they got the full force of her gaze. They looked at each other in mock confusion. Noah shrugged and sat beside her, just as Clio managed to look surprised.

"I haven't the slightest idea of what you're talking about. Anyway, you have tea on Garrett? Spill?" Calli perched her glasses on her head and leaned in, lowering her voice conspiratorially.

"Well, he's been seen around town, trying to get information on us. He's tried to buy off a few officials to get his ship the okay to sail, but with Titus's connections, that was never going to happen. Anyway, last night, Mina and Teri went to one of the local restaurants to blow off steam, get a couple of drinks, you know. And they run into a couple of the old crew members, they start drinking and having fun telling the girls how much they miss us. How they wish they could get out of their contract, blah, blah, blah." She paused to take a dramatic sip from a fruity drink, slipping her sunglasses on to cut down on the glare.

"Get on with it, Cal." Clio moaned. Calliope took her time, making a show of putting her drink down before she spoke again.

"They go one and on, spilling that they think Garrett's out of his depth and that he really doesn't know what he's doing. He's taking his cues from this -so called- historian who is just as clueless as he is. They're depending on the pages they have from the journal and luck to find what they need. But Garrett isn't as good at translation as he believes himself to be, so he's getting frustrated. The crew members said they googled this guy and all they found were a couple of articles massacring other people's work. He's a total blow hard but has deep pockets, his family has money. They call him Captain Jack Hole." She giggled, and Noah felt the hairs on his neck rise.

"Jackson Blake? The historian, is his name Jackson Blake?" Noah asked.

Both women turned to look at him, a bit confused and somewhat surprised. Calli nodded, slowly removing her glasses.

"Do you know him?" Clio asked. Noah slammed his fist on the counter, spilling their coffee. Clio hastily moved the computer to avoid the splash, but he didn't seem to take notice. "I take that as a yes." Clio looked at her sister, who was trying to see what was happening from her limited vantage point.

"Of all of the...that sick little arrogant bastard. He's the one who debunked my research and got my funding taken away. He used to be a student, not a very good student. That privileged little...he's had a vendetta against me since I gave him a C on his final paper. He tried to get me fired then because I told him his work was derivative, unoriginal and that I'd been generous in grading him that high. He was a mediocre student, and a terrible person in general. That little asshole."

"Well," Calli sighed, "looks like both of you have a reason to find this shipwreck first. You've both been fucked by the competition." She howled with laughter before signing off, the screen going black.

∞∞∞∞∞

He'd been pacing for a while, his hands balled into fists. Clio watched him while she cleaned the stickiness left by their spilled coffee. He prowled around the room, his jaw set, nostrils flared every muscle in his body seemed taut with rage. There was a vein throbbing at his temple and he gently punched the air as he paced and cursed under his breath. She sat at the counter, watching him while she finished what was left of her coffee.

"I can't believe that weaselly little-" He stopped and looked at her, taking a deep breath. "And he's teamed up with your old partner? Is it me or does that feel like a set up?" He asked, and she thought about that for a moment.

"How could it? It's just some weird coincidence. The archeology field is really small, Noah. It just so happens that my jerk of an ex is working with your ass of a former student. It's totally random." He seemed to think about that for a moment and deflated.

"I guess you're right. It's just so damn frustrating to know that piece of - he decimated my career and is attempting to use someone else's work to make a name for himself. Again. He's a privileged, spoiled leech. And now he's found another leech to try and take credit for something neither of them has any right to." He growled, an honest to God growl. He was seething, the heat from his anger rolling off of him. He looked like a warrior, bare-chested, his hair loose around his shoulders, his brow furrowed in anger. She'd never seen him like this and it took her to a dark, sexy place. All of that passion redirected could be very exhilarating. Her entire body prickled at the thought of it.

"I think I may have something to cheer you up though." She slipped off of her seat and went into the bedroom. When she came back, she was holding the slip of paper and key they'd found, as well as the journal. She sat on the floor beside the coffee table and motion for him to join.

"While you were still sleeping, I started to read the journal to try to get an idea of what these coordinates might be in reference to. I looked on the map, trying to match them to a spot in the Caribbean but there isn't one. I can't do it without the rest of the page." She flipped to a page in the journal she'd marked. "Listen to this, it was written in 1827 but I can't figure it out. *I sent the coordinates to Renato today as he still lives in New Orleans. It will be safe with him until Jean Pierre comes to stay in the spring. Under Boyer, Haiti has become a unified nation, and my sweet Angeline has asked I stop privateering as it has become more dangerous. She asks so little of me I must oblige. The unrest has made us nervous, so we have set sail to Puerto Rico at her insistence. I've notified Renato and have heard the stories of my "treasure" being lost in Grand Isle and Barataria Bay. My friend is a talented teller of tales. Almost as talented as my brother was a blacksmith, perhaps even better. Alas, what lies in wait for me has does not wait at the bottom of the sea. The way has always been with Pierre. It waits with the prayers to our lady as all good Catholics know.*" She closed the journal and looked at him.

"I know that Jean Pierre never made it to his father. He later goes on to say that he and Angelina did eventually move from Haiti to Puerto Rico after he'd been notified of his son's death around 1833. Renato never went to him and he never came back to New Orleans. He couldn't."

"So, whatever he was talking about may still be there." Noah looked at the stone key, then at the coordinates on the page. Clio waited as he seemed to think about the passage she'd just read. He frowned and shook his head.

"I know that it's a church, but I have no idea which church. Who is our lady?" She was getting a head ache trying to figure it out when all she wanted to do was climb into Noah's lap. She looked at him sitting with his back against the sofa. He wasn't wearing those ridiculous glasses and she could see the deep mahogany of his eyes. He ran a hand over the stubble of his unshaven jaw and she found herself focusing on his mouth. Why did he get to look so damned sexy when she knew she looked like a deranged Muppet? She couldn't think with him sitting next to her looking like early morning sex in grey sweat pants. She stared at his crotch her body growing hot at the realization that he wasn't wearing anything under those damned things. It was like he was taunting her.

"Could you put on a shirt please?" She snapped, and he looked at her, his brows raised. Frustrated, she lay on her back on the carpet.

"What?" He half smiled, as confused by her outburst as she was.

"Put on a shirt. And underwear. I can't think with all- this in my face." She motioned towards his bare chest and general vicinity of his lap. He looked down then back at her, grinning devilishly. Oh boy, she thought, she was in trouble now.

"Oh, am I distracting you?" He was on his hands and knees, crawling toward her, that sexily seductive smile giving her butterflies. She shook her head and stared at the ceiling.

"We have work to do, Noah." She said, when his face appeared in her field of vision. He straddled her slim hips, his hands on either side of her head, trapping her in place. He was warm, the feel of him hovering above her oddly sensual. She tried to relax, but every nerve in her body was awake and begging for the slightest touch from him.

"So, you get to tantalize and tempt me all day long, with those big beautiful eyes and sexy little walk but I go shirtless once and I'm distracting? How is that fair?" He was close to her, his mouth inches from hers. He smelled of coffee and his soap, a spicy heady scent that made her catch her breath. He gently pressed into her and she could feel him growing hard against her.

"You think I have a sexy walk?" She swallowed hard, trying to get the words out of her dry mouth. His eyes moved over her face, one hand hovering over her breast until her nipples hardened in anticipation of his touch.

"I think everything about you is sexy, Clio." He leaned closer still. "Everything." She closed her eyes, her lips parting for the inevitable kiss.

"It's the Old Mortuary Chapel." He said suddenly, and her eyes opened in surprise. He was still close, but his smile was pure wickedness. "The place he's talking about. It was first called the Chapel of St. Anthony of Padua or the Old

Mortuary Chapel. It was built in 1826 and used for the victims during the yellow fever epidemic. Now it's called Our Lady of Guadalupe, it has a grotto dedicated to the Lady of Lourdes. It's on Rampart street." Then he was gone, leaving nothing but cool air in his place. She rolled onto her side as he got to his feet and headed into the bedroom.

"That was a dirty trick, professor." She called after him. He peered at her from the bedroom door, that silly smile still plastered on his face.

"Come on, get dressed. Let's go check it out." He winked, and she had to fight back her smile. Damn it, if he didn't make her stomach flutter.

∞∞∞∞

Noah sat staring out of the window of the streetcar as it clanged along St. Charles avenue. He'd silently taken her hand, pulling her closer as they moved through the city. Watching him experience things she'd done a thousand times made everything seem new and exciting. He seemed lighter than the man who'd driven her home a few days ago. And he'd given up those stupid glasses. He didn't need to hide from her. She rested her head on his shoulder and enjoyed the ride with him as if it were her first time.

Her phone buzzed in her pocket and she fished it out, not wanting to lift her head. She didn't even look when she swiped to answer.

"Birdie," The deep accented voice of Titus St. John filled her ear and she instinctively sat up.

"What's wrong?" She asked trying not to panic. Titus rarely called her especially when Calliope had been keeping her informed on what was going on. Titus was always too busy to get too deeply involved in her shenanigans, as he called them. So why was he calling her now.

"Nothing is wrong," He laughed, "Can't I call to say hello?" She sighed and relaxed a little but didn't let her guard completely down. Something was up with him.

"Of course, you can but usually, when I'm prepping for a trip, you only call me to tell me I'm doing something wrong or if something is too expensive. So, which is it?"

"Nothing is wrong, and I've paid for all of your expensive crap. Are you still flying out tonight? Calliope said you'd found something and that you and this professor-"

"And there it is." She said, slapping her thigh. "Okay, I'm fine and I will see you when I get there tonight. Bye, Titus." She was about to hang up, but he stopped her.

84

"I'm sorry. Okay. Just...Calliope said this is the guy from college. The one ..."
She looked at Noah, then slowly slipped into a seat on the other side if the car,
lowering her voice to a whisper.

"I know who he is Titus. And I've let all of that go because quite frankly, I need
him. I can't do this on my own. Please don't get all brotherly on me and ruin this."
She mumbled through clenched teeth.

"So, you're over all of the heartbreak, the months of you crying and not talking
to any of us. What he did -you were already so fragile-" He stopped talking, his
voice filling with emotion. She remembered how she had been then, already taken so
many hits and that night had been another blow. It had taken a toll on all of them.

"It was a long time ago Titus. I'm over it. Can you please, please, please please
stop worrying? I'm fine." He made a noise she was very familiar with, a low
grumble that was usually followed by a creative curse in his native Creole.

"So, you've already slept with him? Damn it, Clio." He barked then slipped back
into Creole.

"I'm a big girl, Titus and I can take care of myself. Don't worry about me. I'm
fine." He was silent for so long that she'd thought he'd hung up on her. He sighed,
and she could picture him pinching the bridge of his nose the way he did when she
exasperated him. She'd even begun referring to it as the Hummingbird pinch.

"But that's the problem, Birdie. I do worry about you. All the time." The
tenderness in his voice melted her cool reserve for a moment and sit was her turn to
sigh.

"I know, and I love you for it."

She ended the call and stared at the phone for a while, before slipping it back
into her pocket and returning to the seat beside Noah. He took her hand again, his
childlike enthusiasm slightly subdued, but he was still smiling. She could see the
question in his eyes and waited until he was comfortable enough to ask. She didn't
have to wait very long.

"That was Titus?" He asked. She nodded. "Is everything okay?"

"Everything is fine." She could see him try to remain nonchalant, to make his
next question seem like breezy small talk.

"So, who is this Titus anyway?" She smirked and turned in her seat to face him.

"Titus St. John is someone I've known most of my life. He's good with money
and he can get things when I need them. That's his job. Sort of. We don't really
discuss what Titus actually does." He put an arm on the back of her seat, his fingers
gently playing with the strap of her tank top.

"And he just freely gives you money and cars?" He met her gaze.

"Occasionally." She said, "When the mood strikes him. Sometimes I have to
actually write down what I need the way you would with any standard grant. But he

is easier to deal with. Why? Are you jealous?" She teasingly tugged on the waist band of his jeans. He shook his head and snorted derisively.

"No." He was lying. She could tell by the way he avoided her eyes. He was jealous she liked that. "Were you jealous when Catherine called last night?" She tilted her head, trying to keep her expression blank, unreadable. She wasn't really sure how she felt about that.

"Did I act as if I were jealous? I mean after all; you were in my bed. Why should I be jealous?" He lifted one eyebrow and nodded.

"Exactly. I'm not jealous of Titus. I don't even know the man. Come on, I think this is our stop." He pointed to the church coming up and pulled the stop cord to signal the driver. "Let's get going, bae."

"I never called you bae." She said. Had she?

"Of course, you didn't." He agreed

Chapter 7

Like most things in New Orleans post-Katrina, the church had been restored. A lot of the original architecture had changed but the grotto remained intact. Clio pushed the iron gate open that led to the small stone alcove dedicated to the Lady of Lourdes. They stepped into the dank heat of the tiny space which housed a wall of prayer candles in colorful glass. The flickering glow cast a kaleidoscope on the wall and smelled of dried flowers and wax. The other walls were covered in what looked like handmade crosses.

They waited until an elderly woman completed her prayer over a candle in a bright green jar. She crossed herself and kissed the rosary and eased out of the little space, eyeing them curiously.

"So," Clio sighed looking around the little room, "Where do we start?" Noah watched her scan the room. She wore a skimpy white tank top, a loose skirt that hung low on her hips and bright red Converse sneakers. The candlelight gave her an ethereal glow, casting a halo of gold around her. She looked up and fire flickered in her eyes and his chest hurt at her stunning beauty.

"Hellllooo." She waved a hand in front his face and he snapped back to reality.

"Yeah, what?" He blinked and looked at her, trying to focus on her question. She was staring at him with a strange expression on her face. It was as if she had a question on the tip of her tongue but decided against it.

"I asked where we should start?" He looked at the stone walls surrounding them trying to think, but all he could think of was Clio standing so close. She smelled like sugar and reminded him of sunflowers, bright and lively. She was simply amazing. He turned in a slow circle, trying to focus on the task at hand when he noticed something that seemed slightly out of place.

"Do those stones look weird?" He asked, pointing to a cluster of rounded stones high in a corner. While most of the stones were worn and smoothed by time, the ones high in the corner were more jagged, except in that spot. They looked strange to him, far in the shadows, obviously not part of the refurbishing efforts.

"They look like stones." Her trusty flashlight appeared in her hand and she focused on the area he'd been staring at, slowly panning the beam of light across into the darkness. "This is where the grotto connects to the church." She panned across the ceiling, then back at the stones. They were a different color as well, not as new and smooth as the others. She and Noah eased into the little used corner, where he touched the out of place rocks and to their surprise, the wall moved.

Noah and Clio stared at each other before he pushed harder, putting all of his weight into moving the wall. Slowly, a dark narrow hallway swathed in cobwebs, smelling dank and moldy appeared before them. Clio shone her flashlight into the void, highlighting the stone walls and dirt floor. She swung her bag from her hip to her back and eased closer to the entrance. Noah grabbed her arm.

"You're not going in there are you?" She looked at him as if he'd said something ridiculous.

"One of us has to and it's not like you can." He looked into the narrow passage and realized he wouldn't fit. He'd had to walk hunched over and sideways just to get through the doorway.

"How long do you think it's been since anyone's been back there?" He turned to look at Clio to find her pulling the hem of her skirt between her legs and tucking it into her waist band creating makeshift harem pants. She pulled her hair back into a heavy band that magically appeared, the flashlight held between her lips.

"Well," She finally said, preparing to go into the dark abyss, "If I find someone back there, I'll ask."

"That's not funny." He snapped. She looked at him for a moment, then stood on tiptoe and kissed him.

"I'll be fine. Watch the door." Then she was gone.

He watched after her until the beam of light got smaller, then disappeared altogether. When he could no longer take staring at the darkness, he watched the grotto entrance as she'd instructed. As he waited, his stomach twisting with anxiety, his phone vibrated in his pocket. He answered, grateful for the distraction and the thoughts of Clio being killed by some ridiculous *Goonies* worthy booby trap.

"I have been trying to call you all morning. Where have you been?" Raina barked into his ear.

"What?" He looked over his shoulder for signs of Clio, but the corridor remained dark and still.

"I called this morning, trying to apologize for that wench calling you last night. What happened anyway, she was ranting and pitched a complete hissy fit this morning. Oh, she spent the night here, by the way. I swear that woman-"

"I heard you got the internship. I knew you would." He stepped into the alley outside of the grotto, a cool breeze blowing across his sweat drenched back. Raina quickly began to prattle on about her internship, the party the night before and finally Catherine's rantings about him "*sleeping with a psycho*".

"You would think you'd hooked up with an ax murderer. But I must admit, I'm impressed. You locked that down quick." He managed a short laugh.

"Sorry to break it to you, Raina, but Clio doesn't do boyfriends." He saw the beam from Clio's flashlight growing as she approached. He could hear something, a muted thumping that made the ground shake beneath him.

"But she's doing you, and that's all I care about." Raina was saying, but he wasn't listening.

"Raina, I'm gonna have to call you back." He could hear his sister protest before he hung up. The light was growing brighter, bouncing as the sound of Clio's footfalls became louder. Somewhere, glass shattered, and someone screamed, candles fell from the alter and some of the crosses clattered to the ground. Clio burst into the room an explosion of dirt and rock accompanying her dramatic exit. The stone opening sealed shut behind her by falling rocks.

"Time to go!" Clio called as she sprinted past him. He instinctively followed, a million questions fighting to be the first out of his mouth.

∞∞∞∞

"So, are you going to tell me what that was about?" Noah finally asked when they were safely back at her apartment. Clio looked at him, smiling through the grit and dust that coated her from head to toe. They had been panting, dripping in sweat and grime, her laughing hysterically after she'd flagged a taxi and got them safely away from the chaos. But now as her rush of adrenaline had subsided, she was able to breathe without coughing up a cloud of dust.

"That was amazingly dangerous." She laughed, but she could tell he was not amused. If anything, he was horrified. Ignoring his obvious disapproval, she went into the kitchen and poured them each a glass of water.

"What happened?" He asked taking the glass from her. She drank her water in great gulps, easing her parched throat. When she finished, she poured another glass and gulped that down as well, watching Noah over the rim.

"Okay," She finally put her glass down and leaned against the kitchen counter. He sat at the bar, his glass still in hand, untouched. "Well, the tunnel wasn't very long, after maybe twenty feet there were stairs that led to what I assume was some sort of make shift basement mortuary. It was full of coffins, old pine boxes and some makeshift tombstones with a small alter like room off to the side." She took another drink. "Anyway, that little room was almost like the grotto, but smaller."

She described the darkened alter covered in melted candle wax and faded pictures of those who'd died in the yellow fever epidemic. The stones that lined the wall were just like those that covered the hidden door. And as she scanned the small space with her light, she'd found the Lafitte mark on the corner of a handmade crucifix. She pulled it from the wall and noticed two things about the cross. First, it was a cleverly disguised puzzle box and that there was something on the stones behind it.

"I took a picture with my phone and that's when it happened." She sighed. Noah looked at her expectantly, still silent in his judgment. "Apparently, I backed into a rotting support beam and it cracked, splintered and the ceiling started to crumble. It must have been directly under the alter of the church, because I could hear people screaming. I started running out, and so did the parishioners which must have set off some sort of chain reaction because the entire room started to fall apart around me. I was halfway up the stairs when I saw the entire vestibule fall."

"And that's when you came flying out of there like a bat out of hell?" He asked, finally drinking his own water.

"Pretty much." She said, reaching into her bag. "But I did get this." She gingerly retrieved something wrapped in a cheesecloth and placed it on the counter between them. She motioned for him to open it, and he carefully pulled back the cloth to reveal the hand carved cherry wood crucifix. He stared at it, as a somber awe seemed to fall over them. "It's beautiful isn't it?"

Noah used the cloth to turn it over. He stared at the tiny symbol at the base of the carving and slowly met her eyes. He was staring at her, a look on his face that she couldn't read.

"What?" She asked, her heart sinking to the pit of her stomach until he smiled, then laughed.

"This," He pointed to the symbol, the same on the brick and in the journal. "This is the mark we've been looking for." He ran his fingers across the symbol that had been carefully, meticulously carved into the wood. He lifted it, testing the weight in his hand before looking up at Clio.

"Did you notice how heavy it is?" She shrugged because she hadn't. She hadn't had time to question anything other than how fast she needed to run to get out of there alive. He flipped it back and forth, then, seeming to have discovered something, pulled on the base. It separated, and a sheath of paper and two rubies fell onto the counter.

Noah looked up at Clio who stared at the items on the counter. She unrolled the paper and smiled.

"It's a note to Jean Pierre. It just says, 'Paradise is yours to behold'. It looks like it was torn from another piece of paper. It looks like some writing was cut off." She handed it to Noah who stared at the foreign scrawl, then suddenly stood up and headed toward the papers they'd spread out on the coffee table earlier.

"Where is it? I just saw it this morning." He rummaged through the pages looking for something.

"What are you...?" She was asking when he held up the paper they'd found the day before, the one with what they suspected were map coordinates. "But the coordinates don't match anything on the map. Remember?"

He came closer, matching the jagged edges of the pages so that she could see the full picture.

"They are." She stared at the letters and numbers in the curling handwriting she recognized as Lafitte's. She stared at the pages, then remembered there was still another piece to the puzzle. One that had been scratched into the wall.

"Where's my phone? The picture I took of what was behind the cross is in my phone. Where is my damn phone?" She dumped everything from her bag and the phone slid across the kitchen counter. She snatched it up and began scrolling through until the picture popped up. She stared at the words crudely cut into the wall, sharp jagged slashes that formed three words.

"Well, what does it say?" He asked impatiently.

"Vieques, Culebra, Muertos."

∞∞∞∞

"I don't know. That's why I sent the pictures to you guys." Clio had been on the phone with her crew for the better part of twenty minutes as she and Noah rode through the city toward the airport. After she'd read the words from the picture, she'd sent them as well as pictures of the wall and the papers to Calliope and the crew. With that task completed, she'd turned to him, covered in soot and dust and smiled brightly.

"We are seriously in need of a shower. I'll bet we have sand and dust everywhere. And I mean everywhere." She'd looked up at him with big innocent eyes, well as innocent as she could with that sexy little smirk of hers. She played with the buttons on his shirt and looked at him through her lashes.

"I'll try not to use all of the hot water." She turned to walk away, but he'd picked her up and tossed her over his shoulder and gave her rear a playful slap. She erupted into a fit of giggles as he carried her into the bathroom where they'd shared a long steamy shower.

After, they'd lay in bed, the late afternoon breeze from the open windows chilling their damp skin. Clio rested her head on his chest, her fingers tracing designs on his skin. He'd drifted in and out of sleep, feeling more relaxed than he'd been in years. Clio made him feel free and light, like he could do anything. It would be so easy to be with her like this all of the time. He supposed he'd ruined any chance of a serious relationship with her years ago. But that hadn't explained her aversion to relationships.

"Tell me something," He sighed. Clio rested her chin on her hands so that she could look at him. "What exactly happened between you and your partner to make him turn on you?" She shrugged.

"Who knows. Garrett was always a glory hog, maybe he wants the spotlight for himself." She sat up, running her fingers through her hair, her bare back to him. He ran a hand over her skin.

"You do shine kind of bright, like a shooting star." He kissed her bare shoulder, and she looked back at him, her expression shaded. He moved closer, intent on pulling her back down beneath him on the bed.

"Believe me, that shine fades fast. We better get moving. We have a plane to catch." She'd disappeared into her closet before he could say anything else. She avoided any further conversation on the subject by deftly changing subjects. Finally, she'd stopped and tossed him the keys to her never used car, giving him a smile that was somewhat consoling.

"Come on," She said, letting him take her bag. "Let's go find some treasure."

He'd enjoyed taking the car out on the highway, rolling through the city on a sweltering summer evening, Clio beside him looking as gorgeous as ever. He'd figured she was trapped now, she'd have to talk to him. Instead, she'd taken out her phone and called her sister, spending the entire ride going over plans with her.

As they pulled into the parking lot, she pointed towards a hanger. Frustrated, he swung the car around and followed the narrow rode to the row of hangers and small private planes that sat waiting. He looked at her and frowned, because of course it would be a private plane.

"This one." She pointed, finally disconnecting her phone call. He eased toward the hanger and stopped but kept the engine running. She smiled and tried to open her door to find it locked. She pushed the button to unlock it, only to have him lock it again. They repeated this little song and dance until she turned in her seat to face him.

"Professor, we have a plane to catch." She tried her best to look stern, but he wasn't buying it.

"We are not going anywhere until we clear something up." She folded her arms across her chest and waited. "I will not have you shutting me out. I've spent the better part of three hours with you completely avoiding any conversation with me. Instead, you've deflected or ignored me, when you weren't yapping away on your phone. I don't know what happened with you and your last partner, but I need you to trust me. I need you to respect me enough to treat me as an equal and I need you to not shut me out when things get a little uncomfortable for you." He didn't know what he expected, but her response was calm, almost cold. The ice in her stare physically chilled him and he involuntarily backed away.

"Okay, but that goes both ways professor. You can't hide from me either. Not ducking behind those ridiculous glasses or acting like an arrogant asshole. You can do that shit with other people, but not with me. You want me to trust you, you have to trust me as well." He shook his head.

"I am nothing but honest with you." She snorted and sat back in her seat, her arms across her chest.

"No, you aren't. You aren't even honest with yourself, Noah." She snapped. "You rather hide than be who you want to be, who you actually are."

"Oh, pot meet kettle." He snapped back. "Talking about honesty, why don't you admit that this ridiculous *"no relationship"* rule of yours is to keep people at arm's length. So, they won't get close to you and maybe have you get close to them, maybe love you. You're so scared of being hurt that you even keep your distance from your own family." She shot daggers at him, and for a moment he felt that he'd said too much.

"And you pretend to be someone you aren't to make everyone else around you happy. What are you hiding from Noah?" Her voice was low, and he knew he'd hit a sore spot but wasn't sure what it was. Her expression was intense, her body rigid as she faced him. "We all have our demons, professor. I suggest you deal with your own before you go poking at mine." She got out of the car, slamming the door so hard that he winced.

Well, he thought slowly getting out of the car, that was not what he expected. He walked to the trunk to help the flight crew get the luggage. Clio glared for a moment before going up the short flight of stairs and disappearing into the dim interior of the G6. He stared after her, letting the young man beside him take their bags and disappear somewhere with them. He figured they would be stored somewhere beneath the plane and reemerge when they landed. He also figured that this plane ride was going to be long and uncomfortable.

∞∞∞∞

She was yanking at her seatbelt when he finally made his way onto the plane. She gave one more tug and the hard medal end attached to the end of the belt swung up and hit her on the top of the head with a thunk. She winced but refused the yelp in pain like she wanted to. She wouldn't give him the satisfaction. Instead, she just snapped it into place, thankful that it had been the flat side instead of the corner. She was also thankful that she had ten pounds of hair to cushion the blow. The last thing she needed was to be pouring blood from a self-inflicted head wound.

He took a seat across from her and belted himself in as the door closed and the pilot took his seat in the cockpit. He stared out of the window, watching them taxi out of the hanger toward the runway. She noticed that those damn glasses had

93

reappeared. His posture was rigid, as if an iron rod had replaced his spine, and he clenched his jaw, she could see the muscles working. Her anger began to ebb, giving way to a sort of sadness.

He'd let his guard down with her, let her peek behind the curtain, as it were. She seen glimpses of the real Noah, sweet, sunny, sexy and if she were totally honest, one of, if not the best lover she'd ever had. She liked that Noah, not the caricature he pretended to be.

The plane stopped as it waited for clearance, and she used the time to remove her belt and ease into the seat beside him. He didn't say anything as she buckled in, or when she rested her head on his chest, one hand playing with the buttons on his shirt. He relaxed a little, but still didn't look at her.

"I do trust you, Noah." She said in a small voice. "I've always trusted you. And as much as I hate to admit it, I really like working with you. I'll try to be less of a jerk if you try to be less of an ass." He remained silent but put his arm around her shoulders and kissed the top of her head. Exactly where the belt buckle had hit her. She took a deep breath and closed her eyes.

"Garrett, that's my former partner, left because he said I was a selfish, emotionally bankrupt succubus that had ruined his life. He said, and I quote, 'you are draining my soul, sucking the joy from my life, you relentless harpy.'" He didn't move or speak so she decided to continue her purge.

"That was after he'd asked me to make our occasional arrangement into a permanent partnership, that he was in love with me. He was offered a job teaching at some private university in northern California. He asked that I go with him, make this our last trip and start a life together on the west coast. Get a house, get married have kids..."

"And that's not what you want?" He asked.

"Sure, I want it, but to be a stay at home mom, or even being tied to one place would make me crazy. I told him that. I guess he took my research as a way of showing me that since I didn't need him, he doesn't need me either." Noah buried his face in her hair, his arm tightening around her.

"Or he's trying to hurt you the way you hurt him." She looked up at him, needing him to see her face, her expression and understand the seriousness of her next statement.

"And that is exactly why I don't do relationships." She closed her eyes and let her head fall against his chest.

∞∞∞∞∞

"Are you serious?" Noah bellowed as they approached the 'boat', pausing to watch a deck hand take their luggage up the gangplank. Calliope stood on deck in a brilliant white romper, her hair pulled up in her usual ponytail. Her bright green eyes were shielded from the afternoon sun by a pair of cat-eyed sunglasses her face was awash in before unseen freckles.

"Ahoy mateys! Welcome aboard." She saluted then disappeared.

"Isn't it cool?" Clio was saying taking his hand.

"This is Titus's boat? I thought you had a salvage ship, not this. Clio, this is a freakin yacht." He said. She looked at it, then looked at him and shrugged.

"Yeah, Titus usually rents it to people for private charters when he isn't using it. I think there may be a smaller one, but this one can accommodate our equipment better. Besides, why buy another boat when we have this one? Come on, I'll show you around really quick." She gave his hand a tug and he followed, trying to take in the resplendence of what had to be at least 290ft of yacht with the name *Red Bird* painted prettily on its aft. There were large cranes and wenches on the side that looked as if they had just been installed, and he wondered how the hell they'd managed to turn a luxury yacht into a research ship in such a short amount of time. When he'd asked Clio all she said was.

"Titus has the ability to get stuff done quickly. It's what he does." As if that were an answer.

They started on the lower deck where she showed him a small gym and sauna, before taking him to the bridge to meet the captain and his first mate. The level below the bridge was called the owner's deck, which was where the living room and master suite were located.

"Titus works a lot, so he'll probably be here most of the time. I'm actually surprised he's not here now. He's probably on the upper deck, that's where the bar and Jacuzzi are. We'll spend most of our time on the next level down."

She explained while leading him down a staircase to the main deck. On this deck she showed him a large living area that had been set up as their base but would also act as the dining area. It reminded him of her apartment, light colored furniture that had been polished to a high gloss. There were several sitting areas, a dining table and a television hidden behind a panel in the wall. It also opened onto an opened deck with a bar and smaller dining table. She took him towards the bow of the ship and a hallway lined with bedrooms. There were six rooms in all including three single rooms and two doubles. One double was occupied by Teri and Mina who always roomed together because they were usually awake before everyone else. Javi was in the other double.

"This is Calli's room. You can take this one." She pointed to the door across from Calli's and he opened the door to peer inside. It was done in pale blue and a bit small. He frowned and turned to look at Clio.

"So, we're together?" He asked flopping on the bed.

"Uh No. That would be highly inappropriate. This, is my room." She tapped the wall at the end of the hall. He looked at it, then at her expectantly. She reached down and pushed a lever that blended into the dark paneling perfectly. Someone would have to know exactly where to look to find it. A door slid open and she entered waving for him to follow.

Clio's onboard suite was elegant and soft, decorated in shades of gold and beige. The sitting area was already filled with metal boxes, specialized equipment, maps and files. There was a table in the center of the room that had been set up with a computer and three monitors, all of which were scrolling numbers, weather predictions and nautical measurements. This was her base, he realized. It was why she had the biggest suite she had enough hardware to furnish a small IT department.

"This used to be another lounge and dining area, but we re-purposed it. We will probably do most of the work on deck, but I need the space to work. On these trips, I keep strange hours and this way I don't disrupt the entire boat."

He peeked into her bathroom which was relatively small but had a shower and a large round tub that faced tempered windows and the view of the bluest water and sky he'd ever seen. Her bed faced a great glass wall and a private deck at the bow of the ship. Fresh flowers overflowed from vases on either side of the bed; and sitting the center of the bed with a bright pink bow was a large white box. He managed to glance at the card and saw that it was from the mysterious, *'brotherly'* Titus to his *'hummingbird'*. He fought the urge to knock it to the floor because that would be childish and petty, and he was neither of those things. He walked closer and magically, the windows lifted. He was about to ask why they couldn't share this room, when a deep voice caught his attention.

"Hummingbird," He turned to see not one, but two men enter the room. On was older, but built like a stone wall, his skin had been bronzed by years in the sun, his hazel eyes bright. He had short white hair and a neatly trimmed beard and mustache in the same snowy shade. She squealed and jumped into his arms.

"Uncle Z," She laughed as he swung her. When he put her down, she went to the next man and Noah felt his stomach drop to his toes. The other man wore white board shorts and nothing else. His skin was golden, there was no other way to describe it. His dark hair was cut short, his eyes were as dark as midnight but when he smiled at Clio his entire face brightened. Noah had seen him briefly during one of their video chats, but to see him in person, he was even better looking, if that were possible. He reminded him of a matinee idol from the 1930's only with muscled arms covered in dark spirals and curves of elaborate tattoos. When he smiled, his face became boyish, softening the edge of his strong jaw line and defined cheekbones. He looked like a prince of some island nation.

"Hummingbird," He said in accented English. She hugged him, resting her cheek on his bare chest and Noah felt as if he'd been punched in the gut. When the man kissed her cheek, the pain intensified to agony. What the hell was wrong with him?

"Doodlebug," Clio said, looking into the face of Titus St. John with pure love and adoration. Titus held her with an obvious affection that made Noah envious. Titus looked at him, his eyes narrowing slightly in recognition, before he smirked and held Clio tighter.

Noah hated him immediately.

∞∞∞∞

Music throbbed around them, a primitive beat that had Clio and Calliope on their feet. They danced together in the VIP section of one of Titus's favorite night spots. After they'd settled in, Titus had taken them all out to dinner and now dancing and drinks. It would be their last night out before they set sail on what he referred to as Clio's wild hair.

"Hey," Calli leaned in close so Clio could hear her over the music. "What's going on over there?" She nodded toward Noah, who sat watching her, a drink in his hand. She had to admit, he was the sexiest man in the place in all white against chocolate skin. His locs were loose around his shoulders and occasionally, he would run his fingers through them to push them off his face. When he did, his sleeves would tighten around his bicep and a thrill of excitement rolled through her in a lusty wave. She'd seen women watching him since they'd walked in, a couple trying their best to get his attention.

But he'd been quiet and somewhat sullen all night. At dinner, while they were raucous and lively, he'd remained silent. She'd nudged him affectionately trying to get him to join in the fun, but he hadn't. He'd basically pouted the entire time, picking at his food.

"Dr. Toussaint, is the steak not to your liking?" Titus asked, addressing Noah for the first time since their arrival.

"Actually, it's delicious." Noah offered, "I'm just not very hungry tonight."

"Would you like something else? Maybe something lighter? I'm sure the chef would be more than happy to prepare anything you'd like." Titus offered, but Clio got the feeling that his pleasant demeanor was masking his animosity towards her guest. Noah declined, but Titus continued to watch him throughout dinner, trying to engage him in conversation, but Noah didn't bite. In fact, Noah's only responses where monosyllabic and rather terse.

He hadn't even cracked a smile when she told them about their scavenger hunt through the French Quarter and subsequent damage to a historical landmark.

"Look on the bright side, Birdie," Titus laughed, "You probably initiated some well needed renovations." They had all laughed, everyone except Noah.

Even with his antisocial behavior tonight, Clio was about ready to jump on him, wrap herself around him and ride him all night long. Maybe it was the music or the drinks or the fact that he looked like something out of a romance novel, she wanted him. He looked every bit the alpha male.

She left her sister and crew on the dance floor, moving past the velvet rope with one thing on her mind. She eased beside him on the dark leather sofa, her hand high on his thigh.

"Come dance with me." She leaned close, her mouth inches from his ear. Her fingers danced lightly across his inner thigh, but he didn't even flinch. Instead, he just covered her hand with his.

"What's wrong? Don't you want to dance with me? Get all hot and sweaty?" She asked, leaning closer. She touched his cheek, her eyes searching his face. He glanced past her, and she followed his gaze to Titus who watched them intently.

"I think I may just be jet-lagged, that's all." He gave her a tight smile, gently stroking her cheek with his thumb. "I think I'm going to head back to the boat and get some rest." He stood to go but she held his hand.

"I'll come with you." He shook his head.

"No, stay. You're having fun." She frowned but stood when he did, anyway, picking up the little silver clutch Calliope insisted she bring. She's also insisted that she wear the skin-tight latex pants that were sticking to her like a second skin. She couldn't wait to peel them off.

"I'd have more fun with you. You can help me get out of these ridiculous pants." His eyes moved down the length of her, slowly taking her in. He stepped closer, leaning in for a kiss perhaps. She would never know because Titus chose that particular moment to interrupt.

"He's right, you stay. I'll walk him back. It will give us a chance to get to know each other." Titus had placed a hand on Noah's shoulder and was steering him toward the exit before she could protest. Watching them disappear into the crowd, she had the feeling that this would not end well.

Chapter 8

Noah hadn't been able to refuse Titus's offer. Not that he really wanted to, they needed to hash out whatever was going on between them in order to work together. They had danced around each other all day, giving each other looks and making snide remarks to each under their breath.

They stepped into night air that smelled of the ocean, music and lights fading as the moved through the streets. Noah said nothing as they walked, waiting for Titus to begin. After all, this little stroll was his idea.

Titus lit a cigarette, inhaled deeply, and blew out a plume of fragrant smoke. It smelled of cloves and spice, not the tobacco he'd expected.

"I know who you are." He finally said. "We all know. That is why it amazes me that she even asked you to come on this little adventure of hers. She assured me that you were different, that you had changed, grown. So, I promised her that I wouldn't kick your ass. At least, not until I saw for myself."

"So, that's why you decided to walk with me? To kick my ass?" Noah asked, preparing himself for whatever came next. Titus shrugged, exhaling a cloud of smoke into the breeze.

"I haven't decided yet." He said, turning to look at Noah. He shoved his hands in his pockets, the cigarette dangling from his lips. As much as Noah hated to admit it, Titus was the definition of cool. Everything from the subtle tailoring of his clothing the easy swagger to his stride and French creole accent screamed debonair. Beside him, Noah felt every bit the country hick he was. "I think we need to come to an understanding, have a discussion, man to man, before we spend however many weeks in close quarters."

"So, you're coming with us?" Noah tried to make the question seem casual, but by the look Titus gave him, he knew he'd failed. Titus tapped the ash from the end of his cigarette but didn't comment.

"I know Clio and I have history but that was years ago. And I already apologized. It was a stupid mistake made by a stupid kid." He sighed, tired of rehashing this yet again. Every time Clio had introduced him to someone in her world, he had to explain and apologize. At this point, he was fed up. But he also understood, Titus was more than just a friend, he was like Calliope. He was Clio's family. He could be a great ally. Or he could be his downfall. It all depended on what happened in the next few minutes.

Titus looked at him, his dark eyes sharp, his expression menacing. Noah had a few inches on him and out weighed him by about twenty pounds, but something about Titus St. John's demeanor made him wary of the man. He exuded a powerful confidence and hint of danger that was ingrained in his DNA.

"You'd think that, but it was more than that." He stopped walking, turning to face Noah. "You did more damage than you realize. She was so sensitive, and you crushed her." Noah snorted confused.

"I hardly think I damaged her. She was hurt and maybe embarrassed but..." Titus flicked his cigarette to the ground and cursed.

"You nearly broke her. Do you know about her parents? Her baby brother?" Noah shrugged.

"They died in a car accident." He said, and Titus nodded.

"So, you know why she doesn't drive and why she's always early for everything?" Noah shrugged. He didn't know why, he just assumed they were personality quirks. Everyone had their strange little idiosyncrasies, why couldn't those be hers. By the way Titus spoke, he knew that wasn't the case.

Titus continued walking, Noah falling into step beside him. He lit another cigarette taking a deep drag to seemingly calm his nerves.

"Clio is smart, but even as a teenager, she had this capacity that was beyond her years. She's never been one to pass on any opportunity. When she was a senior in high school, she was accepted for an exchange program where she would spend three months in Italy. Calli was already at NYU and Clio was so excited. It was her first trip abroad alone and she would get to explore Rome and even planned a weekend trip to Greece. The night of her flight, she was running late, which back then was the norm for her. She hadn't finished packing until a few minutes before they actually left the house." He took another drag on his cigarette before flicking it into the night air. They'd managed to get to the docks, the lights from the boats illuminating the water. Titus stopped and leaned against the stone wall barrier along the edge of the water.

"It was raining that night, a real downpour. They piled into the car and headed to the airport, rushing of course. On the interstate, an eighteen-wheeler hit a patch of water and hydroplaned across the median into oncoming traffic. They were hit head on. Her father and little brother Archie were killed on impact. Her mother made it to the hospital but died in surgery. Clio was the only one to make it, with only a broken arm, collapsed lung and some cuts and bruises." Noah felt as if he'd been punched in the gut. He could feel that whatever Titus said next was going to be devastating. "She was driving."

And there it was.

"That's why Clio doesn't drive. It's not that she can't, she won't because she still feels guilty. She blames herself because she was the driver. She feels responsible for that night. It took her so long to get pass that. For months she didn't talk to any of us, she wouldn't let us get close to her. We were so scared for her. She wouldn't eat, she wouldn't sleep, she was so thin and frail, it was frightening. We were all a little shattered. And she thought we blamed her, which we didn't, but she didn't believe us. Or she couldn't." Noah swallowed hard when he realized what Titus was going to say next.

"Six months later, when she went to college, we were terrified. But she insisted, she said she needed to try to start over, get some perspective and focus on something other than the darkness. We tried to convince her to go to New York with Calli or to the islands with Z or me, but she said no. She wanted to go to school so we let her. And then she met you and for a while, she was our old Clio. She was alive again, and back to herself."

"Until the night of the party," Noah finished for him. Titus nodded, giving Noah's shoulder a pat.

"She was so hurt, so broken. You were the one person she was finally opening up to. She had even convinced Z to invite you down for Thanksgiving. But that night, you broke her heart. When she said you were coming on this trip, I thought she was joking. But when I heard about Garrett, I thought maybe she was using you. That she'd devised some sort of payback for that night. Hurt you the way you hurt her."

"I never ever wanted to hurt her, Titus. I didn't know any of this. Why didn't she tell me?" Noah scrubbed a hand over his face. Titus steered him down the dock toward their home for the next few weeks. There were lights on in the cabins of the lowest deck where a few of the dozen or so crew had their quarters. There was laughter and music floating into the quiet of the night as they approached.

"Because," Titus sighed, "Clio isn't what we would call a sharer. And she'd never tell you anything like that anyway."

"Why not? Why didn't she tell me back then? If she had just stayed, or answered my calls or emails..." Titus looked at him as if he'd sprouted a second head.

"For someone so smart, you are completely stupid. Or blind. Clio's in love with you. She has been since college."

∞∞∞∞

Clio sat watching Noah and Titus disappeared into the crowd, when a familiar face moved into view. Was she drunk or was she actually seeing what she thought she was seeing? A cold chill of dread ran through her and she grasped Calliope's thigh. Calli, who'd been sipping a glass of champagne yelped.

"Cal, look." Calli gasped, letting Clio know that she saw as well. She wasn't drunk.

"What the hell is he doing here?" Calli snapped.

"It's an island, Cal. We were bound to run into him sometime." Garrett Matthews stared after Titus and Noah before turning in their direction. His look of confusion cleared when he spotted them seated in the VIP section, a smile spreading across his too pretty face. Clio swallowed hard as he came towards them, looking as dapper as ever in pale grey slacks and a white button-down shirt. He'd let his dark hair grow out and sported a goatee, his olive skin had darkened into a summer tan, accentuating his Latin heritage. She hated to admit it, but he looked good.

He cleared the velvet rope and came to stand at their table, a glass of vodka in one hand, the other in the pocket of his slacks, pulling them tight across his crotch to emphasize what he felt was his best asset.

"I thought that was Titus. And where there's Titus St. John there is always a Jean-Noel sister or two."

"Hello, Garrett." Calliope snarled through clenched teeth.

"Calliope, you look as interesting as ever." He motioned to her bright red cigarette pants and boat neck t-shirt. Calli gave him the finger and a tight smirk. He ignored her as he often did and took a seat beside Clio.

"You look gorgeous as always, Clio." He leaned closer, his breath tickling her ear. She pulled away, turning to meet his smoky gaze. He bit his lip and moved closer still, his eyes moving over her as seductive as a caress. He'd perfected this sultry look, and, in the past, she'd always given in. But tonight, she just wanted to punch him in his smug face.

"I heard you found a historian, a disgraced professor, on your crew. Is he the new me? Your new lackey?"

"Actually," She sighed, "he actually contributes something meaningful to the process. Unlike you, he knows what he's doing. I hear you found another incompetent leech to work with you. How's that going to work? With you both sucking and all?" She took a sip of her drink, watching his face redden beneath his tan. On her other side, she heard Calli chuckle. He looked past her at her sister, who went to join Mina, Javi and Teri to watch from a distance. They hadn't approached but by their expressions, it had taken everything in them to stay away.

"You know, I would love us working together again. I can let everything go, I'll even apologize." He ran a finger over the bare skin of her arm. "The crew misses you."

"I'll bet they do. Don't touch me." She pushed his hand away.

"We were an amazing team. That Dr. Toussaint doesn't hold a candle to me and you. We are the dynamic duo. Don't throw that away." He had moved closer again, his hand on her thigh. She had to give it to him, he was really laying it on thick.

Shaking her head, she wondered how she'd fallen for this in the first place. She leaned into him, smiling as seductively as she could.

"We were a great team, weren't we? But you ruined that when you went behind my back, stole my crew and my research. Good bye Garrett and good luck. You're going to need it." She tipped her glass, emptying the contents on his groin.

He was on his feet, his attention on the icy wet spot as she went to join the others. She felt the fire in her spark anew with determination to beat him.

"Guys, it's time to get this show on the road." She said looking back at Garrett as they made a bee line for the door. She couldn't believe that she was ever attracted to such a clueless ass hat. He wasn't even that good looking, not compared to the walking fantasy that was Noah Toussaint. Just the thought of him made her catch her breath for a moment.

"Damn it, Clio!" Garrett was shouting from across the room. Looking at him she felt that she'd definitely upgraded. And she was ready to take full advantage of it.

∞∞∞∞

He lay on the bed, his arm thrown across his face, not bothering to look at her as she stood watching him from the open doorway. She sighed heavily and shifted, leaning against the door frame. He hadn't taken a shower, he hadn't even taken off his clothes, instead he'd developed a massive headache. He heard Clio and Calliope board. They were laughing, their shoes clip clopping on the wooden planks of the dock. She softly tapped on his door, and when he didn't answer, she eased into the small dark room.

He felt her ease onto the bed, crawling across the bed before straddling him while dropping soft kisses on his neck and chest. Her hands moved quickly to unbutton his shirt, so that she could run her tongue from his sternum down to his navel. She bit him, gentle playful nips at the skin just above the fly of his pants. Everything in him wanted to touch her, to pull off the pants that had tempted him and every other man in a fifty-foot radius all night.

"Nooooaaaah," She sang. "I know you're awake. I can feel you getting hard." She chuckled as she reached down to cup him. He peered at her from beneath his arm but said nothing. She sat up, rocking her hips against him until he inhaled sharply. They locked eyes and she slowly pulled the thin white tank top over her head. She took his hand and brought it up to cup her breast. "I want you to make me come." She moaned, leaning over to kiss him, her hips undulating against him.

"Clio," He held her still. It took every ounce of will power in him not to succumb to her effort. "Stop,"

103

"You don't want me to stop. Not when you're so hard I can feel you throbbing against me. You want me, Noah. You want me so much it hurts. I can help with that." She giggled, her mouth on the hollow of his throat. She undid his fly, releasing him before moving down his body. He inhaled sharply, grasping her shoulders as her breath caressed him.

"Clio, stop. Wait." He lifted her so that they were face to face, but he could still feel her, soft and wet against him. But he had to know, he had to ask before he could no longer form rational thought.

"What?" She sighed impatiently. "What is so danged important, man?"

"Are you sleeping with me as some sort of revenge plot for what happened in college?" He rose to his elbows, so he could see her face in the moonlight. She sat up, her expression more confused than annoyed now.

"Of course not. Don't be ridiculous." She gave him a playful shove. "Why would you ask me something like that? Did Titus tell you that? He's such an asshole. He's just messing with you."

"Are you sure, because you fell into bed with me pretty fast." He lifted her off of him and settled her on the bed beside him. He stood up, but she took his hand, lacing her fingers with his.

"You're really doing this now? Seriously, professor?" She asked.

"Do you do this on every expedition or excavation? I know you slept with your old partner. How many others have you had this no relationship- relationship with?"

"Is that what you really think of me?" She asked. She managed to not change her expression, her calm demeanor still firmly intact. But he noticed that shade falling into place as it always did when things got too serious for her.

"Honestly, I don't know what to think, Clio. But this seems to be your M.O. Is that what you think of me? I'm a good fuck buddy until the next trip, the next partner? When this is over, I don't see you again for another ten years?" He choked back his anger, watching as she pulled her shirt back on.

"It's easier that way. No one gets hurt when it's over. I told you, I don't do relationships." She said, rising to leave.

"You mean so you don't get hurt. Why did you even bring me here? You got what you needed from me, I helped point you in the right direction. Did you drag me along as your personal fuck toy?" He was beginning to yell, but he couldn't help it. She sat watching him without moving.

"Hey, that's not fair and it's not even close to the truth. I wanted you to be a part of it because if anyone deserves to go down in history as discovering Lafitte's sunken ship, it's you. You've spent so much time on the research, you deserve this more than anyone else here." She said evenly.

"And you sleeping with me is the way you keep me here? Make sure that I want to be a part of this? Just string me along until you're done, then off to the next adventure? The next man? The next arrangement?" He spat, and she flinched. "Is that how you get what you want? Tantrums and bullying don't work so you sleep with me? Is that why Titus is funding this trip?" She stood suddenly, that fury he'd seen that last day in Baton Rouge back. Her gold green eyes flashed, and she pursed her lips.

"I have *never* slept with Titus. Never have, never will. And I don't use sex to get my way. In case you haven't noticed, I can be pretty damned determined and even more persuasive. I have never been the type of woman to use my ...vagina to get ahead. I don't negotiate on my knees and I don't compromise on my back, you enormous self-righteous ass." She stood on the bed, so she could look him in the eye, her nostrils flaring with her growing fury.

"I have sex with you because..." He looked at her, waiting for her to say it, but she just stood before him fuming, her expression completely unreadable. But he noticed something, that shadow that usually masked her emotions had fallen away. There was no more of the false calm, she was furious and something else. Her eyes glistened with tears that she stubbornly held at bay.

"Because what, Clio?" He asked. She was hurt, he realized. He had genuinely hurt her, and it made his heart ache. Damn, could this little hellion really care about him, he wondered. Or had Titus just lied to him to make him feel worse about hurting her.

"Because... shut up." She growled brushing past him to leave the room. Noah took her hand, sitting on the bed so that he wasn't looming over her. The size of him in the small space could be intimidating and that was the last thing he wanted. What he wanted, was her to talk to him.

"Why Clio? Stop running and talk to me." She looked at him, those beautiful eyes of hers solemn. She held her head high, threw her shoulders back and stared him square in the face.

"The same reason you slept with me, professor." Her voice was almost a whisper. A tear escaped, rolling down her cheek in complete opposition of her demeanor. "Because as much as I hate to admit it, the more time I spend with you the more I want to spend with you. Because I like you. I really, really like you." She looked into his eyes, her expression pained and confused.

"You big stupid, jack-hole." She mumbled before making her escape.

He sat on the bed, smiling like an idiot. But he couldn't help it, Clio might actually still be falling in love with him. If that were the case, he was going to do everything in his power to make sure she fell as hard for him as he had for her.

∞∞∞∞

What was she doing? Clio thought as she paced the private deck off of her bedroom, a bottle of beer in her hand. She stopped along the rail and stared out over the still darkness of the sea and inhaled. She showered and washed her hair, gently combing the tangles out before dressing in a pale green silk chemise and matching robe. She didn't even know why she'd packed it. She never slept in anything frilly or lacy, yet here she was dressed like a damned fool, the chill of the Caribbean breeze cutting through her.

"Hey," She started at the sound of Calli's voice and nearly tossed her beer at her.

"You scared the shit out of me." She breathed and dropped into a chaise.

"Sorry, but I have news. We just found out Garrett is sailing out tomorrow morning, so we're leaving tonight, as in now." Calliope sat on the chaise beside her and crossed her legs at the ankle. Her thick auburn hair hanging in loose waves around her make-up free face. Clio looked at her sister and smiled, she never understood why Calli covered up those glorious freckles with makeup. With her auburn hair, cafe au lait skin, green cat like eyes and face full of freckles, Calliope Jean-Noel was an exotic beauty. It didn't help that she had the voluptuous curves of a pin up girl. Clio had always felt slightly underdeveloped next to her big sister. She was a sweet heart and nurturing just like their mother. She looked and acted so much like her, that sometimes it broke Clio's heart. She wondered what if felt like to look in the mirror and see the face of their mother looking back at her? She wondered if their little brother would have grown to look even more like their father. Clio had the luck of looking like neither parent but some combination of both. She and Archie had their father's hazel eyes, high cheekbones and dark curly hair. While she and Calli shared their mother's slightly slanted eyes, and full lips, but Clio had inherited her petite figure. She knew that next to her sister, she would forever be seen as the "cute" little sister while Calli was the beautiful sexy one. It was a fact she'd learned to live with long ago.

"Awesome. Mina already mapped our course." Clio sighed.

"Why aren't you more excited? You should be more excited." Calli said.

"I am excited. It's just been a really long day I mean I did destroy an entire church and all." It was meant to make Calli laugh, but she didn't. She just sat quietly waiting. When Clio didn't speak, she groaned.

"Okay, so are we going to sit out here and act like there's nothing going on?" She sipped her freshly uncapped beer and leaned back on her lounger, her legs crossed at the ankle. She was barefoot, the gold from her ankle bracelet catching the moonlight.

"Nothing is going on. I mean other than Titus opening his big stupid mouth about things that aren't his business."

"Him? I think he was very respectful and cordial." Calli snorted. "Your professor was being a pouty little toddler."

"He was not, and since when do you take up for Titus?" Clio snapped.

"Since when do you take up for Noah?" Calli snapped back. Clio looked over at Calli, narrowing her eyes in the pale light cast from the lamps of her bedroom that cast a shadow over her face. Something wasn't right here.

"Is something going on between you and Titus?" She nearly choked on the words, feeling a little sick to her stomach. She had always thought of Titus as an older brother. She could never, ever picture him as anything else. And she'd thought that Calliope saw him the same way, but maybe she'd been wrong.

"No, don't be ridiculous. He's...Titus." Calli sighed and faced her little sister, "Now are you going to tell me what that was all about? At dinner I mean?" Clio watched her, knowing that there was something she wasn't telling her. Something about the way she said that, the tone, Calli was hiding something from her. She could just feel it. But she knew better than to push, if she did Calli would dig in and stand her ground. She would let it go. For Now.

"I have no idea what you're talking about." Clio insisted and continued drinking her rapidly warming beer. Strange, she thought, the night air felt chilly to her, but the warmth from her body seemed to be taking the chill off of her beer. Stupid body reacting to the mere mention of Noah. Stupid Noah.

"Okay, so I guess I shouldn't bring up the fact that you called him bae." Calli sipped her beer.

"We have an arrangement," Clio began, not wanting to be reminded of that little slip up. Why had she called him bae anyway? It was probably because she'd slept with him. No, she corrected, slept was very little of what they'd done. A smiled teased the corners of her mouth at the memory. Nope, very little sleep.

"Oh lord, not another arrangement. That's what got you into the situation you're in now. Trying to beat one of your "arrangements" to your own discovery. You really should just give up the 'arrangements' and try to have an honest to god real life adult relationship." She sat up, shaking her head.

"It ends fine. And it's not like it happens a lot. He's only like the third or fourth."

"And what happened to the first, second and third? Not pretty, Clio. It's never pretty. But you wouldn't know that because I have to clean up the carnage once you've found a new dragon to chase into the ether. I'm the one who's left to tell these poor sweet guys, that you've gone. I'm the one who has to listen to them go on about how they thought what they had with you was real. You wreck men, Birdie. Look at Garrett." Calliope snapped, and Clio closed her eyes.

"You don't even like Garrett." Clio mumbled.

"That's not the point. Yes, I think he's a self-promoting leech and a manipulative troll, but he has real feelings for you. Why do you think he's pissed enough to try and snake you out of this particular find? Because if he does, it would hurt you the most."

"This is different, Noah and I are adults." Calliope shook her head in frustration.

"You cannot expect people to be as emotionally stunted as you are." Clio was on her feet, the beer bottle slammed onto the small table near her chair with enough force that she was sure she'd cracked it.

"I am not emotionally stunted!" She was yelling, she knew it, but she couldn't stop it.

"Okay," Calli conceded, "not stunted. Unavailable. You have completely detached yourself from everything and everyone around you. You can't drag men into your orbit and not expect that at least a couple will actually feel something for you."

"Why not? It happens all the time." She mumbled, picking at the label of her beer bottle feeling as if she were being chastised.

"Not the way you do it. They get to be around you twenty-four seven, they can't help but feel something for you. Clio, you are sweet and funny and beautiful and smart. Believe it or not, you are pretty damn fantastic. What man wouldn't fall all over himself for you if given half the chance?" Clio stared at her sister, her anger subsiding. Stupid Calliope, always being rational and good at being an adult, while she was still acting like a petulant child.

"You have to say that. You're my sister." She flopped down on the chaise, her bare legs erupting in goose flesh as a cool breeze blew up from the water. They'd left the dock and were drifting away from the lights of the city. The stars grew larger, the moon brighter as they coasted away.

"Don't get me wrong, you're a stubborn, impulsive, quick tempered pain in the ass most of the time. But you have so many good qualities, Birdie, that someone like Noah Toussaint is going to fall for you."

"I told him not to." She mumbled and Calli laughed, a hearty sarcastic laugh if ever there was one.

"You told him not to? And how's that working out for you?" Calliope sat on the chaise, wrapping and arm around her little sister and sighing. "I think that ship has sailed. The problem isn't him. The problem my sweet, irrational sister is that you are falling for him and you can't stop yourself." Clio let her head rest on Calli's shoulder and stared into the starry night sky. She remained still, knowing that Calli was right. She'd all but admitted that fact to Noah already. Her problem wasn't the falling; it was the stopping.

"I know you're trying to figure a way to stop it, Birdie, but you can't. You just have to ride the wave and see where you land." She frowned but remained silent because she knew where she would land. It was where she always landed, in a shattered heap all by her lonesome.

Chapter 9

Noah sat at the small table in the galley, eating an apple. Clio had feelings for him. His dilemma was getting her to accept it. Lord knew that he'd been crazy about her since the moment he'd met her. After he'd come to that realization, he'd also realized he'd been starving.

"Professor. I assume it was you arguing with Clio." Zeus Jean-Noel strolled in, drink in hand. His voice was deep, tinted with an accent that Noah could only assume was an amalgam of years living in the Caribbean and New Orleans. It was distinct, unique and in such a large and gregarious package, endearing. Noah shrugged sheepishly at the older man and smiled.

"I didn't know anyone else was awake. Umm, yeah. We had a little disagreement."

"We all have had our fair share of disagreements with Clio. At least she doesn't pinch anymore. Fingers like a lobster claw." Noah snorted, and Z laughed.

"I guess she really likes you. You're still on the boat. That's saying a lot because that one has a temper. Mean as a rattlesnake sometimes." He chuckled and poured himself a glass of bourbon. Z sat across from him, watching him with eyes reminiscent of Calliope and Clio, but with a distinct twinkle.

"She's like a five-year-old." Noah grumbled before taking another bite of his apple. Z inspected Noah as if he were some alien species. Noah paused with his apple midway to his mouth and returned the stare.

"Pretty much." Z agreed. "She's a very passionate and spirited girl. Always has been our little daredevil, our adventurer. Clio has never really been afraid of anything or anyone. She'd circled the globe at least twice by the time she was nineteen. Always searching, digging through ruins, walking and living with people who know nothing of the modern world. She's our citizen of the world."

"She is passionate; I can give you that. Her enthusiasm is infectious, but she's so damned pig-headed." Noah admitted. He could see a familial resemblance between Calliope and the infamous Uncle Z, they shared the same cafe au lait complexion and freckles. But something about his demeanor, that devious twinkle, that was all Clio.

"She really got under your skin, didn't she? Big Ant said she was dragging some fool around by his short hairs, but I would have never expected you. Not after the way you two started out." Z stared at him, narrowing his eyes.

"What does that mean?" Noah asked, finally biting his apple. He wished he'd waited when Z next spoke.

"I mean the *Incident.*" Noah winced at the mention of that night. Now her entire family had created a code word for it. *The Incident.* It sounded so ominous, so dark and depressing. He felt shame whenever someone mentioned it. They'd all eyed him suspiciously from time to time, even the crew keeping their distance.

"It means," Z continued, "you're the type that goes for the prettier package. I would have expected you to go for someone like Calli. She's more agreeable, beautiful, great sense of humor. That one is a catch. Clio is like getting too close to fire, she's cute and funny but get to close and she will incinerate you." Noah stared at him, his anger rising at this man who claimed to love Clio.

He chewed slowly and swallowed hard, willing himself to remain calm. How dare he speak of her that way, Noah thought.

"Why wouldn't I want someone like Clio? A prettier package? Calliope is gorgeous, I will give her that. But so is Clio, distractingly so. She has always been the smartest person in the room and she's sweet and funny. Have you ever taken a really good look at Clio? I mean a really good look? Her eyes are absolutely stunning, like golden sunlight. Haven't you noticed how absolutely beautiful..." Z sat back and smiled, a twinkle lighting his eyes and a broad smile on his face. It made him look younger and a bit ethereal, like something from a Dickens' novel or children's book.

"Uh huh," Z smirked. "Just what I thought. Tell me the truth, that party."

"I swear I would have never taken her to that damned party if I'd known what it was. That's the honest to god truth." Noah felt a strange sense of calm around him, a had a sense that he could purge his deepest feelings and Z would accept it without judgment or comment. Z winked, and he knew that what he thought about him was absolutely true.

"You lied to her." Z said, his bright eyes narrowing as he studied Noah. He squirmed a little, feeling like Z was reading his mind. He leaned closer, lowering his voice to just above a whisper.

"I never..." He started to stammer, but Z just laughed and shook his head.

"Yes, you did. You told her you didn't remember her when you first saw her, but you did. You knew exactly who she was, and you were embarrassed. It's hard to forget a name like ours, Jean-Noel is a very distinct name. And how many Clio's have you met who spell their name with an I instead of an E? There is no way you didn't recognize it, not someone like you. You couldn't block it out if you tried. You didn't want to admit that you remembered her and that you'd hurt her. Just like you were back then. That's why you never looked for her. You thought she would reject you and you couldn't stand if she did. Not again. Even after all of these years, you saw her and all of those old feelings, those wound burst wide open. You tried, put up quite a good fight. She was ready to give up on you and go it alone. But you..." He shook a finger at Noah who sat stunned. He was chilled to the bone, his eyes locked on the older man's as he spoke. Noah's mouth went dry, and he found it hard to find his voice, fearing that whatever he said, Z would contradict. Somehow, this man he'd only just met, had been able to guess the truth.

"I...I..." He was at a complete loss for words. The truth was, he had remembered Clio the moment she'd walked up to him in the coffee shop. He'd tried to pretend that he didn't, tried to treat her the way he treated the pretty co-eds who flirted with him. But looking into that face, a face that he'd burned into his memory had made his stomach twist in knots. Even in those ridiculous glasses that made her look like a baby owl, she had been adorable.

"No use denying it, son. I knew from the moment you agreed to come on this wild goose chase that you'd known who she was. You just needed an excuse, a little creative thinking to make it okay to do what you're doing. Test the waters so to speak, see if she really has forgiven you and that maybe this time you can do it right."

"What are you some sort of psychic? How ...'

"Because I have eyes and a fully functioning brain. You, my boy, have a long road ahead of you with that one. I saw that the minute I laid eyes on you. When Titus hugged her, you looked like a bull about to charge. You watch her, you know? I don't think she notices how much, but I have. And so, has Titus. He's very protective of those two. Always has been. Always will. But I think you can handle him." He gave Noah a gentle pat on the shoulder as he stood. "Besides, he's got his hands full with the other one."

"Don't let her push you away and she will try. She's really good at it. And as you know, she doesn't fight fair. She's like a tiny ninja." He chuckled and disappeared down the narrow hallway, glass of bourbon securely in hand.

∞∞∞∞

She didn't stir at the soft tapping on her door, or the soft creak as it was gently pushed opened and closed again. She shifted only slightly when he slipped beneath the covers, his weight making the mattress dip. She moved closer, sharing the warmth of his body, feeling safe in his arms. He kissed her neck and she sighed, fitting perfectly against him.

"I know you're awake," He whispered against her cheek.

"I'm sorry." She whispered. He kissed her ear.

"I can handle your little tantrums. And I know why you did it, so it's fine." He assured, resting comfortably on the coolness of the pillow. Her cloud of hair had been twisted into shining coils that hung to her shoulders and her skin smelled of flowers and cool night air. He ran his hands over the cold silk of her chemise to the warmth of her skin. He skimmed her breast with the palm of his hand, her nipples aching from the whisper of a touch.

"You do, huh?" She asked, her voice husky. She could feel him grow hard against her rear end, his hands moving under the silk to feel smooth naked skin.

"Yes." His lips brushed her neck and followed his hand as he pushed the thin strap of her gown off of her shoulder. She melted into him, her body reacting to every touch. When his palm moved down her stomach, his fingers resting on the lace waistband on her panties, she held her breath. He gently slipped his hand down the front of her panties, his fingers finding the hot moisture at her apex. The fire that had slowly smoldered there ignited her entire body. She was liquid heat against him, her body soft and yielding to his touch. He cupped her, long hard fingers gently caressing her until she rolled onto her back to give him better access.

"Why did I do it, professor?" She asked on an exhale.

"The same reason you wore this." He was watching her, his eyes darker, more intense. He leaned closer, nuzzling her neck when one finger slipped inside of her. She inhaled sharply, her hips moving against his hand. She drew her knees up and parted her thighs, urging him to go deeper.

He drew the covers back and shifted so that he was kneeling between her parted thighs. Slowly, he moved his hand and she whimpered in protest. He stripped her panties away, tossing them somewhere in the darkness. He looked at her, his hands moving down her thighs to her hips, pulling her closer. He eased himself down onto the mattress, his eyes still on hers and kissed her just below her navel and the muscles in her stomach contracted. He moved lower, achingly slowly, his fingers digging into soft, warm chocolate flesh.

"Because you know that I'm going to make you fall completely in love with me, Clio Jean-Noel. You will be mine, all mine and there is nothing you can do to stop it." She was ready to protest until his tongue flicked the most tender part of her and she bit her lip to keep from crying out. His mouth was so hot, his teeth gently grazing the tightened nub at her center. She clutched a thick thatch of his hair, knotting the long locs around her fist as he teased her. She felt her hips moving against him, wanting to feel every delicious stroke of his eager tongue.

He put one palm on her stomach, the other cupping the fullness of her ass while his mouth, his teeth and his glorious tongue made her cry out in pure ecstasy.

He continued licking and suckling until her body began to shudder. Clio twisted, turning her head and biting the pillow as another wave of pleasure rolled through her. Her skin was on fire and with each new pleasure she felt as if she were going to sink into the depths of this euphoria and never resurface. Just when she thought she could stand no more, he stopped.

"I have to have all of you, Clio. I want all of you." His voice sounded far off and dreamy. She parted her lips, intent on assuring him that he did in fact have all of her, then felt the unmistakably beautiful pressure of Noah slipping deeply inside of her and there were no words. He covered her mouth in a kiss that tasted of apple, and she could no longer think, just feel. He was hard and smooth, every inch of him heated. He said nothing as he drove deeper and deeper into her, her own body welcoming the feel of him. She gripped the mattress, her legs wrapping around his waist. She wanted to cry out, to verbalize what she felt but the only sounds she could make were grunts and nonsensical gibberish.

He sat back on his haunches, lifting Clio until she was straddling him, his hands on her hips. She rocked against him, her arms around his neck, her face buried in his hair as she rode him hard and fast. He tried to slow her pace, but it was too late, she was too far gone, her body slick and hot. She held him tighter, her hips rocking as she took all of him, her body convulsing in the most seductive way. He was watching her, and it excited her even more, if that were humanly possible.

She could hear him cursing under his breath, his breathing labored. He grunted when she rotated her hips, taking him deeper, her downward thrust and writhing hips forcing moans from him. She raked her nails down his damp chest, her fingernail stimulating already sensitive nipples and he made a noise she didn't even think was human.

She grasped his face, kissing him, her teeth tugging at his lower lip. She whispered something to him, something she knew he couldn't understand, but she no longer cared. She just wanted to feel and taste every muscled inch of Noah.

Unable to hold himself back, Noah grasped her hips and drove hard, trying to match her feverish pace, when she shook, every muscle in her body tightening as she came, her body coiling inward as wave after wave of indescribable joy washed over her. Noah was soon lost in his own release, his groan animalistic as he rocked forward, his hands going out to brace his fall and to keep from crushing her under his weight. The lay still, every few moments, one or both of them were shaken by tiny tremors of aftershock, before they settled. Noah rolled onto his back, one arm still under Clio while they tried to catch their breath.

"If you're going to do that every time, we have an argument, I'm going to be picking a whole lot of fights with you, professor." She kissed his neck.

"Good to know." He chuckled and kissed the top of her head seconds before she heard soft snoring against her hair.

After a long while, once she heard his breathing low and even, she rolled closer, resting her head in the crook of his arm, one hand gently playing in his hair. She'd found the blanket and covered their partially naked bodies. Noah still wore his pajama bottoms, he had just pulled them down, so now they were twisted around his thighs. She also realized that she had one breast exposed and her gown was in a tangle around her waist. They smelled of sweat, sex and sea but she couldn't care less. She could barely control her limbs, her entire body felt like gelatin that had been left out in the sun. She was sure that if she did anything besides lay here, close to this man, she would drift away. Instead, she snuggled closer and drifted off to sleep.

∞∞∞∞

He lay still, staring at the ceiling long after Clio had drifted off to sleep. The gentle rocking of the boat and the sweet breeze of sea air that wafted into the room relaxed his body, but his mind was racing. He couldn't for the life of him, figure out how her uncle Z had hone in on the truth so quickly. He'd stared at him, into eyes that seemed ancient compared to his smooth nut-brown face. Z had to be in his late 50's maybe even his early 60's, it was hard to tell by looking at him, but his eyes, like Clio and Calliope's had seemed so old.

From the moment Clio had come back into his life, he'd tried to fool himself into thinking that he could get away with a facade of ignorance, that if he pretended, he hadn't remembered her he wouldn't hurt her again. He thought he could get close to her, to find out more about the women who had once been an intriguing girl that he'd lost before he'd gotten a chance to really know her. He had no idea when he'd gone to her hotel room that he would feel so strongly.

Sure, he'd been drawn to Clio in college when she was a quirky little neo-hippie. But Clio as a woman was fascinating. He looked down at her curled beside him. She was tiny, her thick hair brushing his cheek. She had her fingers laced through his locs and her face on his bare chest, one velvety brown leg across his thigh.

He'd wanted to see if there was still a spark, and know he knew that it was more like a blazing inferno, an uncontrollable force of nature. Clio Jean-Noel was it for him. She had always been his ideal even before she had become the woman she was now. He just had to make her realize that they belonged together, to make her break her own rule. It was simple, he would just have to make her fall completely in love with him.

Simple as that.

∞∞∞∞

"What do you mean it's not enough information? It's plenty of information." Clio was bellowing when Noah made his way to the aft deck the next morning. The entire yacht crew, including Titus and Z were watching as Mina and Clio argued over a map that had been carefully laid out on the table. Javi and Teri anchored the table, all were looking at the map that had a transparent overlay to show the names used for locations during Lafitte's time.

"I mean," Mina was saying as calmly as she could muster, "that these coordinates are for three different locations on three different islands. We have no idea where to go first or where to start looking." To emphasize her point, she stabbed long pins into each of the coordinates on the map. Her dark hair was pulled away from her face in a severe ponytail, her brilliant blue eyes narrowing as she stared down the elfin woman before her. She stood at least five inches taller and had a good thirty pounds on Clio's tiny frame. Yet, Clio didn't flinch.

"Then we will go to the first one first and we do some soil cores. Once we analyze that, we'll know where to dig. Easy peasy." She stabbed her own flagged pin into the map.

"The first one is on a wildlife preserve Birdie. We are not allowed. As a matter of fact, all of these are national parks. We can't just go digging around willynilly." Javi sighed. Calliope waved Noah over to where she sat on a sofa basking in the early morning sunlight. She wore a white one-piece swimsuit, her eyes shielded by white heart shaped sunglasses. He joined her, nodding a good morning to Uncle Z, who sat on the other side of Calliope sipping what he assumed was a glass of orange juice. By the face Z made when he took a sip, he knew he was wrong.

"So what they're national parks? Some of the best stuff is found on restricted land. And who says willy nilly?" Clio turned those fierce eyes on Javi who rubbed his own and shook his head.

"Who says easy peasy?" He countered. From everyone's posture, he knew that this argument had been in progress for some time now and neither side was relenting. Clio was only five feet, but her presence was powerful, she dominated any space she was in and this was no exception. She placed her hands on her hips and looked at the three of them, waiting.

"So," Teri chimed in and for the first time, Noah noticed the deep southern drawl that was not native to New Orleans. There was too much twang. Her accent dripped with Georgia honey. Her tone was gentle but firm, her eyes never leaving Clio's face. "We could get arrested."

"For what? We aren't going to poach turtles or destroy a barrier reef. We're just going to look around and see what we see."

"What we'll see is the inside of a jail cell." Javi muttered and slumped in his chair.

"We'll be seen, Birdie. They have hundreds of tours there every year for snorkeling and scuba diving, but it is strictly enforced that no one set foot on some of these islands." Teri tried in her calm, passive tone. Clio shrugged.

"It's not like its booby trapped- wait- Is it booby trapped? Is it like that shock collar you put on a dog, so he won't leave the yard but in reverse? Is that a thing? I think that's a real thing." She looked at Titus who looked completely confused.

"Is any of what you just said a thing?" He asked.

"Yes. So, if there isn't an electrified force field, we can go check it out."

"There isn't a force field but some of these were once used for survival training by the military and there are unexploded bombs and mines all over the place, so I guess, yes, it is booby trapped." Titus sipped his drink, his eyes darting to Noah, a smirk on his face.

"So, we use the radar thing and the infrared what's-it that Javi has and only three of us go onto the island."

"Radiation detectors and laser bomb detection devices. I do have something that can detect bombs and other inorganic materials buried thirty to sixty feet deep." Javi nodded, reluctantly admitting to that fact. Clio looked at her team triumphantly.

"What's happening?" Noah asked Calli, who watched with less interest than the others. She was more interested in the magazine in her lap and the drink in her hand.

"You were right about all those things you two found in the Quarter. Those were map coordinates. The three words, *Vieques, Culebra, Muertos,* they're islands. And Clio, being Clio wants to start looking before Garrett tracks us down and follows. We ran into that little mosquito last night. He tried to convince Clio to work with him again."

"And?" He swallowed hard, knowing that she obviously declined but it still gave him a tinge of jealousy. Calli snorted, her eyes still on the glossy pages of her magazine.

"And... she poured a drink in his lap and came back here to climb into yours." He looked at her out of the corner of his eye, his cheeks heating from embarrassment. He cleared his throat and brought the conversation back to the issue at hand.

"Do you think it's safe? Those islands, I mean." Noah mumbled to Calli. She glanced at him briefly and shrugged.

"Doesn't really matter. Clio is going to get her way no matter what. Arguing with her is like ramming your head against a brick wall. She's a little pit-bull, once she locks in, she's freakin relentless. She lived in a tree house for six weeks to keep our dad from cutting down a tree. Wouldn't even come down for food or bathroom breaks. That tree is still in the yard at our grandmother's house." Calli casually sipped her drink. He glanced at Z, then Titus who also had similar nonchalant attitudes about the impending danger. Any resistance against Clio was clearly an act in futility.

"They love this. It's how they work," Calli was saying. "They give her the reasons why something shouldn't happen or why she can't do it. And Clio proves them wrong." She took another sip of her drink.

Noah could feel her staring at him and turned to look at her. She tilted her head inspecting his profile. He met her gaze, expecting her to turn away. That's what most people did when they were caught staring. Well, normal people. But from what he'd already discovered, the Jean-Noel's were not normal people. She continued to look at him as if she were staring at an abstract painting.

"What?" He finally asked, when he could no longer take her open scrutiny.

"You really like Clio, don't you? I mean you really care for her, don't you? More than you'll admit out loud." He frowned, wondering if this was going to be a repeat of the freaky conversation, he'd had with their uncle the night before.

"Yes...I..are you all weird and semi-psychic like your uncle? Because he and I already had the conversation yesterday." She pursed her lips and shook her head.

"Z isn't psychic, just very intuitive. He is weird though. I know you care about Clio. I see the way you watch her. Just let her tell you how she feels first. If you go letting out your feelings, she's going to bolt like a scared rabbit. So just don't go blurting out that you're in love with her."

"I never said I was in love with her." He half laughed, shaking his head. Was he sweating, he felt as if he were sweating. Suddenly, his face was hot, and his palms were wet. His stomach felt as if it had dropped to his feet.

"You never said that you weren't either." Calli smirked and turned a page in her magazine.

"Okay, so what else do we have to worry about?" Clio asked, leveling Mina with her determined gaze. Noah had to admit, watching her in her element, seeing Clio be Clio was definitely a turn on. There was just something so sexy about a woman who was so confident and sure of herself. She didn't flinch, didn't blink as obstacle after obstacle was tossed at her.

"Uh...prison, maybe? They must have security patrol to make sure crazy people don't stomp all over the place." Mina said, clearly losing steam. She took a seat and looked at the map again.

"It's patrolled by the coast guard and wildlife and fisheries. They circle the island every hour or so to make sure no one wanders onto the beach from the diving charters. It would probably be best to check it out at night, less chance of being seen, especially if you go at it from the east. The wildlife and fisheries department usually do only one pass per night a little after dark, then not again until dawn. The coast guard only once near dawn, if that." Uncle Z offered.

"How do you know that?" Calliope asked. He shrugged as he walked past them on his way to the bar for a refill.

"I know stuff." He mumbled.

"So, this is doable." Clio said and the other three threw their hands in the air.

"If we're caught, Birdie we will be arrested. That is if we don't get blown up first." Mina practically growled through clenched teeth.

"We are not going to blow up when we have *Ja-Gyver* on our team." She pointed to Javi who laughed. "We've been arrested before and for dumber stuff than this. Besides, I take a helluva mug shot." If there was one thing Noah had learned about Clio in their short time together, it was that she was tenacious and determined. She would not relent. Not when she was so passionate, so bold. She was a tiny force of nature. He watched her crew look at each other then Mina threw her hands up in defeat.

"Okay then, I'll let the Captain know. Titus, get ready to bail us out, because we're all going to jail." Mina reached for a walkie talkie that was clipped to her hip.

"Love you!" Clio yelled after Mina who gave her the finger as she spoke to the bridge from the deck.

"I guess I'll go check the equipment," Javi sighed and grabbed another walkie from its cradle near the bar on his way down the stairs. Teri remained seated, happily taking a drink that Z offered her.

Clio turned then, acknowledging Noah for the first time. She still had her hair in twists, but they were pulled away from her sun kissed face. She wore denim cut offs that left nothing to the imagination and a teeny-tiny white bikini top. Her skin was covered in a fine sheen of oil that he could only assume was sunscreen, her feet were bare. She looked like all of his teen-aged fantasies brought to life and it took everything in him to not pull her onto his lap and kiss her. Damn, he thought, damn, damn, damn.

"Good morning, Professor." She said in the same husky tone she'd used in bed the night before and the effect was immediate. Noah casually crossed his legs and nodded to her. He wished his body wouldn't react so strongly to her. He no longer had control of his hormones, like a teen in the throes of puberty. He wanted to touch her, to take her in his arms and hold onto her, protect her keep her safely with him, forever. That thought was like ice water down his spine. It also succeeded in ebbing his growing erection.

"Good morning, Clio." He managed to keep his tone even, neutral as he spoke to her.

"So, the two of you are matching now?" Calliope asked referring to the fact that Noah wore white swim trunks and a faded blue t-shirt. "And why do you smell like flowers?"

He shrugged knowing it was because he'd shared a shower with Clio that morning.

"Did you sleep well? I know this was your first time on a boat." She said, a teasing glint of mischief in her eyes. "Calli is going to do a couple of scuba lessons with you today. If you're up for it."

"I'm up for anything and I slept very well, thank you. Something about the sea air I suppose. Or the motion of the boat on the water put me right out." She nodded, unable to hide the cute little smile that teased her soft lips.

"Would you like something to eat first? I know you didn't have much dinner last night–" Clio started and Noah took his opening, as it were.

"I ate just fine last night. What I did have was very, very satisfying." He said and watched her nipples harden, pushing against the thin material of her bikini. She inhaled sharply, and he could practically feel the heat of her skin. Calli's brow lifted and Clio crossed her arms over her chest. Noah could feel Calliope looking at him, but he couldn't take his eyes off of Clio. She swallowed hard and licked her lips, ready to speak when Z groaned in disgust.

"Who do you two think you're fooling? We sleep in close quarters and the walls are very thin."

"What?" Clio asked, turning to face all who remained on the deck. They all nodded, but at least the yacht crew had the tact to look slightly embarrassed.

"I haven't heard so many shouts to the lord since I went to that Southern Baptist revival with your Aunt Athena four years ago." Z said, and everyone laughed. Clio turned to look at Noah who was trying to blend into the furniture. He had never been so mortified in his life. When Calliope playfully nudged him with her elbow, he couldn't help but smile.

"Oh, sweet Jesus," Clio groaned.

"Yup, sounds about right." Z said before draining his glass.

∞∞∞∞

Noah watched Clio as she strapped a weight belt around her hips. The white of her bikini against glistening chocolate skin captivated him. His eyes moved from the pink polish on her toes, up muscled calves to tone thighs, over the curve of an ass that fit perfectly in the palm of his hands. He smiled as he moved higher, to pert breasts that begged to be kissed. She was chewing her bottom lip, her face scrunched in effort as she tried to secure the heavy clasp. He wondered if she knew just how gorgeous she was, how sexy.

"Hey, I'm talking to you." Calliope snapped her fingers and he turned to look at her, slightly annoyed. "I asked if you can swim?" she said, her hands on her own ample hips where she also wore a weighted belt.

"Yes," he said, his attention back on Clio when she bent over to inspect the gauge on her oxygen tank. That ass, he thought, that ass was meant to be held, caressed, kissed...

"Hello," Calli stepped into his line of vision, blocking him from staring at her little sister.

"Dude," she barked, and he physically jumped.

"What?" Calli turned to see what had him so enthralled and laughed.

"You are so gone." She chuckled. He looked at Calli and attempted to look offended. She lifted one eyebrow and shook her head, a sympathetic smile on her face.

"I can tell you a secret." She glanced back at Clio then moved in closer, lowering her voice. "She'll never admit it, but she feels the same. I've never known her to be this open with a relationship. Whatever you're doing is working. Keep it up, we're all pulling for you." She winked at him and he felt his cheeks heat. He'd never blushed so much in his life.

"Are we ready?" Clio asked, watching the two of them curiously. Her hands on her hips, goggles resting on her forehead.

"Not quite. I'm trying to get the Professor's level of expertise in the water." Calli sighed.

"I can swim. Really." He assured, securing his own weight belt. Calliope pursed her lips.

"Can you swim, or can you actively not drown?" She asked.

"I worked as a certified lifeguard during summers while I was in high school. I can swim in salt water, lake water, pools and I've worked at a water park. I can swim." Calliope looked at Clio who shrugged.

"Okay, let's go." Titus said, his tanks already in hand. Calliope looked at him then Clio who again shrugged.

"I didn't know you were coming. Why are you coming? You're already certified." Calliope stared at him in confusion. Noah looked at Titus, watching his eyes as they shifted from Clio who was gathering flippers and adjusting her face mask, then to Calliope and realization hit him like a ton of bricks.

While Titus was very protective of Clio, it was more of a brotherly affection. The taunts and smirks at his expense had been his reaction to the woman he saw as a little sister bringing home a suitor. It was his way of being Clio's big brother, her protector.

He did not feel the same way about Calli. When he looked at Calliope it was with a heat and passion with which Noah was all too familiar. Whether she knew it or not remained to be seen. But Titus was in love with Calliope.

Noah eased away from them, going to Clio who held out a pair of flippers to him as soon as he approached. He grasped her wrist and pulled her close, his hand going to the small of her back to hold her close to him.

"What are you doing?" She said breathlessly, her arms encircling his waist.

"Do you know how sexy you are? Can we skip the diving lesson?" She chuckled, then looked up at him, her head tilted as she studied his face.

"What's happening with you? I haven't seen the glasses or witnessed Dr. Toussaint lately. That stick up your butt finally dislodge?" She gave his butt a nice squeeze and he laughed.

"I just feel good, happy. You make me feel good without wanting something in return. No schmoozing possible donors, no status…nothing. And besides, this is fun. Right? I see why you love doing this. It's a real-life pirate treasure hunt, without the scurvy and lice. And I get to do it all with you. What could be better?" His voice was low, and he felt a knot form in his stomach as he spoke.

"Yes, it's fun but not everyone can handle it. Living out of a suitcase, always on the move. And just so you know, I do want something." She teased, pulling at the waist band of his trunks and it was his turn to chuckle. "But let's get this done first? Okay?" He was ready to protest when Z came over handing him a cell phone.

"There's a Raina on the line for you. I picked up your phone by mistake." He said, eyeing Noah suspiciously.

"Oh damn, I forgot to call her last night." He mumbled taking the phone, but never released Clio. He tapped his phone and Raina's lovely and excited face popped up on the screen. She was just about bouncing with excitement.

"Tell her Hi for me." Clio said, then looked at Z and shook her head. "Relax, Raina is his sister." She said before he could start what Noah was sure to be a litany of questions and accusations.

Noah turned the screen so that Clio and Raina could see each other. They spoke briefly before Clio went to help Calli with her equipment.

"So, I hear you're blowing up churches." Raina teased.

"How did you know about that?" He asked in a harsh whisper.

"It's all over the news. I mean a church collapsing in the French Quarter is kind of a big deal, Noah." She said. "It was national news. You really should pay more attention to current events, Noah."

"How did you know it was me?" He chuckled.

"You're on the inter-webs. Someone named Calliope has you and Clio all over social media. There is a picture of the two of you covered in soot the same day the news reported on the church. I put two and two together. In case you didn't know, I'm kinda smart. Not to mention, someone took a grainy cell-phone video and I spotted you in the background." She waggled her eyebrows at him.

"Anyway, Catherine is losing her shit because you are the talk of the campus. The faculty is like going ballistic. News outlets are contacting them, and me and even the ice queen trying to get info on your little excursion. She hates that she can't reach you, something about you blocking her number, which I think was a smart move. The university is trying to cover their asses because you, my dear sweet brother, have gone viral. Doesn't hurt that you're supposedly hot and Clio's like certifiably hot. Her body is like hashtag goals."

"How do you know about her body?" He asked, looking up to see Clio standing on the deck in her bikini.

"Because Calliope?" She waited for him to fill in the blank.

"Clio's sister." Noah motioned for her to continue.

"Posted pics of the two of you this morning. I told you, you've gone viral. The interns here found out you were my brother and have been hounding me about the two of you. It's actually sickening how gorgeous you are together. Catherine can't stand it. She's like stalking my social media for clues. I have never seen the ice princess so freaked, it is frightening to say the least. I love it." She giggled.

"Hey how's the internship going anyway, Pooh Bear?"

There was silence on the line and he looked down to see Raina staring at him. If it weren't for her blinking, he would have thought the screen had frozen.

"What did you say?' She asked.

"How's the internship?" He repeated, and she shook her head no, slowly, her wide brown eyes still on him.

"You called me Pooh-bear." She said.

"I've called you Pooh-bear since you were five." He chuckled.

"And you haven't called me that since I was thirteen. What's going on with you?" He thought about it and looked up at Clio who turned to him and smiled. He felt as if the air had been knocked from him, butterflies danced in his stomach as something he knew deep down finally hit him.

"Raina, I'm going to tell you something and I need you to remain calm." He knew that what he was going to say would send his sister into hysterics and she did not disappoint. Once the words left his lips, she screamed in a pitch so high and piercing, he thought it would shatter the screen.

"I think," he said, a knot forming in his throat as he spoke a truth, he'd known from their very first kiss. Hell, he'd know it since she'd come crashing back into his life. "I'm in love."

Chapter 10

Titus spit into his face mask and rubbed the lens before putting it on. Noah watched him, frowning at the prospect of spitting into his own mask. He stared at it, then looked at Calliope and Clio who were doing the same.

"Tell me again, why I have to do this?" He asked.

"It keeps your mask from fogging up underwater. What's wrong professor, scared of a little spit? Wait until you have to take a pee in a wet suit." He grimaced, and the sisters giggled. They were always giggling at him, sharing secret looks. Sighing, he followed their lead. He had agreed to this after all. He looked up at the sky from the lowest deck, still amazed by the sheer size of the floating castle and squinted. A storm cloud hung low, darkening the sky in the distance.

"It looks over cast." He turned to watch the women fasten their scuba tanks, both testing their regulators and gages. Calli looked up at the sun and clear blue sky, then at the storm clouds on the horizon.

"There is a storm heading this way, but we'll be okay. We have a couple of hours at least." Calli assured, tugging on Clio's scuba harness and double checking her tanks. When she was satisfied, Calli came to do the same for him. At the side of the deck, Titus and Clio were talking for a moment, before he sat on the edge of the deck. He adjusted his mask, put his regulator into his mouth, gave her a thumbs up and fell backward over the side and into the water.

"Okay," Calli was saying, "everything looks good. Let's go." She gave his shoulder a pat and handed him a pair of flippers.

"Do we have to go over the side like that?" Clio looked over her shoulder at him, the sun at her back giving her a bronzed glow. She shook her head, turning to Calli who laughed. Clio sat on the edge of the deck, her flippered feet disappearing into the blue depths of the sea and dipped her regulator into the water before putting it into her mouth. She glanced back at them, giving them the thumbs up and slipped into the water.

"You could. Or you could be a normal person and use the ladder." Calli headed toward the edge, her flippers slapping against the damp lower deck. She motioned for him to follow, and after putting on his own flippers, followed them into the sapphire blue water.

With Calli's instruction, it had taken him a few minutes to adjust to the weight around his waist and on his back. Not to mention breathing through his mouth and silence that cocooned him. The only sound was his heart beat and his own breath as the regulator fed him oxygen. He waited, letting his body acclimate to this new state of being, then it was easy. He was buoyed in the gravity free water, clear and clean he could see each of his companions swimming in the same area before Calli motioned for him to move.

He followed them around the reefs, watching the colorful fish and plant life sway. He looked up to see the sun overhead, shimmering light cascading onto them. He drifted away, maybe for a minute, may be more, exploring the world beneath the world. He swam deeper, examining the reef, he even spotted a small shark that swam inches away from him, he reached out to touch it. It was so small, and fast, darting around him, scattering the colorful fish that lived near the reef. It didn't acknowledge him, swimming away in search of something more appetizing, he supposed. He stepped back, his back brushing a rock and he felt a slight sting but thought nothing of it because he saw her. Clio moved close to him, effortlessly gliding through the water, smooth chocolate skin that seemed to glow under the water, the white of her bikini dazzling. His stomach twisted into knots and he felt a wave a nausea that he brushed off as excited nerves.

She came closer, taking his hand and pointing toward something she wanted him to see. He nodded, swimming after her when dizziness overpowered him. He tried to shake off the feeling that something was wrong either nerves or anxiety. He closed his eyes, just for a moment when a pain set his body on fire. He needed to just close his eyes for a second, he would be okay, the dizziness would pass, the pain would subside, and he would be fine.

All he needed was a moment.

∞∞∞∞

"Careful," Clio could hear the panic in her voice and tried to calm herself while she struggled to undo the harness that held the oxygen tank to her back. Z, Javi and Titus hoisted an unconscious Noah onto the deck, his limp body still, his breathing ragged. Calliope practically sprinted up the ladder shedding her tank and mask as quickly as she could so that she could help.

"What happened?" Z barked, carefully removing Noah's mask. His lips had turned blue and his breathing was strained as if his throat was closing.

"I don't know. He was fine. Once he got comfortable with the weight and breathing through the regulator, he was great. We were looking at the reef, then he started to flail, he spit out the mouthpiece and screamed. He was bleeding and then nothing." Clio said trying to get closer, to help him, to touch him. She couldn't get the image of him thrashing in the water, his eyes wide with terror. He'd spit out his regulator, a silent scream lost to the sea. She grabbed the regulator, trying to force it back into his mouth, but he was seizing, his body too large for her to hold still even in the weightlessness of the water. The bubbles that escaped the regulator and her frantic movement alerted Calliope and Titus who'd come to help immediately.

She had never felt so helpless in her life.

Before that, before the horrific incident, he'd been so happy, excited to discover the world beneath the surface. The crystal blue water, the colorful fish, it had all been so new to him. He'd taken to scuba quickly and proved to be a better swimmer than both she and Calli, which was impressive. They'd spent summers and vacations in these waters, snorkeling and playing for as long as she could remember. Noah, as always, had surprised her. He was always surprising her.

She pushed to get through the men huddled on the deck, but Calliope held her back. Gently removing her from the situation. Clio fought to see him, fought to be at his side.

"He needs me, Calli." She repeated over and over even as she felt herself moving away.

"Let Uncle Z have a look. He'll know what to do." She was saying. That didn't make sense to her. She needed to help, she needed to hold him and let him know that she was there, that she would always be there. That... her knees went weak and her heart twisted.

"How can he know? He doesn't know, Calli. Noah needs me. Just me..." She was screeching, her chest hurt, and her eyes stung from unshed tears. She couldn't understand why Calli couldn't get it through her thick skull that she needed to be with him. Calli pushed her into a chair and knelt in front of her, willing her little sister to look at her.

"Birdie, what does Uncle Z do? What is he?" She stared at Calli for a long time, the question swirling in her head. She knew the answer, but she couldn't get it past the knot in her throat. She looked at the group again, Javi had joined them and so had a steward and someone else. Was that Teri? Why was Teri here? Why were so many people running around the deck, in and out of the cabin? Why was Noah shaking again, his feet and hands thumping against the fiberglass floor?

"Clio look at me. What does Uncle Z do? What is he?" She repeated. It took her a while to focus. When her vision cleared, she could see her sister, freckled face and wet red hair, a nervous smile on her pretty face. Calli had always been the pretty one, she thought absently.

"He's a doctor." Clio heard herself saying. "Uncle Z is a doctor." Teri and Mina ran past them into the cabin, then down the narrow hall where they disappeared into the darkness. She could hear Z talking and Titus responding, but the words were garbled.

"And who will do whatever he can to help?" Calliope asked, but she was watching the steward run across the deck with a medical bag. Z's bag.

She watched Z put on gloves, the brief flash of a scalpel and her stomach sank even lower. She couldn't breathe, why couldn't she breathe? Because her heart was breaking, she could literally feel it breaking in her chest. It was as if someone had reached in and began squeezing the air from her lungs. She covered her face with her hands and tried to remember how to breathe without screaming.

"Z," she said, trying to once again focus on her sister's face to quell her agony.

"And why do you think he'll do that Birdie?" Calli continued, but Clio was looking past her again.

He'll do it, she thought, because Z is awesome at what he does. He'll do it because he's a kind gentle soul who loves helping. He'll do it because he loves me, she thought, and he knows that I am in love with Noah.

"Yes, that's right." Calli agreed. Clio blinked and looked down at Calli and grimaced. What on earth was Calliope talking about, she wondered. What was she saying?

Noah coughed and was quickly rolled onto his side as he expelled water and vomited. He inhaled deeply and continued coughing. Titus and Z forced him to sit up and he did so, but his expression was pained. Mina returned, saying something she couldn't comprehend then disappeared again.

"Help him into the bath, quickly." Z said, struggling to his feet. He looked at Clio and smiled and she felt relief wash over her in great waves, her body going limp as the tension left her. She exhaled and felt the tightness in her chest begin to ease, but the knots in her stomach remained.

Z caught her as her knees buckled, holding her close and kissing the top of her head.

"What happened?" Calli asked, rising to face him, her hand still grasping Clio's chilly fingers. Z held up three long, narrow black striped spines in his gloved hand. Both women inhaled sharply, immediately recognizing the poisonous spines of the Lion fish. Though they weren't native to this part of the country, they had begun migrating to the region. If she'd have known there was a chance of coming across one, she would have stayed away from the reef. Or at least warned Noah that there was a possibility of running across one.

"He's going to soak in a hot bath to pull out anymore venom and I've' given him a sedative. He had an allergic reaction to the venom, so that's why he was seizing. The spines have been removed and once we get him out of the bath, he will be fine. It got him in the right side of his back and his shoulder, he'll be in pain for a couple of days. I have some pain meds for him and I've given him an epi shot. We're going to take him to the hospital. Just to be on the safe side. I've already had Teri radio ahead to let them know we're coming. He'll be fine. See, it's good to have me around." He kissed Clio's forehead and ran a hand over her wet hair.

She nodded and looked down at her shaking hands. Why was she shaking she wondered? She looked up at the darkening sky as storm clouds moved in. Lightning struck in the distance and a cool breeze rolled towards them. She was cold, chilled to her bones save the hot tears still streaming down her cheeks. Calliope held her face and gently wiped her tears away.

"Come on, let's get you out of these wet clothes." She felt herself being turned toward the cool shelter of the interior of the yacht just as the sky opened drenching the deck and the still, silent crew.

∞∞∞∞

She was showered and dressed in warm fleece pajamas when Z and the others finally left her with Noah. Z had given him a sedative to help him sleep until they transported him to the hospital. On his way out he'd suggested that she have one as well. She'd thought he was joking, but she wasn't completely sure. She never was with Z.

She sat on the edge of the bed, gently stroking his stubbly cheek. His skin was feverish, his breathing slow and even through the oxygen mask covering his nose and mouth. She watched him, openly inspecting every delectable inch of him undisturbed. His body, she knew, was chocolaty muscled succulence, his hair silken ropes that smelled of sea water and coconut oil and his face, his face was absolute perfection. He had soft full lips that felt like heaven when he kissed her. His teeth, brilliant white, but there was a slight chip in one of his front teeth, not something obvious, but she'd noticed it. He also had a small scar just above his left eyebrow that was practically imperceptible but again she'd noticed. She noticed everything about him.

His eyes had been the kicker, the thing that had thrown her off course. They were as dark as a cloudless midnight sky, piercing, hypnotic and so beautiful. Add that dazzling smile and she had turned into a bug-eyed pile of blathering idiotic mush. Something had happened between the first time she'd known him and this man. She'd had a crush on the sweet, self-effacing, hidden nerd of a boy, but what she felt for the man was deeper, more palpable. He'd always been sweet, but now he was more protective and so kind. When he let his guard down, he was smart, funny and he didn't take any of her shit. She even liked when he pulled his Professor Toussaint act, a defense mechanism he'd nearly perfected. But she saw through that, she saw the real Noah, her Noah.

"Don't you dare," she told herself, "don't you dare think you can keep him."

There was no point in her even letting that into her head. He loved his life, teaching and studying. He'd worked so hard for it and this, hopefully, he would get it all back. And then some.

He'd go back home, a hero, a superstar in his field. He would be able to teach and write and be the man he'd worked so hard to become. He'd go back to Raina and ... Catherine.

She swallowed hard at the thought of him returning to her. But he would. He couldn't live his life the way she did, jumping from one adventure to the next, never spending more than a few months at a time in one place. It was a hard life and she wouldn't put him through that. Hell, he'd been with her for a week and she'd nearly gotten him killed.

And what would Raina say? She was going to have to call her, of course. That conversation would be fun. *"Hey Raina, I know I've only had your brother for a week and this is the second time I've almost killed him."* Looking at him, laying so still, so peaceful for the first time she wished she were different. He couldn't survive in her world. No matter how much she wished he could.

"Stop it," She whispered. *"Just stop it."*

He stirred, his eyes drifting open and slowly coming to focus on her.

"Hey, you," She whispered, her hand still cradling his cheek. "How do you feel? You thirsty? Z said the pain meds would make you thirsty and a little groggy." He clasped her fingers, a sleepy, dreamy smile on his lips.

"Your eyes are so beautiful. I've thought that from the start, even behind those stupid huge bug-eyed glasses. I never forgot them. I never forgot you. I could never forget eyes like yours, not if I tried. I always liked you, I even had a crush on you in college. But now, I think I love you, Clio." His eyes remained on her face, intense and dark, his brow furrowing in confused realization. He was looking at her, but she wasn't sure he was actually seeing her. He yawned then, his lids drifting shut as he fell back into a medicated slumber.

Clio sat stunned, unable to think or even breathe for that matter. She stared at him, tears burning her eyes and her heart felt as if it would burst from her chest. Noah sighed, holding her hand to his chest as his eyes drifted closed once more.

She stared, her hand-held captive, her skin prickly. What did he just say? He couldn't have said what she thought he'd said. Maybe she was a little delirious herself because he couldn't have just said that. Could he, she thought as panic welled up from the pit of her churning stomach. What the absolute hell? She pulled her hand away and stood backing away from him as if putting space between them would erase his words. This wasn't supposed to happen. He wasn't supposed to do that. He wasn't supposed to care that much or at the very least admit it.

"Damn it, Noah Toussaint, you are going to leave a mark." She whispered.

∞∞∞∞

Lightning struck close enough to briefly light the room, waking Noah from a fitful sleep. He opened his eyes and winced just as thunder clapped long and loud around him. He sat up and pain shot through him, turning every nerve in his back into a lightning rod of agony. He inhaled sharply and grasped the bed rail. Confused disoriented looked around the small room and realized he was in a hospital. He looked down at his arm, at the IV that was pumping a steady flow of fluids into him. He tried to remember what had happened to warrant a hospital stay.

"Afternoon professor," Calliope said from her seat in the corner of the room with her laptop on her lap, a glass of what he suspected was whiskey and an unlit cigar in her hand. She smiled brightly and put the butt of the cigar between her teeth, made a face and took it out again.

"How are you feeling?" She took her time putting the laptop on a nearby table with her drink and cigar before coming over to him. She moved on unsteady legs that he suspected was due to the drink. He looked different, not her bubbly effervescent self and she looked, if his eyes would focus correctly, as if she'd been crying.

"Where's Clio?" His voice was gravelly, tired as if he hadn't used it for days. His head hurt, and his muscles ached. He sat up, throwing his legs over the edge of the bed and immediately regretted it. He braced himself, inhaling deeply to quell the growing nausea that roiled his stomach.

"Well, I'm fine too, Noah. What am I doing you ask? Well, I was here getting some writing done and keeping an eye on you while Clio takes a break to get a shower and some sleep. She thinks she's figured something out. She always thinks she's figured something out. The curse of being too smart for her own damned good." Calliope's toned dripped with sweet sarcasm and he couldn't help but smile.

"I'm sorry, Calli. How are you? What are you working on?" She was crossing the room, a bottle of water in her hand. She handed it to him and pressed a cool palm to his forehead.

"I am working on my next book. Well, I'm supposed to be, but I'm blocked. This trip was supposed to jump start my creative juices." She stood with her hands on her hips. "But between this storm, my nut-case of a sister, this treasure hunt, you and Titus the pompous — I can't seem to get anything done. Too many distractions, you being one of them at this very moment." She sighed. "How are you feeling? Really?"

Noah looked up at her, taking in the strained expression and lack of Calliope fashion flair.

"I could ask you the same thing." He said, and she stared at him, blinking in confusion.

"I'm...just tired is all. So, you're feeling better? You look better." She sighed, rubbing her eyes.

"I feel a little punch drunk but I'm okay. What happened?" He ran a hand over his face and felt what had grown into a full beard. His mouth tasted gross and he imagined his breath and body odor weren't much better.

"You, my friend, were assaulted by the new scourge of the sea. The dreaded Lion fish. You've been out of it for the better part of two days." She wagged her fingers at him and he stared at her, his head tilted in confusion.

"A fish? I got bit by a fish?" He didn't know if he should be amused or embarrassed. Here he was, six foot two, a solid two hundred pounds and he'd been taken down by a fish. A fish that had left him incapacitated for two days no less.

"No, you weren't bit." Calli sat beside him and explained exactly what had happened. Noah sat listening his head in his hands as he realized just how closely he came to losing his life. He was stunned and a little impressed that the laid-back Uncle Z was an actual doctor and had saved him.

The funny thing was, up until he'd blackout, he was having the time of his life. Being underwater, walking along the sandy bottom of a crystalline sea, had been like being on another world. The colors and feeling of weightlessness, the way Clio and Calli darted around him like mermaids, teasing he and Titus as they swam off in different directions. He'd followed Clio, who'd turned to beckon him. She was like a siren, urging him towards the reef. She'd shown him the sea life, the urchins and anemones, the tiny fish that scattered in schools into the distance. She'd brushed the sand with her hand and unearthed a ray fish that swam past him, smoothly. Everything there, the entire world just beneath the surface had been gorgeous and he had seen it all with Clio, who'd absently grasped his hand, lacing her fingers into his to pull him with her deeper out to sea. He'd actually been having the best time since Clio had barreled back into his life.

"Clio wouldn't leave you until your fever broke. I have never seen her that terrified. Well not over a man. She even managed to get behind the wheel of a car. Haven't seen her do that in a while" Noah watched Calli's expression change. It was as if she were trying to tell him something without actually saying it. This family, he realized, tended to do that a lot. Instead of forcing Calli to blurt out what was on her mind, he sighed and changed the subject. The Jean-Noel's avoided emotional conversations, it was infuriating, but who was he to force them to change.

"You know, I've never enjoyed anything as much as I've enjoyed being here with you and Clio. I forgot how much fun she can be." He wanted to say he should have never let her get away in the first place. What would his life had been like had he gone after her immediately when she'd run from that idiotic, mean spirited party. What if he'd been able to catch her before she disappeared and confessed his developing feelings. Would his life had been filled with adventure? Or would he have dragged her into a boring life full of academic functions and college football booster events? With his luck, she'd have gotten bored of the daily drudgery of his life and taken off. Who could settle for a mundane life like his when she was gifted sports cars and traveled on private planes and luxury yachts? She had grown into who he thought she was, a daring, beautiful, smart amazing young woman. He'd known it then but being here in her world now, he understood that Clio was and always had been out of his league.

He looked at Calli and saw the sadness behind her tired eyes. She ran a hand through her hair and looked at him with a melancholy smile. He yawned, and stretched, regretting it immediately when a sharp pain tore through his sore back. She took a deep breath and stood up, motioning for him to lay back in bed.

"You need some rest. The doctor says you will probably be released tomorrow." She yawned, then gave herself a shake.

"Are you okay? I mean really?" He grasped her hand, forcing her to look at him. She sighed and nodded.

"I'm just a little tired. You gave us all a scare, professor. I'm glad you pulled out of it." She went back to her seat and he settled into the bed. While he tried to get relax in a bed that was decidedly uncomfortable, he watched her take a flask from her purse and pour herself another drink.

"How did you manage to get liquor and a cigar in here?" He asked, slightly amused.

"Well, the flask was in my purse and the nurse let me keep the cigar since I promised I wouldn't actually light it. It's more or less a prop or a lucky charm. Titus gave me this cigar right before my first novel was picked up by a publisher. After he read my manuscript, he said, Red, this is going to be a bestseller. He gave me this cigar and bottle of *Perrier-Jouet* champagne. When I made the New York Times list, we drank the entire bottle, but I kept the cigar." She smiled at the memory, then the sadness returned. "He always was my biggest supporter, even when we were kids. He was always my champion, my hero and Clio's protector."

"You're in love with Titus." He finally said. Calli snorted.

"And you're in love with Clio." He couldn't deny it and noticed that she hadn't denied it either.

"We are a sorry pair. They're going to break our hearts you know." She said, and it was his turn to snort.

"I will do everything in my power not to let that happen. So should you."

"I don't think that we can stop it, Noah. It's what happens to people like us who fall for people like them."

"What do you mean people like them?" He asked, not sure if he should be offended.

"People like us, staid, normal, responsible adults always get hurt by the impulsive, adventurous gregarious nomads. They are the unicorns that mere mortals like us spend our entire lives trying to capture. We do get brief moments to bask in their glory before the flame burns out and they move on to the next star struck mortal. We are left in their wake, our hearts broken, and spirits crushed and usually with another broken soul who's been damaged by their own mythical creature."

"Wow," He whispered, "very poetic. I'll bet you're an amazing writer."

"That's what they tell me." She inhaled and shrugged.

"And I hate to burst your bubble, but you are people like them. You are as magical and mythical a creature I've ever seen. Titus would be blind and crazy not to see that."

"Enough of this pity party, you get some rest before the tiny tornado comes in and accuses me of keeping you awake." She said it with such sugar in her tone that Noah could only smile.

"Yes ma'am." He said, letting the painkillers from his IV take hold of him. As he drifted into sleep, his most prevalent thought, the one that kept needling at him, giving him a headache was the one he didn't want to think about.

How was he going to be able to just let Clio walk out of his life when this was all over? How was he supposed to go back to his hum drum life and boring friends after loving her?

∞∞∞∞

Clio sat beside Z as he drove them back to the hospital. As much as she'd hated to admit it, Calli had been right. A shower and a nap in an actual bed had been wonderful. She had finally been able to rest knowing that Noah would be okay. When his fever had spiked, Z had admitted him to the nearest hospital. Sure, it delayed their work, but she hadn't cared. All she cared about was Noah.

When she'd received the call from her sister to let her know that his fever had broken and that he'd finally woken up, she couldn't get back to the hospital fast enough. She'd even managed to get behind the wheel of a car. She hadn't gone anywhere, her knuckles white as she gripped the steering wheel of a car she hadn't even started. She'd been relieved when Z eased her into the passenger seat.

Now, she could feel the weight of the world lifting as she mashed the button for the elevator.

Beside her, Z was speaking, but she really wasn't listening. He'd been talking the entire time he'd been with her. She supposed it was to keep her occupied, but it had become the droning background noise of her day. She had tuned him out, letting her mind drift. That is, until he nudged her to gain her full attention as they stepped out of the elevator and headed towards Noah's room. She turned to look at him and saw exactly why he'd nudged her.

Garrett Matthews stood in the hallway looking into the window of Noah's hospital room, his hands deep in his pockets. Beside him stood another man, younger with a shock of black hair and a rather smug expression on his face. She looked at Z who urged her forward. She stumbled slightly but regained her footing and straightened her back.

"What are you doing here?" She growled through clinched teeth. Garrett looked at her, then Z who folded his arms across his chest and stood at her back. "Why is it you keep turning up like a black cloud of doom? Don't you have treasure to plunder or someone else to double cross?"

"I heard about the accident and came to make sure you were alright." Garrett placed a hand on her shoulder and she brushed it away.

"More like you came to rob my corpse. Are you following me? Of course you are, I mean you couldn't possibly find your ass with both hands unless I directed you to it. That's why you decided to shoot your shot at the club, to see if I would be open to working together. Among other things." She shook her head and sucked her teeth. "Too bad you never took time to learn anything in the five years we worked together. Nothing sunk in? Not even by like osmosis? Shame." She snorted. The young man beside him, laughed before coming closer, his hand out stretched.

"You must be Dr. Jean-Noel, I've heard so much about you. It's an honor to finally meet you. I've followed your work for years. Your article on living with the *Vedda* tribe in Sri Lanka was inspiring. I'm Jackson Blake." Clio sized him up, taking in his carefully orchestrated disheveled hair and neatly trimmed three-day scruff. His clothes, though wrinkled and dry had never seen a speck of dirt, nor had his perfectly manicured nails. He was a smugger version of Garrett.

"Jackson Blake. I've heard of you. You made a nice career for yourself by demeaning the work of others. But I've never actually seen anything you've ever produced. You are quite the intellectual leech." He pulled his hand back as if she'd slapped it, laughed nervously and wiped his palm on his cargo shorts.

"I assure you, I have worked really hard..." He laughed nervously.

"To mock others while you've never really done anything on your own. Garrett is the perfect person to work with your first time out." She said, itching to look over her shoulder at Noah.

"Clio, is that a compliment?" Garrett smiled and for a split second she knew why she'd so easily fallen into bed with him. He was handsome and charming but ultimately, she'd discover that the surface was all there really was to him. He had the depth of a curbside puddle.

"Oh, I'm sorry you misunderstood, let me clarify in terms you may understand. You are perfect for someone like Mr. Blake here because you both have succeeded by riding the backs of other more talented people to achieve your success. The saying is true, we all rise to our level eventually. Too bad your level is mediocrity." She turned to enter the hospital room, her hand on the door knob, when she snorted derisively.

"And to think of the years I lowered my standards for you. I would say I'm better for having known you, but we know that would be a lie of epic proportions. But if you hadn't been the underhanded belly crawler you are, I wouldn't be working with Noah, the best partner I could have asked for. I guess I have you to thank for that as well, Mr. Blake. Thank you both for being the attention seeking, inept wastes of DNA that you are. Screwing us over was the best thing you could have done."

∞∞∞∞

Noah heard Clio's voice and Calli curse under her breath. Curious, he turned to look out of the small window near the door to his hospital room and spotted Clio, Z and two very unexpected guests.

"What the hell is Garrett doing here?" Calli was moving across the room. He was fully awake immediately, a slow roll of anger overriding both his pain and medication. He sat up and ignored the shooting pain that wracked his side. He looked into the face of the man who'd wreaked havoc on Clio's life. He'd stolen from her and hurt her. He was going to kick his ass.

He was nearly to his feet when another, more familiar face came into view.

"And who is this dick?" Calli asked. Noah watched Jackson Blake extend his hand to Clio and she completely ignored it. Calli looked at Noah before silently cracking the door open so they could hear what was being said. He leaned in, smiling as Clio cut both men to the quick without raising her voice.

He listened, and his anger gave way to a feeling of pride. He could feel himself sitting up a little straighter, his chest sticking out as she told them off. He didn't even speak when she walked into the room, Z behind her still chuckling with mischievous glee.

She smiled when she saw him sitting on the edge of the bed, and his heart filled to bursting. She crossed the room, relief washing over her, lightening the room.

"You're awake. How do you fe-" He reached for her, taking her in his arms to kiss her. He pulled her against him, sinking one hand in her hair, the other pressing her lower back. From the moment he touched her his heart pounded in his chest and he felt a giddy elation that made him a bit woozy. It could be the drugs, but he didn't think so. This feeling was too pure to be drug induced.

"What was that about?" She asked breathlessly when he finally released her. He touched his forehead to hers and sighed. "Not that I'm complaining."

He wanted to blurt out everything he was feeling but couldn't bring himself to do it because she didn't feel the same. She'd told him several times, she didn't do relationships or boyfriends. She most certainly wouldn't do love. So, he exhaled and plastered a smile on his face even though that realization hurt him more than the stupid fish venom ever could.

"You are by far the most amazing person, I've ever met. I'm just grateful to be here with you." He said instead. "Even if I was nearly taken out by a fish."

Chapter 11

Clio happily pushed Noah's wheelchair toward the exit and the car Titus had waiting for them.

"I can walk you know." He insisted, but she ignored him. She'd also ignored him when he said he could dress himself. But he'd insisted when she started to zip his pants, he could imagine what a fiasco that could have turned into.

"Doctor's orders." She said before lifting her feet and coasting down the incline toward the car and driver that waited for them. He got the impression that it was the only reason she'd urged him into the chair to begin with. Her squealing, "*wheeee*" on the way down just punctuated that theory.

She did let him ease his way onto the back seat on his own, before sliding in beside him. She took his hand and sat quietly, her attention on something outside of the window. He waited until they were on the road, heading toward what he now considered their home on the water.

"You comfortable?" She asked, resting her head on his shoulder.

"I'm fine." He said. She sighed dramatically, and he couldn't help but smile, knowing she had something to tell him. Calliope had told him Clio'd found something while he was unconscious. She'd poured over the journal and maps as she held vigil in his room, even confirming it with Mina once she was back on the ship.

Again, the heavy dramatic sigh and he gave in.

"What did you fi-" She straddled his hips, her eyes alight with glittery excitement. She looked over her shoulder and met the driver's eyes in the rear-view mirror briefly, before hitting a button and a privacy partition slowly rose eliminating his prying eyes.

"I thought you'd never ask. I found which island he was referring to in that note we found in the church. Those three islands were mention a couple of other times in the journal, but he said he ran ashore on one. Apparently, he was sailing under some other flag at one point and ran afoul of some Spaniards. He and his crew were there for about a month. He mentions the other islands but just in passing, like the flora and fauna, but this island was where they spent a significant amount of time. I want to check it out." As she spoke, she dropped soft kisses on his neck, her fingers working to quickly unbutton his shirt. She was trying to distract him, not that he was complaining. She rocked against him, the hem of her sun dress rising above her hips. He put his hands on her thighs, loving the feel of silken skin, letting her continue her oh so obvious seduction. He could just feel the *but* and waited for the proverbial other shoe to drop.

"And?" He urged, inhaling sharply when she released the fly of his pants, one hand moving down to stroke him. His eyes drifted closed, but he could feel her smiling against his neck. Her hand moved in slow, languid strokes bringing him to the brink. It felt like forever since he'd touched her, kissed her. He cupped her rear-end, pulling her against him, his hips rocking to meet every stroke.

"It's the one with the undetonated mines." She blurted in a rush.

And there it was.

"Then there is no way you're going out there." The words were out of his mouth before he could stop himself. Clio sat back, narrowed her eyes and clinched her jaw. He shouldn't have said that, he knew that the tiny pit-bull in her would take it as a challenge.

"And who's going to stop me?" She asked, and it was his turned to feel challenged.

"I am. And apparently, I'm not the only one. This little passion play of yours is because everyone else told you not to go there because it is a horribly dangerous idea." He sighed.

"I didn't do it because I was worried about you. And this little 'passion play' is because -I kinda missed you, you big stupid." She lowered her voice and his brow lifted in surprise. This was a new tactic.

"You missed me?" He asked, running his fingers along her outer thigh. She eased him out of his pants and moved against him. He realized that she'd forgone panties when he felt her sleek and wet against him. He closed his eyes and tried to fight the urge to sink into her. It felt like ages since he'd made love to her. His need overrode the pain that still tormented his tender, healing back.

"I did. I've gotten use to you snoring and stealing the covers. Your big, hot, hard body draped all over me. That bed got very cold and very lonely without you." She sighed, her hips swaying against him, teasing him. "You scared the life out of me."

"Don't think you're distracting me, Clio. I don't want you going to that island. We have enough to go-oh damn." He mumbled. Again, she moved against him and he had to catch his breath.

"Me? Would I do such a thing?" She took him in her hand, slowly easing him into the heat at her core. They both exhaled, Noah cupping the back of her head, drawing her closer so that he could capture her mouth. He did miss this; miss her after only a few days. How bad would it be after a few weeks or months? Would he be able to live without her ever again?

"Look at me," He barely recognized his own thick raspy voice. She did as he asked, her lids slowly lifting. "I still don't want you to go to that island alone. It's dangerous, Clio."

"Your concern is duly noted." She dropped a kiss on his lips before she slipped off of his lap, breaking their intimate connection.

"What does that mean?" He adjusted his clothes, just as their driver opened the door on her side of the car, letting the afternoon sunlight shine into the darkened interior.

"It means, that I understand." She took the drivers hand and stepped into the sunlight. He followed, knowing that her acknowledgment was just that. Clio was going to do what she wanted no matter what anyone had to say about it.

∞∞∞∞

She was wiggling into a wet suit, her butt poking into the air as she struggled to pull the latex above her thighs. For a second, Clio wondered if she had grabbed the wrong suit until it finally gave and slipped easily over her hips. Relieved, she pulled it on, zipped up and began to check her gages and tanks. She'd found herself alone on the deck, just as the sun peeked out briefly from behind the dark clouds that lingered in the late-night sky. Everyone else had gone up for dinner and a movie. After their ride home, Noah had been drained and had taken a long nap. She on the other hand, had been full of nervous energy. She couldn't sit through dinner without fidgeting and felt as if she were going to burst out of her skin if she didn't do something. She turned to look into the darkness of the deck's interior and found it empty. Shrugging off her paranoia, she continued preparing her equipment.

The fact that Noah had admitted he loved her had her on edge. Sure, he'd admitted it while in a medicated stupor, but he'd said it with an earnestness that could only have been genuine. When he said it, she felt it down to her bones. And it terrified her.

Now whenever he looked at her, it was as if he could see into her soul, as if he could see past all of her stubborn bravado to the real Clio. She liked and feared that kind of connection. It could only end badly. It always ended badly for her.

She'd just reached for her oxygen tank when the voice from behind startled her, making her jump into the air and scream loud enough to scare herself.

"What do you think you're doing?" The tank hit the deck with a metallic thud before rolling away. She turned to look at her visitor, stopping the rolling tank with her foot.

"Jesus, Titus you scared the shit out of me. Stalker." She snapped.

"I hope that you aren't about to do what I think you're about to do. The captain wants to go back to port, the storm is supposed to get bad tomorrow." He said, his arms folded across his chest as he stared down at her. His expression was firm, scolding as if he were a disapproving father chastising a child. Clio mimicked his stance, her lips pursed in aggravation.

"And what do you think I'm doing?" She asked haughtily

"I think that you are going on a night dive. Alone. In the middle of a storm. But of course, you couldn't be thinking of doing something that stupid."

"Did you just call me stupid?' She asked and tried her best to look completely offended. Titus wasn't buying it. He lifted one eyebrow and smirked.

"If you're about to do what we both know you're planning, then yes, I am calling you stupid." He said.

"I, Titus St. John, am very far from stupid and you know it. I would never do anything-"

"Reckless? Childish? Irresponsible? Impulsive? Completely ridiculous and unnecessary? Yes, you would, and you have. You always do. It's kind of your M.O., Birdie." She rolled her eyes before bending over to stand the tank up.

"I have a tether-"

"You are about to go out in a damn storm. Alone. Without telling anyone because you're too bullheaded to admit that this little fling of yours is more serious than you intended. I know you, I know how you work and from the moment you got this bug up your ass about sunken pirate ships and helping that man-" She shushed him as his voice rose loud enough for it to carry to the upper deck.

"I told you not to talk about that." She hissed her blood running cold.

"About what? That you practically stalked Noah Toussaint for months to get him to do this? You've known about that journal for three years and now suddenly you have to go and find it? Please, Birdie. I know you better than you think. I know that Z planted that bug in your ear about Noah six months ago. He's been needling you, dropping hints to push you into this. I know he told you about Wainwright cutting his funding and his pending ouster from the university. I know Z and I know you. The two of you are always trying to save lost souls. But maybe this time you're the soul Z is trying to save-"

She put her hand over his mouth to ebb the flood of information that he felt he needed to spew now where anyone could hear. She pushed him back until he collided with a bench and forced him to sit. She narrowed her eyes and leaned closer, speaking through clenched teeth.

"You be quiet. My soul is far from lost and you promised that you wouldn't say anything. We made a deal. This will be over soon enough, and you will never have to see Noah Toussaint again, okay? He'll get his job back or an even a better one and we will find a sunken treasure. Then I will move on to the next thing leaving him with hopefully a great memory and the recognition he deserves. Win-win for everyone." He gently removed her hand from his mouth, his expression stony, his tone low.

"Win-win how exactly? You have been harboring some sort of infatuation with him since your freshman year. And do you think he's just going to walk away? Sorry Birdie, this one isn't built like your usual playthings. He won't heal, stay like a whipped puppy—"

"You don't even like him." She hissed. "Why do you care anything about him?"

"I am him! I have been him for the past ten years, for Christ's sake." She stared at him and watched the pained expression play across his face. "He is not going to be able to let you walk away from him. I know a kindred spirit when I see one." She sat beside him, her heart hammering in her chest.

"Jesus, Titus. I--" She stammered, suddenly at a loss for words. He read the expression on her face and rolled his eyes in irritation.

"Don't get a big head. I'm not in love with you. That would be weird." He snapped, and she stared at him relieved but confused. He snorted and shook his head.

"Calliope. You and your sister have this uncanny ability to avoid meaningful relationships at all costs. It's like as soon as someone shows interest in you outside of sex, you scatter to the far corners of the world." He said, and she gasped as reality slapped her in the face. If she hadn't been caught up in her own self-inflicted drama, she would have seen it. Titus made a point to always be near her sister. The unexpected visits to the city, the insistence to be where ever she was and the constant checking in with them. She'd always thought he was just being a big brother, and maybe that was how he felt about her, but with Calliope it was different. Hell, he'd dropped everything to come on this trip when he found out her sister was coming along. How had she missed it? Because she was an idiot, that's how.

"Titus," She sighed with a pitying tone she hadn't meant but had escaped her, nonetheless. He grunted but remained sullenly silent. Clio leaned closer, resting her head on his shoulder and sighed.

"How long?" She finally asked as they watched the rain blend into the darkness.

"Since I was fourteen years old. She was my first major crush. You remember that night my dad brought me over to your family Christmas party?"

Clio smiled at the memory. It had been at their grandparents' home on the coast of San Cristobal in the Dominican Republic, the same home Z now called his own. Titus and his family had been invited when his father had invested in their father's business venture. It was a very special occasion.

She had been ten and forced into a party dress that was stiff with crinoline and lace. Her hair had been forced into a sleek bun and she had been told that under no circumstance was she to take off any article of clothing until all the guests had gone. It had been miserable, and she had spent most of the night itchy and uncomfortable. Calliope, on the other hand had been radiant. She was thirteen and beautiful. Clio recalled how her sister had seemed so grown up in her ten-year-old eyes, especially because she was given a sip of champagne by their father. She'd worn a pale pink party dress with a full tulle skirt and kitten heeled pumps. Unlike Clio, Calli's hair hung to her shoulders in thick dark auburn waves and she was even allowed a bit of pale pink lipstick and mascara.

"I had been dreading that night. We were moving from Port au Prince to New Orleans and my dad insisted we go to that party. I complained the entire time, right until he rang the bell and Calliope opened the door. She was so mature when she greeted my parents. I remember my dad introducing us and she shook my hand, still smiling and said, '*what's the story morning glory?*'. I had no idea what it meant so I just nodded. She laughed and tucked her arm in mine and escorted me into the living room, chattering a mile a minute, but all I could do was stare."

"My sister has that effect on men." She sighed, taking his hand.

"Don't be so humble. You've had many a man groveling at your pretty little feet." It was her turn to snort with laughter. "Don't give me that, Birdie. You have men dropping everything to follow you on these hair-brained adventures. You go out of your way to find these sad sacks, disgraced and broken men. You take them on these real-life *Raiders of the Lost Ark Indiana Jones* treks then send them away."

"I do not." She protested, but knew it was the truth. She had a knack of finding just the right partner for her expeditions when they were at their lowest. She would swoop in and whisk them away, promising adventure and romance and delivering in spades. Then when it was over, she would walk away leaving them happier and wealthier than they ever imagined. She enjoyed being a muse of sorts, it suited her lifestyle, and no one got hurt. Well, usually.

"You do, and you like it. Look at what just happened with Garrett. You managed that little twat alright, but this time, this one I think you're in over your curly little head." She looked up at him, her mouth twisted in deep contemplation. He was right. He was always right in his annoying way. He and Calliope had that in common, they were better adults than she would ever be.

"I think I can nip it –" Titus laughed, a full guttural sound that echoed across the water. She pursed her lips and put her hands on her hips waiting for him to finish. When he did, his cheeks were a ruddy color and tears filled his dark eyes. She wanted to kick him, to twist his nipple until he howled, but she knew that would just prove that once again, he was right. Instead she rolled her eyes and mumbled how much she disliked him.

"It is much too late for that Hummingbird. Your professor is already in love with you. That one, you're not going to be able to shake, and you know it. Deep down, I don't think you want to shake him. I saw your face when we pulled him out of the water. You're stuck, baby girl. And there is no way to get out of it."

"I'm not what he needs. Or even wants, not for the long term. I'm just fun and different, a passing fancy. He'll get bored and go back to his comfortable life with the kind of woman who can cook and clean and look pretty on his arm when she needs to. That's not me. Never has been never will be." She whispered, and Titus growled.

"You know, you and that damned sister of yours are the most aggravating women I have ever met. You are the dumbest smart people I know. You and Calli are surrounded by this mysterious cloud of black girl magic, and whenever someone gets a little too close- Poof you disappear. You don't see how wonderful, magical and perfect you are. Sometimes I just want to ..." He practically roared in frustration and she instinctively recoiled. He was angry, truly angry with her, with both of them. She wanted to protest, to tell him that it wasn't true that he was completely wrong about them.

But of course, he was right. She and Calli pushed people away, clinging to each other desperately. She knew why she did it, but Calli...she had no idea why her sister would push men away. Especially Titus who knew them better than they knew themselves. Maybe that was it, Titus knew them too well. Clio took a deep breath and shook her head, her eyes drifting to the island in the distance. Noah had said he loved her. Albeit in a drug induced haze, but he'd said it and it cut her to the core. She glanced at Titus who leaned back in his seat, an arm thrown across his eyes.

She didn't want to hurt Noah the way Titus hurt. She couldn't bear to see him in so much agony. Shaking her head, she gave Titus's thigh a pat.

"We are a sorry pair. But I think you have a better shot with Calli than you realize." She sighed, getting to her feet. Titus sat up, his eyes narrowing as he watched her.

"And still you want to go out into the darkness by yourself?" He asked throwing his hands up in defeat.

"That is the plan." She mumbled, continuing to check her gages. She reached past him for her weight belt and Titus watched for a beat longer then exhaled sharply. "We're losing time and the storm could shift the soil on the island. According to the captain, we're going to have to go back and dock the boat tomorrow before the storm gets really bad. It may be our last chance for a week or two before we can get back, Titus. It's now or never."

"Of course, you've spoken to the captain." He mumbled. Slowly he got to his feet, watching her. "And I supposed you've had Javi hack into some government file to find out where the explosives and undetonated mines are buried."

She tried to look as innocent as possible, stretching her eyes wide and making a perfect O with her mouth.

"I would never ask Javi to do such a thing. That would just be completely unethical and totally illegal. Titus, how could you even suggest such a thing?" It was his time to give her a look of disbelieving exasperation.

"You're going to go no matter what I say aren't you?" He finally asked. She put her hands on her hips and raised a brow.

"Well shit, wait a minute. I'll go with you, so you don't get yourself killed."

∞∞∞∞

Noah sat stiffly in his chair at the dining room table. Around him the crew laughed at Z's raunchy jokes and ate the best conch salad he had ever had. Yet, something was off. He could feel it in his bones, something was wrong.

"Where are Titus and Clio?" Calli asked the moment she entered the room. Noah noticed that she looked more relaxed and refreshed than she had earlier in the day. She'd returned to her retro clothing, perfectly coiffed hair and bright red lips. She took her seat beside her uncle, her eyes scanning the room for the errant duo. Noah had noticed they were missing as well, but it hadn't seemed unusual. A few of them were missing from this dinner, but this felt especially off.

The captain had docked the boat closer to the cluster of islands after Clio insisted, they were shielded from the storm in the shadow of Mona Island. He was apprehensive about it; the right wave or errant stone could sink them where they were. He'd also heard the crew murmuring about returning to the dock. The storm was going to get worse and from what he'd heard it was going to be prolonged, at least two days. They needed to get on dry land within the next twenty-four hours, or it could become dangerous.

"Last time I saw them, they were on the lower deck, that was a few hours ago." Javi said around a mouth full of his salad. He lifted his fork, put it back on the table. The expression on his face let Noah know that his growing anxiety was warranted. Noah watched Javi run off, his face creased with worry. Something was wrong.

"Did anyone tell them dinner was ready?" Z asked, watching as everyone shook their heads. Noah looked at Calli, who seemed slightly worried and he knew why. Since he'd known Clio, she had never missed a meal. She was always eating something, chips, fruit or a candy bar. When they had meals, she always had seconds, which was amazing since she had to weigh no more than one-hundred pounds soaking wet.

Since he'd been back on board, she insisted he'd take a long hot shower and a nap. He'd obliged, knowing that she would be busy, going over plans and coordinates. She was sure that Garrett was following her, which made her more determined to find whatever was on that island sooner rather than later. But Clio missing a meal was a huge red flag.

"I'll go get them," Calli turned to leave, but Z grasped her wrist.

"Sit. Eat. I'll go wrangle those two." He'd only taken two steps when the chaos began.

"The god-damned dinghy's gone." Javi said storming through the room, rushing toward the outer deck, a walkie talkie in his hand. Mina angrily pushed her chair away from the table, cursing under her breath as she rose. Teri jogged up the steps from the lower deck, her face furrowed in what he could only assume was frustration or even slight anger.

"We're missing some scuba gear. If she..." She was cut off as something exploded nearby.

The noise was deafening, cracking through the patter of rain and thunder. Noah looked at Calli whose eyes had gone as wide as saucers. Her face paled and he knew she was holding her breath. He knew because everyone in the room was, they were all still, quiet as if someone had put the entire world on mute. No one moved, no one so much as blinked for what felt like eternity. He dropped his fork, the sound of the metal clanging against the china of his dish seemed to jump start time again.

"Clio!" Calli screamed, she was running through the door to the sun deck. Mina, Teri and Javi were already there standing in the downpour looking in the direction of where they thought the explosion had originated. Mina took her own walkie from her hip and began to bark orders to the bridge, moving with a calm urgency toward the upper deck.

Noah's heart hammered, his mouth dry a chill running down his spine. Calli was beside him suddenly, gripping his hand, her eyes scanning the inky horizon for some sign of life. He followed her gaze, waiting. Around them people moved, yelling at each other, barking instructions but they remained still.

"Titus," She whispered, one hand going up to her mouth and Noah looked at her. The expression of sheer terror made his own heart beat a little faster. He felt a sickness in the pit of his stomach, a fear that he'd never experienced before made it hard to stand, so he clung to Calliope, holding her just to keep them both on their feet.

He'd spent the afternoon watching Clio from a distance. He'd managed to corner her in the tiny hallway outside of her bedroom, filling the space so that she had nowhere to run. There was no computer or maps, no gadget or journal to distract her.

"Please don't do whatever it is you're planning to do." She'd looked up at him with those cat-like eyes, so wide and innocent. She jutted out her chin and pursed those soft full lips that felt like silk against his skin and sighed.

"Whatever you think I'm doing, I'm not actually doing. Besides, you don't have any say in what I do. Remember, this is business and a little bit of fun. That's all." She's said. He'd cupped her cheek, supple skin against his cool palm, his thumb stroking the skin along her jaw line. Leaning in close, his lips brushing her ear and he felt her go rigid.

"And I told you I want all of you. And I intend to have it." He'd let his hand move down her neck, his fingers playing along her collarbone before it fell to his side. As much as he wanted to touch her, to kiss her, something about her dour expression kept him from it.

"And I told you, I don't do relationships." She'd eased past him, glancing back briefly, a perplexed look on her face. He couldn't get a read on her mood but knew there was something there, something holding her back. But he was wearing her down. He was going to get through to her, he had nothing but time and opportunity.

She'd managed to stay away from him for the rest of the afternoon, keeping her head down as she, Teri and Javi worked non-stop on some secret project. He watched them move into a quiet corner, away from everyone with a laptop. They'd argued, albeit silently until finally, an exasperated Teri had walked away, insisting that Clio was a bona fide crazy person. She'd met his gaze then, a sheepish smile playing at the corner of her mouth, before returning her attention back to whatever had been so interesting for most of the day. They'd worked until the sun finally began to set on the dreary afternoon. He'd found her to be the most frustrating woman he'd ever known, but she was also charming and funny. Not to mention the sexiest woman he'd ever met. He still wanted her more than anything else in his life. Permanently, and he needed to tell her that.

He should have told her, now he may never get the chance.

He put those thoughts out of his mind, one arm tightening around Calliope who looked as if she would shatter into a million pieces. She was in worse condition, she stood to lose her sister and the man she loved. He stiffened his back, determined to be strong for her at least.

"They're fine." He said, trying to convince himself as much as he wanted to comfort her as they waited for someone, anyone to say everything was okay. "Clio's like a cat, she always lands on her feet. You'll see, they're fine."

∞∞∞∞∞

"You are about a subtle as a jackhammer," Titus barked as soon as they were back on the dinghy. He tossed his mask into the boat before lifting her in behind him. She was ignoring him, too giddy to be bothered with his bad mood. Clio dropped her flippers and pushed the hood from her hair, raking her fingers through her matted curls.

"You could have gotten us both killed. Do you ever stop and think before you go off half-cocked? I mean really Birdie, you charge headlong into danger like you think you're bulletproof. One of these days your foolishness and impulsiveness is going to bite you in the ass." He tossed his own hood onto the floor before going to start the small motor and head back to the boat.

"I must be losing my mind to follow you out here in the pouring rain in search of buried treasure. We are not the fucking *Goonies*, Clio. Why do I listen to you?" His accent was more pronounced in his anger, the smooth Haitian Creole flowing freely as a litany of curses.

She looked at him, her hands on her hips, the side of her foot tapping the ancient metal case at the bow of the little boat. He grunted and shook his head, trying not to let her see that he was fighting the smirk that teased the corners of his mouth.

"You know everyone on the ship probably thinks we've blown ourselves into oblivion. The entire place is probably in an uproar. When we get back Calli is going to rip you a new one. That is of course, if she can get to you before Z does. Not to mention the professor. I swear I need my head examined for listening to you. You are by far the most insane person I've ever met."

Again, she tapped the case with her foot. In the moonlight he could see her smile, a self-satisfied smirk that proved that she was in fact quite proud of herself. It also hid the small trickle of blood that streamed from just above her left ear. She hoped that her silence masked the fact that she could barely hear a word he was saying.

Sure, she'd done what she'd set out to do. She'd found another piece of the puzzle. But he hadn't seen how close she'd come to blowing herself to kingdom come. She'd followed Javi's map exactly, what she hadn't counted on was the rapid-fire chain reaction she'd set off. She'd stood away from the first detonation, tossing a heavy stone in the direction of an unearthed mine. It had landed perfectly, setting of the bomb and showering her with dirt and grass. She'd been far enough away to be safe from that one. It was the falling rocks and earth that had set one off mere feet from her that had thrown her onto her back. She'd landed with a thud, her head crashing hard on a half-buried stone. She'd felt the flesh break immediately but had no time to think as she scrambled to her feet and charged up the small hill as earth and rock rained down around her.

When she'd found the hole in the ground, the deep gully that had been created by the initial explosion, she'd fallen to her knees to quickly dig into the soft earth for what she needed. It had only taken her a few minutes to find the case, rusted and heavy, half sunken in muddy earth.

She had been struggling to pull it free when Titus grabbed her and pulled her out of the hole. She couldn't hear anything but a low, sustained whistling in her ears, but by the expression on his face and the way his mouth was moving in the moonlight, he was mad. He was still cursing and fussing as he yanked the case free, tossing it easily onto the ground beside her. When he'd climbed out, he'd taken the case as if it weighed nothing in one hand and dragged her by the arm behind him as they rushed back toward the beach.

He, being bigger and stronger, had swum with the case back to the dinghy. She had seen him angry before, and more often than not that anger had been directed at her. But this time, his anger was capped by a fear that was palpable. She had scared him, terrified him to the point of fury. She would have to apologize to him, but not now. Now she had to figure out how to take care of the gash in her head before anyone noticed it. She thanked god for her thick mass of dark curls, at least they could camouflage her wound for a while.

As they moved closer to the Redbird, she could see the movement on the deck, people scrambling just before a high-powered search light swept over the yacht, illuminating the darkness. Her hearing was coming back, the ringing fading and she could make out what he was yelling, but it all sounded as if it were coming from far away. She sat as he steered them closed to the rear of the boat, his walkie in his hand as he spoke to someone in his rich creole.

As if by magic, a partition in the lower deck split open allowing them to ease the dinghy back into its little hidey-hole in the lower deck of the yacht. It slipped easily into its space between storage crates and the as yet unused mini sub.

Once they were inside, Titus cut the engine and waited for the doors to close behind them. Two crew members appeared from a dark, narrow hallway towards them. One worked quickly to secure the dinghy, the other helped her from the tiny boat. Once she was safely out, he took the case from Titus, who leaned in and whispered something to him in Spanish. She could only make out a few words, her hearing, still spotty. But when he in turn, leaned into Titus and whispered she clearly heard the words '*being boarded*'.

"Well," He said, facing her. "Go get changed. Thanks to your little stunt, we have company."

Chapter 12

"Would it help if I said I was sorry?" Clio absently touched the bandage just behind her ear and flinched. On the opposite side of the makeshift cell, six sets of angry eyes stared daggers at her. They hadn't said more than two words to her since the coast guard had taken them into custody. Z had done some quick talking and managed to extract himself from being cuffed. She'd wondered what he'd said to escape the clink, but knowing Z, it hadn't really been a surprise.

"No," They shouted in unison. That made three words, she thought and slumped against the wall, her feet swinging inches above the floor. She was too short to reach the floor on this stupid bench. How demeaning.

"Well, I am." She mumbled, and they glared. Even Noah looked as if he were going to throttle her if she said anything else. Titus touched his swollen lip and it began to bleed again. His nose was also bloodied, and he had a black eye. He leaned forward to stare at Noah, who was seated on the opposite end of the bench nursing a bruised eye and cheek of his own.

She knew that there was trouble when Titus had ordered her to get dressed. He stomped around the lower deck barking orders to the crew to hide anything that the Coast Guard might confiscate or that Garrett might have found interesting. From the start, Titus had been under the assumption that Garrett or Jackson Blake had a hand in their current predicament.

"We haven't done all of this just to have them come and take everything. We'd never get it back." He mumbled, as they moved covertly between decks through hidden hallways she'd never known about.

"Do you use these to sneak Calliope in and out of your room?" She asked. He looked at her and pursed his mouth. "I will take that as a yes," she whispered and continued to follow him. He pushed a panel and a wall in her room opened. She looked at him, brows raised but said nothing before entering. She watched the wall slide closed before changing into a pair of shorts and a tank top and went to the main deck.

She raced up the stairs two at a time, several more explosions echoing in the night as she ascended. Well, she thought, at least now it would be safe enough for tourists. Almost immediately, she was bombarded by questions and blinded by search lights. The coast guard had boarded them questioning everyone on deck, their attention turning to her as she entered the fray. Calliope had rushed her, embracing her as tears of relief rolled down her cheeks.

"Oh, thank god," She sighed, holding her face. Her fingers brushed the wound just behind her ear and Clio involuntarily flinched. "You're bleeding. Why are you bleeding?" Calli's eyes were wide. Z and Noah pushed past Calli to get closer to her, Z won, going immediately into physician mode. Noah watched, his face drawn and tense, until he spotted Titus.

"Looks like a gash on her scalp." Z was saying. Noah's face shifted from worry to anger. Before she could say anything to stop him, he charged, punching Titus in the nose. Titus took a stumbling step backward, Noah tackled him, tossing him to the floor with a bone rattling thud.

"You were supposed to protect her." Noah was yelling as he continued to pummel a still stunned Titus. "She could have died, you son of a bitch." Titus finally responded, striking Noah in the eye and the two continued to grapple until the coast guard interjected and separated the two.

That had been several hours ago. Since then, she'd been looked at by the medic on board the coast guard ship as they were transported back to the Sector offices in San Juan. They'd been questioned by Homeland Security for hours, one at a time until finally, near dawn they were brought into this cell, and here they sat.

"It could be worse." Javi stretched and sighed, "At least it's not like that time she got us arrested in Sri Lanka." He said, and Mina smirked.

"It's not as bad as that bar fight in Cairo, either." Teri volunteered. More titters of laughter from the group.

"Or the skinny-dipping incident in Slovakia." Mina said, and they howled with laughter. Even Titus had cracked a smile. But Noah remained stone faced, his eyes narrowing as he stared at her until finally, he exploded in anger.

"This is funny to you? She got us arrested, the boat docked, and nearly blew her damned head off and you think it's funny? You let her run around like a lunatic, everyone accommodating her irrational behavior and when she could have gotten herself killed, you just laugh it off. What is wrong with you?" He stood up and paced in front of them, throwing an accusing finger in her direction as he ranted.

"Let me? They don't *let* me do anything, professor. In case you failed to realize it, I am a full-grown woman and I make my own choices." She yelled, standing on her own bench so that she could look down at him. Being five feet tall did have its disadvantages in an argument. Especially when you were arguing with a six-foot two former middle line man.

"They encourage your recklessness. Hell, they even reward you for it." He barked, stomping over to her. "They let you run off half-cocked-"

"I'll have you know I am always fully cocked–" Clio paused, and shook her head, "That came out wrong but you know what I mean!" Calli burst into a fit of uncontrollable laughter and Noah's nostrils flared. He stomped closer to Clio, who nearly fell from her perch atop the bench. He grasped her arms and drew her close, his voice low, almost a whisper as he looked into her eyes and spoke.

"I was terrified. I have never been so scared of anything in my life. What if it was more than a gash on the head, Clio? What if you'd been hurt worse or bled out before Titus could get you back to us? When I heard that first explosion, my heart stopped. I would die if I lost you, Clio. Don't ever do that again, understand? I would die…" He pulled her into an embrace and she was too stunned to do anything other than let him hold onto her.

She wrapped her arms around his neck and rested her head on his shoulder. He still smelled of coconut oil and sun and his arms felt wonderful around her. She cuddled closer, her head throbbing as her pain medication wore off.

"I'm okay." She said against his neck. "I didn't me to scare you. I'm sorry, Noah. I love you." She could see Calli's shocked expression over his shoulder. She frowned and straightened so that she could see the expression on Noah's face and he looked just as stunned. Her heart had dropped to her feet and she felt a little like she was going to throw up. What in the world was wrong with her? Of course, something was wrong with her, she'd been hit in the head by a fucking rock the size of a small boulder. She was lucky she wasn't in a coma, instead of a mild concussion. What the absolute hell had she done?

"Did you just say…?" He had a strange smile on his face and she felt her face heat. That was not what she'd intended to say. It was the furthest thing from her mind, but she'd said it. She looked over at the bench to see if anyone else had heard, but they were talking amongst themselves, not really paying attention to them. Only Calliope looked as if she were going to burst. Only the three of them had heard her confession. Now what was she supposed to do?

Her head hurt, and she couldn't think clearly, because she would have never said that. Not ever.

She swallowed hard before sighing heavily and lowering her eyes.

"I …a… big rock hit me… in the head." She grunted, and he held her tighter, chuckling. That was it? That was all he was going to do? He wasn't going to say anything? No questions?

Was he going to say it back?

The longer he remained quiet, the more she hated that she had let that slip out. Damn, why had she been so stupid? Of course, he wasn't going to say it back. What kind of future did they have? She was a nomad and he was a staid, reserved academic. She was impulsive and reckless, the injury that was setting ever nerve in her scalp on fire punctuated that fact. Of course, he could never love her, he needed someone stable and level headed, he needed...

"I love you too." He kissed her forehead and every bone in her body melted into him. He loved her back. Her stomach fluttered, and her heart was so full that she was sure it would burst.

"Okay you clowns," A guard shouted as the cell door slid open, "You're free to go. Looks like pretty boy has connections." He looked at Titus who rose slowly, a self-satisfied smirk on his bruised but still handsome face.

"It's about time." Titus grumbled before standing, making a show of straightening his torn and rumpled shirt.

"Shall we?" He bowed allowing the others to file out before him. Noah took Clio's hand as they made their exit. She walked a step behind him, looking up at his stunning profile and felt as if she were floating.

He loved her too. She hadn't thought it possible, but he actually loved her. As the cell door slammed shut behind them, she sighed and leaned against his arm. Noah Toussaint loved her.

Oh man, was this going to be a complete disaster

∞∞∞∞

"I knew from the moment Z called that this had something to do with you." M. Jameson St. John stood in the waiting area, his private security at his back. He was tall, an older more dignified version of his son with neatly cut salt and pepper hair and tobacco brown eyes. He was talking to Clio who released Noah's hand to go over to him and was immediately enveloped in a warm embrace. He tilted her head so that he could get a better look at the bandage behind her ear.

"Z said that you were up to your old tricks. Still trying to be Lara Croft?" He laughed, and she shrugged.

"Thank you, Jameson," Calliope stepped closer, smiling up at him. "God only knows how long we would have been in there, thanks to *Wrong Way* here."

"Calliope," He put an arm around her and kissed her temple, before turning to his son. He frowned, looked at Titus's face, then at Noah and shook his head. Titus shrugged but said nothing. "I see you've rounded up the usual suspects. Mina, Teri, Javi good to see you again. Titus,"

"Hi Papa," Titus gave his father a hug. Noah watched as they shared a quick whispered word and laughed.

"No Garrett? But I see you have a new member," He extended his hand to Noah who stepped forward to shake it.

"Jameson, this is Dr. Noah Toussaint," Clio was saying, "Noah, M. Jameson St. John."

"Pleasure," Noah said and waited.

"No," Jameson looked at him, then at Clio then back at Noah, "No, the pleasure is all mine. I'm glad to see that Clio finally dropped the dead weight. Fresh blood is needed every now and again." He had a strange expression on his face, a look of familiarity or some recognition. Noah felt his heart sink as it had done every time Clio introduced him to a new person. But if he recognized him, he never said anything. Instead he clapped his hands together and smiled.

"I know you all are probably hungry and tired. Come, let's go." He turned and put an arm around his son's shoulders as they headed for the door. Everyone followed, silently whispering to each other.

"Hey," Noah pulled Clio close to him as they lingered behind. "How did he get us out? This is the military? Is he some kind of politician or something?" Clio looked confused by the question and shook her head.

"No," She nearly laughed as if the notion was completely absurd. She shook her head and followed the others outside.

"Then how did he do it? I mean we should be locked up. I mean, this is federal..." She stopped at the door, turned to look at him and sighed.

"Remember when I told you that we don't discuss what Titus does? That goes for his father as well. Just know that no matter what happens, the name St. John carries a lot of weight in most parts of the world. Let's just say the St. John men have ways of making things happen. We don't question how we are just grateful that they do." She pushed the door open and he saw three large black SUV's each with two men dressed in dark suits standing watch. Noah paused for a second before following.

He stepped into the misty night air and watched as they all climbed into the back of cars. Titus, Calli and Jameson, riding in the first, while the rest of the team climbed into the second. He stood, rain dripping down his face as he tried to grasp what was happening. Clio sat in the back seat of the third vehicle waving for him to join her. Slowly, he got into the car, flinching as the driver slammed the door closed behind him.

Beside him, Clio had produced a beach towel from the dark recesses of the seat and began drying her hair.

"Where are we going?" He asked, realizing that the boat had been docked. "Hotel?" She snorted again, and he could see the glazed sheen of her eyes. Her concussion had made her slightly loopy, but coherent. He hoped she was coherent, she'd just told him she loved him after all.

"Home." She said simply.

"Back to New Orleans?" She yawned and touched the bandage wincing in pain.

"No," She rested her head on his shoulder. "Here., We have a house in San Juan. Right on the water. It's like fifteen minutes from here." She closed her eyes and yawned again. The driver was listening to soft music which relaxed him even more than the heated seats. He looked out at the night sky, the rain making a staccato rhythm on the glass. He ran a hand through Clio's damp hair, being extra careful of her wound and closed his own eyes.

In all of this craziness, he had so many questions still. But at least he knew that Clio was safe, in his arms where she belonged. And that she loved him. Whether she admitted it in the morning was another story, but she'd said it and that was all that really mattered.

She loved him.

He let his head rest on the back of the seat and slowly began to drift off to sleep when a question popped into his head. One that should have come to him sooner than it had.

"Wait, what do you mean "*we*" own a house?"

∞∞∞∞

"Your description of things is woefully lacking." Noah mumbled when the car finally came to a stop in the circular driveway in front of what he imagined would be referred to as an estate. The house, as she called it, was a sprawling villa with a separate guest house and a wing with its own private entrance. He followed her into the foyer and stared at the double staircase, marble floors and elegant chandeliers.

"How many rooms are in this place?" He asked. Javi gave his shoulder a pat as he walked past him.

"Ten bedrooms. And I am going to mine now. Night." Javi mounted the stairs, Teri and Mina trudging along behind him. Noah saw Z emerge from the kitchen, a drink in his hand. He smiled, tipping his glass to them.

"You're here. Good. Get some rest." He kissed Clio's forehead then walked past them down a narrow hallway. He looked for Titus and Calliope, but they had disappeared somewhere in the rear of the house. Clio took his hand and pulled him towards another hallway that he realized led to the separate wing.

"I need a shower." She was saying, "And bed."

"You still haven't told me who owns this house. And I don't have any clothes here."

"We, Titus, Calli, Uncle Z and I own this house. Together. And right now," She pushed a door open and leaned against the door frame. Behind her, in a dimly lit room that smelled of Jasmine, was a California king sized bed.

It was late, and it had been a very long night. The thought of climbing beneath those crisp, cool sheets, Clio's warm, naked body draped across him, was enough to distract him from all of the questions rattling around in his head. "You won't be needing any clothes, professor."

They could talk tomorrow.

∞∞∞∞

Clio rolled onto her stomach, letting her head rest on Noah's chest as they both tried to control their breathing. The sun had just begun to peak over the horizon, bathing the room in a hazy glow. She'd pulled the curtains, muting the light. A palm leafed ceiling fan ticked quietly chilling their naked, sweat drenched bodies. Clio felt luscious, her body still trembling from their love making. She absently played with Noah's hair, her fingers moved deep into the thick locs.

"I wish we could stay like this forever." She sighed. He pulled her up so that she lay fully on him, her face inches from his. He smiled, his hands cupping her bare bottom, the sheets tangled around their legs.

"We can." He said, his voice low. "We can stay right here, just like this, for as long as you want." She stroked his cheek, a pain twisting in her chest.

"No, we can't. Once this is over, you're going to go back to your life and I will be on the next thing smoking. I told you Noah, I don't do relationships. The two of us would never work."

"I happen to believe we work pretty well." To prove his point, he moved his hands down to her inner thighs and gently spread her legs so that she was straddling him. "I believe that you think you're going to push me away. But it's not going to work." He kissed her shoulder and she shivered.

"Noah," She started, but he shushed her.

"I told you that I would have all of you, Clio. I lost you once, that will never, ever happen again. I love you Clio," He whispered against her ear. "I've always loved you. From the very first time you stumbled into my world. I lied. I never forgot you. I could never forget you. You told me you love me, Clio. Now, I'm yours forever. I wouldn't know how to be without you. And I don't want to be without you ever again." She felt herself relax against him because she knew he meant what he said. He was hers and she was his and there was no way around it.

"Say something," He whispered. She cupped his cheek as she stared into his dark, searching eyes. She found his lips, kissing him until he wrapped his arms around her.

"I love you, Noah Toussaint. God help me I do, and I don't know what to do about it." He smiled and kissed her again. In his arms, she felt the world melt away.

"You don't have to do anything other than let me love you back." He kissed the tip of her nose. "Maybe talk to me before you make an impulsive decision. Oh, and occasionally let me make love to you. You know, just to keep me interested." He couldn't hide the cheeky smirk and she playfully slapped his chest.

"Stop it, I'm being serious. How do we do this professor?' He sighed and grazed the bandage behind her ear, his expression suddenly solemn.

"Well, we can start by not scaring each other to death. I don't ever want to feel the way I did last night. If you were half as scared as I was when I was nearly taken out by a fish..." She smiled, brushing his hair off of his shoulder. "How about this?" He leaned in so that they shared a pillow. "How about we stop trying to figure out what to do? How about we just enjoy being with each other? Okay? Everything else will work out. I promise."

"So," She yawned, "We'll just be us? Just the Hummingbird and the Professor?" He chuckled.

"You make us sound like mystery solving cartoon characters." He laughed.

"Okay, then I'll be Indy and you be Short Round." He actually guffawed.

"If anything, you would be Short Round because ...well." She gave his arm a playful slap.

"Well, we are kinda like that, I guess in a weird way." She said in all seriousness. "We are trying to solve a mystery. I even found something out there...." She sat up, suddenly remembering the case. "Shit, I did. I found something." She jumped out of bed in search of her clothes before turning to look at Noah. He was leaning on his elbow watching her with lascivious fascination.

"Are you listening? I guess the bump on my head made me forget, but I found something, Noah. A metal case, I think Titus stored it somewhere on the boat. Come on, we have to see if it's still there." She headed to the door and had her hand on the door knob when Noah called to her. She turned to look at him. He was sitting up in bed, the sheets pooled around his hips, a bright smile on his face. Lord, he was a beautiful man.

"Sweetie," He sighed, "As beautiful and sexy as you are, you might want to take a second and put some clothes on."

∞∞∞∞

Noah stood on the opposite side of the bed slipping on a pair of jeans, his eyes on Clio as she gingerly dried her hair. They had shared a shower before going to join the others and he stood watching her with fascination as she dressed. He was still watching her slip into a pair of barely there lace panties when his phone rang. Raina was calling, and from the looks of it, had been calling him for quite some time.

"Hey Raina," He said, distracted by Clio who was fastening her bra before turning to face him. She smiled but walked past to the closet where Jameson had their clothes delivered and put away. Jameson had taken care of their every need, and though generous, Noah found it slightly unnerving.

"Thank God, Noah I've been calling you for hours. What the hell..." She was shouting, finally drawing his attention from Clio who was slipping a bright yellow sun dress over her head.

"Calm down. Why are you yelling?"

"I'm yelling," She said after a deep exhale, "because my phone and email has been going crazy. You are all over social media, Noah. There are photos of you yachting, actually freaking yachting. And scuba diving with two gorgeous women like your life has become a rap video. Then I get a call about you being in the hospital..."

"Yeah," He sat on the edge of the bed and rubbed his eyes. He meant to call her, but he'd forgotten in the chaos. He'd gotten caught up in the adventure, the excitement and of course, Clio. "I got stung by a lion fish. I'm fine. Clio's uncle is with us, he's a doctor."

"Who's the other woman? In the pictures?"

"That's Clio's sister. I told you..."

"Everyone at the university just about lost their shit when the pictures hit. The entire campus is talking about you and Clio. I mean just looking at the pictures of you guys-It's like something out of a movie, Noah. The entire saga is like everywhere. News shows, entertainment shows, sports shows, you're even on the freaking history and science channels. Do you know how big this has gotten? What's going on?" She finally stopped talking long enough for him to get a word in.

"It's a really long story," He sighed.

"Oh my god, Noah, you should hear some of the voice mails I've gotten. The faculty is like hounding me to get in touch with you. Not to mention Catherine stalking me on social media. She's obsessed, I think she may be cyber stalking you, too. Or Clio. Maybe both. Noah, this thing between you and Clio, is it serious?"

He watched Clio a goofy smile on her face as she slipped on her shoes, her eyes dancing with excitement and his heart sped up. His stomach fluttered, and he had to catch his breath. He'd waited so long to feel this way and it was with Clio. His beautiful hazel eyed adventurer. He never thought it possible to love someone so much, to want to spend every waking moment in their presence.

"Extremely" He said.

∞∞∞∞

Clio sat eating her second stack of pancakes when Z pulled up a chair beside her on the patio. Everyone else seemed to be working on something or other while she sat eating. Noah was with Javi and Teri trying to remove some of the rust from the metal box looking for some way to open it without using a crow bar or mallet. Upon closer inspection, they found that the box was in fact a trunk, small and wooden with heavy metal studs and straps. Mina was looking over her transit station, a computer program that creates a map of the site, using GPS and spatial data which records exact locations and heights of specific points, Titus and Jameson watching as she explained what they were looking at. Clio decided she would ignore Z, who watched her in silence, a ridiculous grin on his face. He'd been grinning like a fool ever since he'd examined her and diagnosed her concussion. He'd even given her a quick check this morning, making sure she was still in her right mind. Now, it just felt weird with him watching her the way he was.

"So," he said, trying to spark a conversation. "How you feelin?" She turned to look at him. He was grinning so wide that it was comically maniacal, he waggled his eyebrows at her and she shook her head.

"I feel the same way I felt twenty minutes ago when you asked me the last time." He sighed heavily before pressing forward.

"This could be a good thing." She turned to look at Z who seemed entirely too happy in her opinion. She turned in her seat to look at him, giving him her full attention. "You can take a break, get some rest maybe help Calli write that book the two of you are always yammering on about. Spend some time with your Uncle Z who misses you so much when you're gone."

"Last night you said a couple of days rest and I will be fine. Besides, you know if I stay in one place too long, I become completely obnoxious and annoying." Z snorted and looked at her.

"As opposed to what?" She shot him a look that she hoped would make him recoil, but he just chuckled and shook his head.

"I will have you know that I have a sparkling personality and a winning attitude." She said and this time he laughed so loud and hard she thought he'd pass out. His cheeks had turned a nice shade of red and his eyes watered from the effort.

"Are you saying I don't?" She folded her arms across her chest and waited for him to finish laughing. Z looked at her briefly then thought for a moment.

"You are engaging, loving and captivating," He agreed, she started to thank him, but he continued. "You're also headstrong, determined and a little pushy. You can be a little pit-bull and at times, downright ornery. But we love you for it. He loves you for it." He motioned toward Noah who was now having a rather animated conversation with Calli, who'd suddenly made a very un-Calli like appearance in blue jeans and a boat neck t shirt.

"We aren't talking about him right now." She ran her hands over her dress, smoothing it over her stomach and thighs. Instead of fidgeting, she linked her fingers and dropped her hands into her lap, her mind slowly drifting until Z snapped her right back.

"Well damn it, maybe we should. You keep saying that the two of you will never work, but you work pretty damned well from what I can see. He loves you and you love him. You need to admit that you've been in love with him since college. And don't you try to deny it." Z barked, "I just want you girls to realize that you have really good men in your lives. Men who love and want to take care of you. But you're too stubborn or pig headed to let them."

"So, you know about Calli and Titus?" He gave her a quick wink, that mischievous glint in his eyes.

"Birdie, I know everything there is to know about you girls. I know that you think you're destined to be alone, you and your knuckle headed sister, but I know different. You have got to get yourself out of this self-imposed relationship purgatory. You do deserve happiness. I have been around a lot longer than you two and I know love, real love, not just bunny humpin sex, when I see it. I would hate for either of you to be so stubborn that you let the love of your life slip through your fingers. I did that, I let the best woman I've ever known walk out of my life and I have never met anyone like her again. Please, Hummingbird, learn from this silly old man." He cupped her cheek and she felt his sincerity, his anguish over a lost love.

She'd never known Z to be anything but a happy bachelor, always single. Now that she thought about it, she'd never seen Z with a woman.

Ever.

She turned to look at Calli and Noah and marveled at how comfortable they were together. They laughed and talked easily, like they'd known each other for years. If it had been any other woman, she would have suspected that she was flirting. But with Calli he was more familial, he treated Calli the same way he treated Raina. They genuinely liked each other. Her small, close knit family had embraced him as one of their own and he had done the same. It was obvious, but she hadn't seen it happen. They loved Noah as well, to them, he was already family.

∞∞∞∞∞

Clio was sitting at a table on the patio, her glasses perched on the edge of her nose as she studied several maps and all of the data Mina and Teri had gathered while she had been tending Noah when he was hospitalized. Nearby Titus, Javi, Mina and Teri struggled to open the trunk. They'd searched for a key hole, hoping they finally had a lock for their key. But there wasn't one, not one they could see anyway and the latch holding it closed had rusted in place. Calli sat on the edge of the pool her feet in the water, a laptop sitting precariously on her lap. The sun was setting, casting an amber glow over the entire scene. Noah stood back watching the breeze pick up the edge of her dress giving him a peek of toned chocolate thighs.

"Are you going to stand there staring all night, professor?" Clio hadn't bothered looking at him, but he instinctively straightened. He walked over to her, leaning over her shoulder to get a look at what she was working on. She'd spread out transparent maps, one over the other, each representing a different time period. She'd used a marker to note changes over the years. Everything from the flow of the current to shore erosion was marked in a different color and the map coordinates had been written in pristine print on one side.

"How are you feeling, Clio?" He looked at her bandage which had been recently changed. She shrugged.

"I would feel better if everyone would stop asking me that." She sighed.

"Sweetie, you cut your head open last night. That isn't normal especially after you, miss-I-don't-do- boyfriends, admitted that you love me. You've been acting a bit off. Is it more than just a bump on the head?" He sat beside her chair so that he could look her in the eye. She put down her markers and turned to him, her expression a mask of indifference. He watched her face and then something in her eyes, flickered. It was a mild shift, but he felt it, something she was hiding.

"Clio?" He took her hand, and for a moment he thought she was going to say something. She was going to tell him something that was eating at her. Instead, she smiled and shook her head.

"I'm fine, Noah. Just a bump on the head that was a little harder than Z thought. That's all. I'm fine. I promise."

He was going to push it further, but the ringing of the doorbell distracted him. Everyone stopped what they were doing and looked at each other curiously. When it rang again, and no one moved, Z slowly rose sighing heavily.

"Who the hell is that? Everybody is already here." He grunted and made his way inside. Clio and Calli looked at each other before following trailed by the ever-present Titus. The others continued working on the trunk unaffected by the distraction.

They'd just entered the living room when Garret and Jackson Blake were escorted in by the housekeeper, who looked a bit confused. Z spoke to her in hushed tones, before looking at his nieces.

"She thought he was still part of the crew. I'll show them out now." Z sighed before giving the woman a reassuring nod and letting her go back to her room.

Garrett Matthews looked every bit the smug opportunist Clio made him out to be. He was dressed more like someone who spent most of his time sipping cocktails on a yacht than any one who dug in dirt for a living. Now that he thought about it, he wasn't even sure that Garrett really was an archaeologist. Clio had never said he was, he'd just assumed it to be true. Behind him, Jackson Blake looked around trying to look nonchalant, but it was obvious that he was surprised and impressed by their digs.

"Gentlemen," Z turned to escort them out only to have Blake side step him and move toward Noah.

"Dr. Toussaint," Blake said with a much too toothy smile. "Good to see you back on your feet."

"Jackson, good to see you're still as smarmy as loathsome as ever. That fake smile has gotten better, though." Noah said in what he hoped to be an un-bothered tone. He must have succeeded because Blake's smile evaporated.

"You." Calli snarled. "I swear you're like an STD, annoying as hell and hard to get rid of." Titus stifled a laugh, and Noah liked him a little better in that moment. "Why are you here anyway? Haven't you done enough to this family?"

"I just wanted to check on Clio. I heard she got arrested, by the Coast Guard no less. Really, Birdie-"

"Don't call me that." She snapped. Noah instinctively grasped her hand, feeling that she would charge at him at any moment. "You don't get to call me that ever again." She practically snarled.

"Come on, Bi-Clio. We can at least be civil about this. I mean we used to be friends." He moved closer to her with each word. "We were even closer than friends. Once this," he gave Noah a meaningful once over, "is all over we can kiss and make up. We always do." He looked pointedly at Noah, who clinched his fists, ready to punch the other man in the face. But before he could, Titus spoke up.

"How did you know about the arrest?" Titus asked.

"Excuse me?" Garrett took a step back as Titus approached.

"I mean, it wasn't like we were marched through the center of town. We aren't celebrities so there was no paparazzi following us around. It wasn't by the local police, so it wasn't on the blotter. So how did you know?"

"Well," He stuttered, "you go around blowing things up, you're bound to get the attention of the coast guard."

"Again, how did you know that? We were miles off shore, no one else anywhere near us. So, how did you know? Were you listening in on our radio frequency? Or did you follow us?" Garrett tried to laugh it off, but it came out in a high-pitched giggle.

"Follow you? Why on earth ..." Titus stepped closer. But Noah moved in front of him.

"So, let me get this straight. You knew exactly which club Clio and I went to that first night. You knew when I was taken to the hospital, you knew about the explosions and you knew about the coast guard taking us into custody. Are you psychic?" He asked.

"No, I-"

"Did you plant a GPS somewhere on Clio's person?" Titus stepped in, adding to the line of questioning.

"No, I-" Garrett stumbled backward, trying to get away from the advancing men. Noah assumed they were quite the menacing duo. The terror in Garrett's eyes told him that.

"So, you either listened in on our radio transmissions, had a spy or, and I think this is by far the most plausible scenario, followed us. You did because you knew that you had no idea what you were doing. You couldn't possibly do it on your own. And even though you had Jackson here in your camp, he's just a cyber bully with no actual talent or skill. Am I right?" Noah asked.

"I think you're right." Titus agreed. "I think this little piece of shit actually thought that if he proved himself as her equal that Clio would come running back to him because when he proposed, she laughed in his face." Noah felt as if he'd been gut punched. This lowlife had actually proposed to Clio. It all made sense now, why someone who'd worked with her for years had suddenly, seemingly out of the blue, decided to steal from her and try to take credit for her work. It also made sense as to why Jackson Blake had eagerly joined his cause.

Credibility. It was their way of legitimizing themselves in a community that they longed to be a part of, not just a part of but superstars. Like Clio. Like he was once upon a time.

"So, this is some sort of twisted plot to gain credibility and get Clio's attention. Show her that that you're worthy? Garrett, you thought by stealing her work, her family history and popping up whenever she's at her most vulnerable was a way to show her that she needs you? And you Mr. Blake," Noah spat the name as if it left a nasty taste in his mouth, "this is how you wanted to make your mark on history by siding with a thief? Frankly, it's just–"

"Sad." Calliope finished for him. Noah looked back, forgetting that she was still there.

"Exactly." He agreed.

Chapter 13

There had been no more sputtering or explaining from either man. There had been no disputing the facts, they had been caught. Jackson Blake was the first one to break, realizing that with this little scheme they'd bitten off more than they could chew. He'd shushed Garrett when he begun to confess, letting everything pour out of him like water from a broken spigot. He'd admitted that Garrett had contacted him after he'd discovered that Clio had gone to Noah for help.

Taken in by Garrett's charm and seeming expertise from his perspective, it had been the opportunity of a lifetime. After all, Garrett had proof of who he was and a proven track record. Clio had given him credit on everything she'd done over the past five years. He was someone with stellar accolades. On Paper.

When it came time to put that expertise into practice, everything had gone downhill rapidly. Within the first week, most of the crew had quit, a few days later, the boat had issues and had been in dry dock for weeks. By the time Clio and her crew had arrived, their funding had been taken and they were lost.

"He said that he could convince Clio to take him back. He said she would do anything for him. He said they'd been in a five-year relationship and she would jump at the chance to work with him." Jackson had blurted. Clio and Calliope looked at each other incredulously but said nothing. In the end, it had been Z who'd shown them to the door with the promise of litigation.

"Okay," Titus clapped his hands and rubbed them together. "Now since that has been handled, back to work." Calliope nodded as she and Z followed. Clio turned to leave as well, but Noah reached for her hand.

"We'll be having a talk about this later. Right?" She looked up into those tobacco smoky eyes and nodded.

"Yes," She said, knowing she had no intention of doing that. The last thing she wanted to do was be interrogated by Noah about Garrett. Why couldn't he have just slunk away like all other dejected men. No Garrett had to be Garrett and make promises he couldn't keep. He had to try and *"win"* her back, even though he'd never actually had her. She'd never loved him. He was convenient and at times fun. She didn't want to tell Noah that, especially after she'd made a big deal about not doing relationships. She'd had a long term, though one-sided, relationship with Garrett.

She'd basically used him. They used each other. She didn't want to admit that to him.

Now she sat on the patio, thoughts of the inevitable conversation rattling around in her head as Titus, Javi and Noah tried to muscle the trunk open.

"Maybe you should get some hydrochloric acid and burn the latch off." Calli suggested in passing. She lounged near Clio, two glasses of chardonnay in her hand. She'd offered Clio a glass and when she'd declined, Calli had helped herself to both.

"I don't keep acid on hand." Titus grunted.

"Like you couldn't get it. The great and powerful Titus St. John can have and do anything. Isn't that right? Any old thing he wants is his." Calli's tone had a bit more bite than it needed. Clio wanted to think it was because of the wine, but had a feeling that like she and Noah, Calli and Titus had issues of their own. Titus handled it much better than she would by ignoring her little jab.

"Ha," Titus yelled and began cursing in creole. He and Javi had used a crowbar to create a small opening in the case. They put all their weight on the handle, Noah adding his to the effort.

"Careful guys, this could have some historical value." Clio warned.

"You could do it yourself if you weighed more than eighty pounds." Titus grumbled. They strained, putting all of their combined weight on the crowbar, until it began to creak and give way. Rust and dirt began to crack and pop off, sailing through the air in several directions.

There was a loud crack, the hinges snapping off as the lid came free. They stood staring at it, no one moving or even breathing as they waited. Clio looked at everyone, then eased closer to the table. She leaned forward and peaked inside, frowned and took another step, then another until she was staring into the dark interior. She frowned then smiled and reached inside.

They all leaned closer, trying to get a better look at what she'd taken out, but all they could see was dark burlap. Noah moved closer, leering over her shoulder as she gently uncovered what was hidden underneath. Clio held it to the light so that thy all could see, and the mood went from excited anticipation to confused disappointment.

She held in her hands a hinged case roughly the size of a shoebox with a key hole. "Noah, where's the key?" She asked. He handed it to her and she said a silent prayer as she put the key in the hole and slowly turned. The latch gave way and she gently lifted the lid. She reached inside and removed a ten-inch-long stone that was heavy enough that she had to hold it with both hands. It had been shaped into a crescent, five oddly shaped holes in the surface. In the arch of the stone was a large circle and tiny markings like the ones they'd found on the bricks in New Orleans. She felt as if that had been so long ago, but those moments led them to this. Holding it in her hands, it looked almost like a roughhewn and somewhat rudimentary boomerang. It was smooth on both sides, but the side with the symbol had worn lettering chiseled into it as well. Noah moved closer to Clio, taking it from her hand to study it closer.

"Is that what I think it is?" Clio asked, clutching Noah's arm. He looked at her, then at the table where she had been working. His own voice trembling with excitement.

"One way to find out." He swallowed hard and went to the map, Clio at his side.

"What is it?" Titus asked, going to look into the box himself before he and the others followed. Clio straightening her maps out and Noah place the stone in the center.

"Can you read it?" He asked. Clio squinted at the long-ago faded wording, trying to decipher what had once been full words. She tilted her head and looked at the left corner of the stone.

"What is it?" Titus repeated. They had all gathered around the table to get a better look.

"It's a cipher key." Mina said after getting a good look at it for the first time.

"A what?" Calli chimed in.

"It's like an X without marking it on an actual spot or map. It marks a location by using landmarks or points on a map. The key is knowing how to read it. It could lead us exactly where we need to be." Clio said, staring down at the stone.

"Looks like something that ends in C or E, but it's really hard to read. But this," She spoke to Noah answering his question and pointed to the scratchy lettering just right of the curve. "This says Honduras. So, this must be Port au Prince?" Noah placed the stone on the corresponding points and the holes lined up with several tiny islands. The space at the apex remained empty. "We were searching the wrong side of the island. We were looking on the ocean side, we need to be on the gulf side of the island. Somehow, we got everything turned around. Look at the map coordinates," He motioned to the numbers Clio had scribbled on one of her maps. "They're backwards. He wrote them backwards."

"There's nothing there." Clio mumbled, shifting the stone. "I don't get it." She whispered, her heart sinking.

"Maybe after all these years, what was there is gone." Noah said.

"Wait a sec," Mina came to stand between them. "Look at this." She pointed between a tiny cluster of islands. She opened her laptop and accessed her transit station and pin pointed the area. Mina zoomed in, her smile widening as they saw a tiny patch of green come into focus.

"There." She sat back folding her arms across her chest. "It's not on the map because it's an atoll." She announced. "We've been searching for an actual inhabited island when what we should have been looking for was this little sand bar. There is actually," She hit a button and the view flipped, giving them a 3D side view. "A deep crevasse around it. It's really close to the oceanic rift line. There are rock formations along this axis. And see this- it's an oceanic transform fault, it shifts over time and there have been cases of caves being created when the faults shift. I think that's what could have happened. See how the water gets darker, that means the water is deeper there. Being this close to the fault, it's very possible that there is a huge fissure or drop off in the area. From the aerial maps we can tell it's pretty deep. Without going down there it's hard to tell exactly how deep though. Could be anywhere from 30 to 30,000 meters." Mina said as she moved through screen after screen. She could see things that they couldn't pointing out certain points of interests and rattling off numbers so quickly that they all stood stunned.

"Okay, slow down. Now, in English for the slow kids." Teri said. Mina looked at Clio, who felt her heart stop.

"Clio, I think we may have found our site." Mina said with a huge grin.

∞∞∞∞

She was standing at the bow of the sun deck, looking out over the sea as the sun began to peek through the clouds. They had packed up and set sail almost immediately, Jameson clearing the way with his connections with the coast guard and government officials. After triple checking the equipment and plotting their course, everyone else had crashed. Only she remained awake, enjoying the early morning solitude. She could feel Noah come up behind her before he put his arms around her and kissed the top of her head. She relaxed against him, enjoying the quiet comfort of being in his arms.

"Are you excited?" He finally asked.

"I am. Are you?" When he didn't answer, she craned her head around to get a good look at him. His expression was one she'd never seen before.

"Are we going to discuss Garrett?" She sighed and turned in his arms.

"There is nothing to discuss. We worked together for years. He used me to get where he wanted. We slept together-a lot-because he was there. It was understood that it only happened when we worked together, and it was just casual. He thought that it was more serious than it was and when he proposed I said no."

"Don't tell me, it was big." Noah asked, and she nodded.

"He proposed during an NBA game on the Jumbotron. I should have known, I usually don't go to sporting events and never with Garrett. It was out of the ordinary, but I went. He'd made a big deal of getting floor seats and It was bad, but I had to say no. As awful as it sounds, I'm glad it all happened because it brought me to you."

"I was never in love with Garrett." She was quiet waiting for Noah to speak. He seemed to contemplate what was said, his eyes on the rising sun on the horizon.

"But you love me." He said.

"Yes." She swallowed the lump that had formed in her throat. "I do." He kissed her forehead and smiled.

"Good. Because I love you too, you little nut-bag. These last few weeks with you have been amazing. I'm not ready for it to end."

"I thought you said that we were just going to live in the moment, that we were going to just be us." She wrapped her arms around him, giving, what she hoped was a sexily teasing smile. "Don't think so much about the end, think about the now. Right now, we are on the verge of what could be a career making discovery. This is what all of the hard work, late nights doing research, the theories and questions, all of that could be answered and you're going to be right in the middle of it all."

"We are going to be in the middle of it all." He corrected. He looked past her at the skyline, his expression somber. She gave him a little shake, trying to bring him back to her. As much as she dreaded telling him about what she did to Garrett, she didn't feel like that was the issue. Something else was needling him.

"Yes, we are." She agreed. "What's going on with you?"

"I'm fine, sweetie. I just...I guess the possibility of all those years of work coming to an end has me feeling a little conflicted. Don't get me wrong, I am excited, but at the same time it feels like an end."

"But it's not. It's the beginning of everything for you, Noah." He looked down at her and managed a small smile.

"I know." He agreed.

"You can at least act like you're excited." She teased. "Come on, let's get breakfast before the others wake up." She started to walk toward the stairs, when he grabbed her hand and pulled her back to him. He kissed her, long and hard with an urgency that made her heart race. She rose to her tiptoes and put her arms around his neck, holding on to him. When he finally released her, she was flushed and breathless.

"Breakfast?" He asked taking her hand. She followed blindly, still dazed by the intensity of his kiss.

∞∞∞∞

"Okay," Mina clapped her hands to get their attention. "We're as close as we can get to the atoll without running aground. We've been using my transit station to remotely plot our course and what we've discovered is that I was right. There is a rather deep crevasse about two miles out and maybe 800 meters down." She looked at Javi, flashing a bright smile. He rolled his eyes and sighed.

"Anyway," Javi continued. "Using the cipher key, we estimate that the 'dig' should start right here." He indicated a point on the map that was between the atoll and their current location. "Since we don't know how deep or how wide Mina's crevasse is..." There was a tittering of laughter and Mina looked at him with disgust, "you know what I mean, we'll take the sub down. We figure, Teri and I are going because, duh. But since you can't go Birdie, it will just be Noah..."

"Wait, who said I couldn't go?" Clio stood putting her hands on her narrow hips.

"Well," Teri said looking at Z, "your doctor did." All eyes turned toward Z who had the courtesy to look perplexed and a little shocked. They waited as he took his sweet time finishing his orange juice and wiping his mouth before he spoke.

"You have a *head* injury." He spoke slowly, deliberately.

"I'm *fine*. You said all I needed was rest. I'm rested." She said calmly. "I've worked too hard to miss this, Z. I need to be down there." He sighed and scrubbed a hand over his face. She waited for him to protest, to say that she was just recovering from a concussion and that she shouldn't be doing what she was doing.

That wasn't what she got.

"Okay." He said. She rolled her eyes, her hands firmly on her hips as she prepared to argue her case to her uncle when she paused.

"Wait, what?" Z shook his head, approaching her slowly.

"You, little hummingbird, are going to do whatever the hell you want no matter what I say. So, go. Find your treasure. But if you feel so much as a little light headed, I want you to surface immediately. Do you understand me?" He held her shoulders, making her look up into his face. She nodded, giving him a hug.

"That goes for you too, Javi. If she so much as blinks funny, you bring that little bubble back to the surface." Javi saluted him. Z, seemingly satisfied, headed into the interior lounge, patting Noah on the back as he went. The two shared a look that held some meaning, but Clio wasn't sure what exactly. But she didn't spend too much time dwelling on it. There was work to be done.

∞∞∞∞

"Explain to me again why I need to wear a wet suit if I'm in the sub?" Noah tugged at the cord attached to the zipper at the back of his suit. Clio, who wiggled into her own suit looked up at him, blowing a stray curl out of her face.

"Because the deeper you go, the colder it gets, even in the sub. You ready?" She grunted, struggling to pull the suit closed over her hips and stomach not really watching him. He'd offered to help and even suggested that perhaps she try a larger suit earlier, but she had given him a look that sent a chill through him.

"It's fine." She'd snapped. Now she had gotten it on and was tugging at her zipper.

He was grateful for the distraction because if she was really paying attention to him, she would see his apprehension. He hadn't really seen the sub until Javi had pushed a button in a control panel in the wall of the lower deck that sat between a light switch and an intercom. The floor of the lower deck had opened, beneath it was a black mini-sub with a viewing dome that reminded him of a fish bowl or giant bubble. The frame of the sub was lined with high powered flood lights and he could see control panels along the back wall with buttons and levers all with in distance of the pilot seat at the back of the dome.

He watched Javi and Mina climb into the back of bubble and take their seats.

"Okay, let's go." Clio said, looking at Noah with an excited smile. He took a deep breath and managed a tight smile before following her into the sub.

He sat beside Clio in the small, but surprisingly roomy interior. In front of them sat Mina, who calmly and quietly navigated. Behind them in the pilot chair that was slightly higher than theirs, was Javi who went through his check list while the sub's door sealed. Inside of the small space, Noah could hear the muted voice of Teri and Titus as they spoke over the intercom system. Clio secured her seat belt and he followed suit, listening to the engine come to life before they detached and began the descent into the deep blue depths.

Mina and Javi spoke to each other in technically nautical terms that he partially understood, while Clio clicked away on the computer tablet in front of her. They all seemed oblivious to the beauty that surrounded them. Noah looked up at the sun, diluted through the water it looked like a quavering spotlight, dimming as they sank deeper. Brightly colored fish darted past them, looking for refuge from these strange invaders. The colors seemed brighter here, more vibrant. Anemones danced in the darkening depths, creating their own light which magnified under the high beams of the sub.

"We're approaching the gap." Mina said, and Teri said something back, her voice scratchy over the intercom. Clio looked up, the interior of the dome darkening as they began their journey into the crevasse.

"I can't really see anything yet," Teri said, the whir of cameras moving overhead. Clio moved forward in her seat, her hand on Noah's pulling him with her. They both stared into the abyss, waiting with bated breath for something to happen.

"It gets too narrow down here, but ..." Mina paused, looking up from her radar screen to look into the darkness. "What was that?"

"Javi, move the light again. I think I saw something." Teri said excitedly. The lights moved, slowly sweeping the darkness between the narrow opening in the rocky wall. There was a tiny glint, a flash in the darkness and Noah's heart stopped.

"There!" Teri and Mina yelled in unison. Javi focused on the spot, the light reflecting off of something metal. "Can you get closer?" Teri was asking. Her voice sounded even further away, Noah supposed it was because he was so focused on the light in the darkness. Clio gave his hand a squeeze. He turned to look at her, those brilliant hazel eyes of hers blazing with excitement, the lights overhead making her appear angelic. His chest tightened, and he had to exhale slowly.

"Not if we want to get back out. It's pretty tight. I'm sending out the rover." Javi said while flipping buttons on his massive control panel. From a small compartment somewhere beneath them a small metal drone with a camera mounted on the front emerged. Noah looked back at Javi to see him navigate the machine using what looked like a high-tech joystick. Javi watched a screen in front of him. The rover moved through a school of jellyfish, the glow of pink and green from their bioluminescence reminding him of tiny spaceships moving through the darkness. They scattered when Javi turned on the rover's lights.

"Look," Clio eased closer to Noah, her tablet in hand. She was using it to get a better view of the live feed that was being watched on monitors on the ship's deck. Along the bottom and side of the picture was a running scroll of depth, temperature and pressure in addition to some scientific jargon he didn't understand. They watched the rover dive between the rocky walls for a few feet before it entered a large cave. Javi navigated around the space, coming to rest on a rock wall.

"Look at that." He whistled. Noah stared at the tumble of rocks blocking the far wall of the cave.

"Rock slide. Looks like this used to have another entrance. What's the depth on the rover, Javi?" Mina said.

"It's hitting five." He said, and she nodded

"Five?" Noah asked.

"Five thousand meters." Mina answered. "The sub is at 980 meters, which is far as we can go without compromising the hull. The rover can go as far as ten thousand." She never looked up at him as she spoke, her eyes on the monitor as she worked. She was staring at a screen that Clio had told him was like a high-powered metal detector. As the rover moved further away, he heard a clear, although muted, beep.

"Javi, go right a little. Now down, right there...zoom in..." He did as he was instructed, the rover hovering over the sandy floor of the watery cave. As he did, the beeping became louder, the intervals coming closer until it was simply one prolonged beep. The sound filled the small space, making his ears ring, but his excitement overrode any discomfort.

The little machine landed on the sandy bottom, it's fan and engine kicking up a dust cloud that took forever to dissipate. When everything settled, and the dust cleared, they remained silent, all of them staring at their monitors in awe. Clio, being the smallest, stood up and walked to the front of the dome. She turned to look at him over her shoulder and Noah could swear she had tears in her eyes, a smile on her lips. Noah's heart hammered in his chest, he was sure they could all hear it in the eerie silence. The stillness and quiet here was unnerving, almost frightening.

There in the sand, the rover had unearthed a 4 x 10-foot piece of waterlogged wood. It was damaged, with great chunks missing, but the word that had been burned into it was unmistakable. Noah scooted closed to Mina, who had a sonar picture, grainy and sepia toned on her monitor. She looked up at Clio, then back at Noah, smiling for the first time since he'd known her.

"We've found it, professor." Mina said quietly. "We've found the *Pride*."

∞∞∞∞

The sun had set and was on the verge of rising on the new day before they finally took a break. The sub had reemerged, and the crew had gone into immediate overdrive. He hadn't realized how long the process would be, that they would have to set explosives to widen the opening in order to get their equipment into the cave entrance. Before they'd surfaced in the sub, Javi had carefully used the Rov to place explosives in the craggy rock wall that blocked their narrow path. The explosives hadn't been detonated until they were back on board, safe and sound. Once the way had been cleared, it had taken hours for a larger rover, one lowered by the massive crane that had been installed on the sun deck of the ship, nearly five hours to make the journey from the wreck and back to the ship.

By dawn they were on the fifth descent and Noah could no longer hold his eyes open. Clio had dozed almost the moment they'd stripped out of their wet suits. Now he found himself staggering to bed, when Z stopped him.

"Hey, professor. You have a call on the ship to shore." One of the ship's crew said in passing. Changing direction, Noah climbed the short flight of stair towards the bridge to answer a call he could only assume was from Raina.

Once on the bridge he'd been directed to a small room off of Titus's suite that was used as an office. He sat at a desk that seemed too neat to ever have been use and picked up the radio.

"This is Noah," He said sleepily, his eyes on the stack of file folders sitting neatly on the corner of the desk.

"Noah, this is Wilson Bradford. You are a very hard man to track down. It took lots of string pulling to get this number." He frowned at the radio but listened as his former boss began speaking to him.

"Dr. Branford, what can I do for you?" He yawned and rubbed his tired eyes and listened as the man on the other end of the radio began to talk. Raina had been right when she'd told him that his photos on social media had made the university take notice. Now Branford wanted him back, the dean was on him to get him back whatever the cost.

Noah really wasn't listening because a name on one of the folders caught his attention. He pulled the folder from the pile and slowly flipped through the pages, his drowsiness disintegrating as he did. He was suddenly fully awake, as he read his confusion giving way to hurt and then anger.

"So, Professor Toussaint, what do you say?" Brandford was saying.

"I need to get back to you." Noah said, leaving to room with a sheath of papers crumpled in his fist. He stalked down the narrow staircase, his blood boiling as he stormed past Titus and Z who watched him go. He nearly collided with Calli as she made her way out of the galley.

"Whoa, where's the fire?" She joked, but he had no time for her. He was too angry, his blood too heated for pleasantries. "Hey," Calli called after him, but he didn't stop, instead he barged into Clio's room where she lay on her side in the fetal position sound asleep.

He turned on the lights and she groaned pulling a pillow over her head.

"You want to tell me what this is?" He barked. She mumbled something incoherent but kept the pillow over her face. He yanked it away, tossing it to the floor. Clio sat up dazed and irritated.

"What? What is?" She yawned. "What are you yelling about?" He tossed the papers into her lap and began pacing the floor as she stared at them. "What is this?" She asked flipping through the pages.

"That is a memo about the cancellation of a grant from the Wainwright-Magnus Endowment Foundation." He spat. She looked up at him still groggy and utterly confused.

"Okay," She said rubbing her eyes.

"It was MY grant, Clio. How could you do that? Was it a ploy to get me here? You uprooted my entire life..."

"Noah, why are you yelling at me about this? Where did this come from anyway?" She spat back.

"Are you serious right now? How can you look at me and lie? Was this your plan all along? Was this some sick game you and Titus cooked up as payback? Twisted revenge?" She stood up, her face twisting in anger.

"First of all, I have no idea what you're talking about. Second, I haven't spent all these years plotting revenge on you. You, my self-righteous friend, hadn't been so much as a passing thought in over ten years. I haven't wasted my life worrying about you, thinking about you or giving two flying sideways fucks about you or your life. And I have especially not spent the last- what month and a half...dragging out some elaborate revenge plot against you."

"So, it's just a coincidence that Titus is on the Board of Directors of Wainwright-Magnus?" He held up a page and pointed to Titus's name included in the header with the other board members. "It was his call to cut my funding, Clio."

She yanked the page from his hand and read the memo again.

"What? What is this? This can't be right." She said in a low voice.

"Come on, Clio. Is this your way of pushing me away? This ..."

"I had nothing to do with this. How was I supposed to know who was funding your expedition? All I knew was that it was pulled." She snapped back.

"And how did you know that, since I wasn't even on your radar? If you had nothing to do with any of this how did you manage to pop into my life just when everything was falling apart? How did you know to come look for me?"

"Because I told her to." Z's voice came from the doorway. "After I had Jameson pull your funding. When Jameson mentioned your name and your grant, it was right around the time Garrett stole Clio's research. It was a perfect opportunity and it all kind of fell into place. It was all my idea. He just helped a little."

"What? His name isn't on this..." Noah was saying, but Clio covered her eyes with her hand and shook her head.

"Yes, it is." Clio said, pointing to the name at the very top of the list of board members. "Magnus Jamison St. John. Wainwright is Titus's mother's maiden name. Son of a bitch. Z, what did you do?"

"I did it for you, Birdie." Z said simply. "I knew that you would never move on to a real relationship until you got over what happened with Noah. After that fiasco with Garrett, I knew something needed to be done. You needed closure so that you could move on. Both of you."

"So, you're a psychiatrist now, too?" Clio snapped.

"Birdie, you love him. You weren't going to magically get over him. I just wanted you to be happy. I'm not going to be around forever, I would like to see you happy and loved. You deserved someone who cherishes you the way Noah does. You've always loved him and now with everything working out the way it has..." Clio gave Z a warning look and he stopped talking, his eyes going to Noah then back to Clio who fumed before him. All five feet of her seethed and Noah didn't know if he should be upset with her or hug her.

"I can't believe you. You had no right to interfere with my life. You ruined Noah's life... you made me humiliate myself chasing him...you made this seem like it was the most important- I had other plans Z. He had a fiancée." She turned to look at Noah. She looked so small and vulnerable, like that day he'd made her cry on campus and his heart ached. Her green gold eyes glistened with tears and he could feel her hurt. Z had embarrassed her and there was something else, but he didn't know what it was.

"I'm sorry. I didn't know he'd done this." Was all she said before leaving the room. Noah stared at Z who sighed before trying to explain his reasoning. He didn't care, all he cared about was Clio. He went after her, seeing her slip into Calli's room. He was following her when Calli blocked the door and shook her head.

"I need to talk to her Calliope." He said.

"Not now, Noah. She's too upset. Just let her calm down for a bit, okay?" He looked into Calli's serene green eyes and nodded. The sun was just peeking over the horizon and he could still hear the hum of the larger, more powerful Rove, continue bringing up the treasure he'd spent so long searching for. He dreamed of the day he would unearth Lafitte's treasure, how all of his hard work had led to this discovery. Z had duped them both, manipulating them. But that didn't matter either. He could deal with that later. Right now, all he cared about was Clio. He wanted to hold her and tell her that he understood, that it wasn't her fault.

"Tell her... I love her." He said. Calli nodded and closed the door leaving him in the hallway. He sighed and sat on the floor, his back against the wall as he waited. He drew his knees up and rested his head on his folded arms, his eyes drifting closed.

He just needed to rest for a moment, clear his head.

∞∞∞∞

"Coffee?" Noah smelled the rich aroma before he opened his eyes. He looked up from his position on the floor, the sun high enough to cast the person handing him a white cup in silhouette.

"Thanks," He gladly took it and watched Titus ease down beside him on the floor. "You didn't spit in this did you?"

"No," Titus laughed and shook his head.

"Poison?" He asked, again Titus laughed and shook his head. "Really wouldn't matter at this point." He took a sip and looked out toward the deck. "The Rove still going?"

"Yup. I think it may be getting close to the end. Javi said about three more dives and then we head to shore."

"What time is it? Where is Clio? I need to talk to her." He struggled to stand, every muscle in his body stiff and aching from sitting on the cold hard floor all night. His joints popped, his bones cracking as he stretched and struggled to rise but Titus put a staying hand on his shoulder.

"It's a little after three." He said, "And she did what the Jean-Noel women do when confronted with real life. She bolted. She and Calli took the dinghy a little after dawn and motored out of here. She should be boarding a plane to New Orleans right about now." Noah let his head fall back and closed his eyes, trying not to let the knot in the pit of his stomach or the ache in his chest kill him on the spot.

"Why didn't anyone stop her?" He knew the answer to that question before it left his lips. Because Clio was Clio and when she made up her mind there was no stopping her. It was part of what he loved about her.

"Why didn't anyone wake me?" Again, he knew the answer to that, because she hadn't wanted them to. He looked at Titus and realized something.

"You funded this expedition, why didn't you stop her? I mean you paid for all of this and to have your lead researcher disappear before it's done..." Titus frowned then shook his head.

"Well, her team is top notch, in case you hadn't noticed. And there is nothing left to do except get it back on dry land and have it authenticated. Clio has already spoken with a couple of people at the natural history museum in New Orleans, as well as one in Baton Rouge and New York, they will be coming into to appraise everything once we get it to a warehouse back in San Juan. Secondly," Titus smirked, "the money to pay for all of this isn't mine. Clio has made a very good living doing what she does. I manage her portfolio, as well as Calli's. You know she writes those C.J Waterhouse mysteries...of course you didn't because why would they tell you." Titus sighed. Noah was stunned. Calli being CJ Waterhouse was astonishing news. Her books about a girl who discovers she's a mermaid queen, had sold millions and had been made into a series of hit movies. Though the author had given several print interviews, her identity had been a mystery. To discover that it was the vibrant and vivacious Calliope Jean-Noel was earth rattling. But then, it made perfect sense. Who better to write about a mermaid than a unicorn.

"Wait, so all of this," He waved his hands around, spilling coffee on the floor, "the apartment, the cars, the boats, the house, they paid for?" Titus nodded sipping his now cooling cup of coffee. "When I asked what you did to make all of this money..."

"Let me guess, they gave the ominous, *we don't discuss what Titus does,*" line, right?"

Noah nodded dumbly. "It's because as smart and as savvy and full of black girl magic as they are, finance gives them fits. I'm their money manager. If I let them handle it on their own, they would buy any and everything that they saw. They're kind of like magpies, attracted to any shiny pretty thing. And just and FYI, my father is also in finance." Titus gave Noah a moment to let that sink in. Drinking his coffee as they sat in the dimly lit hallway.

"So, what am I supposed to do now?" Noah asked no one in particular. Titus grunted and looked him in the eye.

"You're going to go after her and tell her you love her, that she is the only person you want. You're going to tell her that you've loved her for years and that no one comes close to her. She is the one for you and you will accept nothing less than forever. And you're going to pray to God that she realizes that she feels the same way too." Titus got to his feet, crumpling his paper coffee cup in his fist.

"Think she'll listen?" Noah asked, struggling to his feet. His legs had gotten stiff from sitting for so many hours. Titus gave him a pat on the back and shrugged.

"I hope so. Because that's what I plan on doing the moment I see Calli. I'm going to marry that woman."

Chapter 14

"So," Calliope sat beside Clio on the patio overlooking the busy avenue below. Clio didn't look at her sister instead she continued to check off items on an inventory list. Teri had cataloged everything they'd salvaged from the wreckage and now, Clio methodically ticked off every item. She paid no attention to her phone which vibrated on the table between the two of them.

"Are you ever going to answer your phone? He's been calling you for weeks, you need to talk to him Birdie."

Clio pushed her glasses up on the bridge of her nose and shook her head.

"Nothing to talk about." She mumbled.

"Really? You can't think of one thing you need to talk to him about? Not one?" Calli teased, putting a finger under Clio's chin and forcing her little sister to look at her. "Clio, he loves you. And you love him..."

"If he loved me, he would have made a point of seeing me, Cal. Like Titus," She lifted Calli's hand, the light catching the dazzler on her finger. "Titus knows that he wants you and he made sure you knew it as well. Noah got what he wanted. He got the recognition for an amazing discovery. He got job offers, book offers, interviews and offers for lecture tours. And he got the woman who fits into that world, one who didn't need her uncle to force him to be with her. I can't face that look again, Calli. When he found out what Z had done, the look on his face was just...it made me feel like I did all those years ago. It made me feel unworthy and sad and ashamed. What we had, it was fun while it lasted. Our arrangement ended just like they all do. No muss, no fuss." She turned back to her work, avoiding the pitying look she was sure Calli was giving her.

"Birdie, if all of that were true, he wouldn't be blowing up your phone the way he is." Calli sighed. "Every time he's tried to see you, you've bolted like a skittish colt."

"I think it's more that he wants me to go to some talk show with him. You know, promoting our find instead of going to the gala the museum is throwing in our honor. He's being the media darling while I do all of the work. It doesn't matter what I do, I'm not a former pro baller. I'm just an archaeologist. He isn't worried about the taxes or the paperwork-" She stopped, feeling her blood pressure rise. She closed her eyes and counted to ten, taking slow calming breaths. Finally, she exhaled, long and deep before going back to her list. "I need to finish this before Titus and I go to our lawyer's office in like an hour."

"You have people who do this work for you. You're making excuses. It's been two months, and you haven't been my Hummingbird since we got home. I miss you, Birdie."

"I'm right here, Calli." She said.

"No, you're not." Calli sighed, a resigned sadness in her tone that hurt Clio's heart. "Just talk to him. And call Z too. I'm sick of him giving me the puppy face every time I video chat with him." Calliope waved a hand at her sister, rising to go back into the apartment. Clio was grateful for her departure, needing to focus. She didn't want to hear anyone's opinions on what she should do. They had already wrecked her life, the least they could do was leave her alone.

"I'll talk to him when I'm ready." Clio mumbled.

"Which him?" Calli asked.

"Whichever." Clio mumbled, praying Calli would just leave her to her work. She heard the patio door slide open, then close as Calli went into the living room. She waited a beat before turning to see her sister hugging Titus who sat on the sofa. He kissed the top of her head and they sat talking to each other, looking at each other with love in their eyes. Clio turned back to her paperwork, paperwork that she had completed hours ago. Now, she was just distracting herself, avoiding the conversations that Calli and Titus insisted on having. She had buried herself in work whenever either of them had tried speaking to her about anything dealing with Z or Noah.

As if he'd heard her thoughts floating around in the ether, her phone buzzed, and Z's jovial face appeared on the screen. She picked it up and actually thought about talking to him, but it stopped ringing before she'd made a decision. She really wasn't angry with Z anymore. She was embarrassed more than anything.

She'd let herself believe that it had been fate that she and Noah had been brought together after all these years. She let herself believe in destiny. She let herself start to hope that maybe this time, she would have her happily ever after.

To discover that her uncle had manipulated the entire situation to get her over some perceived block or failure to move on. She'd known that she and Noah weren't suited. She had seen him on that campus and knew that he loved it there. He loved working with the students and his life. He enjoyed the recognition. Sure, he'd had fun with her. Everyone had fun with her, that was her appeal. But she'd known from the start it was temporary. It was just, towards the end, she'd actually started to believe that he'd fallen for her the way she had fallen for him.

"Completely and all at once." She mumbled, closing the portfolio she'd spent the better part of two months categorizing, having authenticated and inventoried.

Each item had been photographed and numbered before pieces were to be shipped to museums around the world. She gathered the legal papers Titus had gone over with her, the documents allowing the bulk of the Lafitte collection to be displayed in the New Orleans Museum of Natural History. She hated this part of her work, the tedium of paperwork, but with Titus's help, she managed.

She rose slowly, rubbing the growing ache in her lower back, stretched and looked out over the city. She'd been sitting in the same spot for entirely too long, her feet had fallen asleep and she had completely ignored the beauty of the view that spread before her. The sun was high above her, the sky a clear cloudless blue, a gentle breeze cooling the early fall air. Below people bustled through the streets, music blared from somewhere and she could smell the mingled aroma from several restaurants on her block. She loved this city, loved being home in brief bursts. But now, it was time to get to work. She had a collection to view and a gala to plan. Then she would be off on her next adventure, this one taking her to the other side of the world for the next four months. A project she'd pushed back to go on Z's treasure hunt. She'd be back for Christmas, she always was.

It would be a relief to get back to normal. She would have a different crew, a different team of historians and technicians familiar with Indonesia. She would be on her own for this one. No Calli or Javi, no Teri or Mina, who'd all booked other jobs, banking on their recent discovery to move forward in their careers. She couldn't blame them, they would be in demand and she was proud of each of her friends. She knew that on her own, she'd would be fine.

Eventually.

∞∞∞∞

Noah stormed into the small apartment, nearly toppling a stack of boxes that lined the entry hallway, before stumbling into the living room, cursing under his breath. Catherine had finally sent the rest of his things and now they crowded the tiny apartment.

"Those boxes wouldn't be an issue if you put them in storage." Raina called from the Livingroom. Angrily, he tossed his briefcase onto the floor, raking his hands through his locs, trying to stop himself from punching a wall.

"How about I put you in storage, you little s-" He started before entering the room.

"Watch your language, Noah. We have a guest." He froze, his mouth open when he spotted the guest beside Raina on the sofa. She rose, a wicked grin on her face as she greeted her brother. The man beside her wore a bright Hawaiian print shirt and cargo shorts, his usually jovial smile nowhere to be seen.

"Z?" Noah looked at Raina who's smile seemed to be even wider. "What are you doing here?"

"I came to talk some sense into you. Since I can't get Clio to listen to me." Z said, and Noah felt his brow raise.

"I'll get coffee. You two talk. No," Raina stopped mid-stride. "You talk." She said to Z. "You," She turned on Noah so suddenly that he nearly took a step back. "Listen."

Noah motioned for Z to take a seat when his sister exited the room and headed for the kitchen.

"So, how have you been Z?" Noah asked, trying to force a smile though that was the last thing he wanted to do. He wanted to ask about Clio. How was she? Did she ask about him? Why wouldn't she answer his calls?

"Cut the crap, professor. You know damn well I didn't come here for small talk. I came here to find out why you're dragging your feet. You left Clio in limbo for the better part of ten years and now that you finally have her, you walk away." Z snapped.

"She doesn't want to see me. Z, I have called, emailed, text- I've even driven to New Orleans at least ten times and every single time she stone walls me. She refuses to see me let alone talk to me."

"I never figured you to be a quitter, Noah." Z looked him in the eye and Noah was struck by how much they reminded him of Clio's. No one could match the fire in her gaze, that was all her, but Z had the same determination in his eyes.

"Neither did I." He said, feeling every bit defeated.

"Do you love her, Noah? I mean really love her?" Z asked. Noah looked at Z, never flinching as he focused on the older man.

"Hell, I've spent the better part of eight weeks trying to get her to talk to me. I love her more than I ever thought I could love another person. I have always loved Clio." Z smirked, his mood lightening, that twinkle in his eye returning.

"That's what I thought." Z said. "She's hurt and embarrassed but that was my fault. I've tried apologizing, but she isn't speaking to me either. I think I went a little too far this time. And I really must apologize to you as well. I only did what I did because Clio was never going to let anyone close to her until she dealt with what happened between the two of you. As much as she claims she hadn't thought about you for years, she actually followed your football career. And I know she read a couple of your papers, so I knew there was something there. Something she needed to deal with if she ever wanted a real, meaningful relationship. When she finally got rid of that human barnacle and I read about your trouble with Blake, I knew it was time. I won't be around forever to look out for those girls. They are so stubborn, I had to do something to push them in the right direction. For Calli, she needed to be somewhere to just listen to Titus. For Clio, it was you. I know she loves you, always has, but Clio being Clio, she's just so pig headed. I don't know where she got the idea that she's destined to be alone. She's not. And I have a plan." Raina returned with refreshments, coffee and cookies on a silver tray.

"Great. I love a good plan." She said, setting the tray carefully on the coffee table before sitting on the floor. "Where do we start?" She asked. Z looked at her and winked.

"We start with you two packing a bag and coming with me. I have something I need to show you." He sipped his coffee. Noah and Raina shared a look but nodded, waiting for Z to reveal all.

∞∞∞∞

"You're being awfully quiet for someone who just signed papers of ownership for millions of dollars in sunken treasure."

Titus said, nudging Clio in the elevator. She remained silent, giving him an aggravated look. He was annoying her. He had been since he'd shown up on their doorstep to profess his undying love to her sister. She had admitted that it had been beautiful, and she'd managed to shed a tear. But at the same time, she felt the irrational pangs of jealousy.

Of course, she was happy for Calli and Titus. They were two of her favorite people in the world. What she couldn't bear was the blissful bubble of happiness that surrounded the two.

"Did you even look at all of it? I mean it was such a good salvage, you should be very proud. I must admit, I am very impressed. You out did yourself, Hummingbird." Sure, she'd found a fortune in gold and silver, but the feeling was hollow. She'd just signed papers to allow it all to be displayed in museums worldwide. She hadn't even kept one piece, one token to remind her of what they'd accomplished. She'd even handed in her journals and maps to the New Orleans Natural History museum's archives.

"Hey, Birdie." He gave her another nudge and she looked up at him, knowing he could read the sadness in her eyes. Titus was always able to read her emotions. He hit the stop button on the elevator before embracing her, pressing her face to his chest.

"Okay Birdie, just let it out." He said into her hair and she burst into gut wrenching sobs. She couldn't hold back the pain and anger any longer. In the moment Z had admitted what he'd done, she felt like that awkward kid again, like everyone was laughing at her, or worse. They pitied her.

But Titus hadn't. He never had. Just as he'd done before, he'd rescued her from the humiliation and hurt. Back then he'd arranged for her to transfer to a university on the other side of the country. He was always her protector, even when she was being a bullheaded brat, Titus still had her back.

When she'd finally calmed enough to wipe her tears away, she looked up at him and smiled.

"You are the best big brother in the world." She said. He smiled and kissed her forehead.

"And you are the most infuriatingly lovable little sister. Now, are we ready to face the world or do you need a minute?" She sniffed, wiped her face and took a deep breath. Nodding, he restarted the elevator.

"Alright Dr. Jean-Noel, where are we off too next?" He asked.

"Shopping. I need a dress to wear to this shindig." He nodded.

"Shopping it is. Then maybe lunch? I'm starving." He straightened his tear streaked shirt, tucking it neatly into his slacks. Clio looked up at him sheepishly, but he didn't seem to mind. In fact, he acted as if everything was perfect. She loved Titus even more in these moments, if that were even possible. He was and always would be, her rock. She wrapped an arm around his hips and smiled up at him.

"Me too. And I know the perfect place." Titus laughed, draping an arm around her shoulders.

"Of course, you do."

∞∞∞∞

"Clio, we're leaving," Calli stood in the living room adjusting Titus's tie when Clio burst from her bedroom still in her robe, her hair in tight pin curls and one eye sporting soft pink eyeshadow.

"What do you mean you're leaving? I'm not ready." Calli sighed and turned to her with that look only an older sister could pull off. Clio noted that Calli looked stunning as usual, in a deep burgundy gown. Beside her, Titus looked dapper in a suit in a deep wine shade, with a black shirt and tie. Together they looked amazing, they were absolutely stunning. Titus put a hand on Calli's hip, his eyes adoring every inch of the woman at his side.

"You never listen when I talk." Calli clucked. "I have to some contracts to sign at our lawyer's office. I forgot to do it earlier today and they have to be notarized and sent to New York tonight. I told you all of this earlier." Clio suspected that was a lie, but she honestly had no reason to doubt her sister.

"So how am I supposed to get to the gala? Taxi? Uber?" Again, Calli sighed.

"There is a perfectly good car in the garage." Titus muttered, and she rolled her eyes at him in mock disgust.

"You should really listen when I tell you things. We've already arranged a car to pick you up. It should be here in an hour. We will see you there. Don't be late." Calli kissed her cheek just before Titus put her wrap around her shoulders.

She stood for a moment, staring at the door that closed behind them, leaving her alone in her living room. Sighing, she went back into her bedroom to get dressed. She sat on the edge of the bed, staring at two ratty and fully packed duffel bags. She needed new ones, she knew that, but she couldn't bring herself to part with these canvas bags that had seen better days. Because they had seen her through just about every adventure she'd ever been on.

Her eyes drifted to the dress she needed to wiggle into for this party. She could, she realized, stay right where she was in her bathrobe. Who was to stop her from curling up on the sofa with a pint of ice cream and a good movie?

Calliope Jean-Noel, that was who. If she didn't show up her sister would be here in a hot second, toss her into that dress and drag her out of the house. She had obligations and commitments that she had to honor. Besides, it wasn't every day she was honored at a gala. There would be paparazzi, music and of course, food. Her stomach rumbled at the thought of tiny puff pastries full of crab and stuffed mushroom caps.

"Okay," She said to herself, "let's get fancy."

She'd just fastened her bracelet when her favorite doorman Neil buzzed her intercom, letting her know that her car had arrived. Taking one last look at herself in the mirror, she ran a hand over her smooth curls, then over her hips. She supposed this was the best she could do, which wasn't half bad, grabbed her purse and headed down to the door. She just had to get through this night. One more night then she would be far away from here. Far away from the heart ache and the pain.

She crossed the lobby, nodding at her trusted doorman on her way to the black town car that waited for her on the curb. She was surprised that the driver wasn't holding the door open for her but didn't have time to think about it for too long, because ever faithful Neil was there. She slipped into the dark interior, mumbling a hello and nearly jumping out her skin when the door was slammed behind her. The doors locked immediately, and the car slowly moved into traffic, the driver never turning to face her. She tilted her head, looking at the darkened figure who navigated smoothly through the busy Saturday night traffic and rolled her eyes.

"So, is this where I get a halfhearted apology and a convoluted explanation?" She said through clinched teeth.

"Hello Birdie." He met her eyes in the rearview mirror and winked.

"Okay Z," She said, calmly. She held his gaze, knowing that Calli and Titus were behind this ambush.

"Let's hear it. Come on, I'm trapped back here for the next twenty minutes. That's plenty of time for you to try to convince me that what you did made any kind of sense. I mean what were you thinking? What if I hadn't gone to Baton Rouge? Or what if your lunatic of a pilot friend hadn't flown off with...oh my god you planned that too, didn't you?" She would have slapped her palm against her forehead if she hadn't spent the better part of an hour perfecting her smoky eye. She hadn't realized the lengths Z had gone to in order to put her in Noah's orbit.

"I did. I made sure that Ray flew off with your bags, your ID and I made sure Derrick didn't have time or opportunity to drive you back home. I got Calli stalled in New York and when Ray returned your bags. I got Titus to convince her to leave you two alone for that night before you two came home. I did it all. Yes, after that fiasco of a proposal, I set the entire thing in motion. I planned every detail to get you two together." Z seemed to say it all in a long deep exhale, like he'd saved up for months, so he could breathe it all out at once.

"And I'm not sorry. Not one little bit." He smiled at her in the mirror. She narrowed her eyes, wishing she could truly shoot daggers from them. "You know why? Because what happened is what I knew was going to happen. You fell in love."

"That didn't give you the right to do what you did." She could feel the anger welling in her gut.

"It all worked out..." He started, and she shook her head.

"In case you failed to notice, it didn't. And it never would have, Z. I was alone because it works for my life. You manipulated Noah and I into a relationship that was based on a fantasy. It's not real for him, he got to go on this adventure, find buried treasure and a little bit of fun. But now that it's over he'll go back to his normal, stable real-world life."

"You don't know that. You haven't even spoken to him since you ran off. How do you know?"

"Because it's what they all want, Z." He pulled to the side of the road, then turned to look at her. She didn't want him to see the fresh tears in her eyes or hear the pain in her tone. "I know that any relationship I have will be short lived, Z. At least until I stop doing what I do, and I don't see that happening anytime soon. Yes, I love Noah. I probably always have and more than likely, I always will. But that doesn't change the fact that he has a life and ambitions of his own. Here."

"Clio," Z's tone was soft, reassuring in the way that always made her feel better. She managed to look at him, willing to tears not to fall. "How do you know that if you won't even talk to him? I know he's come to see you, called, sent emails and texts. If anyone isn't giving the two of you a chance, it's you. You're the only one who doesn't believe you deserve love. And sweetie, I've seen how Noah looks at you. He's come a long way from that kid you met in college. He wants to be with you. You're the one getting in your own way. You always have been. I just wanted to give you a push in the right direction. What you need to do now, is stop trying to anticipate the end before you give him a real chance."

She knew that he was right. She'd let her hurt feelings and embarrassment interfere. She had never even given Noah a chance to make his own decision on what he wanted to do. She'd done what she always did when things got too close to what she wanted it to be. Noah hadn't walked out on her during that party all those years ago. She'd been the one running and hadn't stopped running for over ten years.

"Birdie, it's time to stop running." Z turned, shifted the car into drive and eased back into traffic.

Clio exhaled, digging into her clutch for a tissue at dab her eyes. Z was right, it was time to put on her big girl pants and suck it up. There would be no more running for her. It was much too late for that.

∞∞∞∞

She took Z's hand as he waited for her to exit the back seat of the car before the valet hopped into the driver's seat. The museum looked lovely in the moonlight, the soft lights that illuminated the Greek columns that lined the facade. Situated in the art's district of downtown New Orleans, the scene drew slightly curious glances from people moving along the narrow side street. A bright red streetcar clanged past them, packed with people on the warm evening, the noise of traffic from Canal street drowning out the jazzy melodies that poured from the building before them.

Z tucked her hand into his elbow as they mounted the stone steps toward the entrance which was bookended with two banners announced the historic Lafitte collection. She couldn't help but feel a bubble of pride as they moved inside.

Once inside, she caught her breath at the site of it all. The treasured legacy of her family was on display in the main hall. What felt like hundreds of roped off displays highlighted the gold and silver artifacts, the ship's huge wooden masthead and a brass name-plate were mounted behind heavy glass. At the center, the focal point of the entire collection sat on a dark velvet riser on a podium was the journal that had started the adventure of a lifetime.

There were photos of her crew, images from their expedition, portraits of her ancestors, her mother, father, grandparents, Z and even she and Calliope. She'd been to many receptions where her work was on display, but this was different. This was personal, this was her life, her heritage and she wanted to weep. Damn, she was a mess. Stupid hormones. Stupid emotions. Stupid Noah.

Just as she thought of him, of how much she wanted to be with him, to share this with him, she spotted him across the room. He looked debonair in his dark navy suit, his long dark locs secured at his nape. He stood in profile, speaking to someone, his smile bright and easy. She had thought him gorgeous before, but she had never imagined he would look so downright panty dropping sexy. Her stomach did somersaults, and her mouth went dry as she stared, willing him to look her way. She didn't know why she assumed he wouldn't come. This was partly his discovery. He'd been there with her through it all. She could feel Z trying to tug her forward, but she was glued, watching Noah with an intense need she'd never known possible.

She was ready to release Z's arm and go to him, to tell him how much she missed and needed him. She wanted to throw her arms around him and have him hold her close, her fingers sinking into those thick locs as he kissed her, when the woman he was speaking to moved closer, her fingers on his lapel, her head tossed back in light laughter. She was absolutely stunning, and Clio felt as if someone had punched her in the gut.

"Clio, the museum director is waiting." He said distractedly. Clio looked at Noah and the beautiful woman one last time, then let Z pull her away. She was too late, she thought, looking down at her shoes.

"Sure," She answered an unasked question, grateful to move away from the scene playing out before her.

"Let's go," She put on her best smile. She would radiate with joy tonight and graciously accept her accolades. There would be time to wallow later.

∞∞∞∞

Noah stood watching the door, knowing that Clio was due to arrive at any moment. He'd left Raina with Derrick, her new kind-of boyfriend as she put it, almost as soon as they'd entered the room. Calli and Titus had greeted him before being ushered away for photo opportunities with the rest of the crew. He barely recognized them in real clothes, having only seen Javi, Mina and Teri in either swim wear or shorts and t-shirts for the better part of two months. He had to admit, they'd cleaned up nicely.

He'd found himself standing before a picture of Clio standing on the sun-drenched deck of the ship. Her curls blowing in the wind, her face upturned, her skin glowing. He had never felt as alive as he did when he was with Clio, his little hummingbird. He hoped that Z's plan finally worked, and she would talk to him. She'd just bolted like a terrified colt. He gently patted the object in his breast pocket, making sure it was still there. This had to work, he thought.

He'd been staring so long, he hadn't even noticed the woman who'd sidled up beside him until she gently nudged him.

"Hey stranger," He turned and was surprised to see Catherine beside him, looking radiant as ever. He didn't know how to react, so he just stared, his jaw slack as he waited for her to speak. She took one look at him and laughed.

"Don't freak out, I'm not here to ambush you. I just wanted to say hello." She said, her face softer, happier than it had ever been with him. She looked relaxed, and she was down-right glowing. "And congratulate you. It looks like you finally did it." She smiled, turning to look at the picture that had held him in such awe.

"So, this is the infamous Clio Jean-Noel?" She said, nodding. "You finally found your muse."

"You could say that." He said, not sure where this conversation was going, but intrigued.

"I can. You never looked at me the way you look at her. She brought something out in you that I never could. I mean, just look at these pictures. You never smiled like that when we were together."

She turned to him, her expression solemn. "I'm sorry, Noah." She said, and he began to tell her there was no need for apologies, but she held up a hand to stop him. "No, I do owe you an apology. I was so intent on trying to force you to fit what I wanted you to be, I didn't even care that we weren't working. You didn't love me the way I needed to be loved and I clung to you because...well because look at you. And when I saw you being the man, I wanted you to be, I tried to hold you back. I panicked." She chuckled. "I'm sorry that I handled things so badly. You deserve someone who makes you happy. We both do."

She held up her hand, showing him a modest, yet beautiful diamond ring. "And I found it."

She laughed. Relief washed over him, and he leaned in to give her a kiss on the cheek. He was congratulating her, listing to her as she filled him in on all that had happened in his absence when he saw a flash of color from the corner of his eye.

He turned just as Clio was being guided across the room by her uncle. The sight of her took his breath away. She was stunning in a royal blue dress, moving with the grace of a dancer, her back straight, eyes forward as she was introduced to someone. Excusing himself, he cut across the crowded dance floor towards her.

"What are you doing?" Titus stepped into his path, blocking his view of Clio's retreating back.

"What do you think I'm doing? I'm going to talk to Clio." Titus wagged a finger at him.

"It's not time. You're about to ruin everything." Noah frowned, then sighed. Of course, Titus was in on this. They all were. The only way Z could make this work was if he had everyone involved. Noah involuntarily touched his pocket again. "Come with me." Titus took his arm and guided him away from the party. They walked towards a room that was roped off. A sign on the wall near the heavily curtained entrance announced this new exciting exhibit coming soon. Titus pulled back the curtain and usher Noah into the dimly lit room.

"Whoa," he mumbled as he saw what had been hidden behind the curtain, taking in the scene.

"Wait here." Noah looked around the room, turning to ask Titus a question, but found that he was already alone.

∞∞∞∞∞

"There you are," Calliope was coming toward her with two glasses of champagne. "I have been looking all over for you. Wow, you look amazing." She handed Clio a fluted glass and she obligingly took it. "Isn't this amazing. But I guess you're used to all of this stuff, right? "

"Not really. This one is more personal. I mean, look at it. Our family is all over the place." Clio pointed to family portraits that went back generations. Calli stood beside her, both taking in the milestones in their history. They held hands, staring at a photo of their parents on their wedding day.

"You look so much like Mom, Cal." Clio said, looking into her mother's smiling eyes.

"I may look like her, but you ...you are more like her than you realize. You have a lot of Daddy in you too. You did good, Hummingbird. You did really good." Clio felt herself puff up with pride. Standing there in a room full of music, laughter and conversation, she felt as if she and Calliope were the only people who truly understood the gravity of what they had accomplished. And they'd done it together.

"There you are, Dr. Jean-Noel," They both turned when the museum director, a man in his mid-fifties with a penchant for colorful bow ties, approached. "I need to steal you away for a moment. I want to show you what we've planned as a permanent space for the collection." He looked at Calli and if Clio didn't know any better, she would have sworn that the two of them had shared a look. It wasn't something overt, but it had been there, a quick look, an acknowledgment of some sort. Clio looked between the two, waiting for some other indication that she'd actually seen something. There wasn't anything. Shaking off her apprehension, she nodded and followed the chatty man out of the room.

"We chose this space because it's large enough to house the collection. We hope you will really like what we've done." He led her to a section that had been cordoned off, a heavy red curtain shielding the unfinished exhibit from curious onlookers. They crossed the barricade and he held the heavy curtain allowing her to enter before him. "I think you'll be impressed by our uniquely magical interpretation."

She stepped into the room which glowed amber with soft candlelight. She was slightly confused and turned to say as much, only to find herself alone. Soft music floated down to her from unseen speakers as what must have been hundreds of tiny lights hung from the ceiling, mimicking the night sky.

188

The floor had been covered with sand strewn with white candles. Palm trees lined the walls, lush greenery filling the space, a breeze of ocean air wafted towards her. At the center of the room, beneath the thatched roof of a shelter was a candlelight picnic surrounded by large pillows. She spun around taking it all in with wonder and amazement, her heart hammering in her chest. She turned back to the picnic and knew he would be there, watching her.

She inhaled sharply, her eyes filling with tears when she met his gaze. He didn't move, he just watched, his hands clasped together in front of him. She half floated toward him, a million questions in her head, but when she was finally face to face with him there was only one word.

"How?" She threw her arms out, forgetting that she still held the champagne flute until the cool liquid splashed on her bare arms. He smiled, looking around before his eyes rested on her.

"It was all Z. He figured this was the only way I would get you to talk to me. And he was right. I had to go big to prove to you that what he did to get us together doesn't matter. All that matters is that I love you. And you love me, and we belong together. I don't care how he did it, I'm just happy that he did. I'm never as happy as I am when I'm with you. You are my muse and I am completely captivated by you."

"Noah," She started to say all of the things he needed to hear, to tell him how much she loved him when he kissed her. He held her face, looking into her eyes, his expression serious and for a moment she thought the professor was about to rear his ugly head.

"I lied to you." She blurted, needing to say something. "I lied when I said I didn't know anything about your life. I knew everything. I followed your football career. I went to the games, watched on television, I was even there when you got that scar on your knee. And I have loved you since college, even after that stupid party. I was just too ashamed to face you. Just like I was when I found out what Z did to get us back together. He was right. I was never going to get over you." He stroked her cheek and smiled.

"I know. Just like I know that I've never loved anyone like you. You are a very tough act to follow, Clio Jean-Noel. No one was ever going to live up to you. No one ever could. You stole my heart all those years ago, and it took Z and this trip for me to realize that I never stopped loving you. I never will. You are in my blood. I can't live without you. The last two months without you, without hearing your off-key singing in the shower, or watching you eat like a trucker or laying with you in my arms, has been torture. I need you, Clio. You are my everything." He said.

"But your life here..." She began only to be shushed again.

"My life is where ever you are. I know that you thought I wouldn't be able to live like you do, traveling the world making new discoveries. But Clio, I have never been so alive in my life. You make me want to be a better man. You make me a better man.

I wasn't really living until you. You are the spark, you are fire and I love you with everything in me. I would go to the ends of the earth with you. Two months without you nearly killed me. I never want to be without you again. Not even for a day. Not for an hour." He reached into his pocket and her heart raced. He was going down on his knee and she felt her own knees give.

"What are you doing?" She asked, tugging at his jacked as if to pull him back to his feet.

"I'm trying to propose and you're ruining it." He chuckled.

"You're trying to propose what?" She asked, knowing that she sounded like a complete imbecile.

"I want to marry you." He said taking her hand. "I want to be with you forever, Clio. Just you and me."

"You want to marry me?" She watched as he placed the ring on her finger. It was gorgeous, a cushion cut emerald surrounded by pave diamonds in a platinum setting. She looked at the ring, then at Noah.

"Will you marry me Clio?" He repeated, and she felt tears streaming down her cheeks.

"Are you sure? Because you know I can be stubborn and a little bossy. I'm impulsive and reckless and have a tendency to go off half -cocked ..."

"And I wouldn't have it any other way." He said.

"And I'm rich. Like really, really rich. I should have told you sooner," She blathered.

"And that's supposed to be a deterrent?" He chuckled.

"Yea, I guess you're right. Ask me again." She said, wiping her eyes.

"Clio Jean-Noel, will you be my wife? Will you marry-" She practically launched herself at him sending them tumbling into the sand. She kissed him, her mouth covering his, peppering him with kisses.

"Is that a yes?" He asked.

"Yes!" She squealed. "Of course, I will marry you, Noah Toussaint." He got to his feet and helped her up.

"We need to celebrate." He grabbed a bottle of champagne that had been chilling in a bucket ready to pop the cork when she put a staying hand on his arm.

"Before you do that," She ran her hands over the front of her dress, smoothing it against her slightly rounded belly. He stared for a moment, then met her eyes, a slow smile spreading across his face. "There's just one more thing."

Epilogue

"Whose stupid idea was this?" Clio's heel sunk into the scorching hot sand, the wind and spray of salt water ruining her hair. "Who decided a wedding on the beach in a million-degree heat was a good idea?" Noah held her hand, helping her walk towards their seats. She was dripping sweat, her feet burned and the straps from her sandals were cutting into her ankles.

She hated this stupid dress, she hated these stupid shoes and she hated the unrelenting heat.

"I believe this was your idea." Noah reminded her. She looked at him, rolling her eyes in exasperation. Her back hurt, and pain shot through her with every few steps. She'd woken up that morning feeling horrid, the pain in her back and hips making her crankier than usual.

"I said a beach at sunset theme, in an air-conditioned venue. Not on an actual beach in the blazing sun on the freaking equator. Damn it." Her foot sank deeper into the sand, her weight pushing her ankle deep. She groaned in frustration.

"Okay, come on." He easily lifted her into his arms, cradling her close as he effortlessly sauntered towards their seats just before the floral decorations of the alter. "At the rate you're going we'd miss the entire thing."

She wanted to argue, but he was right. She hated when he was right.

He sat her down before taking his seat. Titus looked at them, tugging at the collar of his crisp white shirt. Beads of sweat had formed on his forehead and upper lip, but Clio knew it wasn't because of the heat. It was because of the vision coming toward him in an ivory gown.

A string quartet began to play as Calliope was escorted down the makeshift aisle on Z's arm.

Jameson gave his son a pat on the shoulder as they all marveled at what a beautiful bride Calliope made. When Z placed her hand into Titus's, Clio began to quietly cry, tears running down her face, mingling with the sweat on her cleavage. She was miserable, and as if he could feel her discomfort, Noah took her hand, kissing the heated skin. Another pain shook her, and she squeezed his hand until he grimaced.

"Are you okay?" He whispered. She nodded between calming breaths.

"Yeah, just a cramp." Before the words left her lips, another pain hit her. "Must be the heat." She said through clinched teeth. Noah didn't look too sure about that. "I'm fine, don't give me that look." She waved at him.

When the minister pronounced them man and wife, Titus dipped Calli low and planted a romantic stage kiss on her, the shutter of cameras capturing the moment. Clio stood, taking the tiny satchel of what Calli had deemed eco-friendly confetti, and tossing handfuls in the air as they exited down the aisle to cheers.

Finally, Clio thought, taking Noah's hand. They would go into the beach club Titus and Calli had rented out for their reception. And blessed air conditioning. God how she needed air conditioning. She was dripping in sweat and she had to pee really badly.

Noah took her hand just as a spike of pain shot down her back. She stopped, leaned forward and tried to catch her breath while she gave Noah's hand a squeeze tight enough to crack his bones. He yelped in pain, drawing the attention of everyone around them. Everything seemed to stop for a moment.

Clio looked up, meeting the eyes of curious onlookers as the unthinkable happened on her sister's wedding day.

"Clio, are you okay?" Noah asked. She nodded, her focus on getting into the cool air. "Clio,"

"Just a little cramp." She breathed, following the bride and groom towards the opened doors of the reception venue. She could see the flowers, feel the manufactured air cooling her hot skin.

"How long have you been having these cramps?" He whispered, trying to get Z's eye.

"Um...since last night. But they're getting worse..." She stopped just as the stepped onto the hardwood floors, she grasped his forearm and bent over as yet another pain gripped her. Noah howled this time, finally drawing Z's attention, along with everyone else's. So, she thought, she didn't have to pee after all.

"Noah," She looked at him her eyes wide a puddle at her feet. "my water just broke."

Everything moved in fast forward from then on, the entire bridal party reminiscent of the Keystone cops ushering Clio into the back of a limo. Calli, Titus and Z climbing in to ride with her, the remaining guests following in a convoy of cars. She could have sworn she heard police sirens at one point, but she wasn't sure because every few minutes another round of bone cracking contractions blinded her.

"How long have you been having contractions?" Z asked. "How far apart are they?"

"They started late last night. They've been about two minutes apart since the middle of the ceremony." Clio said, before groaning as another pain gripped her. Z pushed Noah aside, so he could examine her and cursed under his breath.

"What? Why didn't you say something?" Noah asked, his voice coming from somewhere over her head. She was leaning against his chest holding his hand waiting for Z to answer. Instead, he lifted her dress as discreetly as he could in the back of the car, his face pale.

"I just thought it was gas or a cramp. The baby moves a lot at night and with the wedding..." She grunted and concentrated on breathing. "I think I've been in labor since the rehearsal dinner." She said.

"What?" Titus and Calli screamed and she remembered that they were there. She saw the two of them looking back at her from the front seat of the limo and she gave them a weak smile.

"Thought it was nerves." She half-heartedly chuckled.

"You've been in labor for over twelve hours?" Noah choked. "Twelve hours?"

"I didn't want to ruin Calli's wedding." She breathed, twisting as another pain ripped through her.

"She's coming now." Z said, and another pain urged Clio to push.

"Wait, what?" Noah's voice hit an octave she'd never heard before.

"She's been in labor since last night. She's fully dilated, contractions are a minute apart- the baby's coming now!" Z said and there was a cacophony of raised voices but all she cared about was pushing. She leaned forward, baring down as another contraction ripped through her. She didn't understand anything except Noah, in her ear telling her how good she was doing and that they were almost to the hospital.

It didn't matter.

By the time they reached the hospital, Phoebe Jean-Noel Toussaint had made her debut as only as Jean-Noel woman could, screaming to high heaven and unexpectedly.

She was wrapped in Noah's shirt, cradled close to her mother's chest when they finally arrived.

Noah touched her cheek and she opened golden green hazel eyes. He'd counted all of her fingers and all of her toes and ran his hand over a thatch of dark hair that waved against soft skin.

"Isn't she perfect?" Clio asked as they wheeled her into the emergency room, a parade of people in formal wear following her as if she were the leader of some strange confetti covered parade. There were pictures being snapped, Z talking to the staff in animated fashion. The limo driver was asking Titus about payment to get his limo cleaned, and she thought she heard someone popping a bottle of champagne.

And Noah, standing shirtless beside her, linking his hand with hers, their wedding bands glinting in the harsh lights of the ER.

"Look at all of the commotion you caused." Clio sniffed kissing the baby's head. Noah kissed her, then planted a gentle kiss on his daughter's cheek.

"Just like her mommy," Noah said, and Clio realized that he also had tears in his eyes. She reached up, brushing away a tear with her thumb. "Life with the two of you is always going to be an adventure, isn't it?" He asked. Phoebe cooed, yawning and grasping his finger with her tiny hand.

"And you wouldn't have it any other way." Clio said, blocking out the chaos all around them.

About the Author

Tanisha Jones grew up in the greater New Orleans area. She received a BA from Southern University, New Orleans in Literature.

She still lives in the New Orleans area with her daughter, the Mississippi River on one side, the bayou on the other. When not reading or writing about gods, goddesses and all thing magical, she's cooking, baking or spending time with her rather large loving family. She is also a proud Breast Cancer survivor.

Follow her here:

Website: www.tanishadjones.com

Twitter: @tanishadelill

Facebook: https://www.facebook.com/DelillPublishing/

Instagram: tanishadelill

Other books by Tanisha D. Jones

The Fallen Series
Fans of J.R. Ward and Anne Rice will love this exciting new series!!!

When the body of rock star Nicky Sky turns up missing, Dt. Elijah Cain is on the case, until the case is ripped out from under him by some powerful higher ups. But Eli has a little secret, he knows things, and he knows that Nicky Sky walked away from his own coffin. With the help of Nicky's best friend, the sexy and intriguing Dr. C. Keegan Kent, he is drawn into a world of supernatural creatures, a world that he never imagined existed. His connection to the tantalizingly exotic Doc runs deeper than Eli realizes and leads him on a path to the truth.

With the shadowy Collective on the hunt to destroy Nicky and the wicked creature that turned the rock star against his will, Eli and the Doc team up to find the malevolent creature who is also hunting them. The chase puts them on a collision course with their destiny... or their destruction.

Karim of Tyre once rescued Celeste from a watery grave. But he later abandons her with dire consequences. Years later, he's returned. But she has been pledged to another.
Celeste is again drawn to the dark and noble Karim. He ignites a passion that has smoldered for eons. And an anger that has burned just as long.

Torn apart by his betrayal, she still longs for the only love she's ever known. But she's been promised to a man she doesn't even remember. Unbeknownst to either, a plot's been set into motion to push Celeste toward a destiny that could lead to the destruction of their entire world.